DEAD ARMY

OTHER LIVING DEAD PRESS BOOKS

DEAD ARMY

ANTHONY GIANGREGORIO

WHAT HAS COME BEFORE

Over two years ago, a deadly bacterial outbreak escaped a lab to infect the lower atmosphere across America, unleashing an undead plague on the world.

With rain clouds now filled with a killer bacteria, to venture outside in the rain was tantamount to suicide.

To get caught in the rain and exposed to the bacteria would be an instant death. But that wasn't the end. Once dead, the host body would rise again, becoming an undead ghoul, wanting nothing more than to feed on the flesh of the living.

Time passed, and eventually the bacteria burned off in the atmosphere. But mankind still wasn't safe. The virus then mutated inside the host, and to be bitten by one of the living dead was a death sentence. Sickness followed by a painful death, only to return as one of the undead.

The United States was torn asunder; civilization collapsing like a house of cards in the weeks after the dead began to walk.

But mankind survived, eking out a dreary existence, always keeping one eye open for the attacking dead.

Only two years after the zombie apocalypse, the world has become a very different place from what it once was. Gone are cell phones, the internet, restaurants and shopping malls; now all lost relics of a culture slowly fading into history.

In this new world, the dead walk and a man follows the rules of the gun, where the strong are always right and the weak are usually dead. Major cities are nothing but blackened husks, nothing but giant tombs filled with walking corpses.

Across America, towns have become small municipalities with makeshift walls protecting them from both living and undead attackers. Strangers are not welcome and are either shot on sight or made to move on, that is, if they are not exploited by the rulers of the towns.

Through the destruction of what once was walks a man, crushing death beneath his steel-tipped boots. Before, he was an ordinary man, living a quiet life with a wife and a career, but the rules have changed and, so too, has he adapted, becoming a warrior of death who wields a gun with an iron fist, but shows mercy and wisdom when it is needed.

His name is Henry Watson, and with his fellow companions, Mary, Jimmy, Cindy, Sue and Raven by his side, he travels across a blighted landscape, searching for someplace where the undead haven't corrupted everything they touch; where he and his friends can lay their heads down in safety.

Though life is fleeting, each breath means the possibility of one more day of survival, and a better future for all.

Prologue

Deep underground, somewhere in the Nevada desert, a government redoubt ran void of human life. No lights illuminated bare walls and polished floors, and no alarms or gentle beeping from computers filled the air. The place was on autopilot, running independently of human interference. On the lowest level, the nuclear reactor continued to make power, the state-of-the-art computers monitoring control rods and water flow.

The cafeteria was empty, as were the dorm rooms.

Well, they were empty of *living* beings anyway.

Wandering the hallways and trapped in offices were the undead, most nothing but decrepit, desiccated skeletons, many barely animated, with a few loose ligaments or strips of flesh to hold them together. Some of the more lively ones still moaned and groaned, their hoarse voices echoing off the stark walls.

It wasn't supposed to be like this.

What was supposed to happen was that the military and scientists that were holed up within the redoubt would wait out the zombie epidemic, and perhaps even manage to find a cure. Protocols had been put into place to make sure the infection stayed outside and would never breach the cold stone walls of the underground bunker, as days became months and soon years—two years and six months to be exact.

But as in most plans, the human element was to be their downfall.

On a scouting mission outside the redoubt, a scientific team—along with military soldiers for chaperones—was exploring the closest town to the bunker.

At first the town seemed deserted, but in no time the soldiers and scientific team found themselves surrounded by the walking dead. But rotting flesh was no match for bullets and blades and the soldiers soon destroyed the score of undead.

During the battle, one of the researchers was bitten, the sharp teeth of the ghoul tearing through the fabric of his hazmat suit. Acting fast, the terrified scientist sealed shut the tear in his suit.

Later, upon returning to the redoubt, he made sure to keep the area hidden from inspection. He knew what would happen to him if it was discovered he'd been bitten and he also knew what his fate would be. But he prayed that he might be different, that he would be immune to the virus. It was a false hope, but a drowning man will cling to whatever is offered to him if it will save him from drowning.

Two days later, lying in the darkness in his small room, the scientist found out that he was not special, and after becoming sicker with each passing hour, he finally succumbed to the virus and died to reanimate; his last thoughts were for what he'd done to his fellow scientists by selfishly withholding the bite and subsequent infection.

Upon reviving as one of the undead, he stumbled around his small room, not smart enough to figure out how to open the door. That night, when one of his co-workers came to check on him, knowing he had been out sick for the past two days, the friend was greeted by a snarling zombie as soon as the door was opened.

In no time, the friend was killed and fed on, to then revive as one of the undead. Both zombies soon found more unlikely victims, and before anyone knew what was happening, the entire redoubt was filled with the walking dead and the living were dwindling by the second.

A few scientists, who were close to a breakthrough in the zombie virus—or so they hoped—barricaded themselves in a lab and began experimenting on one of their own who had become infected—a man who had been part of the janitorial staff. The hope was that if oxygen was continually supplied to the brain, upon death, the host would remain a thinking, rational person, and not a mindless zombie. If this could be perfected then the undead wouldn't be mindless eating machines and then wouldn't want to eat the living.

But before the scientists could finish their tests, with the test subject strapped to a metal table with wires and hoses connected to his naked form, the door was broken in by a horde of zombies that flooded the lab and devoured the scientists.

Though scientists may have been intellectuals, they weren't pacifists, and they managed to kill almost all of the ghouls before they were killed themselves. Those ghouls that remained functioning fed on the hapless white coats, then satiated, stumbled out of the lab in a mindless daze.

As for the test subject, he had been ignored in the chaos, and with oxygen suffusing his brain, he slowly died and then began to reanimate.

Eugene Gornick opened his eyes, unsure of where he was, or for that matter, *who* he was.

He could hear breathing—a dull, rasping sound—and it reminded him of a death rattle.

As he took inner stock of himself, he felt *weird*. He couldn't put his finger on it but there was something *off* about him.

As his eyes adjusted, he saw that he was looking up at a ceiling covered in acoustic tiles. There was some kind of splatter on the ceiling, dark brown or the color of rust by the look of it. He turned his head to the left and saw carnage on a level he never would have imagined in his life.

The walls were covered in blood, and body parts and internal organs were scattered everywhere, along with more than a dozen corpses, all in different states of destruction. More than an inch of congealed blood coated the floor and every appliance had a generous coating as well, though it had been long since it had been wet and sticky. It reminded him of old paint.

The first thought he had was, *I'm not cleaning this mess up*, as he stared at the charnel house of gore, but then he focused on other matters, namely the tubes and wires connected to his naked form when he looked down at himself to inspect his body.

Carefully, he sat up, then with first the right hand and then the left, he pulled the wires from his skin, surprised when he didn't feel so much as a twinge of pain.

With his legs dangling over the side of the table, he slid off it, his feet sinking into the congealed blood as if it was mud. There was a folder soaked in blood on the floor by his feet. He picked it up and perused it. His name was in there and his description, such as height and weight, and as he read this, his memory came back of who he was.

Dropping it to the floor, he looked for the exit. One step at a time, he wadded through the corpses until he was at the door, only detouring to take a blood-splattered lab coat from a mostly intact corpse. It was mostly intact, because other than having no head and arms, the body looked fine.

Near the door were the bodies of two soldiers. Eugene picked up one of the fallen soldiers' handguns, a .45 if Eugene was correct. He had never been much of a gun nut and so didn't know much about guns. He had always thought that men who went gung-ho for guns were probably compensating for their small penises. After all, a real man didn't need a gun to kill, which was a coward's way in his opinion. Now a knife, there was a weapon for a warrior. Sinking the blade into an opponent's chest as you watched the life slide from his eyes.

Though just a janitor, Eugene had always believed he was destined for greater things, but those *things* never happened. Not bright enough to go to college and with parents who wouldn't help with the finances of doing so, he had gone off to sling burgers in a fast food chain until coming across an ad in the local newspaper about opportunities in the government. Of course, he hadn't thought of being a janitor at the time, but the pay was good and he got full insurance and other benefits that came with a government job. So he'd taken the position.

He had never thought that position would mean he would be one of the few people picked to be stationed at the redoubt, and when the shit hit the fan with first the deadly rains that turned people into flesh-eating zombies and later when the virus mutated, he found himself safe and sound a half mile beneath the earth.

And now, while walking through the empty hallways filled with more bodies and chewed parts and copious amounts of dried blood, he found himself once more a very lucky man.

He came upon his first zombie on the next level. Stepping off the elevator which was for all personnel, he came face to face with a ghoul with half a face and only one arm. The creature moaned loudly at the sight of Eugene, who screamed in terror and fired the .45 into the face of the ghoul as he squeezed his eyes closed in fear. The first bullet struck the zombie right between the eyes, the second going through the forehead as the gun rose slightly with each shot Eugene fired. The third bullet missed the ghoul completely, going over its head to hit the wall behind it. But the two rounds were enough, the back of the ghoul's head exploding outward to cover the wall with even more blood, bone and brain matter. Eugene turned away in horror to escape as the body slumped to the floor behind him. He found he couldn't run and so had to settle for a fast walk. He wanted to go faster but his legs wouldn't let him. He didn't give it much thought, however, only wanting to escape.

Coming to another elevator, he saw that this one needed an access card. As his mind raced with where he was going to get one, he glanced down to see there was one pinned to his dirty lab coat, the one taken from the dead scientist.

The name on the card was John Lazarus.

Swiping the card, the elevator door opened and he stepped inside. Pressing the button for the uppermost level, he rode the elevator to the top. The door opened onto a massive atrium made of stone and poured concrete. At the far end was a ramp. At the end of the ramp was where the bay doors were located, and where supplies were driven into the redoubt. Eugene knew there was a pedestrian door there also, to allow foot traffic in and out of the bunker.

He crossed the atrium, trying not to look at the carnage surrounding him. Once more, bodies and parts were strewn everywhere, more than one corpse missing its head due to the high impact rounds the soldiers had used to defend themselves. Eugene tried to remember what had happened at the beginning but it was all fuzzy. He remembered being attacked and bitten, and then later being taken to an isolation room where he was poked and prodded for days. With each day he'd felt sicker and sicker until he could barely keep his eyes open, as well as vomiting continuously.

He should be dead. He knew that right away but for some reason he wasn't. Maybe he was immune to the virus? That had to be it, or how else could he be still alive?

The odor of spilt blood made his stomach began to growl and he felt a ravenous hunger within him but ignored it. Right now he simply wanted to escape the redoubt, to get outside where there was clean air and sunlight.

When he reached the large bay door and pedestrian exit, he saw there was yet another keypad for both. He tried to use his ID card but the light remained red. He knew there was an override code but he didn't know it, nor would he have ever had a reason to. Panicking that he would be trapped in the bunker forever, his eyes began to scan the wall and surrounding area, and that was when he spotted seven numbers scrawled on the wall near the floor. There was a dead soldier lying on the floor with half a head and the dead man's right arm was stretched out so that his bloody index finger was no more than an inch away from the wall, right where the numbers had been written—in blood.

Eugene read the numbers, his lips moving as he did this, and then shrugged and punched the code into the keypad.

Immediately, the small red light turned green on the keypad and he heard the soft sound of a lock disengaging. Going to the pedestrian door, he pushed it open and stepped outside.

The light hurt his eyes and he had to blink profusely before he could see better; though the pain never seemed to leave his vision. He found himself in the middle of nowhere, in an austere field filled with nothing but tall grass and mountains surrounding him on all sides. He began to walk and soon reached the end of the field. When he turned around to see where he'd come from, he could barely make out the doors of the bunker, as they were camouflaged to look like nothing more than a large hillock amidst a field of grass. Even though he knew right where to look, the entrance to the redoubt was all but invisible—and the weeds had grown back quickly to mask any tire tracks from vehicles entering or leaving the bunker. It reminded him of that picture, where if you stared at it long enough, an image would take shape.

He began walking again, not knowing where he was going but knowing he needed to find shelter before the day ended. By the position of the sun in the sky, he knew it would be dark in a few hours.

He walked for two hours, surprised that he never felt tired, his legs never weakening. Though he still felt odd, he also found this indefatigable state exhilarating.

The sun had just begun to set when he detected an odor in the air, one of cooking meat—and another odor, one he didn't quite understand but found appetizing. He followed the scent like a bloodhound, weaving his way through the forest until he came to a small, open glade.

In the center of the glade was a family of four. A fire was going, and on a spit over the flames was a cooking rabbit, the grease from its fat dripping into the fire to sizzle and crack. The odor wafted into the air and Eugene figured that odor was what he had been smelling and had followed to the glade.

As he stepped out into the open, the family stopped talking amongst themselves and looked up, their faces taking on a look of fear. Eugene opened his mouth to speak, assuming that his disheveled state, the gun he held, and the blood-splattered lab coat he wore, had panicked the family. He was going to tell them he wasn't a danger to them, but the father of the family reached to his side and raised an old hunting rifle.

Seeing this, Eugene panicked and raised the .45 he still carried. Both men fired at the same time and Eugene watched as the man fell over with a bullet hole in his chest, dark blood seeping out to soak into the dry ground. Eugene felt a gentle tug at his stomach but there was no pain.

The rest of the family began to scream, the mother grabbing her two children to her—a girl and a boy of around seven and eight— and they huddled together in fear. Eugene stepped forward and raised his free hand to try and calm the family. As he did so, he glanced down at himself and it was then that he saw a small amount of congealing blood seeping from a hole in his abdomen, just below his belly button.

Forgetting the family for a moment, he stared down in shock to see that he had been shot after all. As he examined the wound, he slid his index finger into the hole and moved it around. He felt no pain, none at all. He didn't understand what was happening to him, why he felt nothing, not even a slight pressure as he explored the wound. Now why was there no blood?

He caught movement in the corner of his eye and he looked up to see that the mother had gone for her husband's rifle and was even now raising it to shoot Eugene.

Seeing this, Eugene didn't think, only reacted, and he raised the .45 yet again and fired at the woman. He didn't aim very well and the round ended up hitting the small boy first, going through his neck before it then entered the mother, hitting her in the almost exact same spot as Eugene's bullet wound.

The boy fell to the ground, gagging as blood geysered out of his torn neck to splatter hotly onto his screaming sister. The mother fell over as well, her bullet fired from the rifle going wild and high into the treetops as she crumpled to the ground, more blood seeping into the thirsty soil. Her left arm landed in the fire and she shrieked in pain, to then end up rolling right into the fire. Her clothes went up in seconds, and as she flailed her arms, she began to cook, her flesh blistering, her eyes melting in their sockets from the heat of the fire. She finally sucked in enough heat and fire and died, though the crackling of her body as the fire consumed it continued. The sweet smell of cooking human flesh permeated the glade.

The small girl was screaming uncontrollably as she stared at her dead family that only a minute ago had been laughing and talking with her.

Eugene was in shock, too. He'd never killed anyone before and now there was the blood of three people on his hands, one a child. Not knowing what to do, he stepped forward, wanting to calm the screaming child, to tell her how sorry he was, that it was all a mistake.

He was only a few feet away when an overwhelming hunger consumed him. He glanced at the rest of the now dead family, seeing their blood spilt, the coppery odor in the air, the mother burning, and the stench of scorched flesh filling the air as well.

At first he figured it was from the aroma of the cooking rabbit or even of the cooking woman, but as his mind raced, he realized it wasn't those smells at all and that those aromas did nothing to inflate his craving. That what he was detecting and now craving was the little girl. The *living* little girl. It was like he could see her life force, sense her heart beating within her, and he wanted it for himself—needed it.

In three quick steps he crossed the distance separating him from her, grabbed her, and held her close to him, so that her face was even with his. She kicked and screamed, tears running down her cheeks, her mouth open in a perpetual shriek.

Before he even fully understood what he was doing, he bent his head down and sank his teeth into her tender neck—the skin was soft and supple from youth. She was a pretty girl and if she'd lived, no doubt she would have become a beautiful woman one day.

Blood squirted into his mouth and Eugene moaned in pleasure. The little girl's legs kicked a few times before going still, and she faded into death by exsanguination, blood pattering to the ground beneath her.

Eugene continued to feed, that is until he heard something scratching at the ground behind him. Dropping the little girl, he turned to gaze down at the father, who was still alive, though holding on by a thread. The man was dragging himself across the ground towards Eugene, his eyes on his daughter as she lay limp on the ground. Eugene watched with curiosity at the man who refused to die.

When the father was only a foot from Eugene, the man reached out and grabbed Eugene's bare leg, the grip surprisingly firm for one so close to death.

Raising his head slightly, his eyes shifting to look up at Eugene's down-turned face, the man spoke in a rasping, hoarse voice: "*Why...did you...do this? Who... are... you?*"

Eugene thought about it for a moment, thinking of his name and how he'd always despised it. How when he was a child in school, the other kids had called him mean names made up from his own name.

But as he looked around him at the glade, now covered in blood and bodies, he realized it was a new world, a world where he could be anyone he wanted to be.

Glancing down at his blood-covered lab coat, his eyes focused on the ID card still there, the one he'd pinned back onto his coat after using it to gain access to the elevator. He read the name again and then looked down at the slowly dying father.

"My name is Lazarus," he said with a grim smile, and then went to his knees so that he was standing over the man. He took the father's head in his hands, and began to twist with all his might. The man screamed in agony as the newly-christened Lazarus continued turning the head, as if it was the cap on a soda bottle. The father's legs and arms flailed about wildly as his voice reached a crescendo of suffering. It went from a low decibel to incredibly high-pitched, as vocal cords were torn asunder. Then, the head was off and the decapitated body dropped to the ground, blood squirting from the jagged neck hole, as fingers curled and uncurled, nerve endings sending their last signals.

Lazarus held the severed head aloft, staring into the eyes that still saw with sight, and would for a few more seconds as the remaining oxygen still kept the man's brain alive. Lazarus was amazed at his strength and how easily it had been to tear off the man's head. It all came together in that exact instance, too. The bite, infection, experiments, the bullet hole in his stomach, how he felt no pain and craved human flesh, and now, his incredible strength.

He was a zombie, but for some reason unknown to him, he was still a thinking, reasoning entity. He looked down and to the right, where there was a puddle of blood, the sheen so clear it was like a mirror. When he peered into it, he saw his face, but it was different from the one he had known for his forty plus years on Earth. This face was pale, the eyes sunken into their sockets, the forehead protruding slightly. The lips were cracked and there was a patina of jaundice around the eyes.

He casually tossed the severed head into the flames just as the light went out in the father's eyes. The black hair began to burn immediately, curling in on itself, the eyes then bubbling as they were steamed in their sockets like hardboiled eggs.

The sound of the footsteps of many people moving through the forest filled the air and Lazarus looked up in time to see more than a dozen zombies stumble out into the glade, more than one tripping on its feet to hit the ground hard, to then pick themselves up. They had heard the gunshots and the mother and father's screams, as well as the girl's death cries.

They had come in search of fresh meat and had found it. They hadn't eaten in weeks and though the bodies were dead, they were still more than fresh enough to feed on.

Lazarus, upon seeing the ghouls, reverted back to who he once was and terror filled him at the sight of the zombie mob. His mind yelled, *STOP*! to the ghouls, not wanting them to get near him.

To his amazement and surprise, they did just that, halting in their tracks to remain immobile.

Lazarus watched them as they remained still and then began to hear something in his mind. It was hard to describe it, but the best way was that there was a sound in his head, like radio static. After a full minute he came to understand that this 'static' was really the minds of the zombies, that he was somehow able to tap into their dead brains.

He tried something.

Take one step forward, he thought to the zombies.

They did just that and then stopped.

Another, he thought.

They did.

To an observer watching at the edge of the glade, it would have looked like a silent game of *Simon Says.*

Lazarus began to smile, one so large it threatened to crack his face in two. Somehow, whatever had allowed him to remain a thinking entity also allowed him to tap into the zombies, to control them. Telepathy was the first word that came to mind, but whether that was what it might truly be was unknown. Not that it mattered. He could do it, *that* was what mattered.

He thought back to when he had first appeared in the glade and how the family had looked scared at the sight of him. He had assumed it was because he was a man carrying a gun who had come upon them suddenly, but now he realized that they had been terrified because he was a zombie. And he knew other humans would feel the same way, just as he had felt like that before he'd become infected.

Humans would want to kill him, to destroy him…unless he destroyed them first.

And now he had a way.

"Go 'head, my children, feed, eat all you want," he said to the zombies, and in his mind he told them to go ahead and eat the family of corpses.

The zombies moved instantly, shuffling to the four bodies, to then tear at them, pulling off limbs, sinking teeth into flesh still warm.

Just to make absolutely sure of his dominance over the undead, he willed them to stop feeding, and to his pleasure they did stop, though they continued to chew the bloody gobbets of flesh in their mouths.

It's all right, my children. Go 'head and keep feeding, he thought and they resumed their consumption, the sound of rending flesh and cracking bones filling the glade.

Lazarus began to laugh, and in that laughter was the sound of true madness, for what man could be turned into a zombie without going insane?

"Things are going to be different now!" Lazarus yelled to his undead soldiers. "I'm not a lowly janitor anymore. Now, I can be a king! And you will be my army, my dead army. With all of you and more of our kind that will soon join us, we'll become unstoppable! I'll gather all the dead across this state, and then the next, and then the next, thousands of them—no, millions!—and we'll wipe the humans off the face of this planet, either by feeding on them or by killing them and converting them to our cause, for every one that dies becomes one of us!" He raised his fists into the air, his sunken eyes alight with madness and power. "Soon, I will rule this world, this undead world!

As he laughed manically, the sounds of the zombies feeding joined in, a bitter portent of things to come.

Chapter 1

"What the hell, that ain't a fair trade!" a man in a worn leather jacket yelled angrily. He was coated in dust with a face that resembled road kill left out in the hot sun. Acne and blackheads covered him like a road map.

"It's a fair trade, mister. I swear, that's the best I can do," the old woman pleaded for reason from behind the counter of the trading post. "We need to make a living 'round here, too, ya know." The trading post was located on the outskirts of the small town of Battle Mountain, Nevada.

"Bullshit, that's bullshit and you know it," the man spit. "You're tryin' ta screw me, and now that I know about it, you're tryin' ta deny it."

Before the old woman knew what was happening, the man drew a battered Browning from his jacket and aimed the muzzle of the gun directly at the woman's forehead. Her eyes went wide as she came to the realization that she was about to die.

"So now I'm gonna take everything you got and leave you with a fucking hole in your head!" the man yelled, spittle flying from his cracked lips. He'd been on the road for more than a month, narrowly escaping the walking dead multiple times. He'd killed more men than he could count since the first contaminated rain fell, changing the world forever, and almost all of the men hadn't deserved it, not even close. He believed in this new world of the walking dead. That only the strong survived, and goddammit, he was the fucking strongest! A malevolent smile crossed his lips as his finger began to squeeze the trigger to blow the old woman's head clean off her shoulders.

Knowing she was dead, the trader closed her eyes and waited to feel the lead slug impact her skull. She jumped when the gunshot filled the inside of the trading post, but a split second later, she realized she was still alive...and she wasn't shot!

Opening her eyes a tad, she caught the end of the life of the man threatening her.

A bullet had impacted the back of the man's head, sending the upper half of his scalp and forehead flying into the air. As the man fell forward, the Browning fell from his grip to clatter on the counter. The man's brains blew out and around the old woman to spray the wall pink and red. Miraculously, not one bit of brain matter landed on her. The fresh corpse was slammed forward and then it rolled to the floor, the man's eyes still open, not understanding what had occurred.

The smell of cordite and blood filled the trading post as the old woman glanced past the counter to the stranger standing in the doorway before her with a 9mm Glock in his hand, smoke still drifting from the muzzle.

He wasn't overly tall, a shy over five eight, but his broad shoulders and grim visage gave him the look of a man six feet plus. His muscular arms were visible, the tank top he wore also showing off his powerful chest and the few gray chest hairs peeking through above the line of his shirt. As the old woman's eyes went higher, she saw a strong chin, slightly covered in stubble, and as she looked even higher, she saw the cold eyes of a killer. But there was something else swimming in those steely orbs, something that reminded her of mercy, of compassion.

His hair was cut short, and the once brown locks were now splattered with gray, giving him the look of a man much older than his forty-plus years. On his lower hip was a sixteen inch panga, the sheath worn, the handle looking as if the blade wasn't just for show but had seen hard use over the years.

"You all right, ma'am?" the man asked as he took a step closer, one eye always on the corpse just in case the man was somehow *not* dead.

"I...I'm fine, yes, many thanks. I thought I was a goner."

He grunted in reply and moved closer to the counter. Kneeling down over the corpse, he rifled through the man's leather jacket. He pulled out some spare ammo for the Browning, found a hunting knife and a few odds and ends, such as a cigarette lighter and a small box of toothpicks. He also found a roll of cash, hundred dollar bills by the looks of it, and as he rolled the wad in his hand, he casually tossed it aside. He had toilet paper, he didn't need any more.

"Do you have a name, mister?" the old woman asked, still shaky from her brush with death.

"Sure, the name's Henry Watson."

"Well, Mr. Watson, you're welcome to anything in my store as a thanks for saving my life."

Footsteps from the main entrance caused the old woman to look past Henry and to the doorway, where five people were crowding to get inside, all with concerned looks on their faces upon hearing the gunshot.

"Relax, miss, they're with me," Henry said as he stood up.

"You okay, Henry?" Jimmy Cooper asked as he burst inside the trading post, the first one in. "We heard a shot." Jimmy was in his twenties with a wiry frame and long brown hair. In his hand was a pump action shotgun and on his hips were a .357 Colt Python and a Bowie eight inch hunting knife, each having seen battle recently.

Right behind Jimmy was a beautiful blonde woman holding an M-16. Covered in dust from the road, Cindy Jensen was still gorgeous and wouldn't have looked out of place on the cover of a fashion magazine. In a pair of dirty BDUs and a button-down shirt, she was still a vision of beauty. The muzzle of the M-16 was pointed into the trading post, her finger on the trigger.

"I'm fine, Jimmy, everyone, stand down," Henry said as the others in the group of travelers shuffled inside, though the immediacy was passing with each second.

After Cindy came Mary Roberts, a brunette beauty in her own right. In her right hand, gripped tightly, was a .38 revolver, but when she heard Henry say things were fine, she quickly lowered it.

Behind Mary was Sue Anders. Forty plus a few more years—only Henry knew her true age—her blonde hair was tied back in a pony tail, making her look twenty years younger. She held a .22 in her right hand and the confidence in her eyes told anyone she knew how to use it. It hadn't always been that way before, but over time Sue had come to realize the benefits of being armed in a world where the dead walked and other humans either tried to eat or enslave you for profit.

As everyone gathered by the doorway, a head poked out from around Cindy's waist. The face was that of a teenage girl, with dark black hair and a pretty face. Raven swept her eyes across the inside of the trading post, took in Henry and the corpse, and then quickly ducked back out, satisfied that nothing interesting was happening, or it had already occurred.

With the exception of Raven, who stayed outside, the four companions shuffled forward to join Henry, so close together that Henry flashed a smile, finding the image humorous. He slid the Browning taken from the counter into the waistband of his BDUs and put the spare bullets in a lower pocket on his leg. "This guy didn't want to pay like the rest of us," he said and kicked the corpse.

Jimmy knelt down by the body and wrinkled his nose. "Whoa, this guy hasn't bathed in months," he said while waving a hand across his nose.

"How can you tell?" Cindy asked. "He shit his pants when Henry shot him."

"Trust me, the nose knows," Jimmy replied and stood up.

More footsteps were heard on the wooden front porch of the trading post, and a second later, two men in their sixties came charging in with rifles leading the way. They took one look at the six companions and leveled their weapons. Henry and the others did the same and for a split-second it looked like there was going to be a firefight in the store, but the old woman ran out from behind the counter and got between the two warring parties. "No, Jed, stop! These people saved my life!"

Jed, one of the men, came up short and pointed his rifle at the floor, the man beside him doing the same. Henry and the others kept their guns aimed at the two men, not assuming anything.

"This man," the old woman said and gestured to Henry, "shot that bastard on the floor when he tried to rob me. If it wasn't for him, I'd be dead right now."

Jed seemed to consider the woman's words for a second, then his eyes shifted to Henry. "This true, stranger?"

Henry shrugged and kicked the corpse. "That guy's dead and the woman isn't, so what do you think?"

Jed's mouth creased tighter but he didn't let on that Henry was getting to him. Instead he said, "Well, then, I guess you and your friends deserve a hearty thank you." He walked over to Henry and held out his hand. Henry stared at it for almost three seconds, then he holstered his Glock and took the older man's hand.

"It really wasn't that big of a deal," Henry said. "I was in the right place at the right time."

"And it's a good thing you were, too," the old woman said with a grin.

"Amen, Maggie," Jed added. He glanced down at the body and then to Jimmy. "Would you mind helping Earl get that piece of shit out of here, son?" He gestured to the other older man, who was Earl.

Jimmy shrugged. "Sure, I can do that." He slung his shotgun over his shoulder and went to the corpse's legs, while Earl went to the head and picked the body up by the shoulders. With both men grunting slightly under the dead weight, they carried the body out of the store.

"So where you all from?" Jed asked as he leaned against the counter.

Maggie had walked away and she came back a minute later with bottles of homemade beer. She popped the top off three of them and placed them before Henry and Jed, Cindy taking the other and sharing with Mary. Sue joined Henry and everyone stood at ease.

"Here and there," Henry said cryptically.

Jed's jaw tightened slightly but then it relaxed. "Mind if I ask ya what's your business here?"

"We're just passing through," Cindy said.

"That's right," Henry agreed. "We heard about your trading post and seems we needed a few things, we thought we'd come by. Once we get what we need we'll be moving on."

"Whatever you need is on me, Mr. Watson," Maggie said again. "I owe you a great debt." She was washing the brain matter off the wall with a dirt rag.

Henry reached into his pocket and pulled out a slip of paper. He handed it to her. "What we need is on this paper. The stuff circled is what we really need and the rest is stuff we'd just like to get."

Maggie nodded. "I'll get right on this." Then she was off to the back of the store, the sounds of her digging floating back to the others seconds later.

"Are you gonna visit Battle Mountain before you go?" Jed asked.

Henry took a sip of his beer, wincing at the bitter taste, then he shook his head. "No, there's no need."

"Besides," Mary added, "whenever we go to towns and the like, it seems we always get into trouble."

"Amen," Cindy added. Mary handed her the beer after tasting it, not liking the taste. Cindy on the other hand drank half in one gulp.

"How is it around here for deaders?" Sue asked, wanting to get in on the conversation. "It seems pretty quiet."

"What's a deader?" Jed asked and then he figured it out. "Oh wait, do you mean the *goners*?"

"Goners?" Henry repeated.

"Sure, like that guy's a goner," Jed explained, referring to the removed corpse.

"Oh, okay sure," Henry replied. "We call them *deaders* if they're local ones, and the ones you see out on the highways roaming around searching for food we call *roamers*."

Jed thought that one over, then smiled. "Roamers, I like that. Mind if I steal it?"

"Be my guest."

Jimmy returned with Earl, the two joining the others at the counter. Maggie appeared as if from nowhere and two more beers were in her hands. She handed one to Jimmy and one to Earl, both men saying thank you.

"I think I have most of what was on your list, Mr. Watson," Maggie said. "Should have it all together in an hour or so."

"That's fine. Thank you," Henry said.

Jed was talking to Sue, answering her question. "Up here in the mountains, the *goners* are few and far between since we killed most of them already. Every now and then one wanders into town, but we take care of it easily. Now, down near Vegas, that's where the biggest hordes are. Go there and you'll see thousands of them."

"We don't plan on going near Las Vegas," Henry said, the others agreeing. Raven was at the door now, watching everyone, but she didn't want to join the group. She liked being on the outside, watching. She was like a cat, her eyes lazy to the casual viewer, but at a moment's notice she could pounce. She tapped one of her long, razor-sharp fingernails on the doorframe. All her fingernails were sharp, a honed edge on each of them. They were weapons by themselves, and Raven could slice a man's throat before he knew what had happened. She was a mystery to the others, even Sue who had been with her when the companions had found the two of them tied up in the bathroom of an old Greyhound bus. Raven didn't talk much, but preferred to listen.

"That's a wise thing, mister," Jed said and finished off his beer. Wiping his mouth on the back of his arm, he nodded to Maggie who had reappeared after disappearing again. "I'm gonna be off, Maggie, it looks like things are all set here."

Earl joined Jed, as if he was a faithful sidekick or a loyal dog. With a nod of his head to Henry and a glance at the others, Jed turned and left the store with Earl, leaving the companions alone— with the exception of Maggie, who could be heard digging in some part of the store for supplies.

"So what next?" Jimmy asked.

"We get stocked up and move on. What else is there?" Henry said to Jimmy and the others, who all agreed that was the next thing to do.

"We could visit Battle Mountain," Sue said. "Jed told us we could."

"Not this time, Sue," Henry said. "We'll be able to get what we need from Maggie, then we'll hit the open road, bypass Vegas completely, and see what's in Oregon."

"At least we're not walking," Jimmy said and received a harsh glare from Henry to shut up. Not taking chances, they had hidden the beat-up Ford pickup a mile and a half down the road. The pickup had half a tank of fuel and another five gallons in an old metal gas can in the rear bed. Once that ran out, unless they came across more fuel, it would be back to walking, which was never a good thing when an undead horde could be just around the next bend.

"Okay, let's tally up everything I have for you," Maggie said, popping up behind the counter with an armful of supplies.

Stepping around the already congealing blood on the floor, the companions did just that.

Chapter 2

Loaded down with supplies, the six companions walked back to their hidden pickup truck after leaving the trading post behind.

"Wow, Maggie sure was appreciative of you, Henry," Mary said as she slogged along, the heavy backpack filled with dry and canned goods weighing her down. Normally, none of the group would ever carry so much gear. Being weighed down would mean a person would be slow on the draw and even a second too slow to pull your gun could be fatal, but it was a short walk to the pickup, where they could then put it all in the rear bed.

"I know," Henry replied. "Who would have guessed when we went there that we'd end up getting all this for practically nothing?" Maggie had almost everything on Henry's list, and when it had all been wrapped and tallied, Maggie had only asked for a few of the companions' spare bullets in payment, the rest being a gift for Henry's good deed of saving Maggie's life.

Henry had given her half the clip from the spare he had from the Browning taken from the man he'd killed, so in reality the supplies had been totally free.

He felt no guilt for taking that man's life. Henry had never been one to think too much about the meaning of life. He believed in the good and bad of all people, and if a person tried to take the life of another in cold blood, then that person forfeited their life if someone like Henry came along to stop it.

He'd killed many men and women since the dead began to walk and if he wanted to keep on living, no doubt he would kill even more. But his inner sense of justice kept him from crossing that line where he became a coldheart, but he also knew he would cross *any* line if it would save his friends from pain or death.

The pickup was exactly where they'd left it, hidden in a small copse of trees, the branches having been cut to cover the vehicle in the exact same position.

Cindy had set up a few traps as well, such as twigs leaning at odd angles and other such ways to identify if the pickup had been found, but everything was as she'd left it.

In no time, the supplies had been taken off weary shoulders and tossed into the rear bed, then everyone climbed aboard with Henry in the driver's seat.

The pickup shot out of the copse of trees to spray branches in all directions. With a spinning of tires, it was soon lost from sight.

Two hours later, Henry slowed the pickup and pointed up the road. Beside him in the cab, Sue saw what he was pointing at.

"You think he's friendly?" she asked as she eyed the man standing in the middle of the road far ahead. The man was waving at the pickup. "Or do you think he's a decoy of some kind?"

Henry felt a swell of pride rise up in him when Sue asked these questions. When he'd first met her she'd been rather passive and wouldn't even hold a gun. Now she was thinking like a warrior, like someone who wanted to stay alive and would do what was needed to remain that way.

"There's no way to know unless we go forward and spring the trap," Henry said. The man lowered his hand and stood still, waiting to see what Henry was going to do. Henry watched the man for a full five minutes, ignoring Jimmy's questions when he called down to Henry from the rear bed.

Henry took in the way the man stood, his posture to be exact. If the man was a decoy, his body language said otherwise. Henry had seen many men when they were about to attack him and they always had a certain look, like a mousetrap ready to snap shut. This man seemed the exact opposite. Never a man to ignore his gut instinct, Henry began to drive forward, while calling out the window to Jimmy, "Stay sharp back there, Jimmy. I don't think we're gonna have trouble but let's not take any chances." The other reason Henry was concerned was that this was the only serviceable road heading west to Oregon, and Henry wasn't about to stop, turn around, and backtrack to find another route simply because there was a man standing in the road. The companions came across travelers like themselves all the time and more often than not the people were friendly. But the few times they hadn't been...well, those were tense times where more often than not blood was spilled. Luckily, so far none of it had been the companions'.

"Got it, old man," Jimmy called back. "If those trees along the road hold anything other than trees, the people in there are in for a surprise." The sound of guns being cocked and checked filled the air and floated down to Henry. Beside him, Sue also got her .22 ready and Henry felt even more pride fill him at the sight.

As he drove closer to the man, his eyes took in the sides of the road and the desiccated corpses lying there. At some point in the past, the bodies had been tossed there. Whether they had been zombies or were just people gunned down was unknown. Once a body began to rot, whether it had been walking before it was put down for good couldn't be seen. A few buzzards fed on the jerky-like flesh, and what was left of the bleached skeletons.

Henry stopped the pickup a good thirty feet from the man, who smiled and waved again. Henry held his Glock in his hand, which rested on his lap, and if so much as a leaf moved in a tree on either side of him, the man would find a bullet in his chest before said leaf had stopped moving. The trees were sparse here, dry and thin, as the mountains became the desert and flatland encroached to the road.

Opening his door, Henry stepped out, looking in at Sue. "You stay put. If anything happens, you slide behind the wheel and get out of here."

"But what about y..."

"No buts, just drive away." He began to walk towards the man after a quick look at Jimmy and the others, who with a simple nod knew what to do. After years traveling together, the companions could pass volumes of information with a glance or a nod, each knowing what the other was thinking. Cindy was kneeling in the rear bed with the M-16 resting on the roof of the cab, the muzzle aimed directly at the chest of the man who was now walking towards Henry with a wide smile on his lips. Mary and Jimmy had their eyes focused on each side of the pickup, watching for movement along the road, while Raven looked in all directions, her eyes squinting in the harsh sun, her mouth set in a tight grimace. Her black hair flew around her head like a halo of ink and she had to push it down with a hand so she could keep her vision clear.

"Hello there," the man said. "I'm Shaun. Shaun McAllister. It's good to see other humans. I was beginning to think I was the only one living around here."

"You alone, Shaun?" Henry asked. " 'Cause if anything comes at us, I promise you that you'll be the first one to die." Henry aimed the Glock directly at the man's heart to prove his point.

Shaun blinked at that but he shook his head no. "I'm alone if that's what you mean. There's no one hiding in the brush waiting to attack you."

Henry saw that Shaun carried a rifle and he gestured to it with the tip of his Glock. "You have a gun. So why did you simply wave to me? For all you knew, me and my friends were coldhearts that would have killed you to take what you have."

Shaun nodded at that. "True, but I also saw there were way more of you than of me. I highly doubt I could have held you and your people off for too long with just my rifle if I had to."

"Yeah, but you could have tried. So instead you just decided to be friendly and roll the dice that we were too? You know what would have happened if we weren't, right?"

Shaun visibly relaxed at Henry's statement, as he now knew that his gamble had paid off and Henry and the others weren't going to kill him. Shaun smiled as he said, "I guess you would have shot me dead and taken my meager possessions... what there is of them, that is." He pulled off his backpack. "Myself, I don't think I have anything worth killing over, but then..."

"Buddy," Henry said. "I've seen men killed over a sip of water or less. Trust me, if we were coldhearts, we wouldn't be having this conversation."

"Fair enough."

"Hey, Henry!" Jimmy called from the pickup. "Everything okay?"

Henry tuned slightly to call back to Jimmy, but he never took his eyes off Shaun—just in case he was wrong about the man. "It's fine, we'll be right there." He turned back to face Shaun completely. "You want a ride?"

"Depends. Where're you headed?"

Henry pointed down the road. "That way."

Shaun chuckled slightly at that, seeing that was all he was going to get out of Henry. "Well then, after such a detailed explanation of your destination, sure, I'd love a ride."

Henry waved and the pickup began to move, Sue driving. The entire time Henry had talked to Shaun, the deadlands warrior's eyes had been scanning the sides of the road. Not one leaf had stirred.

As they waited a few seconds for the pickup to reach them, Henry gave Shaun the once-over one more time. He appeared to be in his late twenties, with sandy-brown hair, a strong face and piercing blue eyes. He was handsome in a surfer boy kind of way. He wore a faded pair of jeans and a plaid shirt, both covered in dust. A baseball cap with no insignia on it adorned his head to keep off the hot sun. He hadn't shaved in at least two weeks, the beard scraggly in a few places, reminding Henry of a teenager that was trying to grow a beard, but it wouldn't grow well in all the right places on his face. Other than the rifle and backpack, he carried nothing else.

Sue slowed the pickup a few feet from the two men and Henry waved Shaun to follow him to the vehicle. All guns were on Shaun, despite Henry's relaxed posture.

"Guys, this is Shaun. We're gonna let him ride with us for a while."

"Hey," Shaun said to the gun barrels pointing at him.

"Hey, yourself," Mary said, a coy smile on her face. Henry saw that smile and wondered if Mary was attracted to Shaun, but then put it out of his mind. If she was, that was between the two of them, not him. Though he sometimes felt like Mary was his daughter, in truth she wasn't, and he had to let her make her own decisions.

With help from the others, Henry and Shaun were pulled into the rear of the pickup, then Henry slapped the cab and Sue began to drive. For now she could drive alone, as Henry wanted to talk some more with Shaun.

Shaun was happy to oblige, and he quickly told the companions his tale of survival, how he'd been in college till the zombie outbreak and had gone home, only to then run from his town when it became overrun by zombies more than a year ago, and how he'd been traveling alone ever since. A few times he'd come across some tight scrapes, but luck had seen him through in one piece.

"And here I am with you people," Shaun finished as the companions looked at him and each other.

"Shit, Shaun, you're one lucky bastard," Jimmy said. Though Cindy had looked at Shaun with admiration, Jimmy couldn't help but like the man despite a twinge of jealousy. But when Shaun had answered a question from Cindy—and had flashed his blue eyes at her—Jimmy had made sure to wrap his arm around her, the gesture telling Shaun clearly that Cindy was his. Shaun had merely smiled slightly and continued talking.

"Yes, I guess I am. And now I found you people," Shaun said.

"You sure did," Henry added. "But don't think you're one of us just yet. That's gonna take some time."

Shaun smiled at that, the gesture going to his eyes and making everyone around him like him even more. "I wouldn't have it any other way."

Chapter 3

The small town of Bishop, Nevada had done well since the zombie outbreak. With underground wells and solar power, they'd managed to keep the town safe, especially after building a ten foot wall around the entire town.

The mayor had seen to everyone's needs, setting up a roster for standing guard, along with the local police. There were even crops being grown in greenhouses so as to keep the plants out of direct sunlight, unless it was absolutely necessary. Nevada wasn't known for its crops but the town of Bishop was changing all that. Totally self-sufficient, the town was even beginning to prosper and replace the lost population that had died from first the contaminated rains, and later from the walking dead.

It was just coming on four o'clock in the afternoon on this humid day, something the populace wasn't used to. Usually the heat was dry, and the thickness of the air made everyone sleepy, especially as they didn't have the power to spare on fans or air conditioning. The solar panels on most of the houses were only so strong and the batteries in basements that were charged by the panels only so big.

So the residents of Bishop had to try and find a cool place in the shade to weather the heat; a few children were even lucky enough to have small pools half-filled with water to play in. The pool water was also used for showering and watering crops and was collected from rainfall using intricate pipes and aqueducts connected to every roof and flat surface in the town. If desperate, the water could be drunk after boiling or by using purification tablets.

The pools were then covered to protect against evaporation but on a day such as this, the covers were removed so that the children could have a fun day. Even though life was tough, the residents knew there were times when the leash had to be removed and some time for enjoyment allowed.

On the north wall, overlooking Route 88, three men stood guard, nothing but a beach umbrella for each to keep the hot sun off their heads.

One of the men was named John Cummings, and for the thousandth time since he'd come on guard duty, he gazed up at the sky and wished the sun to go down. He had another four hours, give or take a few minutes, on watch. Reaching down to his side, he picked up the canteen filled with tepid water. Taking a swig, he screwed the cap back on and put it down again. To his right, Fred was snoring loudly and John frowned. They had agreed to let each of them sleep for a bit, while the other two stood guard, but snoring hadn't been part of the equation. If the guard captain came up and heard the snoring, then they would all be in trouble. Latrine duty was the usual punishment and John cringed at the thought. Digging holes for toilets in the hot sun at the edge of town wasn't something he looked forward to, but filling in holes full of shit was even worse.

John glanced to his left to see Paul was concentrating on his shirt sleeve, on a loose thread that wouldn't come free when he pulled on it. The thread would slide through his sweaty fingers each time. Finally, Paul leaned forward and used his teeth, yanking the annoying thread free and leaving a run in his shirt.

Sighing at the two fools he was saddled with, John turned and looked back out onto the horizon. But where he expected to see the same sight as always, instead he saw small dots that appeared to be moving towards him.

There were a lot of them, too.

At first he didn't give it much thought, thinking it was a mirage caused by the late-day heat, but as he continued to stare, the dots began to coalesce into even more, and as the minutes ticked by, the first dots began to take on form.

He didn't like what he saw.

Grabbing a pair of binoculars near his feet, he scanned the dots and gasped at what the image that came into clarity. Zooming in, he focused on the first dot in line and his heart began to triphammer in his chest at the sight.

Zombies.

More than a thousand, easy.

He scanned the approaching horde, his mouth sagging open in amazement. There were all shapes and sizes, all minorities—that is, the ones that weren't so decayed that their appearances couldn't be discerned.

He shifted his gaze back to a zombie that seemed to be in the lead, and as he did this, the zombie looked directly at John, as if the ghoul could see John's eyes through the binoculars from a quarter mile away.

Then the zombie stuck up its middle finger and thrust it at John.

"No fucking way," John whispered. "That zombie just flipped me off. It can't be." He wiped his eyes as if that would wash away the image and looked through the binoculars again. Yup. It was the same sight, a thousand-strong horde of zombies was coming straight at him...and the town.

"Oh shit, oh sweet Jesus," John whispered and then turned to Paul who was now studying the fingernail on his right index finger, intermittently gnawing on it to pull out an annoying hangnail. "Paul, hey Paul, look out there!" John yelled.

Paul looked up, as if coming free from a daze. "Huh? What's wrong, John?"

"What's wrong? You fucking moron. Look out there and tell me what's wrong."

Paul did as he was told and his eyes went wide, his mouth slipping open in amazement. "Is that..."

"Yeah, it is. It's a fucking zombie horde. We've got to warn the town."

Fred snorted, awoken by all the yelling. "What the hell's the matter with you two? Why all the yelling?"

"That's why." John pointed out over the wall where the zombies were moving closer. He could see a large black cloud hovering over the marching undead army, and he quickly figured out it wasn't smoke but blowflies, millions of them, all feeding on the decaying bodies.

"Oh my God, are those...?" Fred began and John quickly cut him off.

"It sure as shit is. We've got to warn the town." He picked up a two-way radio and quickly called it in. The dispatcher on the other end took some convincing and told John that if this was some kind of practical joke, he'd pay for it later.

"It's not a joke, damn it," John said into the radio. "Get every available gun on the north wall right now! And sound the alarm!"

Seconds later, an air raid siren filled the air, signaling the town of the emergency.

Within minutes more men and women arrived at the wall, after being directed on where to go by others who had gotten their information from the dispatcher. The town had gone through drills many times for this exact scenario, though no one had believed it would ever happen. In fact, the past few months the amount of walking dead had dwindled to almost nothing, and there had been hopes that the outbreak was finally over.

But those hopes were quickly dashed as each person climbed the wall to see the massive undead horde heading straight for them.

A few began firing as soon as they saw the undead horde and it was John who made them stop. "Wait till they're closer, damn it!" he snapped loudly. "We only have so much ammo, so conserve it. They're too far away right now anyway."

"Jesus Christ, there's so many," a new arrival said from John's side as more and more men and women lined up on the wall. There were so many people on the wall that John wondered if the wall could hold all the weight.

"The more the merrier," John said. "Just more to shoot at when the time comes." From the looks of it, only minutes were left before it would be time to start the barrage of lead. A few had already begun shooting again and this time John let them at it, knowing he could only hold them back for so long. Nervously, he kept checking and rechecking his weapon as the seconds counted down.

Then it was time.

"Fire at will!" John yelled and the reports of over a hundred guns filled the air, John joining in as well. On either side of him, Fred and Paul did the same, shooting at the massive amount of animated corpses.

At first it seemed that the townspeople had the upper hand, taking out zombie after zombie, the bodies then falling to the ground to lie still. But John soon realized this wasn't helping the situation as each time a body went down, other zombies would pick it up and carry it forward. When the first of the undead horde

ANTHONY GIANGREGORIO

reached the base of the stone wall made from boulders of all sizes and cement, the fallen zombies were used like cordwood, their bodies packed against the wall one at a time to make crude steps.

It reminded John of something he'd seen in a barbarian movie, when Vikings were sacking a town. With each body knocked off its feet, the corpse became another stepping stone to scale the wall. John quickly could see what was happening and he tried to tell his fellow residents to stop firing, that they were falling right into the zombie's hands, as hard as that was to believe. For what was happening was that the zombies were thinking, were planning, and simply shooting them in the head wasn't going to work this time, and in fact by killing the zombies, the town was falling into the diabolical plans of the undead. He began going from person to person, yelling at them to cease firing, but no one listened, too caught up in the bloodlust of killing.

Finally, John gave up and was about to get off the wall and try and find the mayor, or the chief of police, anyone he thought he could talk some sense into, when he was knocked off the wall to fall head first to the ground.

At the last second, he managed to tuck in his head, but he landed hard enough to be knocked unconscious. The last thing he heard were the gunshots as the defenders continued firing, the reports echoing across the town.

As John lay unconscious, the first zombies climbed over the corpses of their fallen brethren and stormed the wall. The fighting quickly became hand-to-hand with the townspeople sorely lacking against a foe that felt no pain.

In the thick of it all stood Lazarus, who was controlling the zombies telepathically. His orders were simple. Kill the humans and feed on them only a little, that way there was more than enough to reanimate and so replenish the undead soldiers that he'd lost in the attack.

The townspeople fought back with resolve at first, but with each loss of their numbers, they quickly fell apart and began to try and retreat. This was a lost cause for the zombies then swarmed over the wall en masse and began moving through the town, taking each resident from their homes to then tear out throats or other grue-some ways to kill each human.

Though Lazarus told his undead soldiers not to eat them all, to his dismay he found that some zombies didn't listen, their blood-lust too strong. These zombies tore their victims apart.

Frowning at this, Lazarus resolved to find a way to make sure it didn't happen again, though he had no idea how he would do this.

John had been left alone during the ransacking of the town, af-ter a zombie had been shot in the head to fall on top of him. Now, as he awakened and pushed the body off him, he gazed up at a crowd of undead faces, all looking down at him. Reaching for his gun, it was nowhere nearby and he realized it had fallen out of his reach when he'd landed. All around him were the screams of his fellow townspeople, as they were killed and converted to the walking dead.

"Why hello there," Lazarus said to John, who blinked in sur-prise. Did a zombie really just talk to him? Figuring he must be delusional from the fall, John said nothing, and only stared at the pale faces leaning over him. In the back of his mind a small thought of wondering why they hadn't attacked him yet came to him, but he pushed it down. He wasn't complaining, not one bit.

Two faces to his right looked familiar, and as he shifted slightly so that the sun wasn't in his eyes anymore, he saw that the two zombies were Paul and Fred. Both had large, bloody holes in their throats and Fred was missing his right cheek, while Paul had a missing eye. Both gazed down at John with a blankness he'd never seen in the undead before. Normally a zombie had hunger in its eyes, and that was it.

The screaming and gunshots had faded dramatically since John had first woken and a sinking filling overcame him at the thought that the entire town had been wiped out.

"I said hello," Lazarus repeated and this time John looked the zombie right in the face, and when he did, the zombie actually *smiled*. As impossible as that sounded that was exactly what he'd seen.

"What's wrong? Cat got your tongue?" Lazarus joked. "Ah, where are my manners. My name is Lazarus, and you've already met my dead army."

"You...you can talk," John said, his voice dry from the dust he'd sucked in.

"I know, right? Isn't it cool?" Lazarus smile widened even more. "And I can do so much more than that, in fact. Why, I can control my army with my mind. Pretty neat, huh? Like something out of a sci-fi movie."

"What do you want with me? My town?"

"What do I want with you?" Lazarus seemed to consider this for a second, as if it was a heavy question that needed long contemplation. Then he said, "Why, I want to turn you all into undead beings like me, what else?"

"You mean zombies?" John asked.

"No," Lazarus said, his voice becoming angry. "I don't like that word, it's soooo... clichéd. No, I prefer the name undead being. It sounds so professional, not like a character in a children's horror story."

"Why am I still alive?" John asked, though he didn't really want to know the answer. It couldn't be good, he knew that.

"Oh, my little man, you're still alive because I like to play with my food." Lazarus turned to Paul and Fred and creased his eyes in thought. A second later, the two newly-christened zombies picked John up and held him tight. John tried to pull himself free but he was helpless. The word *deathgrip* had taken on an entirely new meaning for him.

"Do you have a name, food?" Lazarus asked.

"John Cummings," he said, swallowing heavily but holding his chin up. If he was going to die, he would die like a man, not groveling for his life. The odor of rotting meat was so strong it took all he had not to vomit right there. Blowflies flitted on his head, tasting his sweat, and more fed on each zombie around him as they stood mindlessly still, awaiting orders.

"Go 'head then, you asshole, kill me and be done with it. I'm through talking to you," John said defiantly.

Lazarus laughed, as if he'd just heard the most entertaining joke in a long time. "I agree. This conversation hasn't even begun and I find it already boring. Maybe you'll be more interesting when you're one of my soldiers."

John opened his mouth to rebut but before he could get out so much as one word, Lazarus took a step forward and snapped his head down at John's throat, his teeth sinking into the warm flesh and tearing out skin and muscle, including John's carotid artery. Lazarus leaned back and stood a step to the side, focusing all his mental power on keeping his zombies motionless. He could feel them wanting to move forward and tear John apart, the smell of hot blood overwhelming to them. But Lazarus maintained control and not one zombie moved. Well, maybe one did, but only a little. As John bled out, Fred reached an index finger out, let it become coated in warm blood, then licked it clean like a small boy sucking dripping ice cream from his fingers. Lazarus let it go, knowing there was only so much he could control.

John gagged and choked as he bled out, then his head sagged forward in death. The blowflies went to work on the pool of blood on the ground, lapping up the sticky goodness. Lazarus put out a mental call to all the zombies in town to come to him, that it was time to move on to the next enclave, to continue the cycle again and then again after that.

Lazarus felt a stirring, that of yet another mind joining his, and he turned to see that John's head was up again and he was looking at Lazarus with a blank expression. Lazarus willed Fred and Paul to release John, who stood by himself.

"Ah, John, welcome back. And welcome to my dead army. Now, let's finish up here and move on, there are more humans to kill, and more undead beings to make."

John shuffled to Lazarus' side and the two undead beings moved off, the zombie horde quickly gathering around them and following, leaving nothing behind but blood and death in their wake.

Chapter 4

Jimmy looked around, not understanding where he was. He was standing in the middle of a wide-open plain of seared flesh and burning babies. Not knowing what to do, he began walking, his feet sinking into the fetid pools of gore, the pus and blood sucking at the soles of his boots as he made his way through this nightmarish landscape.

The sky was almost pitch black with rumbling storm clouds overhead. The smell of ozone tickled his nose, as if it would rain at any moment. Small creatures skittered amongst the flesh coating the ground, things with red eyes that peered at him as if he was the alien, the intruder into their world of horror.

Turning around, Jimmy saw nothing but a bleak horizon. At least before him he could make out shapes, and he knew if he was to escape this nightmare, he would have to continue forward.

Eventually he came to a small hill, a single tree with no leaves and gnarled branches atop it. Bleached bones littered the ground like mulch under the tree, and the tree itself was covered with bodies, all hanging like ornaments on a Christmas tree. Many of the bodies were bloated, and more than one had exploded from internal gases, intestines and other organs spraying the ground with gore, to cover the earth with bones of dark color. Rats had crawled up the tree to feed on the corpses, taking the choicest parts, to then scurry off to eat in peace in the bent branches. Crows were there as well, plucking out eyeballs and tongues, going for the softest meat first.

The wind changed direction and blew at Jimmy, and it was all he could do not to double over and vomit, the rancid smell of rotting meat overwhelming him. Breathing through his mouth, he covered his nose with his left arm and continued onward until he had climbed the hill and was directly under the tree. There was a soft patter coming from around him, as if of rain, but it was only the drip, drip of congealed blood seeping from the corpses.

As he stared at the bodies, they begin to twitch and then, one at a time, they pulled themselves off the branches they were impaled on and slid off the limbs holding them.

As they fell to the ground, many broke open, like spilled meat bags, the rest landing heavily to then get up. Those that stood, with broken arms and legs, began to drag themselves closer to Jimmy.

Jimmy backed away, only to trip over the bones beneath his feet and fall onto his butt. He gazed up at the corpses as they shambled to him, eyes missing, gaping sockets now wriggling with maggots, night crawlers sliding out of noses to then slide into open mouths devoid of tongues. Cockroaches poking their heads out of ear canals, to then sniff the air, before delving back within skulls to feed on the tender brains within.

Jimmy didn't know how he knew it, but he knew with all his heart that the dead wanted to eat him, that they wanted to consume him body and soul. And when they were done, there would be nothing left of Jimmy Cooper, he would be just a memory that would soon fade away like smoke in the wind.

He would cease to exist...forever.

He screamed once as they swarmed over him, suffocating him with their foulness. Hands reached out for him, covering him, smothering him, and in that instant, Jimmy knew he was going to die

He tried to fight them, to roll over and crawl away to escape, but there were too many hands on him, holding him down, trapping him.

He watched in horror as the first mouth closed on his arm and teeth began to sink into his flesh. But where he expected to feel searing pain as yellow teeth sank into his skin, he was surprised when it only felt like a pinprick, as if someone had poked him with a needle, albeit a large one.

Before anything else could happen, before more teeth could find his tender flesh, his eyes snapped open and Jimmy saw that the nightmare landscape was gone, to be replaced by a wide open plain of land filled with scrub brush and shrubs, as well as a few cacti.

Though the horrible dream was already fading, he felt pain in his arm where the fictional corpse had bitten him. Glancing to where the pain was, his vision still fuzzy from sleep, he saw a simple bee on his arm, its stinger embedded deep in his flesh. As Jimmy watched, the bee separated itself from its stinger and fell off him to land in the dirt, the bee committing suicide in this violent act, as if it was willing to give up its life if it meant causing Jimmy harm.

Jimmy took all this in with a calm face, as if he was watching a movie. Then neurons fired and adrenalin surged through his body and he was suddenly awake. Jumping to his feet, he yelled, "Henry! I need help here!" Instantly it all came back. The traveling for hours, to then pull over and rest, Jimmy taking a nap after going off behind a line of shrubs to make love to Cindy. After that she had been full of energy but he had wanted to sleep, so had gone to a small tree to get in the shade and had quickly drifted off. Unknown to him, high in the tree, was a beehive, and one particular bee had decided Jimmy being so close to its home was offensive.

Footsteps came running from behind him and Jimmy turned around to see Henry running, Mary and Sue right behind him. From the opposite direction came Raven and Cindy, who had gone for a walk together. Shaun popped up near the pickup truck, where he'd been checking the engine over. It had been running hot and he wanted to see if there was a leak in the radiator or one of the hoses.

"Jimmy, what's wrong?" Henry called out as he ran up to Jimmy, his Glock in his hand.

"I've been bit by a bee!" Jimmy yelled, his face taking on a look of absolute fear.

"So what?" Mary said. "Oh, Jimmy, you're such a big baby. Let me see, I'll get the stinger out for you if it's still in there."

"No, you don't understand," Jimmy said in a slurred voice, already feeling lightheaded. "I'm allergic. I need an epi-pen. If I don't get an injection in the next fifteen minutes, I'm gonna die!"

As the companions surrounded Jimmy, each looked at the other, not knowing how to fix this problem. Zombies they could handle, even cannibals or slavers, but this...this was something new.

None of them had an epi-pen on them, not thinking there had ever been a reason to carry one in their supplies, and Jimmy having never shared this information with the others could now mean his doom.

"Oh God, Henry," Cindy said as she rushed to Jimmy and held him up—his face and arms were already beginning to swell with the allergic reaction. "What do we do? If we can't get him help he's going to die!"

Henry shook his head with concern for his friend. "I don't know, Cindy, I honestly don't know."

Chapter 5

Shaun joined the companions, his eyes taking in Jimmy's swelling condition, only hearing the tale end of the conversation. "What's wrong with him?" he asked.

"Jimmy's been bit by a bee," Mary informed Shaun. "He's allergic; he's having an allergic reaction. In fifteen minutes he'll be dead if we don't get him help."

As if to prove her point, Jimmy began to gasp as his throat closed up.

"We need to find an epi-pen," Sue added and went to Jimmy, too, wishing there was something she could do for him.

"Well, there's a middle school about a mile from here," Shaun quickly said. "They might have one in the nurse's office. That is if it hasn't been ransacked."

"Sounds like a chance," Henry said. He went to Jimmy and wrapped his arm around his friend and began to half-carry him to the waiting pickup. "Come on, let's move. We don't have a lot of time here."

Henry reached the pickup in seconds and practically dumped Jimmy into the passenger seat, Cindy right behind him to slide in next. Then Henry climbed in and grabbed the keys where they were hidden under the mat. It wouldn't do to have one of them have the keys and something happen and another of the group needed to drive it away fast, so the 'under the mat' trick had been decided on. When the pickup had been found, the keys were still in the ignition, the driver nowhere to be seen. The assumption was that someone had stopped on the side of the road and had befallen harm, the pickup left unattended. Someone else's misfortune was the companions' gain, was the way Henry looked at it.

The others grabbed what supplies they had and tossed it all into the rear bed, then followed it all in themselves. Sue was barely onboard when Henry stepped on the gas pedal and the pickup surged forward, spitting dirt and gravel out behind it. Sue would have fallen off if Raven hadn't acted fast, reaching out and pulling her back from the brink.

"Thank you, Raven, I could have broken my neck," Sue gasped as she fell onto the rear bed, the vehicle rocking back and forth like a ship at sea.

Raven nodded in reply, never one to use words when a gesture would suffice.

Shaun stood at the front of the bed, holding on for dear life as Henry shot down the road. Shaun slapped the roof of the cab once or twice and leaned over so he could yell at Henry, pointing the way they needed to go. Halfway there, a zombie lurched out onto the road. It was wearing clothes that were little more than rags, no shoes on its feet. Both eyes were missing and the nose had rotted off more than a year ago. Its mouth sagged open, a dried-out tongue laying there like a dead fish.

Henry didn't swerve, nor did he slow down. The front bumper of the pickup connected with the ghoul and it folded almost in half over the hood of the pickup. It stayed like that for almost a full twenty seconds, then Henry swerved to make it around a tight bend and the body slid off to roll in the dirt on the side of the road. It was forgotten as soon as it slid off the hood.

It took only four minutes for Henry to reach the school. In a spray of rocks, he slid to a stop twenty feet from the brick building, swung open his door, and jumped out. "Cindy, stay here with Jimmy and watch him, the rest of us will check out the school and see if there's anything left in the nurse's office." Henry pointed to the others. "The rest of you with me." As everyone climbed out of the rear bed, Henry pointed to Raven, who was also climbing out of the pickup. "No, you stay here with Cindy. If there are any deaders in the area, she'll need your help taking them down."

In other circumstances Raven might have argued, but she knew time was short for Jimmy so all she did was nod, accepting her orders. The rest of the group was already running at the school, Henry in the lead. He carried Jimmy's shotgun, too, knowing his friend didn't need it at the moment and he did. There was no way of knowing what awaited the companions in the school. Henry said a silent prayer to whatever god was up in the heavens to let the school be empty of ghouls, so that he could get to the nurse's office quickly and return to save his friend.

The double doors he ran at were side doors, and he knew as he moved towards them that there would be no time to check other doors if these were locked. The windows on the first floor had metal mesh over them, put there for both security and to protect the windows from errant kickballs thrown at recess in the large parking lot the school sat on where the kids would play. As he ran at the school, seeing sun-faded pictures in the windows of past holidays, he felt a tinge of loss but quickly pushed it down. There was no time to be melancholy, now he needed to focus on saving Jimmy.

Reaching the doors, he yanked on the handle and wasn't surprised that they were locked. Before any of the others could say anything, he swung the shotgun muzzle at the lock and fired at point blank range. The blast didn't blow the lock out like in an action movie but it did knock it loose, and it was all Henry needed to shoot it a second time, and then yank the right-side door open. It opened easily, and he swung it wide, Mary right behind him to grab it as the others followed behind her.

Everyone filed in, as if they were children late for school and the bell about the ring. When Shaun came in last, his rifle in his hand, the door swung closed behind him. In this part of the school, it was mostly dark, but light filtered in from the hole where the lock had been and from a few windows that weren't thoroughly covered in soot from years of not being cleaned. It let in a suffuse light that gave the hallway a gloom that would have made even the cheeriest person sad.

"It seems quiet," Sue said beside Henry, her .22 in her hand, her knuckles white.

"Yeah, it does," Henry said. "I hope that's a good thing." He was about to tell them to follow him, that they needed to hurry, when the first moan echoed through the hallway, coming from the far end.

Henry held out his left hand like a gate so the others wouldn't walk past him. "Hold it; I don't think we're alone in here."

No one spoke, not even breathed, as each waited for what would come next.

The groan turned into a low moan, followed by a wail, and as the five warriors stood and waited, the first zombie appeared at the far end of the hallway, its shoulder brushing the wall and knocking over an announcement for band practice, one that would never be fulfilled.

More were behind it, many not more than four feet tall. All had been attracted by the sound of the shotgun and all were hungry and ready to feed. Henry counted more than a dozen, but no sooner did he finish than another dozen shuffled around the corner, most the size of children, but still, their teeth were just as sharp and deadly as the adults'.

"Oh my God, there's too many, Henry," Mary said. "What do we do?"

Henry's resolve was firm. In his eyes, there really was no choice. If Jimmy didn't get an injection in the next ten minutes, he was a dead man. Raising the shotgun and aiming it at the first zombie that was no more than fifteen feet away, he fired, taking off half its head in a spray of dark blood and brain matter.

"We go through them, Mary, that's what we do! We're not gonna lose Jimmy, not like this, not by something as stupid as a bee bite." He raised the shotgun over his head to rally his team. "Are you with me?"

A round of hearty cries of agreement filtered back to him, even Shaun chiming in. He'd been with the companions for a very short time but he already liked them all, Mary especially. He hoped in time that he might even have a chance with her, as she didn't have a man in the group.

"Then spread out so you don't get in each other's line of fire," Henry said. "Headshots only if possible. We can do this, people, we can save Jimmy." With one more rallying cry, he began to move forward, shooting from the hip and taking down body after body, the others right behind him. When the shotgun ran out of shells he would use his Glock, and when that clip ran dry he would use his panga, hacking and slashing until every damn zombie was put down and nothing but a pile of rotting meat remained.

He would save Jimmy, goddamn it, or he would die trying.

Chapter 6

Outside the school, five zombies arrived, attracted to the sounds of the pickup, the talking and the shotgun blasts.

Raven was the first to see them and she stopped Cindy from leaving Jimmy, knowing she wanted to stay with her man.

"I got this, Cindy, you stay here."

"Are you sure, Raven?" Cindy asked. Jimmy was looking worse, his face bloated like a balloon, his eyes all but hidden. He was beet red everywhere. His breathing was practically non-existent and she prayed he didn't swallow his tongue and suffocate.

Raven only nodded.

"Okay, then take this at least, I know you don't like guns." Cindy handed Raven her hunting knife, all of the companions besides Henry—who wielded a panga— carrying one.

Raven reached into the cab and took the proffered knife. She looked at it carefully, as if deciding if she really needed it. In the end, she decided to use it, not wanting to get her fingernails dirty with blood and pus from the dead.

Raven's fighting skills were unparalleled. None of the group knew where she'd learned her skills but she was deadly in hand-to-hand combat. Like the wind, she could move in and around her attacker, striking before they knew where she was. Her fingernails were her most deadly weapon, long and razor sharp. She used them like slim blades and could slice a throat open as if she was using a stiletto.

The zombies were at the end of the parking lot, stumbling slowly but with resolve. Raven waved to Cindy and began to jog at the group, her movements so fluid it was almost like she was gliding across the ground.

As if the zombies knew she was coming to attack them, they spread out slightly. The lead ghoul was a man, with a bald pate and sagging flesh that resembled Play-doh. On either side of him were two women, both of indescribable age. Both women were naked, their breasts hanging on their chests like deflated balloons. The last two zombies on the far side of the women were teenage boys, one with red hair, the other brown, both with little to no decay, meaning they hadn't been zombies for long. This wasn't good, for newer ones were spryer and could move much faster than ones that had been stumbling around for years. Though zombies didn't rot completely, the decay still happened and some looked like nothing more than walking skeletons, while others looked fresh as the day they were killed. The idea many people had was that some looked better because they fed more, but there was no one with any real scientific knowledge to confirm this; those people were either dead or walking around beside the ghouls they once would have liked to study.

Raven decided to take one of the teenage boys out first, so she picked the red head. As she got closer, the red head raised its arms to grab her but Raven was moving so fast that the zombie barely touched her arms as she ducked under its grasp and slid the knife directly into the ghoul's neck. She twisted sharply and dragged the knife to the left, practically severing the head from its shoulders. The zombie's head fell back, the hands reaching and grabbing for empty air. The spinal column was still attached and though the world was now upside down, the zombie still stumbled around. Raven ignored it, knowing it was out of the fight. Spinning on her heels, she ducked a groping attack from one of the women and kicked out, snapping a leg, the undead woman falling to the ground. Raven followed up with a blow to the back of the woman's head, the handle of the hunting knife heavy, the bludgeon more than enough to crack the skull and cave in the back of the zombie's head. The body collapsed in a cloud of dust, but Raven was gone, already sighting on her next target.

The brown haired teenager was next, and as she tried the same move she'd used with the first, the teenager reacted differently and Raven found herself caught in a trap, the boy's grasping hands strong enough to make her cry out as they dug into her flesh. The boy's face came at her, teeth snapping on empty air in expectation of feeding, and Raven dodged left and right, avoiding the deadly teeth. Acting quickly, she jumped up, pressed her feet into the teenager's chest, and pushed off, the move too much for the zombie. Raven found herself free, and she rolled across the ground, coming up in a crouch.

The other woman came at her and she swung out her right leg in a sweeping motion, taking the woman down by knocking her right off her feet. As the woman landed, Raven jumped on top of her, then slid the knife into the zombie's right eye. Metal scraped bone as the knife sliced through the eye and into the brain, a pinkish ooze seeping out of the socket. Pulling the knife out with a heave, she got back to her feet and took a survey of her surroundings. Only the man and the brown-haired teen remained.

Deciding she wanted to end it quickly, she ran at the undead man first, jumping up and wrapping her legs around his head. The man tried to bite her but he couldn't get any leverage and Raven used this to her advantage. Swinging herself around, she fell, and carried the man with her, then slammed him onto the ground with her weight helping drive the man's face into the pavement. She let go of his head with her legs upon landing and rolled away to once more come up in a crouch. The dead man was trying to get up, his nose nothing but a bloody paste after being smashed into the ground. Raven ran at him, kicked him in the head, then followed it with a knife to the left ear, the blade slipping into the canal and then the brain. The zombie stopped moving and Raven got off the body and faced the last one, the teenager with the brown hair.

Snarling, the teen came at her and she jumped back, then did a backward somersault over a body in her path and came down on two feet. As the teen came at her yet again, she flipped the bloody blade around in her hand so she was holding it by the point, tested its weight, then threw it right at the undead teen's head. The throw was true and the blade impaled the teen in the left eye, the brain becoming punctured and the teen falling over, limbs twitching as nerve endings shut down. Walking over to the fallen teen, Raven placed a foot on the corpse's chest and pulled on the knife, the blade grating on bone before sliding out. She wiped it on the teen's shirt to clean it, then jogged back to Cindy and Jimmy.

"How is he?" she asked upon reaching them. There was a sheen of sweat on her forehead, otherwise there was no indication she'd just taken down five zombies single-handedly with only a knife.

"Not good," Cindy replied. "If Henry and the others don't get back soon, I think he's gonna die." She was crying, the tears rolling down her face in rivulets.

"Don't worry, Cindy, Henry will come through. He always does in the end," Raven said hopefully.

"I hope you're right, Raven, 'cause if you're wrong, Jimmy's dead."

Inside the school, the air was filled with the odor of blood, rot and cordite as the companions shot zombie after zombie.

The hallway quickly began to resemble a charnel house as dark blood covered the floor, leaking out of every dead ghoul. The blood was sometimes colored black, as if the once, life-giving plasma had rotted while within the zombies.

"Mary, get that one on your right!" Henry yelled as he shot a ghoul in the face. Mary did as instructed, sending a .38 slug into the neck of a stumbling zombie. Half its neck was blown out and the head rocked to the side, as if the zombie was a dog and giving her a gesture of curiosity. A second later, another bullet found its skull and the body slumped to the red-tiled floor.

"Oh my God, so many are children," Sue said while firing at the oncoming ghouls.

"Don't let that stop you, Sue," Henry told her. "They aren't kids anymore, now they're something else."

"I know but still, they *were* children once."

More than half of the small horde was children, many wearing the remnants of what were once their school clothes. But there were no moms and dads to get upset if a knee was ripped or a pen leaked on a once-white shirt. Those days were over.

To Sue, it was the logos on the children's shirts that truly hit home that the small zombies before her had once been innocent kids. Pokemon, Star Wars and Sailor Moon were just some of the iconic characters she recognized, thanks to friends she had once known that had had children. She tried not to think about those friends now, knowing they were probably dead, or worse, were now the walking dead.

The shotgun ran out of shells, and Henry slung it over his shoulder by its strap and pulled his Glock, lining up on the face of the first ghoul to come at him. In skilled hands, a Glock semi-automatic takes seventeen and a half seconds to shoot all its bullets, and after using it for years, Henry was that marksman.

With calm precision, he fired again and again, not stopping until the clip ran dry. But when it did, eight more ghouls had been put down, each with two rounds in their heads, and one extra round that had gone wild when a zombie zigged when Henry thought it was going to zag. Not perfect, but still a damn good score.

It was as he popped out the empty clip, then pocketed it to reload it later, that the gunshots abruptly ceased, as there were no more targets to shoot.

Just two minutes had passed since Henry fired the first shot with the shotgun, and while the last zombie was still settling on top of another one, half its head missing, Henry was already waving the others onward deeper into the school.

"Let's move, people, the clock is ticking." Henry was already stepping over the bodies and turning the corner, the others right behind him.

"Do you think there are any more in here?" Sue asked Henry, her eyes wide from the battle.

"I doubt it," he replied. "Anything that still has ears would have come running after all that noise. We should be fine." There was a map on the wall, covered in plexiglass, and he stopped before it and studied it, Mary and Sue right behind him and peering over his shoulder. Shaun stood a few feet away, watching the hallway. He figured there were enough eyes on the map already, one more set wouldn't do much more than get in the way.

"It's right here," Henry said and stuck his finger on a point at the center of the map, right next to the principal's office.

"It's not far from here, either, down this hallway," Mary added, and as one unit they turned and began running. Henry almost slipped and fell, the soles of his boots covered in blood and making the hallway like ice.

Mary couldn't help but laugh at this. "That's why there's no running in the halls, Henry. You're going to get detention."

"I doubt it," he replied. "Anyone who might want to enforce that rule is probably long dead, so I'll risk it." He flashed her a slight grin that someone who didn't know him well wouldn't have even seen.

"Well, I won't tell," Mary rebutted with a grin of her own and then concentrated on running.

There were more bodies lying prone in the hallway, most so desiccated that they were nothing but shredded clothing and bones. They had died a long time ago. Some were children, and the companions had to look away, not wanting to think about all the innocent deaths.

Half a minute later they reached the door to the nurse's office. The door was closed. Henry reached down to the knob and turned it, pleased that it was unlocked. Though made of wood, the door would have taken precious seconds to break in, time Henry knew he didn't have if he was going to save Jimmy.

"What if we can't find one of those pens?" Sue asked from behind Henry. "Has anyone given any thought to that?"

"Think positive, Sue," Mary said. "That's all we can do."

In any other circumstances, Henry would have paused for a moment, and would never had gone charging into a room without clearing it first, but he was so concerned for Jimmy that he did just that.

His Glock was in his right hand, his left one empty, and if not for this happenstance, he might have been killed right then and there.

As he charged into the room, he ran three steps through the main foyer, and was about to go into the next section, where he hoped the medical supplies would be, when a zombie dressed as a nurse stepped out from behind the door and he ran right into her.

They both fell to the floor in a tangle of limbs, and Henry quickly found himself fighting for his life as teeth snapped at his face and pus dripped onto his forehead. In the blink of an eye, he found himself in a battle for his life, and all the while the seconds were passing on Jimmy's life.

"Henry!" Mary screamed as she ran into the room and watched the tableaux happen before she could so much as move. Then she raised her .38 to shoot the zombie but then stopped. Upon seeing the way its head was bobbing and weaving, she could just as easily shoot Henry as the nurse.

"Don't just stand there, somebody, shoot it!" Henry yelled, his free hand jammed under the nurse's neck, barely keeping the teeth at bay, his other hand—the one holding the Glock—trapped under his body. He could feel the shotgun pushing into his lower back, the pain an annoying reminder of his predicament.

The undead nurse was surprisingly spry. Henry saw that the woman had been obese in life and had a lot of that flab in death, too. As he pushed on her neck, his hand slid into the soft, roiling folds of flesh, the malleable skin sucking his fingers in like rancid dough. He fought the urge to vomit as pus and bile dripped onto his face, as the nurse tried to sink her yellow teeth into his skin. The steady *clack-clack* of teeth gnashing came to him, blocking out all other sound.

Mary and Sue didn't know what to do. They aimed their weapons at the nurse, but were too scared of hitting Henry to attempt anything. Shaun was the last inside the room, and it took him an extra second to figure out what was happening, as he had to push past the two women to see.

The second he did, he went into action, spinning his rifle around and using the butt end as a bat. Just as Henry lost his grip on the nurse's neck and her face dove down to bite him, Shaun swung the rifle like a baseball bat, the base of the weapon connecting with the nurse's head as if it was a baseball. There was the sound of a bat hitting a ball and the nurse's head rocked to the side, which gave Henry the momentum he needed to buck his hips and shove her off. She didn't go all the way off him due to her being so overweight, but it was just enough for Henry to pull his trapped arm out from under him and swing the Glock around. The nurse's mouth was open, a loud hiss issuing from her throat as Henry shoved the muzzle of the Glock between her cracked lips.

"Suck on this, bitch," he hissed and double-tapped the trigger. The report of the pistol was muffled inside the zombie's head but the exit wound more than made up for it. An instant later, after Henry squeezed the trigger, the back of the nurse's head evaporated and sprayed the wall behind in a spray of dark, oozing blood and brain matter. The head didn't even snap back, but remained stuck on Henry's Glock.

"Someone help me, damn it!" he yelled as he tried to extricate himself from the obese corpse, which still straddled him and made it look like she was riding him in some perverse sexual game.

Everyone went to his aid and pushed the zombie off him, then Henry was helped to his feet.

"Are you okay?" Mary asked, looking Henry over for possible bite marks.

"I'm fine, I'm fine, I didn't get bit." He looked at Shaun and held out a hand covered in pus and gore. "Thanks Shaun, I owe you one."

Shaun stared at the filthy hand, unsure whether he should take it anyway, not wanting to insult Henry, and knowing he really didn't want to, when Henry glanced at his gore-covered hand and retracted it. "Oh shit, sorry, I guess thanks will have to do."

"Works for me," Shaun said relieved that he didn't have to touch Henry's filthy hand.

Henry smiled at the young man and then spun around to face the interior of the room. Sue handed him a towel and he quickly wiped his face. "Okay, that's enough of that, let's search this place. We've wasted too much time as it is."

The others did as he said and they began to rip the nurse's office apart, going through cabinets and drawers.

"Once we have what we came for and Jimmy's fine, we need to come back in here and take whatever we can use," Sue said as she rummaged through a file cabinet.

"Agreed," Henry added. "But one thing at a time. Jimmy comes first."

"That's what I just said," she rebutted, while rolling her eyes. She got back to work. *Men,* she thought. *They always have to have the last word in any conversation.*

There were the decayed bodies of five small children in one of the corners, nothing left of them but shreds of skin, bones, strips of material of their clothing, and sneakers covered in dried blood. No doubt they were patients that had never had the chance to escape the office. So the undead nurse had been fortunate enough to have something to snack on while being trapped in the office, which explained why she hadn't wasted away like other ghouls had over the years.

"I found one, I found one!" Sue began to yell as she held up an epi-pen, still sealed in its vacuum-packed wrapper.

"Great job, Sue, give it here," Henry said and she handed it over. With the pen in his hand, he spun around and dashed out of the office, leaving the others standing mute for a moment. Then they also ran out of the office, following Henry, though the man was already halfway down the hallway and turning the corner.

He leapt over the bodies, slid across the floor, but refused to fall, and dashed to the exit doors at full speed. His heart was pounding in his ears as he charged outside and into the light of day, then ran straight at the pickup truck.

Henry could see Cindy inside the cab and a lump of what was Jimmy, but as he got closer, he saw how Jimmy's face was so swollen that he was barely recognizable as a human being, let alone as good ole Jimmy.

With the epi-pen gripped tightly in his hand, Henry crossed the remaining feet separating him from the vehicle, all the while praying it wasn't too late to save his friend.

Chapter 7

Lazarus led his shifting mass of undead humanity across the Las Vegas desert. Just around the bend in the road was the small town of Cherry Creek. Hopping up onto a guard rail, he turned and surveyed his vast dead army.

They were over a thousand strong and soon there would be even more added to the roster; each mile he traveled, he called to more walkers and soon they joined his army.

His *followers* were many and he knew in time there would be nothing like them on the face of the planet. Lazarus would be a god, the ruler of the entire planet. Of course, he didn't know what he would actually do with the planet once he had it, but one step at a time. First he had to take it for himself, then he could figure out how to pass the time as the ruler of a planet of the dead.

He sent out a telepathic command for a hundred zombies to move forward and be the spearhead of the assault. He didn't know what awaited him around the bend in the road nor did he care. There was nothing the people of Cherry Creek could do to stop him. Guns, bombs, fire; it was all for nothing when the army they faced felt neither fear nor pain, and when each time a townsperson was killed, they then returned to fight for the other side.

Before Lazarus was in sight of the town, he heard the gunshots. Quickening his pace, his army did likewise, picking up on his thoughts.

When he rounded the bend in the road, he saw before him a fifteen foot tall barricade surrounding the town. Made of anything the townspeople could get their hands on, he saw such items as washing machines, old tires and even cars and trucks, all piled on top of each other with cement holding it all together. Though ugly to look at, the wall was a formidable barrier.

The wall was lined with men and women, and even a few children, all with firearms of some kind.

Lazarus gave his army the order to attack and they surged forward, coming up right under the wall. They began to climb it, but no sooner did they do this than they were shot off it by gunfire.

Bodies began to pile up, and just like the last town, this actually benefited the attacking undead army, which began to use the fallen corpses as steps to breach the top of the wall.

A *whoosh* to the left caused Lazarus' gaze to shift to that quarter and he saw the tail-end of a LAW rocket as it soared through the air and impacted in the center of his army. Body parts went flying, a few severed heads, too, to spin in the air while bloody gobbets of flesh spun off in all directions. When the smoke cleared, more than two dozen of his army were destroyed, some nothing more than animated torsos with heads. The torsos flopped around, rolling back and forth as they tried to obey Lazarus' command to attack.

Then, where the hole had been made by the rocket, it was swallowed up as more walking corpses swarmed across the land, crushing the body parts of fallen soldiers to a bloody pulp, and turning the dry ground into a slurry of gore.

As before, each zombie taken down allowed the ones behind it to climb higher on the wall and soon the wall was breached, the undead swarming over it like Indians in an old cowboy flick attacking a fort.

The townspeople fought bravely, for they were fighting not only for their own lives but for those of their family, who were even now huddling in fear within the buildings of the town.

Lazarus waited until the last gunshot, the last scream, had faded on the air, then he climbed over the bodies used for steps and onto the wall. From there he climbed down into the town and surveyed his new conquest.

There were a few living citizens being held by his zombies and he nodded at this, glad his soldiers were following his orders. He always liked to play with a few victims before killing and turning them.

With his hands behind his back, he strolled across the ground and stopped before the prisoners. "Ah, an excellent group. And look how frightened they are. That fear makes their blood taste oh so sweet."

"Holy shit, you can talk?" one of the townspeople gasped, a man in his late thirties with thinning hair and a large nose. "That's fucking impossible!"

Lazarus spun around and walked up to the man. "Impossible? Hardly. Do you believe your eyes, your ears? I'm standing before you and talking, so it must be true, right?"

The man said nothing and a few others began to cry. Not all of them crying were women either.

"Well?" Lazarus yelled, his breath rancid from being one of the walking dead.

"Yes, yes, it must be true," the man sobbed.

"Exactly," Lazarus nodded. He turned to face all the prisoners, a total of fifteen, each one being held by two zombies. Even if they tried to run, there were hundreds more of the undead surrounding them. There was no escape.

"You people have been found guilty of the sin of life. There is only one punishment..." He leered at them all. "The sentence is Death."

Many began to cry out, some began to scream.

"But fear not, people, just as you see others around you that were once your friends..." He gestured to the zombies that were once part of the town and were now more of Lazarus' followers. "So too will you join them soon." He smiled then, a gesture that made every human cringe. "But not before I have a little fun first."

He waved to the two zombies holding the man he'd first talked to, and waited as the man was dragged to him. Lazarus didn't bother with any more discussion, but simply sank his teeth into the man's throat, savoring the taste of the hot blood as it squirted down his throat. Pulling back, he chewed gingerly on the piece of flesh in his mouth.

"This one's mine, you may have the rest," he said to his soldiers, while also sending the order telepathically. Like a light switch had been flicked on, every zombie holding a human went into action, attacking their victim, tearing them apart with teeth and nails.

The screams didn't last long, the zombies not pulling any punches, and in no time each of the prisoners was standing side by side with the other animated cadavers—only now with a few choice pieces of flesh missing here and there, and no doubt down a quart or two of blood.

Lazarus barely noticed this, as he was focused on feeding on the man before him. He tore out the man's abdomen, yanking out the long greasy innards, to then chew on them with gusto. The man fell to the ground, screaming, but soon he bled out and fell silent in death. When the man revived, Lazarus watched casually, still chewing on a chunk of intestine. When the man was on his feet again, Lazarus handed him a piece of his own intestine, the newly born zombie taking it to begin chewing with pleasure.

Lazarus nodded at this.

He sent out a telepathic command that it was time to leave, and with his dead army even stronger, he left the town of Cherry Creek behind, to move on to his next conquest.

Chapter 8

The passenger side door of the pickup was open, and Cindy jumped out of the way as Henry approached, her eyes locked on the epi-pen in his hand.

"Oh thank God you found one," Cindy said as Henry raced up to Jimmy, and without hesitation, jammed the pen into his leg and pressed the plunger.

After so much action and trepidation, it seemed weird to Henry that now there was nothing to do but stop and wait. But wait was all any of them could do. Wait and pray they were in time to save their friend.

Henry took a step backwards and let Cindy get back into the seat to hold Jimmy, her hands going to Jimmy's swollen face, caressing him as a mother would her child.

Henry took a moment to survey his surroundings and he spotted the bodies spread across the ground a second later. "Those weren't there before we went into the school," he said casually.

"They came after you went inside," Raven said. "I took care of them."

Henry nodded. "Good job."

The others burst through the doors of the school and ran to the pickup to join Henry.

"How is he?" Mary asked when she stopped beside him.

"Don't know. I gave him the injection, now all we can do is wait," Henry replied.

"I think he's breathing better," Cindy said as she leaned in close to listen to Jimmy's breathing. "Yes, he's definitely breathing better now."

"Does that mean he's gonna be okay?" Shaun asked from Henry's left.

Henry shrugged. "Your guess is as good as mine, but if we want to be positive, then yeah, he's going to be fine." He stepped closer to Jimmy, who had his eyes closed and was barely recognizable. "You hear that, Jimmy? You'll be okay."

A low moan sounded from the right of the pickup and all eyes turned to see a lone ghoul stumble out of the brush lining the parking lot and onto the asphalt.

Henry frowned, not in the mood for anymore zombies at the moment. As the years had passed since the first outbreak, the number of ghouls had dwindled immensely and now they were becoming mostly a nuisance. Every now and then the companions might come upon pockets of heavy resistance, but overall the dead were spread out and as such were easy to take down.

"I'll take care of it," Raven said and jogged away before Henry could tell her not to. He shrugged and let her go, deciding one lone zombie was no match for the spitfire teenager.

The zombie did its usual walk, with hands held out before it like Frankenstein, the hands opening and closing in anticipation of the humans before it. Nothing filled its mind but hunger, so the fact that there were seven humans and only one of it never crossed its dead brain. Raven began to run faster the closer she got to the zombie, and when she was only six feet away, she jumped up and spun in the air, her right foot thrust out before her like a spear. To Henry, it reminded him of a move of a Bruce Lee movie, one of many he'd watched as a child.

The sole of Raven's combat boot connected with the zombie's forehead and the blow was so precise and the ghoul so decayed that the kick took the head clean off the zombie's shoulders. The head flew through the air like a wobbly football, landed near the edge of the asphalt, and rolled into the tall grass to be lost from sight. The headless zombie teetered for a moment and then fell backwards to land heavily, dark blood spurting from the jagged neck hole. Raven came down lightly on her feet, surveyed her work, then jogged back to the others—she was barely winded. She smiled slightly as she joined the others and Henry nodded to her, while Shaun looked on in amazement at the small girl with dark black hair that fought like a martial arts' master.

Henry glanced at Jimmy and saw that in the time it had taken Raven to take down the ghoul, Jimmy's face had decreased in size by half. His eyes were open and he was blinking at the light. "Did I miss something?" he asked, his voice hoarse. "The last thing I remember was getting stung by a bee, then I was here."

"You got lucky, Jimmy," Henry said. "Real lucky. Why didn't you tell us you were allergic to bees?"

He shrugged and winced as he did so. "It never came up before." He managed a wan smile. "Besides, with deaders running all over the place, bees seemed pretty damn low on my list of things that can kill me."

"Good point," Henry grinned, patting his friend's arm.

"Well, I found two more pens before I left the nurse's office," Mary said, holding up the epi-pens still in their wrappers. "So we'll be ready in case something like this ever happens again."

Jimmy was breathing easily now and with each passing minute he was looking more like his old self. They stayed in the school parking lot for another twenty minutes, then Jimmy told Henry he felt well enough to travel, though he asked if he could ride inside the cab of the pickup.

"Of course you can," Henry said and patted Jimmy's leg. "Cindy, you ride in the cab again, too, and I'll drive." He looked at the others. "The rest of you mount up in the back, it's time we got out of here." Half a dozen zombies picked that time to pop out of the brush and step out onto the parking lot.

"Forget them, we're gone from here," Henry said and climbed into the driver's seat, slamming the door as he did, the engine already starting before the door was fully closed. The others wasted no time in climbing into the rear bed.

After glancing in the rearview mirror to make sure everyone was aboard, Henry stepped on the gas pedal and drove away from the school, the zombies still far enough away to barely register as a threat. In seconds, the pickup was lost from sight and on its way.

Inside the cab, Jimmy was sitting up straight, the fire in his eyes returning. "You know, Henry, I saw the concern on your face when I woke up. You were worried I wasn't gonna make it," he said, his voice light and teasing, as if he knew something Henry didn't. Now that the danger had passed and Henry knew that Jimmy was going to be fine, his gruff exterior was back and he frowned deeply, as if what Jimmy had said was the most ridiculous thing he'd ever heard. "Hardly," Henry muttered out of the corner of his mouth, his eyes locked on the road. "I was just worried that if you died then we'd be down a gun, and that's never a good thing these days."

"Oh, please, I saw your face, old man, you looked like you were ready to cry." He nudged Henry's arm. "Come on, Henry, admit it, you love me."

"No I don't," Henry hissed. "I'm just glad for Cindy. For some reason only God knows, she seems to love you." He glanced at Jimmy and said, "As for me, I think you're an idiot."

"Bullshit, old man, you love me. Come on, give me a hug, maybe a kiss on the cheek." Jimmy puckered up and tried to hug Henry, who tried to push him away and ended up swerving the pickup across the road, to the annoyance of the passengers in the rear bed.

"So help me, Jimmy, if you don't quit it, I'm gonna end up driving us into a ditch," Henry said gruffly.

Cindy was watching it all with a sly smile, pleased to see Jimmy was getting back to normal so quickly. He wasn't swollen anymore and his complexion was almost back to its usual color, and if he was teasing Henry, he was definitely feeling better.

Jimmy stopped and leaned back in his seat. "Fine, I'll stop, but I know what I saw. You were worried about me. I know you care."

"Fat chance," Henry said under his breath. But though he would never admit it to Jimmy, Henry was incredibly relieved that his friend was making a full recovery. For some reason even he didn't know, Henry didn't want to think what it would be like traveling across the deadlands without Jimmy. Maybe it was because Jimmy had been with him from the beginning, as were Mary and then later, Cindy. Maybe it was because Henry didn't want to be alone. Either way, if he had a say in it, Jimmy would never know his true feelings for if he did, Jimmy would never let Henry live it down. Besides, Henry knew Jimmy and the others were aware of how he felt about them; it didn't need to be vocalized on a daily basis. Cindy began talking to Jimmy, taking Jimmy's attention off Henry, who flashed her a thank you smile. She nodded in reply. Henry began concentrating on driving, while the young couple chatted beside him.

A few droplets of rain hit the windshield, for the moment nothing to take notice of.

Chapter 9

"Henry, we're getting soaked back here," Mary called from the rear of the pickup. "We need to pull over and wait this storm out!"

"If you can find someplace for me to do that, I will," Henry yelled back as rainwater streamed through his open window. "Just hang on, something has to be around here."

It had been three hours since they'd left the school and it had steadily rained harder with each passing hour until Henry could barely see a foot in front of the pickup. The road was covered with more than four inches of water, and though he didn't know for sure without getting out and measuring it, he was pretty confident it was still rising by the minute. Above, the heavens rocked with thunder and lightning as the sky released its payload.

The pickup rocked on its springs as the front bumper hit something in the road. Henry thought it was an old wreck left there for years but it was gone before he could tell for sure. Everyone in the rear bed cried out for a moment as the vehicle tipped, then it was free of the obstruction and moving onward.

The defrost on the old pickup was terrible, the heater barely working, the fan barely blowing. Condensation beaded up on the inside of the glass and Jimmy had to continually wipe it away so Henry had a chance in hell of seeing out of the windshield as he struggled behind the steering wheel.

With visibility so terrible, Henry never realized he had drifted onto the shoulder of the road until it was too late. The pickup jerked forward and sent everyone in the back tumbling across the rear bed, screams of surprise overriding the patter of rain on the cab roof. Then the right rear tire began to spin as it shot out mud and water behind it, the vehicle vibrating as the engine surged—the pickup failed to move forward.

"Shit," Henry muttered.

"We're stuck, aren't we," Jimmy said by his side, Cindy next to him.

"Yeah, we're stuck."

Henry's head snapped to the left at the sound of someone pounding on the driver's side window. He saw the faces of Sue, Raven, Mary and Shaun peering in at him from outside. All were soaked to the bone, droplets of water running off their noses and chins. The image of four drowned rats came to mind but Henry kept his mouth shut, not wanting to aggravate the situation any more. It wasn't his fault that only three people could fit into the cab of the pickup.

Henry rolled down the window and was immediately pelted with rain. "You guys okay?"

"Other than being soaking wet and freezing, sure, we're all great," Mary said, speaking for the rest.

"We're stuck in the mud, that's why we stopped," Henry said.

Mary nodded. "No kidding, we all kind of figured that out when you sent us flying to the floor of the truck!" She had to yell to be heard over the pounding rain. The water was up to her ankles and still rising. She could feel a gentle current, too, and tried not to think about what would happen if the water rose even higher.

"We need to find shelter," Shaun broke in. "We get flash floods in Nevada all the time. If we stay out here in the middle of no-where, we may find ourselves washed away."

"I hear you. Why don't you and Mary get to the back and I'll join you in a second," Henry said. "Then we can see if we can get this truck free of the mud."

Shaun nodded and he and Mary left the window. Henry opened his door and brought Sue into the cab as he jumped out. Her hair was plastered to her head and she was shivering.

"Hang in there, Sue, we'll get through this," Henry said. "You take the wheel and when I yell for you to gun it, you gun it." He looked at Cindy and Jimmy over Sue's head. "You two join me outside; we'll need all the muscle we can get."

"Oh, uh, gee, Henry, I'd love to help but I don't think I'm up for it yet," Jimmy said, acting like he wasn't well yet. "I'm still pretty weak from the bee bite."

Henry went around to the passenger side, passing Cindy who had already gotten out of the cab. "Jimmy, either you get out here or so help me I'll pull you out and drown you with my own two hands. You're fine, you've been fine for hours."

Jimmy opened his mouth to protest but Henry raised an index finger and pointed it at Jimmy, Henry's mouth nothing but a slit on his face, his eyes creased as water pelted his sopping wet hair, the gray more pronounced now that his hair was wet. The gesture on his face was clear: *try me.*

Reluctantly, Jimmy hung his head in defeat. "Okay, but if I catch a cold, don't blame me."

"I'm willing to take that chance," Henry said and he and Jimmy walked to the rear of the pickup, where Cindy had already joined the others. Each had picked a spot on the rear bumper and Jimmy and Henry took the middle, only Henry didn't realize it but he was more to the right than he would have preferred. As everyone got into position, Henry found himself getting shifted more to the right than he would have liked, until he was basically on the corner of the bumper, right behind the rear right tire. Lightning flashed across the sky, followed immediately by the crack of thunder. The air sizzled with electricity.

He barely noticed that the water was almost up to his knees, as he was focused on the task at hand. "Okay, people, on the count of three!" he yelled and then called out to Sue, "On three, Sue, step on the gas—and make sure it's in drive! If you can hear me okay, honk the horn!" The horn honked a second later and he knew she'd heard him.

"Okay, one...two...*three*! Push!" Henry yelled and they all began to push and lift up on the rear bumper of the pickup.

At the same time, Sue stepped on the gas pedal and the right rear tire began to spin, spraying Henry from head to toe in sticky mud. It got into his nose, his mouth and even his left ear when he tried to turn his face away.

Henry was blinded and he didn't see what happened next, though he quickly figured it out when he could see again. As the rain drove down on the companions' heads, the pickup surged free, and as Sue shot out of the mud, she immediately lost control, the vehicle swerving back and forth until she drove straight into the ditch on the opposite side. The front end went in hard, sending water splashing in all directions and only the fact that the ditch was filled with water saved Sue from suffering terrible injury, the water cushioning the pickup's landing.

"Sue!" Mary yelled and ran onto the road, splashing through the water as fast as she could. Raven was right behind her, followed by the others. Only Henry and Jimmy were left behind, Jimmy staying to help Henry, who was sputtering as he stood up.

Mary reached the pickup and jumped down into the ditch, the water going up past her breasts. She found it a strange sensation that the water was warm and not cold, but the temperature was in the high nineties, and with the ground holding so much heat after the long day, it was easy to understand why the water was so comfortable.

It was difficult getting the driver's side door open but with Raven's help, Mary managed to do it. Cindy was there a second later, and the three women dragged a shaky and out-of-it Sue out of the pickup and then back up the ditch. Shaun was waiting and he helped, too, and moments later Sue was lying on the ground, the others surrounding her, their heads and backs keeping the rain off her face. Sue blinked her eyes and looked up at the shadows of faces, unsure where she was for a few seconds, but then it all came back to her.

"Oh no, the truck," Sue said as she slowly sat up, coughing when rainwater slid into her nose and mouth. The rain was coming down even harder and it hurt each time it landed on the companions' heads and exposed skin.

"Sue, are you all right?" Henry yelled. He came running up to her, Jimmy by his side. The rain had already washed most of the mud from Henry's face and clothes.

Sue only managed a nod as she coughed again.

Seeing the back tires of the pickup truck with its wheels spinning in the air, Henry shook his head angrily. "Damn it, that's not getting out of there anytime soon if ever, no matter how hard we push or pull."

"What're we gonna do?" Jimmy asked. With his hair plastered to his face, Henry thought he looked like the cocky teenager he'd been once, the one who used to cut his lawn on Sundays for extra money. That was a lifetime ago in another world, one where there had been normalcy and structure. Now, the world was chaos and death on a daily basis.

62

Henry shielded his eyes with the palm of his hand to see what was surrounding them. He could see nothing. The light was gone, the clouds overhead a solid ceiling of darkness, and only the intermittent flashes of lightning illuminated anything.

"We have to get out of here!" Henry yelled, the water well past his knees. "This flooding will kill us if we stay out here. There's already an undercurrent tugging at my legs. If it gets worse, it'll suck us all down and we'll never come up. We need to get to higher ground!"

"Which way do we go?" Cindy asked, her blonde hair hanging wetly around her face.

Henry flipped a mental coin in his mind and pointed the way he'd picked in his head. "This way! Everyone hold on to the person before you so we don't get separated. That way if one goes down they won't get pulled away!"

They did as Henry said and with Henry leading the way, they moved off after grabbing their gear from the pickup. Behind Henry was Sue, then Mary, Cindy, Raven, Jimmy and Shaun took up the rear. The water was still rising and it was becoming hard to stay standing, the wind so strong it threatened to blow them over. A few times, Henry could have sworn he felt something graze his legs and one time he knew that something had actually grabbed him. He'd used his fist to punch down, had felt something yielding give way, and then it was gone, taken by the current. He didn't dwell on what it might have been, those thoughts could lead to panic. Imagining what was swirling around under the water was too much to take.

As if the universe had been reading his mind, he suddenly felt multiple hands grab his feet and thighs and then he was being pulled under the water.

He barely heard Sue cry out as he was ripped from her grasp. Then he had more urgent concerns, such as keeping the snapping teeth of the two zombies that had been swept up in the current at bay.

The undead didn't need to breathe, but Henry did, and as he fought for his life, he realized he couldn't hold out for long, as he hadn't been able to take in a decent breath before going under.

Already spots swam before his eyes.

It wouldn't be long before everything went dark...forever.

Chapter 10

It was dark under the water, far darker than it should have been, given how shallow it was. It wasn't until Henry tried to open his eyes and felt the stinging of grit and swirling mud that he realized the sediment was suffusing the water heavily.

It was like he was blind, and the way it made him feel vulnerable wasn't a feeling he enjoyed. But he had more important things on his mind than his vision, namely the two zombies that were desperately trying to bite him.

They had been caught up in the raging water and had been dragged for miles until their reaching, grasping hands found Henry's legs. The second they had taken hold, they knew Henry was prey and it was only a matter of seconds before they began pulling him down, into the dark, surging water.

This wasn't the first time Henry had battled zombies in the water. After leaping from a Colorado bridge, he had plummeted to the cold water with zombies all around him. But he had managed to survive that encounter and by God he would this time as well.

In full survival mode, he reached out and felt his fingers sink into the rotting flesh of one of the ghoul's faces. The sensation reminded him of cold porridge as it surrounded his fingers and sucked the digits deeper until his fingertips were rubbing the cheekbones. The teeth were clacking up and down, and even through the water Henry could hear it as well as feel the jawbone moving under his hands.

When the mouth was fully open, Henry slid both hands all the way into the mouth, thus preventing the zombie from getting any leverage and chomping down on his wrists. He was taking a terrible risk, and he knew it. If even one of those teeth scraped him and broke the skin it might be enough to infect him. But he had considered this and decided it was worth the risk. The theory was the dead still created saliva and it was this that was the contaminate that caused infection if a victim was bitten. So, if that was true, then being in the water, where the saliva would be washed away continually, meant that even if Henry was bit, it was highly doubtful he would become infected. Of course, this was all conjecture and he didn't relish the idea of testing his theory he'd made up on the fly.

With his hands fully in the mouth of the zombie, the jaw stretched to breaking point, Henry began to pull his arms apart, unhinging the jaw. He was already beginning to black out as his oxygen was depleted but he still continued to pull, slowly widening his arms until he felt the jaw separate. Then suddenly, the jaw was free of resistance as the lower jaw was dislocated and yanked from the mouth. Only skin held it in place and kept it from coming completely off.

Henry released his hold and was glad to do it. The entire time he'd been working to crack open the mouth, the zombie's tongue had been tickling the back of his hands. He shoved the body away from him and it was swept away by the current an instant later.

But he wasn't safe yet, there was still another zombie attached to him. Bringing his right arm back, he brought his clenched fist forward to connect with the second ghoul's chin, knocking more than one tooth out. The blow would have done more damage but it was severely lacking strength thanks to the drag of the water. Throwing a punch underwater wasn't as easy as it was in the movies, and only a fraction of the energy was there at the point of impact. Before the ghoul could attack, Henry kicked out with his right boot and sent the zombie sprawling away to roll three times before stopping. By then, the current had it and it was gone, rolling even more as it was quickly pulled away.

But that was it; he had no more strength, no more air. He was so disoriented. He didn't even try to stand, he just slowly began to go limp as he let out his remaining breath of air.

Then he was yanked upward and his head broke the surface of the water. Sputtering, he sucked in air and a good mouthful of rainwater as it slid into his open mouth. Coughing and hacking, he felt hands grab his shoulders and help him to stand.

"Henry, thank God, when I saw you go under I thought…" Sue said and trailed off.

"I'm okay," Henry wheezed. "Just give me a second to catch my breath."

The others were gathered around him, too, their faces all wearing the same look of concern.

"If I hadn't held onto your shirt, I don't think you'd still be here," Sue said. "It's becoming so hard to stand; there's a strong current here."

"What happened, Henry? Why'd you go down?" Jimmy asked from his side.

Henry shook his head. "A couple of deaders floated by and grabbed me; took me down. I got rid of 'em but it was close. Damn things don't need to breathe but I sure as hell do."

Lightning cracked overhead, the air rife with electricity. Thunder boomed immediately afterward. The storm was right over the companions' heads.

A waved of water pushed them all a few feet and Mary fell, and would have been sucked away if not for Cindy holding her by the arm. She muttered a quick thanks and Cindy flashed her a smile.

"It's getting worse," Henry said. "We need to get to shelter fast or we might not live through this." He realized he didn't see Shaun. "Where's Shaun? Has anyone seen him?"

Everyone looked left and right, not seeing their new friend.

"Oh God, do you think he got pulled under the water?" Sue asked.

Henry shook his head, water falling from his nose and chin. "No way of knowing."

"Hey, guys, over here! This way!" a familiar voice called from down the road, or where the road once was. Now all that could be seen was water. It was like they were standing in the middle of a shallow lake.

"Is that Shaun?" Mary asked, Cindy right next to her.

"Yes," Cindy said. "It is. How'd he get way over there?"

"Who the fuck cares!" Jimmy yelled over the crashing thunder and wind. "He's calling us, maybe he found something."

"Everyone follow me, let's go," Henry said and began walking. They had to go somewhere; staying still wasn't an option.

Shaun was a good hundred yards away and the going was rough. Every so often, someone in the group would trip over something unseen under the water and go down, only the others holding on to one another keeping them together. As Henry fought for each step he took, he tried not to think of the irony of the situation. Here he was in Nevada, where it was hot and dry, desert basically, and he was dangerously close to being drowned at any moment. He'd heard about how rain came hard and fast and the ground being so dry, it didn't soak up the water and this created flash floods. But to actually be in the middle of one, well, that was an entirely different scenario.

When Shaun was thirty feet away, Henry called out, "Shaun, tell me you have good news!"

"I do," Shaun replied. "I found a place we can hole up till this storm passes." He waved them on. "Follow me!"

With Shaun now in the lead, the companions trudged onward. The water was almost to their waists, with no signs of stopping. Henry bet if he could have checked the history books, there would no doubt be no other storm that had measured up to the doozy he and the others now found themselves in the middle of.

A corpse floated by, followed by another one, but no one acknowledged them, other than to make sure the bodies were truly dead. Rounding a sharp bend in the road, Henry was the first to see a large dark shape looming on the side of the road, directly on the shoulder.

"This way, it's over here!" Shaun yelled and made his way to the dark shape. Sue cried out and Henry turned to see her falling. Snapping a hand out, he grabbed her by the arm and pulled her up. Spitting water, she nodded thanks and they continued onward.

Lightning was all around them, the air sizzling with electricity, the smell of ozone a viable thing. In these flashes, Henry was able to make out the looming shape before him.

It was a Greyhound bus, its tires gone, the undercarriage flat on the shoulder of the road. The front windshield was intact, but that was all Henry could see as he moved closer.

Shaun reached the bus first and he forced the doors open, the sound of squealing hinges overriding the storm. He stepped up onto the first step and out of the rain, then turned around to face the others.

"See?" Shaun yelled, proud of his find. "This'll keep us dry till the storm's over."

Henry agreed completely with Shaun's assessment.

The bus would be decent shelter from the rain and water. Even if a few windows were broken or missing, they would have a roof over their heads and be out of the deadly flooding, where even now the current was growing stronger, and as time passed, the water was filling with debris of all sizes, another danger that the companions would have to deal with if they had to stay in the water.

Henry was opening his mouth to congratulate Shaun on an excellent find, Shaun standing in the doorway with his hands out, a wide smile of accomplishment on his face, when from the darkness behind him hands reached out and wrapped around him.

Shaun had time for one scream, one that came from surprise rather than pain, then he was pulled up and into the darkness.

Only a few feet away from the bus, Henry and the others could only stand there in shock as Shaun disappeared from view.

Chapter 11

"Shaun!" Henry yelled as the younger man was pulled into the darkness of the bus.

"Shit, there's someone in there with him!" Jimmy said. "What do we do?"

The others gathered around, all waiting on Henry's reply. Whatever he said they would do, instantly. He was their leader and they deferred to him. Shaun's screams carried out of the open door of the bus, blending in with the sounds of the storm.

"We go in after him," Henry said. "Shaun is one of us now. Jimmy, Mary and Cindy, with me, the rest of you wait out here. Come on." He began running to the bus, though it was more of an awkward hop as he tried to get through the high water. Jimmy, Mary and Cindy were right beside him. All had their weapons drawn. His Glock had been wet more than it had been dry lately and he hoped the weapon didn't misfire on him. He still had the Browning taken from the man he'd killed at the trading post in one of his lower leg pockets but that gun would be iffy at best, too.

His hand slid down to where his panga rode his thigh, the reassuring feeling of the handle spurring him on. If his Glock wouldn't work, he still had sixteen inches of cold steel to fight with.

Reaching the dark doorway, he jumped onto the first step, feeling the bus shift on its shocks ever so slightly with his weight. He could hear Shaun screaming and the sounds of a scuffle. Jimmy handed him a flashlight the younger man had taken from his pack and Henry turned it on, then charged up the four steep stairs, his Glock in his right hand, the flashlight in his left. The comforting sound of feet on the steps behind him told Henry that the others were directly on his heels.

The windows on both sides of the bus were covered in filth and grime, the inside worse than the outside, though the rain had washed the outside pretty much clean. Because of this, no light penetrated into the interior of the bus, not even so much as a sliver.

As Henry climbed the stairs to the main floor, the flashlight illuminated the ceiling, then the driver's seat. Dried blood coated the seat, and the steering wheel had small bits of what may have been brain matter. Bits of bloody bone flecked the windshield. Even at a glance, Henry could see the gore was long dried. Whatever had happened to the driver had happened a long time ago.

Thunder cracked outside, drowning out all sound for a few seconds, then only the noise of the rain pattering on the metal roof filled the cabin.

Swinging the flashlight around to face the main interior of the bus, Henry aimed it at the floor first. He saw far too many legs and arms before him to be just Shaun. Then one set of legs moved out of the shadows only a few feet from Henry.

He raised the flashlight beam up the legs, to the torso and then the face of the person before him.

Two coal-black eyes gazed back at Henry, both orbs void of feeling, of sympathy, of emotion—of mercy. Below the dead eyes there was no nose, the nostrils lodged in a moist flab of meat. The mouth was open slightly, the teeth yellow and brown, a coating of fresh blood covering the cracked lips, which were pulled back to expose the rotting gums behind it. The face was something taken from a nightmare, only this nightmare was all too real and for Henry and the companions, it was a nightmare they now lived on a daily basis.

The zombie took a halting step forward, and before Henry could react, it wrapped its hands around Henry's throat. That made the deadland's warrior react and he shoved the zombie to the side, bouncing its head off one of the windows, the safety glass cracking with the force of the impact. The body slid to the floor and Henry ignored it.

His eyes took in the rest of the bus, and of the bodies within it, and he cursed under his breath. The damn bus was filled with zombies and he and his friends were outnumbered two to one.

In the thick of the undead lay Shaun, doing his best to fight off his attackers. Leveling his Glock, Henry was about to try and shoot some of the ghouls off Shaun but then thought better of it. No doubt, with point-blank range, any round he fired would only drill through the zombies' bodies and then into Shaun.

Henry glimpsed more zombies in the back of the bus, adding to the already bad odds. Holstering his Glock, he drew his sixteen inch panga from its sheath and prepared to do battle.

The zombie he'd slammed against the window was getting to its feet, a low moan escaping its cracked lips. Though he would have preferred to use the razor-sharp blade of the panga to take off the ghoul's head, there wasn't enough room for a full, sideways swing, not with Jimmy and the others directly behind him. So Henry went with bringing the flashlight down on the top of the ghoul's head. The top of the skull crunched and caved in under the impact of the steel-frame light, punching sharp shards of bone into the ghoul's brain, killing it instantly. Like a light being flicked off, the zombie's eyes rolled into the back of its head and it collapsed, now no more than a sack of potatoes, its limbs twitching feebly as nerve impulses ceased.

Even as the zombie went down, others began to rouse themselves, now aware that there were more humans inside the bus.

"No guns, we might hit Shaun!" Henry yelled. It was hard to believe that only seconds had elapsed since he'd first entered the bus. Behind Henry, the others holstered their weapons or slung them over shoulders and pulled knives, ready to fight the undead.

Where there had once been passenger seats on both sides of the bus, they were now gone, removed, leaving an open living area. Dirty blankets and odds and ends, such as empty food cans, littered the floor. At one time, people had made the bus a home but had abandoned it. Maybe the engine had broken beyond repairing or the bus had become stuck in the mud after another flash flood— all this was unknown to Henry and the others. Not that it mattered.

"Spread out as much as you can," Henry ordered the others as he took a step towards the first zombie, just as it charged him.

Jimmy went to his right, his eight inch Bowie hunting knife in his hand. As a zombie came at him, he stepped into its attack, the eight inch knife leading the way. He began hacking and slashing, lopping off fingers and slicing throats, the blade a blur in his hand. He added a few punches and kicks as well, dealing death wherever he stepped.

Henry pivoted around the zombie coming at him and slashed two-handed at it with his panga. The sharp blade cleaved off both of the ghoul's arms and bit deep into its stomach, spilling rotting entrails onto the floor. He jumped over it and moved deeper into the bus, trying to reach Shaun, who was trapped on the floor, punching and kicking to keep the zombies at bay.

Mary was next in line and she took a step forward to take on a zombie when she slipped on the blood-slick floor. Her feet going out from under her, she fell heavily onto her back, stars floating across her vision. An instant later, she was blinking up at the pale face of a female zombie. The ghoul reached down at her and she rolled to the side, its hands slapping the cold floor.

On her back, with the ghoul hovering over her, Mary knew there was no chance that she would shoot one of the others if her bullets either went wild or through-and-through the zombie, so she pulled her .38 and shoved it into the open mouth of her undead attacker. Closing her eyes and turning her head to the side to avoid any blowback, she squeezed the trigger twice. The report of the first shot was muffled inside the ghoul's head, but the second bullet made some noise as it exited out the back of the zombie's skull, taking half its brain upon its exit. Cold brains spilled out onto the floor and Mary used her free hand to push the ghoul aside as it went limp. Cindy was there then and Mary was helped to her feet by the blonde warrior. There was no time for thank yous now, only the battle, and the two women focused on the bus full of living dead.

Henry moved in on the thickest of the zombies with his panga, holding it like he would a baseball bat, hacking and chopping at the heads, necks and arms of the ghouls.

While Henry, Mary and Jimmy fought the hungry dead, Cindy ducked under the arms of two approaching zombies. Acting fast, she kicked out with her right foot, striking one of the zombies in its kneecap. The limb folded in on itself and the ghoul tumbled to the floor. Meanwhile, Cindy used the butt of her M-16 as a club, pushing in the face of the second ghoul. The nose was flattened, and pieces of broken cartilage were forced into the nasal cavity and then the brain behind it. The body dropped limply to the floor as the pieces acted like shrapnel, slicing into the brain and putting the zombie down for good.

A yell from behind Henry caused him to spin around to see Jimmy with a zombie clinging to his back, its face snapping forward again and again as it attempted to sink its teeth into Jimmy's neck, riding the young man like he was a bull and the zombie was a cowboy.

Fighting to remain upright, Jimmy tripped over a fallen body and crashed to the floor, the zombie riding him coming down as well, its teeth ever closer to his neck. The zombie's full weight came down on Jimmy, crushing him to the floor, but Jimmy hadn't fought and survived battling the living dead for years to be taken down now, in the middle of nowhere in a torrential rainstorm. As he landed, he managed to turn his body slightly, his right hand coming up, the Bowie knife gripped tightly in his hand. He slashed the ghoul's throat, severing the head nearly clean off its shoulders, but still, the zombie refused to die—the spinal cord remained intact. Its hands wrapped around Jimmy's throat and began to squeeze, as its head flopped around on its shoulders. Even as the head slid back off the head, the ghoul tried to force its head forward so it could take a bite out of Jimmy.

Becoming desperate, Jimmy brought the blade back and swung it forward again, plunging the blade into the zombie's neck, then he began to saw back and forth until finally severing the spine. The head remained attached by a thread of skin and it swung back and forth like a ball on a string. Jimmy gasped for breath, the zombie's hands still wrapped around his neck.

Seeing he needed help, Mary went to Jimmy and together they were able to pry the still-strangling hands from his throat. Getting to his feet, Jimmy cursed the semi-headless zombie that almost had been the death of him, and he kicked the head like it was a football. The blow was enough to rip the remaining skin free and the head skittered across the floor to be lost amongst the shuffling legs and limbs of the remaining zombies.

"Fucking deader," Jimmy muttered, rubbing his sore neck with his hand. "The damn thing almost got me."

Henry stepped back and joined the others. "This isn't working," he said, drawing his Glock. "We'll have to risk hitting Shaun. Fire at will. Take the rest of the bastards out!"

"Now that's what I wanna hear!" Jimmy whooped and swung his shotgun around, leveling it at the remaining ghouls. He couldn't see Shaun, the man lost amongst the bodies.

The four warriors lined up side by side in the bus right behind the driver's seat, then they began firing as the zombies came at them. As Henry began to fire, he breathed a sigh of relief that his pistol was working properly. Though it was made to get wet, it was never a good idea to dunk it in water, and the same went for the others' firearms. He knew when there was time and they were all dry, their firearms would have to be stripped, cleaned and oiled.

The onslaught of so much firepower was devastating to the ghouls. Many were blown onto their backs with great chunks of meat taken from their torsos, the bullets climbing up their bodies and hitting them in the face. It took less than five seconds to put every living dead creature down, and as the bus filled with the odor of cordite, the companions lowered their weapons and surveyed the bloody scene before them.

Charnel house was the only word to come to mind. The windows along the sides of the bus were splattered with gore, and bodies were piled three feet high on the floor.

"Cover me," Henry said and began moving forward, searching for Shaun. He went to the last place he'd seen the man and began digging through the bodies, tossing them aside as if they were nothing but cordwood. Finally, after the last body had been removed, he found Shaun lying face down on the floor. Carefully, he rolled the man over and looked down at him.

Shaun's eyes were open; he blinked once at Henry. He coughed and spit blood, then somehow managed a smile. "I guess the bus wasn't as good a place to hole up as I thought, huh?" It was only a whisper and Henry could see talking caused Shaun great pain. On his arms and left cheek were wounds, the marks obviously made from teeth. On top of this, he had been gut shot. Just as Henry had feared, Shaun had taken a bullet by accident.

A zombie stirred to Henry's right and he put a full-metal-jacket 9mm round into its head, then he turned back to Shaun. Cindy and

Mary went to Shaun, too, while Jimmy kept watch over the bodies, making sure all were truly down for good.

"Is there any chance?" Mary began.

Henry shook his head sadly. "No, he's too far gone."

"I...I don't want to become one of those things, Henry," Shaun whispered, a tear sliding down his face. "I don't want to become one of them." He reached out a hand and grasped Henry's arm, the grip surprisingly strong for someone so close to death.

"Don't worry, you won't," Henry said and placed the Glock to the side of Shaun's head. "I'm sorry it had to be like this." Shaun opened his mouth to say something else but the Glock bucked, a round blowing out the side of Shaun's head. "Shit, this sucks," Henry muttered as he leaned back on his haunches.

"Shit, Henry, he was gonna say something else," Jimmy said angrily.

"It didn't matter, better it was quick before he knew it was coming," Henry replied.

The others were quiet, only the sound of the rain and the wind filling the silence.

Footsteps at the front of the bus caused everyone to aim their weapons in that direction, then when they saw it was only Sue and Raven, they lowered them.

"Shit, guys, don't sneak up on us like that," Jimmy said. "It's a good way to get shot."

"The water's getting higher," Sue said. "And when we didn't hear anymore shooting, we decided it was time for us to get out of the rain, too."

Raven nodded, her black hair plastered to her head, making her look like an actor from an Asian horror movie. They got off the steps and onto the main floor and had their first look around the bus, Henry's flashlight the only illumination.

"Oh my God. Are they all dead?" Sue asked, referring to the ghouls.

"Yeah, they're dead," Jimmy said.

"But still, don't take any chances, there might be one playing possum," Cindy added as she joined Sue and Raven. "Shaun's dead," she said flatly.

"Oh no, that's terrible," Sue said. "I liked him, he was a good boy."

"Yeah, he was," Henry said. He stood up and walked over to Sue. He hugged her briefly and nodded his chin at Raven, who replied in a similar fashion. "Okay, we can mourn Shaun later, but right now we have too much to do. We need to get these bodies out of here for starters."

"And where do you suggest we put them?" Jimmy asked.

"Well, we can toss them out the door and the water will wash them away, is one idea." Henry glanced at the stairs to see the water had risen above the second step. Another few inches and it would be covering the floor of the bus, which wouldn't be good. "But I'm open to other options."

The group looked at one another, but no one had any better ideas so it was agreed that out the door the corpses would go.

"What do we do with Shaun's body?" Mary asked with tears in her eyes. She had liked Shaun a lot and it was hard to accept that he had been taken from their group so suddenly.

"Keep it with us for now. Maybe we can give him a proper burial. I doubt it though, what with all this rain and all." Henry sighed. "But one thing at a time."

They got to work cleaning up the bodies, dragging them to the open door and either tossing or rolling them into the water. No sooner did they splash down then they were ripped away by the current. Spent shells were everywhere and they were kicked aside so no one would slip and fall.

It took almost thirty minutes to get all the bodies out. Henry hated wasting the energy doing it, but he also knew the others, and himself as well, didn't want to spend even a minute inside the bus with the bodies if they didn't have to. So though they may only spend a few hours while waiting out the rain and for the water to recede, at least it wouldn't be inside a charnel house.

When the last body was gone, they washed quickly in the water that was now clean from the flowing current and gathered around Shaun's corpse. Henry had taken some clothing off a few of the corpses and he used it to drape over Shaun's body like a shroud, wanting to give the man a modicum of respect.

No one said a word, each looking down at the covered body, thinking about their own mortality, as the rain pattered on the roof of the bus and thunder boomed across the sky.

"Should someone say something?" Sue asked, looking from one face to another.

"I will," Henry said and cleared his throat while gathering some choice thoughts about life and death. "None of us knew Shaun very well, but I think I speak for all of us when I say we all liked him."

The others nodded and Mary was crying again. Henry would have been surprised if she wasn't. She had always been the conscience of the group, and more than once it had gotten them into trouble.

"Though it's tragic he died, the truth is, it could have been any one of us on the bus steps when he was grabbed." He gazed at the others, taking in each of their sad visages. "I'd be lying if I said if one of us had to die, then I'm not glad it had to be Shaun."

"Henry, how could you say that," Sue snapped.

"What, for being truthful? Listen, Sue, you guys are my family, Shaun was someone I'd just met. I barely knew him. Did I want him to die? Of course not. But if it was either him or one of you, then for me the choice is easy."

"Take it easy on him, Sue," Jimmy said. "I know what he means. He didn't want Shaun to die, but if it was either him or one of us, then the answer's simple."

"Well, it's still a terrible thing to say," Sue said, Mary nodding in agreement. Cindy was more practical and remained silent, not wanting to get into a debate. Raven didn't care one way or the other. More might have been said on the subject but suddenly the bus began to tilt and everyone was thrown off their feet.

"What the fuck is going on?" Jimmy yelled from the floor. Cindy had fallen on top of him and her elbow had slammed into his gut. He wheezed as he tried to catch his breath.

"The bus is moving, but how?" Mary asked, she and Raven falling into a pile together.

Henry had grabbed Sue, and they had gone down together, Henry shielding her from being hurt with his muscled body. The two rolled across the floor and came up against Shaun's corpse. The soft flesh of the body was yielding and it saved Henry from hitting the side of the bus and becoming hurt. His side felt wet again and he realized there was water on the floor, an inch, with more filling the bus each second.

Jimmy got to his feet and stumbled to the front of the vehicle. He went to his knees twice but finally managed to reach the driver's seat. The bus rocked to the side and he plopped down into the driver's seat. He ignored the dried gore.

"Jesus Christ, the water's even higher!" Jimmy yelled and reached for the handle to the door. Though automatic, and operated by hydraulics, it also had a manual handle that could be opened and closed like in a school bus. One of the advantages of being an older model bus.

"Get that damn door closed!" Henry yelled. "The water's coming in here."

"What the hell do you think I'm trying to do?" Jimmy snapped back as he yanked on the handle. Finally, with a dull screech of unoiled hinges and rust, the door slammed closed, the sealing of the door taking an extra moment as water rushed in through the shrinking opening. Looking through the windshield, Jimmy didn't like what he saw. "Shit, guys, we're moving, floating by the looks of it." He began turning the steering wheel back and forth as if he could steer the bus as it floated down the road, which now resembled a small river.

Soon, the bus was moving fast and the occupants were thrown from side to side, only Jimmy managing to stay upright as he sat in the driver's seat.

The bus threatened to overturn on more than one occasion as it was slammed into guardrails, boulders and other unseen objects hidden by the rushing water.

Jimmy stared out the windshield at the roiling water. He knew if the companions had still been outside when the water had risen even more, they would have drowned in the raging tempest, and even now their fate was unknown.

When there was a brief lull when the bus didn't rock so bad, the entire group crawled and stumbled to the front of the bus to join Jimmy, so they could see outside through the now-clean windshield.

Only the bits of dried gore and blood on the inside marred the otherwise perfect view, the pounding rain having scrubbed the outside of the bus clean.

"Where the hell are we going?" Henry asked no one in particular, the bus bucking and jumping like a living thing, the water pushing it around like a child's toy in the bathtub.

No one had an answer.

"Hey, look at the bright side," Jimmy said.

"What bright side?" Henry asked. "There is no bright side to this situation."

"Not true," Jimmy rebutted. "The day can't get any worse."

Chapter 12

Duckwater, Nevada was a quiet place to live. Even after the dead rose, the city officials had gathered together and got everyone to work as a team to protect them.

Tall chain-link fences topped with razor-wire—an inner and an outer fence—were built around ten square blocks of the city, the rest left to the walking dead.

As time went by those fences were moved outward, some of the homes destroyed and the land reclaimed for farmland. Not much grew in the harsh Nevada sun, but with the use of underground wells, the residents were able to eek out a sparse living. And subsidized by what they could salvage in other parts of the state, such as canned and dried goods, the population of Duckwater was doing all right for themselves. There had even been plans to reach out to other nearby settlements and try and join resources.

It was raining heavily this night, and only the angle of the land prevented any serious flooding, not like other parts of the state. On every roof in the settlement, gutters had been set up to direct the rainwater to storage tanks buried under the ground. The added water would benefit the residents greatly and many had simply gone outside and bathed in the rain, taking advantage of nature's free shower.

It was well past midnight, and with the exception of the men and women patrolling the perimeter fence, everyone was sleeping, resting up for the hard day that was sure to come when the sun rose. Though there was no flooding, the heavy rain would have done damage and no doubt there would be extra work because of it.

With the cloud cover thick, none of the guards noticed more shadows crawling across the ground towards the outer fence. Nor did they see when these shadows coalesced into human forms. But in form only was the resemblance to humans that the shapes possessed.

Controlled by Lazarus, who was waiting out in the night, twenty zombies each began using metal cutters on the chain-link fence, while behind them, thousands of others waited for the order to follow. With the rain dampening all sound, the zombies made short work of the links on the fence and then pulled the loose flaps back so that the first ones in line could enter.

Once these were through, they too had metal cutters and they began working on the second fence, which would breach the perimeter and allow them access to the town.

Lazarus saw all this in his mind as he saw through the eyes of his followers.

Upon finding the crate of metal cutters in an old department store, he'd quickly formulated the idea of how to take the next town—this after sending scouts to see how heavily it was fortified. Normally, two chain-link fences would have been more than adequate to keep out his zombie horde, but after the last town and the losses he'd suffered, Lazarus had decided it was time to be smarter.

There was nothing that said his army had to come in openly and attack. No, this time he was sneaking in, and by the time the town of Duckwater knew what was happening, they would all be dead and part of his ever expanding army of the living dead.

As soon as the zombies entered into the space separating the two fences, they began cutting through the second fence. Lazarus was straining from the pressure of keeping them all under control, the precision of making so many minds do as he wanted pushing him to the limit of his ability.

But he was doing it.

The second fence was cut into in a dozen places and the undead army swarmed inside the town, spreading out in groups of twos and threes. They entered homes and buildings, careful not to make a sound, and when they were sequestered and hidden, they waited.

More than a thousand undead filed into the town, finding every human as they lay sleeping.

And then it happened, as Lazarus knew it would. One of the guards spotted one of his undead soldiers and sounded the alarm, shooting from the hip at the intruder. The zombie was struck in the chest and it spun slightly from the force of the bullet, but then slowly it turned to face the guard...and began walking towards the man.

The guard fired three more times, but in the darkness, all of his bullets went into the zombie's torso. Then it was too late; the undead soldier reached the guard and began to grapple with him. The man might have overpowered the lone ghoul but more zombies appeared behind him, surrounding and attacking from the rear. The man went down screaming, and died painfully.

Minutes later, the sub-command Lazarus had given the zombies made them stop feeding before the guard was too devoured to revive and move. Slowly, the guard rose from his position on the ground and joined the other undead.

More guards arrived but they were soon surrounded by the undead and taken down, only a few zombies shot in the head and destroyed.

Meanwhile, inside every home where families slept, believing they were safe from the undead menace, the zombies attacked exactly at the same time, thanks to an order from Lazarus telepathically sent to every undead soldier.

Children woke up screaming as they were torn from their beds. Mothers and fathers raced to bedrooms by candlelight, only to be taken down and ripped apart. It was a massacre, with only a few of the residents escaping.

Within one hour of the attack, the entire town was converted into the walking dead.

Lazarus stood on top of what was once a municipal building, gazing down as his dead army filtered out of homes and buildings and into the streets. With the rain making visibility tough, his soldiers seemed more like wraiths than human forms.

Though he didn't have to speak to his followers with his mouth, sometimes he liked to do it, to hear his voice as he proclaimed his destiny.

Spreading his arms wide, he looked down on the undead as they stood about, most staring at nothing, others watching him, while others chewed on mouthfuls of flesh taken from victims before they'd reanimated.

"My army," Lazarus said in a booming voice. "We have come far this day. We number in the thousands and soon there will be so many of us that the humans will never be able to stop us." He paused, as if he was expecting the undead crowd to begin cheering. But of course that wouldn't happen. How could it?

But then again...

Lazarus sent out a telepathic command for the horde below him to begin clapping and cheering.

Simultaneously, the undead horde began to yell and cheer, vocal cords dry from decay rasping out bellows of joviality. Others clapped, their fingers snapping off, the bones brittle from rot, while others merely moaned or groaned, doing their best to obey the command suddenly thrust into their heads.

Lazarus nodded, waving his arms over his heads for the mob to stop cheering. Then he sent out a command for them to be silent. Like a switch had been thrown, the mob ceased its adulations.

"From here we will continue onward, sweeping up the detritus of humankind and absorbing it into my army. Nothing can stop me, no one has the power. For all purposes, I'm God now, in all but name."

He waited for cheering and realized it wouldn't come if he didn't command it. His eyes flicked from one pale and rotting face to another, searching for any intelligence, any at all.

There was none. Only the stuporously blank faces he'd come to know so well.

Figuring there was no point in posturing for an army of undead idiots, he was about to step down and return to ground level when a scream sounded at the end of the street. Looking out over the heads of his army, he spotted a family of four trying to make a break for it, hoping to escape now that the worst of the slaughter was over. But there were too many zombies on the street, and though the family had done their best to sneak away quietly, they were soon spotted and cornered.

"Wait," Lazarus said and thought at the zombies that had surrounded the family. "Bring them to me."

The struggling family were grabbed on all sides and dragged before Lazarus. They were forced to their knees and they remained that way thanks to the dozen hands on their shoulders. Their faces gazed up at the figure of what they thought was a man on the roof of the building before them. From that distance and with the rain, they couldn't see Lazarus' pale skin, the cracked lips, the sunken eyes, only his outline against the dark sky.

"Who the fuck are you?" the father of the family asked, his wife and two children sobbing beside him. "Why haven't the walkers killed you, too?"

"Why, I'm God as far as you're concerned," Lazarus replied. "You should be nicer to me. Your life and the lives of your family are in my hands."

"What the fuck are you talking about?" the man demanded.

"These zombies are my army of the dead and I plan on taking every last life on this planet and making them like me?"

"Like you?" The man shook his head and looked at his wife. "This guy's fucking crazy. Don't worry, honey, we'll get through this, just be brave." He looked past his young daughter to his son of seven. "Tommy, be strong, son, this isn't over yet."

Tommy nodded, the tears sliding down his face. He wanted to be strong like his father but it wasn't easy. He was surrounded by the living dead, he and his family trapped. He didn't see how any of them were going to escape. Though death loomed over him, Tommy still couldn't accept that he might die. As a young boy, to him life was something taken for granted. Children didn't die, it just didn't happen, and no matter how many facts he might have been shown to the contrary, Tommy still wouldn't have believed it. He was a child, and kids just didn't die. Beside him, his younger sister hugged their mother, sobbing softly into her leg.

The father looked up at the roof to see that the man was gone, and as seconds passed he began to grow nervous. Though being strong for his family, he had no hopes of escaping, his family either. He had a revolver with four bullets in the waistband of his pants, hidden by his shirt—one for each of them—but he didn't see how he could kill his wife and kids and then turn the gun on himself and so spare all of them the pain of being eaten alive before the zombies stopped him. He'd planned on using the gun before they were caught but the zombies had surrounded him and his family too fast for him to use it. Now here he was, helpless, and to top it off, there was some lunatic with the zombies—this seeming impossible as zombies killed any human they came across. Why the man on the roof was safe from attack was something the father desperately wanted to know. Maybe he could use the knowledge to save himself and his family.

But any hopes of learning why the man was immune to attack vanished when Lazarus appeared through the crowd, the zombies parting to let him move past them. The man stared in horror as Lazarus stepped up so that he was only a few feet from the family.

"You...you're one of them!" the father gasped as he took in Lazarus' dead visage. "You're a fucking walker! But how can you talk?"

"That's a long story, my sad friend, and you're not worth the time to tell it to," Lazarus said. "Needless to say that it's I who am in control here and after I'm through with this town, I'll be moving on to the next one, and the next after that until the entire world is mine."

"What are you going to do with us?" the mother wept. The words were barely intelligible because of her crying. She was hugging her five-year-old daughter to her chest, squeezing so tight that the girl could barely breathe.

Lazarus looked at the woman and the small girl, then at Tommy and the father. "Why, I'm going to give you to my army. They deserve a good feast. They'll be allowed to devour all of you; there won't be anything left to reanimate. You see, I don't need you four. Besides, really only you and your husband are worthy soldiers for my army anyway. The two children are nothing but cannon fodder, even if I wanted to keep them. So I've decided to relieve you of the burden of living, of your miserable lives. You can thank me if you like."

"You bastard," the father hissed. "You can talk, think, and you do this to your own kind?"

"And what kind is that exactly, hmmm? Mankind? I'm hardly that. I'm more dead than alive anyway, and you know what? I like it like this." He sighed. "I'm done talking with you. I thought it would be amusing to chat but instead I find it very annoying. Goodbye."

He sent a telepathic order to the zombies that they could feed, and they immediately surged forward at the family of four. But there were so many they only pushed and shoved against one another, and for a few precious seconds, the father found out that he was free of bodies and could move. He had to make a decision then, one that if he had more time to consider, he'd probably never have been able to do it. But there was no time for second guesses, or regrets.

Reaching around to his back, he lifted up his shirt and withdrew the revolver and shot the four zombies closest to Tommy. In that split second he had to make a decision, the father decided that only Tommy had the best chance to escape. His son was a fast runner, was strong and healthy. If any of them could escape, it was Tommy.

But before Tommy could try and run for it, the boy needed an edge...and his father provided it for him with his last action on earth. Four zombies were shot in the face, the bodies dropping to the ground around Tommy.

"Run, son, try and get out of here! Go, before they get you!"

Tommy saw his father's face, saw him screaming something, and at first the words didn't make sense, but then his father's voice snapped the boy out of his fugue state and Tommy heard the words crystal clear.

"Go, Tommy, run for it, you have to live!"

Tommy did exactly what his father told him to do. He began to run. Hands reached out for him but he dodged them. When he used to play tag with the other kids, they could never catch him, never lay so much as a finger on him. He was fast, always had been. Now, that talent might very well save his life.

He had already made it twenty feet when a wall of living dead swelled up before him. He looked to the right to see it was also blocked, then the left, where another wall of bodies had developed. They were so close together he could never hope to get through them.

Behind him, he could hear the screams of his family as they were torn apart, their insides ripped from their bodies. Tommy peed himself when he heard his mother's shrieks of agony, followed by his sister's.

Then he spotted a way out, though it was slim. The zombies were standing with their feet apart, the opening like a gaping tunnel to Tommy's eyes.

He had no choice, he had to try for it.

Running at the wall of undead before him, he dropped to the ground and began crawling under the first one, then the one behind it and so on. The first zombies tried to bend over and grab him but missed. Then the boy was gone, lost amongst the rest of the walking dead.

Soon he was seven feet in and still moving, the zombies not even knowing where he was. He kept moving, his knees becoming open wounds as he scraped his legs on the wet ground, his pants becoming soaked in seconds.

He was knocked over, kicked and kneed as he crawled through the horde but none of them laid a hand on him. Once or twice a zombie figured out he was there, but when it tried to bend over, it found the crowd was too tightly pressed together and the ghoul couldn't bend over enough to grab Tommy.

Finally, after what seemed like hours but was in fact only twenty minutes, Tommy crawled out from under the last zombie of the massive mob, where now they were spaced apart more.

Jumping to his feet, he ignored the cramps in his legs from crawling for so long and dashed towards the open gate, easily running around the reaching ghouls, much too fast for their slow gait. He tried not to look too closely at the body parts and puddles of blood everywhere, the latter mixing in with the rainwater to become a diluted pink color.

Once through the gate, he turned to the right and ran even faster, the adrenalin surging through him making him stay moving, even though he wanted to fall to the ground and cry over his lost family.

He continued running long into the stormy night.

Chapter 13

For more than an hour, the bus was tossed and turned through the raging floodwater. Henry was petrified that sooner or later they would end up going over a cliff or some deep ditch that they could never climb out of. The bus filled with water the entire time, seeping in from every crevice of the vehicle. By the end of the hour, the group was knee deep in water yet again. Shaun's corpse floated near the back of the vehicle, banging against the walls as it was thrown from side to side. The water was a dark brown thanks to the blood that had been washed away from the floor and walls to then splash across them; no one liked being in it, but there was no choice in the matter.

As time passed, the rolling, bucking vehicle became almost a mundane thing. Henry even managed to doze off slightly as he held onto a floor-to-ceiling metal pole near the front.

Next to him stood Sue, holding him tightly, her arms wrapped around him in a death grip. Jimmy and Cindy stood together next to Henry and Sue, and Mary and Raven were in the middle of the bus, using handholds on the wall to keep them from being thrown about.

So far, none of them had been sea sick from the motion of the bus, but Sue was looking paler than normal. When Henry looked at her, she only smiled, keeping up a strong facade for him and the others.

Without warning, the bus suddenly slammed to a halt, the front and rear ends wrapping around a boulder as the center began to crinkle like a tin can. The midsection couldn't take the stress and it finally cracked in half, pieces of the fiberglass walls flying off into the wind as the water rushed in to swallow the bus whole.

The companions suddenly found themselves underwater, the current pulling them from within the bus and into the raging floodwaters. Henry had one brief glimpse of Sue as she reached out for him, then she was yanked away to be lost in the swirling waters. After that, it was all he could do not to drown. He would get his head above the surface and suck in a gulp of air, only to be swept beneath the waves once more.

His conception of time was lost as he fought to stay alive, and only when his head struck floating debris and he was knocked unconscious did his struggling cease.

His last thoughts were of Sue, Mary and the others.

Henry opened his eyes and blinked at the harsh sun and the clear blue sky.

For a few seconds he had no idea where he was, or how he'd gotten there. Then it all came rushing back: the storm, the bus, Shaun killed by the living dead, and finally, his wild ride on a bus-turned-boat.

His head hurt, and when he reached up and touched where it hurt the most, his hand came back with spots of blood on it. Sitting up, he touched the area more carefully and felt a small wound and a good-sized bump.

Looking to his left, he was relieved to see the other five in his group, and though waterlogged, disoriented, and exhausted, all were alive. From a casual glance they seemed unharmed other than bumps and bruises.

"That was some ride, huh?" Jimmy said as he got to his knees and promptly threw up.

"You all right?" Henry asked.

"Yeah, I'll live," Jimmy said. "Just swallowed too much water."

"How about everyone else? Sue? Mary? Raven? Cindy? Anyone seriously hurt?" Henry asked.

"I whacked my right shoulder on something," Mary said, rubbing it gingerly. "Other than that I'm fine."

"I'm okay, too, Henry," Sue said. "Thank God we all made it through that alive."

"I figure whatever current there was dragged us all to the same place," Henry mused.

"Now I know what a rubber duck in a bathtub feels like," Jimmy said. He sat on his haunches, wiping his mouth with the back of his sleeve. His shotgun was still wrapped around his shoulder, the strap cinched tight.

Cindy stood up, wiping caked mud from her hair. Her M-16 lay beside her. Through the entire event of the bus breaking open, she'd never let go of the rifle. She picked it up and tipped it so that the muzzle was pointing straight down. Water poured out of the barrel. "This is gonna need a good cleaning," she said.

"All our guns are," Henry said, feeling around for his backpack and finding it behind him. He vaguely remembered grabbing it when the water rushed in and he was washed out of the bus. All in all, things could have been a lot worse. They still had their weapons and he saw Jimmy going through his waterlogged pack, as was Mary. Raven had lost hers but she hadn't been carrying much that couldn't be replaced in time. Mary and Jimmy's were the most important, as they carried the food supplies, and Henry carried any spare ammo they had in his pack.

Feeling his clothes to do an inventory, Henry frowned to see that the Browning he'd taken off the dead man at the trading post was gone. No doubt it was buried in the mud somewhere, either a few feet or a few miles from where he was now.

Standing up, he felt a wave of nausea overwhelm him. He suffered through it, and after waiting for the bout of dizziness to pass, he gazed out over the austere landscape, where only small pools of water remained. The land sucked up what moisture remained from the flood quickly. With the hot sun beating down on the land, and the temperature already at ninety and climbing, it wouldn't be long before there was nothing remaining to show there had ever been a flashflood—that is except the destroyed trees and shrubs and churned-up ground. Not to mention the debris scattered for as far as the eye could see. More than one body could be seen, hapless souls that hadn't been able to stay above water. Henry figured more than one may have once been living dead. Blunt force trauma to their heads while the bodies had been thrown around in the water would explain why the zombies were down for good.

As he thought this, a low moan came from his right and he turned his head to see a zombie no more than ten feet away. It was crawling, and had just dragged itself out of a shallow pool. As it slowly moved across the ground, Henry saw that it had no lower body, that from the waist down, there was nothing, the legs gone, and only a few dried ropes of intestine dragged behind it.

Henry stood there and watched it slowly crawling towards him.

"Shit," Jimmy said and made a move to deal with the slow-moving zombie.

Henry raised a hand to stop him. "No, I got it," he said. "It's harmless."

The zombie was moaning louder now as it made its excruciatingly-slow progress across the ground. Henry waited until it was only a few feet from him, then he walked the distance separating him from the half-ghoul. The zombie reached Henry's legs and grabbed his left boot, trying to pull itself closer so it could take a bite out of Henry's leg.

Almost casually, as if he was merely going to wipe a piece of dirt off his shoulder, Henry pulled his panga from its sheath, raised it high over his head, and brought it down so that it connected with the zombie's head in the exact middle of its skull. The blade went deep, slicing down between the eyes and then parting the nose in two even parts. The knife made it to the upper jaw, where the blade then became jammed in bone and cartilage.

The zombie jerked once and went limp, black ichor seeping out of the thin line that the blade had made.

Placing his foot on the zombie's left shoulder, Henry heaved back, as if the knife had been stuck in a log being prepped for firewood. The knife came free with a squelching sound, droplets of ichor spraying from the blade to glide through the air before landing on the ground. The hard dirt eagerly absorbed it, always wanting more moisture, despite the recent flooding.

"Nice job, Henry. Way to get the deed done. That's one less deader in the fucking world," Jimmy said with a grin. If there was one thing Jimmy enjoyed it was killing zombies.

Henry only nodded in reply. Over the years, killing the undead had become as common to him as combing his hair or brushing his teeth. It wasn't something you gave much thought to; you just did it when it was necessary. He wiped the gore-covered panga on the shoulder of the half-ghoul, and when satisfied it was clean, resheathed it.

"So where are we, anyway?" Mary asked, the question out there for anyone to answer.

"I think I can help you with that," a voice said from behind the companions.

No one had to be told what to do next but they all did the same thing, each of them trained to act first and worry about consequences later. Only Sue was a little slow on the draw as she was still miles away from truly becoming a hardened warrior.

Simultaneously, all six companions spun around to face the origin of the voice, their hands reaching for their weapons, either aiming them or drawing them from holsters. Raven was unarmed but she raised her fists, prepared to fight it out. Henry was the fastest, and he reached for his Glock and pulled it out of its water-logged holster. He hoped it still worked after the even-worse dunking it had just received, but any chance he thought he had of using it drifted away in an instant as his eyes took in the ten men and women standing before him, all with guns drawn and cocked.

"Drop that fucking peashooter now, or you're all dead," the man who had answered Mary's question said. He was tall, well over six feet, with dark red hair and a beard to match. He was heavy set, with at least an extra thirty pounds of flab, a beer belly prominent. But under that flab was muscle. He carried a hunting rifle with an extended barrel for long-range shooting. A sniper's scope was mounted to it as well.

"You tell 'em, Redbeard," another man said as he stood with a pistol in his hand by the redheaded man's side.

Twelve guns were pointed at the companions, a mix of handguns, M-16s and a few Kalashnikovs, the assault rifles looking well-maintained and oiled. Each of the men and women holding the weapons looked tough and mean, and there wasn't so much as a glint of mercy in any of their eyes. The eyes that were devoid of emotion the most belonged to the man who had spoken.

Henry knew he and his friends had less than a half-second to decide what they were going do. If they tried to fight, there was no question some of the new arrivals would be killed, but with two-to-one odds, the battle would be fatal to the companions.

There was really no option but one.

"Do as he says, guys. Drop your weapons. They got us cold," Henry said, and as his Glock fell to the ground, he heard the same sound multiple times as the others followed his command.

Chapter 14

The six companions were quickly taken into custody, their hands shackled behind them. Once this was done, they were quickly padded down for hidden weapons and led to a beat-up bread truck and made to go inside it. So far none of them had spoken, only their eyes showing how they felt about the situation as they looked at one another for support.

The second the double doors were closed, only letting in thin slivers of light through the crack where the doors met, Henry cleared his throat to get the others' attention. "Okay, this is some deep shit we've fallen into."

The truck began to move, the engine rattling something fierce. Either the fan or alternator belt was on its last legs or the water pump was already at death's door. In the back, the six prisoners fought a losing battle to stay standing upright and sat down on the floor. There were a few empty Twinkie wrappers scattered about.

"What do you think they want with us?" Mary asked. Her zip ties were tight and her hands were hurting as blood tried to reach her fingers.

"Could be anything, really," Jimmy said. "They didn't look like cannies. Cannies like to wear trophies around their necks and shit. I saw none of that. Did any of you?"

Everyone agreed they did not, which was a good thing, too. Ending up on a dinner table as the main course, namely *long pig*, was never a way to end the day on a good note.

"Might be slavers," Cindy suggested.

"Or maybe they just don't want to take chances with us," Sue added. "And once they see that we're no harm to them, they'll let us go."

"Sue, honey, have you been living in the same world as I have for the past few years?" Henry asked, his temper rising despite his best efforts to keep it from boiling over. He loved Sue but sometimes her naiveté could be pretty damn frustrating.

"Yes, Henry, and given the circumstances, I don't think it's a bad thing to hope for the best. Despite all we've seen, not everyone in this world is bad."

"Yeah, but most of them sure as shit are," Jimmy said, getting an angry glare from Cindy for his trouble. "Sorry, babe, but it's the truth and you know it."

Cindy had to nod in agreement at his statement, knowing Jimmy was correct. It just wasn't something she liked to think about unless absolutely necessary. Hell, her own uncle had been a Grade A asshole, and it was possible she might have killed him in his sleep one day if she hadn't left him to join up with Jimmy and the others.

"It doesn't matter who they are," Henry said, cutting off the idle chatter. "They took us against our will and that makes them the enemy. So you all know the drill if this happens. We all stay quiet, keep our mouths shut and our ears and eyes open. The first chance one of us gets, we escape and then return to try and get to the rest of us."

"What if that's impossible?" Jimmy asked.

"Cut and run, no other choice," Raven added, Henry nodding to her.

"She's right. If there's absolutely no hope in hell of saving the others, then if one of us or more escapes, run for it and get to safety. If there's still no options after that, well...it was nice knowing you all."

With a lurching halt that sent the companions falling to the metal floor, the bread truck came to a stop. A second later, the rear doors were opened and bright light flooded in, blinding Henry and the others in the group.

"Get the fuck out here, recruits," someone said off to the side of the truck, the command followed by a hard wrap to the steel wall of the vehicle. The vibration filled the interior. Henry was the first outside and he blinked to clear his eyes in time to see that the man who'd spoken held a simple lead pipe. Unoriginal but effective nonetheless. Behind Henry, the rest of the companions stumbled out into the hot sun, their arms completely numb from the zip ties being too tight. Raven had been gnawing on hers the second she had a chance and she was more than halfway through the tough plastic. She was thankful her captors hadn't put her arms behind her back. Not that it would have been a problem for her. She was flexible enough to easily get her arms under her feet and then over so that they were before her. But if it was seen, then they would only make sure to tie her up even better the next time. She knew she only had one shot at escaping, and if she failed, it might mean her death. Still, she had to try; it might possibly be their only chance to escape. She got behind Sue so she was hidden from her captors and continued chewing on the plastic.

"Welcome to Camp Kitchekecamica," Redbeard said, six more armed men standing behind him. "The best damn summer camp west of Vegas." The people around him laughed. "Or it was until the fucking dead began to walk around like tourists and drunks after a night on the strip."

More laughter greeted the man.

"Wow, man, that's some act you got. Too bad Vegas is gone, you could have been a hell of an opening act," Jimmy quipped.

Redbeard frowned at Jimmy, set his jaw taut, and walked over to the young warrior. He looked at the other people watching, then smiled. He turned to look at Jimmy who upon seeing the smile, gave one of his own, thinking Redbeard found him amusing.

Like lightning in a bottle, Redbeard's right arm came up, the hand locked into a tight fist. The blow sent Jimmy falling onto his back, and if his hands had been secured behind him, it was possible he might have broken his wrists from the landing, or at least dislocated his arms from their sockets.

"Speak when spoken to, boy. You'll live a lot longer that way," Redbeard snarled.

"Leave him alone!" Cindy hissed. "Think you're so tough. It's easy to hit a man when he's helpless."

"Cindy, shut up," Henry snapped, not liking where this was going. He'd met men like Redbeard before and taunting a man like him was never going to end well.

"Oh yeah, little lady? So what? You think you can take me?" Redbeard said with a chuckle.

The crowd laughed at this, as did Redbeard.

"A blowhard like you?" Cindy said, sizing the man up with her eyes. "Yeah, I can take you. You look like there's more fat than muscle under that shirt."

Redbeard's eyes went hard. "No one talks to me like that, especially a woman."

"Then do something about it, you fat fuck," she spat.

"Carl, Louie, untie the bitch. Let's see what she's got," Redbeard commanded. "If I don't kill her, I can soften her up for the brothel when she gets put there."

"Don't soften her up too much, Redbeard," Louie said as he and Carl went to Cindy. Louie was a short man with a face covered in acne, despite his age of thirty. His hair was long and greasy. "She's got a pretty face. I want to see it stay that way when I get to fuck her."

"I'll see what I can do," Redbeard said as he stepped into a circle that had begun to form as spectators began to bet on the outcome.

Using a pair of wire snips, Louie cut Cindy's zip tie. "He's gonna fuck you up good, girlie," he said before stepping away.

Carl, a thin man with a perpetually crooked nose from multiple breaks, only nodded and smiled.

Redbeard was posturing for the crowd while Cindy was being freed and this was a mistake on his part. The instant Cindy's hands were cut free, she shoved Louie and Carl out of the way and ran at Redbeard, who had his back to her as he waved to the crowd.

Just as he was casually turning to face Cindy, expecting to see her a few feet away and just becoming free, that she lunged at him, jumping up and wrapping her legs around him so that she was face to face with him. From a distance, it would have reminded anyone of a father and daughter playing, the daughter holding on to the father as he carried her around by the hips.

But this embrace was the farthest from that. As Cindy's legs went around Redbeard's body, she used her fingernails and tried to gouge out his eyes. Instinctively, Redbeard's head snapped back when he saw fingernails coming for his eyes and it was the only thing that saved him from becoming blinded. Missing his eyes, Cindy settled for ripping the man's earring out of his left ear. Redbeard roared in pain and anger as his ear began to drip blood.

Cindy wasn't impressed by his vocals and she punched him in the Adam's apple, making the large man gag and stumble. Not wanting him to fall face first and crush her beneath him, she let go of his waist with her legs and dropped to the ground.

But Redbeard was stronger than most men and he recovered more quickly. While Cindy dropped to the ground, Redbeard was reaching out for her. She tried to duck and spin away but he managed to grab her long blonde hair, yanking it back as if it was a leash.

Her head snapped back and Redbeard's fist was waiting, her face hitting his fist more than the other way around. She was stunned by the blow and saw stars, her vision becoming blurry. Redbeard used her hesitation and picked her up, holding her in a bear hug. He began to squeeze, crushing her ribcage, the pressure on her lungs making her want to black out.

"Oh God, Henry, do something! He's killing her!" Sue screamed.

But Henry knew there was nothing he could do but watch. "She should have stayed quiet, Sue. Mouthing off wouldn't help and now look what she's done," he said, his eyes on the men surrounding him with guns.

The second Redbeard had told Louie to release Cindy, more men covered the companions with weapons. If one of them so much as tried to act, they would be gunned down before they took two steps. Henry's hands curled into fists and he fought to pull free of the zip ties in his anger, the plastic digging into his wrists to draw blood. Though it pained him to admit it, Cindy was on her own.

Cindy tried to pry Redbeard's arms free but she quickly found it impossible. Her arms were still free and she used them to the best of her ability. Pulling her right arm back, she came in with a blow to his face, giving Redbeard a bloody lip.

He licked his lip clear of blood and smiled malevolently. "I'm gonna kill you and then fuck your still-warm corpse, slut." Letting her go and holding her with one hand, he grabbed his crotch, rubbing it a few times.

The crowd roared with laughter, loving every second of it.

ANTHONY GIANGREGORIO

Cindy kicked out with her left leg, her knee going directly into Redbeard's crotch. The man woofed and dropped her, his face turning red as the pain from his crushed testicles filled him from head to toe.

Cindy landed heavily in the dirt, sucking in air as she tried to get up. But she couldn't. Her arms and legs felt weak, her chest sore, and every breath she took felt like her lungs were filling with acid. She wasn't a doctor but she figured Redbeard had cracked a few of her ribs.

"You fucking whore," Redbeard wheezed. "I wasn't gonna fuck you up much, just teach you a lesson for talking shit to me, but now I'm gonna kill you and fuck your corpse raw."

Jimmy was on his feet now, cheering Cindy on. He had a fat lip from the blow he'd taken but he barely noticed it, too focused on Cindy. "Get the fucker, Cindy, you can take him!" he yelled. By his side, Mary seconded him, calling out her words of support.

Cindy heard the words of encouragement as if her head was under water. Shaking her head, she tried to snap out of it, but loss of oxygen had knocked her for a loop and it was all she could do to keep from simply falling to the ground and laying still.

Redbeard reached down and picked her up by the neck, his meaty fingers wrapping around her throat. With an evil yell he began to squeeze the life out of her. Cindy's face began to turn crimson, her tongue sticking out. Her eyes rolled into her head, and though she banged her fists ineffectually on Redbeard's face and shoulders, the man didn't let go. She started to black out, and she knew without question that he was killing her. Tears slid down her cheeks.

Jimmy saw this too and he cried out and tried to run to Cindy, to stop Redbeard from killing his lover, but a guard stopped him, clubbing him in the back of the legs. Jimmy fell face first to the ground. Henry took a step forward, too, but three men armed with assault weapons threatened him. Though it went against every fiber of his being, he halted, knowing there was nothing he could do but receive a beating for his defiance.

Redbeard picked up Cindy off the ground, her legs kicking feebly six inches in the air, her blonde hair plastered to her face as she

98

was covered with sweat from the exertion of the fight. Dust stuck to her as well, coating her exposed skin.

Mary and Sue cried out for Redbeard to stop, that he was killing Cindy. The large man glanced their way, the look on his face telling them that he knew *exactly* what he was doing.

The crowd cheered louder, relishing the kill, wanting to see blood at any cost.

Cindy's life was measured in seconds, her facing turning red to blue from lack of oxygen as Redbeard squeezed even harder. Her kicks became weaker as she passed out, her fall into unconsciousness preceding death.

The crowd cheered even more, everyone knowing the fight would be over at any moment.

Chapter 15

While the entire crowd was fixated on the fight, Raven used this to her advantage. No one was watching her, the guards focused on seeing Cindy being strangled to death. Raven had used this time well and had worked even harder to chew through her plastic bonds.

When it seemed like she would never do it, she yanked one last time and the zip tie broke apart, her wrists wet from blood where her teeth had bitten into the skin. In the space of half a second she weighed her next move. Henry had told her and the others that if they had a chance to escape, they needed to take it. But she knew if she turned and ran before anyone knew she was free, Cindy would die.

So there was really only one thing she could do.

Shoving her guard out of the way, the woman of forty falling to the ground and breaking her nose, Raven dashed through the cheering crowd, directly towards the open circle where Redbeard and Cindy were.

She ran as fast as she could, her legs seeming to glide across the ground, weaving in and around the spectators, and when she reached the edge of the circle, she spotted a man that had been knocked to the ground from the shoving crowd and was just getting to one knee. When she reached that man, she used his back like a springboard, and as she pushed off him, she flew through the air right at Redbeard. In mid-air, her right leg went out before her, and before anyone could stop her or realized what was happening, she kicked Redbeard in the face, sending the man lurching to the side from the blow. Raven was knocked to the side as well. She fell to the ground, rolled three times, and came up in a crouch. Cindy was dropped by the distracted Redbeard and she landed heavily on the packed dirt that made up the circle, where she lay immobile, sucking in air like a fish out of water.

The crowd roared with this new turn of events, only the guard that had been watching Raven seeming upset. The woman with a bloody nose knew she was in big trouble once the fight was over, no matter the outcome. She had let her prisoner escape and no doubt she would be punished for it. Seeing that no one was watching her, the woman slipped into the crowd and worked her way to the back, then took off running. If she was lucky, she could slip out of the camp and be gone long before anyone knew she was missing. She'd take her chances in the desert; at least there she might have a chance. If she stayed in camp, all she had to look forward to was punishment and pain.

There was a large bruise on Redbeard's face where Raven had kicked him. He shook his head to clear it of the fog that had come over him. "What the fuck is this?" he asked angrily, looking at Raven as if she was a wraith that had appeared from out of nowhere. "How'd you get free? Never mind, it doesn't matter. I can take one bitch down as well as two just as easy, and when I'm done, I'll fuck both of your corpses."

"Bring it on, fatso," Raven hissed, her hands out before her. She was already planning on going in fast, ducking his blows, then trying to slice open his jugular with her fingernails. She'd watched the big man fight Cindy and she thought she had his moves down pretty well. He was strong but she was faster. Raven glanced at Cindy, who was sitting up, rubbing her throat with her hands. She was slowly coming around. All Raven had to do was keep Redbeard occupied until Cindy regained more strength.

Redbeard took a step towards Cindy and Raven knew she had to act. With a battle cry to get Redbeard's attention, she charged him, her hands out before her like scythes, ready to slice and cut.

Just as she planned when she reached Redbeard, the man tried to grab her like he had done to Cindy, but she ducked his blow easily and then jumped straight up, her hands lashing out, her fingernails slicing at his throat. But Redbeard was quicker than she thought and he dodged her blows, her fingernails only slicing into his right cheek; one of her fingernails also cut off a half inch chunk of his beard.

He caught her in mid-air and pulled her to him.

"You little bitch, now it's your turn to die," he hissed, his breath smelling like rancid cheese. He began to squeeze the life out of her.

Raven gasped as she felt the pressure on her ribs increase. Already she couldn't breathe. This wasn't how it was supposed to go.

Instead of saving Cindy all she'd managed to do is get herself killed first.

Cindy got to her feet, wobbling back and forth as she struggled to stand and see straight. Before she could get her balance, she stumbled towards Redbeard and began punching him feebly, her only goal to save Raven from his clutches.

He laughed at her, her blows light as air, then he grabbed Raven by the neck with his left hand and reached down and picked Cindy up by the throat with his right hand.

Laughing maniacally, he squeezed their throats simultaneously, knowing it wouldn't be long before the two women lost consciousness and died. He was already thinking about fucking their corpses when a commanding voice boomed out over the crowd.

"Just what in the name of holy hell is going on around here?" the man demanded, his tone one of anger and impatience. It was a voice that said the owner got what he wanted *when* he wanted it.

Every man and woman that had been watching the fight stopped yelling and went silent, all eyes going to the man who had spoken. Even Redbeard turned to face the new arrival, the women dangling from his hands like ornaments on a Christmas tree.

Henry sighed in relief. Whoever this man was, no matter how bad his arrival might be, he'd paused the fight. Hopefully he would stop the fight for good and save Cindy and Raven.

As Henry had hoped, Redbeard immediately dropped Cindy and Raven to the ground, the women already forgotten. Behind Redbeard, on the packed dirt, Cindy and Raven gagged and coughed as they struggled to breath through their sore throats.

Sue and Mary gasped and Jimmy uttered a low curse, and Henry almost let out a gasp also as he took in the imposing figure that had stopped the fight and commanded attention from everyone in the camp. The man was tall, a little over six feet with a powerful chest and a chiseled jaw. His dark brown hair was slicked back, making him resemble a rebel from a 1960's motorcycle movie, the all-black leather outfit he wore rounding out the look. His eyes were dark green, and even from the distance separating Henry from the man, the deadland's warrior could see mercy wasn't something commonly found in those eyes. A silver-plated Desert Eagle rode the man's right hip in a custom leather holster.

But the thing that made Sue and Mary gasp and Jimmy curse was the figure the man had standing docile by his side, held in place with a dog leash connected to a studded black collar, one that looked as if it had been taken from some S&M lover's basement.

It was a zombie. But the biggest damn zombie any of the companions had ever seen. Well, maybe not the absolute biggest. Henry had seen one close to that size, back when he had been forced to fight a zombie in a cage for the amusement of the boss of the town. But where that one had been as tall as a basketball star, this new figure would have topped the latter by at least six inches.

The zombie had no hands, but instead there were razor-sharp blades there, the hilts taken off so that the blades could be pounded into the meat and flesh of the wrists. The mouth and nose was covered with a leather mask, and there were no holes for air. None were needed. The walking dead didn't breathe.

The zombie moaned loudly behind its mask, becoming agitated, and the man turned and used a cattle prod on it, the zombie twitching as the electricity flooded its body. It calmed down almost immediately.

"Well, I'm waiting for a fucking answer," the man demanded, tugging on the zombie's leash to keep it from moving.

"Aww, Murdock, I was just havin' some fun is all," Redbeard explained, a touch of fear in his voice. "I didn't think there'd be any harm in it. The blonde one got lippy and I had to teach her some manners."

"What have I told you about fighting the recruits, Redbeard?" Murdock asked, his eyes creasing in anger.

Redbeard looked down, running a foot back and forth in the dirt. He reminded Henry of a spoiled child caught filching cookies before dinner.

"You said not to do it again," Redbeard mumbled.

Murdock put a cupped hand to his ears. "What was that? I didn't quite make it out."

"You said not to," Redbeard said louder.

"Yeah, I did. And what did you do?"

"I did it anyway," Redbeard mumbled even lower than before.

Henry watched Redbeard and he saw genuine fear in the man's face.

"Yeah, you did, didn't you," Murdock said with what sounded to Henry like remorse. Then, in quick, practiced moves, Murdock reached up and unsnapped the large zombie's mask off, while mumbling a few words of command. Instantly, the zombie went into action, its long legs eating up the distance between it and Redbeard, who looked up and screamed in fright.

The zombie reached Redbeard, wrapped its arms around him, and picked the terrified man up as if he were a child. Redbeard tried to fight but the blows he rained down on the zombie were ineffectual. The zombie opened its mouth wide and sank its yellow teeth into Redbeard's neck, tearing out a four inch chunk of flesh, along with the man's jugular.

Redbeard let out what sounded to Henry like a bleat, much like what a lamb would make. This quickly turned into garbles as blood shot out of his neck and seeped back into his airway and lungs. The zombie took another bite, chewing happily.

The crowd watched Redbeard being eaten in absolute silence, not one whisper, not one exhaled breath. In less than a minute he had bled out, and his legs and arms stopped twitching and his head slumped to the side. Blood dripped on the ground after sluicing down his body, pooling beneath his feet. The zombie kept right on feeding.

Murdock blew a whistle and the zombie stopped eating. The whistle sounded again, this time twice in a row, and the zombie dropped Redbeard to the ground and returned to its master, chewing as it walked.

When it reached Murdock, he stretched up and put the mask back on the zombie, the giant ghoul still chewing the flesh it had in its mouth.

"Louie," Murdock called out. "Where are you?"

"Here, Boss," Louie said, pushing between two spectators and running up to Murdock. Louie swallowed the lump in his throat and tried not to look at the blood-covered zombie.

"You've just been promoted. Redbeard's position is now yours." He leaned forward and lowered his voice. "Do what's expected of you and you might last longer than Redbeard."

"No problem, Boss, I hear ya loud and clear." Louie was smiling. He'd been promoted, and with the new position would come money and power.

"Good. That's very good. Because my pet zombie is always hungry, Louie..." He trailed off, the meaning clear. Murdock glanced over at Henry and the others, his eyes resting on Mary for a few moments before moving on. Cindy and Raven had returned to the group, looking like they had been through the fight of their lives. Sue did what she could for them, which wasn't much.

"Gather the new recruits," Murdock said to Louie, who got the guards into action. "I want to give them a tour of our camp before they go off to their respective places in the camp." He smiled, but the gesture didn't go anywhere near his eyes. "I want them to see what happens to those that don't play nice around here. Redbeard got off easy. I want them to see what pain really is." He began walking over to the companions, and when he passed Redbeard, he said with a dismissing wave of his hand, "Get that body out of here, Louie. When Redbeard reanimates, make him one of my gladiators of death. I have a few ideas that will make him the ultimate warrior for the arena."

Louie nodded and gestured to three men, who ran to Redbeard and dragged the corpse from the quickly dissipating circle.

"Now, for the tour," Murdock said with a cold smile.

Chapter 16

"We've been here for a few years now, ever since the rains first fell and turned people into the walking dead people," Murdock explained as he walked by a small motor pool, with an assortment of motorcycles, cars and trucks, about a dozen in all. "I knew about this place from when I was a kid. I went here every summer." He waved his hand around at the log cabins, the shacks and tents that had been set up as well. He pointed to the small pond in the center of the camp, and the dock where children once used it to jump off and go swimming. Now it was used for women to clean laundry from. "See that long plastic pipe that goes from the pond to one of the cabins? Well, inside there's a water pump. The pipe in the pond goes twenty feet into the water, that way it won't suck in the dirty water from the laundry." He grinned. "My idea."

He was talking to Henry mostly, as he sensed that Henry was the leader of the companions. Henry said nothing in reply. He was a prisoner; he wasn't going to chat with Murdock as if they were old friends.

"Though the lowlands flooded pretty bad last night, it was fine up here, though the water level in the pond has gone up a good five inches, which is a good thing. We're growing by the day here, too," Murdock said. "That's where you people come in. See, any growing city needs a work force, and just like the Romans did centuries ago, I've taken on slaves to see that what I need done gets done." His zombie followed him like a dog, the leash barely needed, it was so well-trained.

"Sounds pretty shitty to me," Jimmy said and was about to get a rifle butt to the gut when Murdock stopped the guard from doing so. "Perhaps, but it's only shitty if you're on the low end of the totem pole. I found out quickly that not everyone I met wanted to be part of my little community, and if there aren't enough people to do the work then the community fails."

"So you decided to become a slaver," Henry said.

"You make it sound like that's a bad thing," Murdock replied.

"It is, it's reprehensible," Mary added.

Murdock turned to face her. "What's your name, woman?"

"Mary Roberts."

"I like your spunk, Mary Roberts. I think you and me should become better acquainted." He pointed to a guard and said, "Take her to my cabin and have her bathed before I return."

"Back off, I'm not going anywhere with anyone," Mary snapped at the guard as the man raised his gun at her chest. She raised her hands before her, and even though they were bound, she was prepared to fight.

Murdock stepped up to her and grabbed her by the throat. "I like my possessions to have spirit, it gives me more pleasure when I break them," he grinned malevolently. "You can go of your own volition or you can be knocked out and dragged, it's entirely up to you," Murdock said.

"Just go with the guard, Mary, and stay sharp," Henry said. "It's too early to make a last stand."

She nodded, understanding what he meant.

"Be careful, Mary," Sue said.

Mary nodded and even managed a wry smile. "Always." She was removed from the group and Murdock continued his tour. "Follow me, people, there are a few more things of interest for you to see before you're put to your tasks." He glanced at Henry. "I would put ideas of 'last stands' out of your head, you won't get the chance, I promise you."

They walked through the camp, all eyes on the new arrivals. Sue walked close to Henry and he held her tight. Jimmy and Cindy were also close together, Jimmy helping Cindy walk; she was still shook-up from her ordeal. A red circle was around her neck from Redbeard's fingers, and though it hurt to swallow, she took a small consolation knowing that the man was dead.

Raven was last in line. Her eyes darted back and forth as she took in everything. Her hands were still loose, no one bothering to put on another zip tie. But there was an extra guard on her now, and if she tried to run, she knew she'd be shot in the back before making it five feet. So she bided her time, listening and watching everything.

"Ah, now here's something that will make you think about trying to escape," Murdock said, stopping in the center of an open area, where there was a six-foot-round hole in the ground. More than a dozen people circled the hole, yelling down into it. One of the men was urinating into the hole, while another sent a large spitwad that was the color of mud, a residue of the chewing tobacco the man chewed.

At the bottom of the eight foot pit was a filthy, bloody man. His mouth was covered with duct tape, wrapped around it so many times that there was no way he could scream. The man wasn't alone in the pit.

He was fighting half a dozen large rats, each the size of a small dog. All the rodents were black, with the exception of one that had a white spot on the top of its head. As Henry peered down into the pit, he saw the white-spotted rat jump up and sink its teeth into the man's arm. The man tried to scream but only muffled sounds came from behind the tape.

"Oh, how horrible," Sue said and hid her face in Henry's chest.

"How so?" Murdock asked. "This man tried to escape and was caught after less than an hour's walk away from camp. He needs to be punished. If he can last a day in there then he's taken out and put back into the workforce."

"And if he can't last that long?" Jimmy asked.

Murdock shrugged, as if the answer was of little consequence. "Then he dies."

The rats were swarming over the man now, sinking their teeth into skin at every chance they got. The man tried to protect his genitals, and that left the rest of his body open to attack. A hundred small wounds from sharp teeth covered his body, each one seeping blood. Henry frowned. Even if the man survived, no doubt he would die from infection, the wounds turning gangrenous. Modern medicine was a thing of the past, and medicine such as penicillin was valued more than gold was once in the old world.

"If you don't want to end up like him, then follow the rules and do what you're told," Murdock said. "I won't stand for insubordination." He looked around the small crowd that had gathered to watch the man in the pit. "Louie, where are you?"

"Right here, Boss," Louie said and pushed his way through the small crowd of gawkers. "I just got through having Redbeard taken where you said."

"Good." Murdock looked at each of the companions, taking them in as if for the first time. His eyes went to each of them before falling on Sue, Cindy and Raven. He pointed at Cindy and Raven first. "Those two go to the whore house." Then he pointed at Sue. "She's too old for the whore house; send her to the kitchen and laundry." His eyes finally settled on Henry and Jimmy. "Those two go to the arena. The older one looks like he might actually survive for a few days. The skinny one not so much, but he should provide good sport until he's killed."

"Right away, Boss," Louie said and began yelling at the guards to get the companions moving.

As they were ushered away, Murdock turned and began talking with some men, the companions already forgotten.

Sue and Henry were separated and Sue cried out, "Henry, I don't want to leave you!"

"Just go with the guards, Sue," Henry said. "Keep your head down and do as you're told. I'll come and get you as soon as I can."

"But..."

"No argument, just do what they say. Don't worry, we'll get out of this."

"Easy for you to say," Cindy said. "I'm going to the fucking whore house. I swear to God, Henry, the first man who tries anything is gonna get a kick to the balls or worse."

Jimmy wasn't happy about any of this. "They're splitting us up, Henry. We could try and make a break for it now before it's too late. Jump the guards and run for it. Maybe steal a car or something."

"Sure, we could, but even if we did, we'd have to leave Mary behind."

"Well, we can't let Cindy get raped and..."

"Jimmy, I know it sucks, but we have to wait for now. We need to see how this place operates and then we can try something."

Cindy and Raven were led off, both women's postures one of defiance. Henry hated to see them being led off to a whore house but there was no way to stop it at the moment.

Henry and Jimmy were led across the camp to the very edge, where there was a wooden shack with boarded-up windows. Two guards stood before the only door, both with assault rifles.

As the warriors were ushered up to the door, one of the guards opened it. Both Henry and Jimmy gagged from the stench of blood and offal that wafted out of the door. Before they could do or say anything, they were shoved from behind by the guards that had brought them to the cabin.

"Welcome to your new home, assholes," one of the guards said with a chuckle.

As the door slammed closed behind them, the guards' laughter could be heard. The floor was covered in shit and mud. Henry sat up, Jimmy as well, both men trying to wipe their hands clean on their clothes where they weren't covered in filth from the fall. Only what light filtered in through the cracks in the door and slats of wood making up the walls illuminated the gloom interior.

"Gee, Henry, you take me to so many nice places. I'm touched," Jimmy said sarcastically as he wiped his hands on his shirt. "I'll say it again though I don't really mean it. There's got to be a bright side to all of this; things can't possibly get any worse."

"This isn't the time for jokes, Jimmy; we're in some deep shit here, figuratively and literally."

"No kidding," Jimmy replied. "We need to get out of here, old man, get our weapons back, and save the girls, and pronto."

The two men were so busy trying to clean themselves off that neither had fully taken in the interior of the shack. But now, deep in the far corner, where the gloom was the darkest, figures began to shift, to slowly move forward.

Henry was the first to hear the shuffling of feet on the floor and he stopped moving and grabbed Jimmy's arm. "Uh, I don't think we're alone in here, pal," he whispered.

Jimmy stopped moving and he looked up from cleaning his arms, his ear picking up the telltale sound of multiple bodies scuffling around. Then his eyes picked up the shifting shadows, of which there was more than one. The two warriors took a step back, then another, until their backs were pressed against the locked door.

"What did you say about things not getting any worse?" Henry asked. "Damn it, Jimmy, you really have to stop saying that."

"Yeah, I couldn't agree more," Jimmy replied.

The figures shuffled ever closer.

Chapter 17

Cindy and Raven were taken to a two-story house set in the center of the camp. Once there, Raven was put in a room on the first floor, and Cindy was locked in a room on the second, then told to wait. Both rooms had barred windows to prevent escape.

An hour later, the door to Cindy's room was unlocked and a woman stepped into the room. Cindy looked past her, thinking she could make a run for it, but there was an armed guard watching the door, his weapon aimed directly at Cindy.

"My name is Dottie but you will refer to me as Madam," the woman said. She was in her late forties to early fifties, with black hair with streaks of gray and far too much makeup and perfume on. The instant she entered the room, Cindy wanted to gag on the woman's perfume. Madam wore a black dress that was cut low in the front, and though the woman was older, her cleavage was still in fine shape. Cindy wondered if that was thanks to a good support bra.

"Oh yeah? I have a few other names I might use instead," Cindy said sarcastically.

The woman clucked softly and shook her head slowly, as if she was putting up with an unruly child. "My, my, it appears I'll have my work cut out with you, too. The dark-haired girl you were brought in with is wild enough to keep me busy for days, and it seems you're both cut from the same cloth."

"You don't know the half of it, lady."

"Yes, well, I will tell you what I told her. If you do as you're told, you actually can have a rather nice life here. You will have a roof over your head and a full belly and nice clothes to wear."

"And if I don't want to cooperate?" Cindy asked, crossing her arms over her chest.

Madam frowned. "Well, I would really not prefer to go into it. Let's just say that if you fail here, there is no place else to go but down."

Cindy said nothing, the threat clear. Play nice or die.

Madam took Cindy's silence as acquiescence and she nodded, a small smile playing across her lips. Cindy saw that the smile didn't go to her eyes. Though Madam might talk like an educated woman and wear nice clothes, Cindy knew the woman was as much a coldheart as any slaver or raider she'd come across on the trail while traveling. If you wrapped shit up in a bow it was still shit.

Madam pointed to a closet. "In there you will find clothes that should fit you. You may wear anything in there. The shower water is hot thanks to a solar water heater so as soon as I leave, I want you to bathe and get dressed for your first customer. But don't dally too long; the water is limited of course."

"Go to hell, you bitch."

Madam frowned. "We'll have to work on your language I think." She took a step back and knocked on the door. The door opened and the guard leaned inside. "If this woman isn't ready for her first customer when it's time, I want you to shoot her. Do I make myself clear?"

"Yes, Madam," the guard said.

Madam nodded and turned back to glare at Cindy. "You have two hours. What you choose to do in that time is entirely up to you." She looked Cindy up and down, sizing her up. "It would be a shame to have you killed. You could end up being one of the more...popular attractions around here." Without waiting for a reply, she turned and left the room, the door clicking softly as the lock was set.

Cindy stared at the door for a full minute, then went to the only window. The iron bars were bolted to the outside of the house. She wouldn't be getting out that way. There was a battery-operated clock on the wall, the minute hand ticking away. A full five minutes went by before Cindy went to the closet and opened it. Inside, all the clothes were the same: short and skimpy, ones that showed a lot of leg and cleavage. She picked out the one she believed showed the least amount of skin, then went into the bathroom to bathe.

For now she had to play along and see how it went. She hoped Raven was doing the same thing.

Two hours later to the minute there was a knock at the door. Without the knocker waiting for a reply to enter, the door opened and a bald, fat man stepped inside. The guard closed the door behind him. Cindy was sitting on the bed, flipping through an old magazine she'd found in one of the dresser drawers. About an ago an old woman had come to take her dirty clothes away, other than that she had been left alone.

"Wow, Madam said you were pretty but she didn't say how pretty," the man said. He walked over to the bed, while already getting undressed.

Cindy wrinkled her nose at the man. He smelled terrible, and when he took off his shirt, she could see dirt within the rolls of fat.

Since Madam had left her, Cindy had debated whether she should go through with what she was told to do, even if it was just until she could figure out a way to escape. Back when she had been staying with her uncle, he had forced himself on her, which was why she had left town with Jimmy and the others. She wasn't a prude about sex. If she had to sleep with a few men while she bided her time, she could have handled it, but wouldn't have enjoyed it. But things had changed since then and she had other reasons why she would never allow another man but Jimmy to touch her. She hadn't been able to talk to Jimmy about it as there had never been a good time to discuss what was on her mind, but hopefully sooner or later she could find a few minutes when they were alone. Of course, all the companions had to escape from the camp first, which didn't seem like an easy thing to do at the moment.

And even if she hadn't been feeling that way, after looking at the fat sack of shit before her, there was no way in hell she was going to let him touch her, let alone fuck her. But she could have jerked him off in a pinch if it would save her life, but she wasn't in the mood. Perhaps she should have reconsidered her next move anyway, and no doubt she might have if she had taken longer to act, but as the man undressed and the rank smell hit her, she let her emotions get the better of her. Cindy often had a bad habit of acting first and then thinking about it second.

The obese man wore a lascivious grin, and was about to climb onto the bed and then onto Cindy, when she slid off the mattress and kicked the man in the groin. Her foot crushed his testicles and the man bent over double, a loud rush of air escaping his lips. He toppled like a felled tree, landing heavily on the wooden floor, taking down a small table placed near the wall. A glass vase with fresh cut flowers were on the table and the vase toppled to the floor, crashing loudly as glass and water spilled across the wooden planks. Seeing the vase break, Cindy bent over and grabbed a decent-sized piece with a jagged edge, hiding it in the folds of her dress, then ran back to the bed and sat down.

The door burst in a moment later, the guard running in with his gun aimed at her, his finger hovering over the trigger. Cindy raised her hands, her eyes staring down the barrel of the weapon, thinking she had made a very big mistake. The guard was about to shoot, she could see it in his eyes, when Madam came in behind him.

"Wait, don't shoot her," she commanded.

"But you said..."

"I know what I said, damn it, and I changed my mind. She's too pretty to simply kill. Maybe I can talk some sense into her. Get *that* out of here." She pointed to the fat man moaning on the floor.

The guard did as he was told. Cindy watched, hoping for a chance to make a break for it but the guard kept one eye on her at all times.

When the guard and the fat man were gone, the door closed. Madam walked across the room to her, and before Cindy could do anything, Madam slapped her hard across the face. Cindy fell onto her side and then sat up, her hand going to her face, her eyes wide in shock. Her cheek was warm where she'd been struck and it was turning red. If it had been a punch, Cindy might have attacked the woman and be damned the consequences, but a slap was different. It wasn't about pain but about humiliation, about showing who was dominant, about who was master and who was slave.

"That was for disobeying me. Actions have consequences, my dear. Just be glad I decided to give you a reprieve." She paused, letting her words sink in. "I may not be so merciful next time."

She turned her back on Cindy, as if the idea that Cindy would ever consider attacking her was the most ludicrous thing in the world, and sat down on a wooden chair across the room and crossed her legs. For her entire career as a Madam, it had never taken her long to break the spirit of one of her whores. She believed this would be the same with Cindy eventually. First she would establish dominance, who was in charge, then she would offer kindness, followed by more harshness. By the time she was finished, the new whore would be hers to control, in mind as well as body. "Clean up that mess and do it quickly."

Cindy did as she was ordered and righted the table and picked up the vase shards, tossing them into a small trash barrel a foot tall. Madam made her put the barrel near the door so it could be taken out and emptied when she left the room after dealing with Cindy. The entire time Cindy picked up the shards, Madam watched her to make sure she wasn't keeping any of them. Cindy was glad she had taken a piece before the older woman had entered. Cindy noticed that she hadn't heard the sound of the lock being redone when the guard had left, and if this was so, then it might be the chance she'd been waiting for.

"Now, young lady, just what am I supposed to do with you, hmm?" Madam asked when Cindy had finished cleaning.

"I don't know, you tell me," Cindy said, walking to the window. It was getting dark and she could see people walking across the camp. They seemed to be heading for the north end. "Where's everyone going?"

"Oh, there is a big show at the arena tonight. Murdock says he has some new recruits he wants to try out. I have to say I'm not much for it all, too violent for me. But the rest of the camp seems to enjoy it."

Cindy thought of Henry and Jimmy and wondered if they were the 'new recruits' Madam was speaking of. Cindy turned and walked away from the window, ending up at the dresser. There was a plastic hairbrush on the top of the dresser and she picked it up. It was dull on both edges, worthless as a weapon, but Cindy had another idea. But first she needed to become an actress.

"Madam, I'm truly sorry about what I did to that man. It's just, well, all my life men have been trying to have sex with me and I was always scared they only wanted me for me body. Because of this..." She hesitated, taking a deep breath, as if she was getting out a terrible secret. "I'm still a virgin."

"Is that so, dear?"

Cindy nodded, pouring it on now. "Yes, it's true. I came close a few times, you know, first and second base, but I never went all the way. Then you sent that man in here and he smelled terrible. I panicked." She walked over to Madam and showed her the hairbrush. "You have such pretty hair; may I comb it for you?"

Madam nodded. "You may." She smiled, thinking Cindy was putty in her hands.

"Maybe the next man you send in could be cleaner," Cindy suggested. "You know, so that my first time isn't with someone who smells like a cesspool. I'd be ever so grateful." She was brushing Madam's hair slowly, getting out the knots, careful not to pull too much and anger the woman. Madam was slowly relaxing, enjoying the feeling of being groomed by her newly subservient whore. "I promise I'll be good from now on. I don't want to die."

Madam was far too overconfident, as she wasn't used to a woman like Cindy and could never imagine there being someone like her, that Cindy could be so tough, that she would rather die than submit to slavery.

"There may be a place for you here after all," Madam said, her eyes only slits as she enjoyed Cindy's caresses.

Madam couldn't see Cindy's hand, nor could she see when Cindy slowly pulled out the large shard of glass she had hidden within her dress.

"That sounds wonderful," Cindy said, her voice becoming hard. Madam opened her eyes, detecting a subtle change in the tone of Cindy's voice, but it was too little too late.

Cindy dropped the comb. Before it hit the floor, she yanked back Madam's head by the hair, exposing the woman's throat. At the same time, she brought her arm holding the glass shard around to the right side of Madam's neck, just below the surprised woman's ear, then slid the shard of glass across the older woman's throat, slicing Madam's neck open from ear to ear.

Madam's eyes went wide as she felt her neck separate and saw her blood begin to shoot out five feet across the room to splatter onto the bed and floor. She tried to call out but all she managed were bloody gargles. Cindy let go, knowing the woman was as good as dead. Madam slid off the chair and went to her knees, her left hand going to her throat to try and staunch the blood. It did nothing, the blood squirting between her fingers and from under her palm. She lay on the floor on her back, staring up at the ceiling, seeing Cindy out of the corner of her eye. She voided her bowels and bladder as she let out one last gurgling sigh, then went still. Blood still spurt slowly from the jagged neck wound, a garish, smiling mouth below her original one.

Cindy waited until the woman was dead, then dragged the body to the bed and pushed the corpse underneath it. A carpet taken from the far end of the room was used to cover the blood pooled on the floor. It wasn't perfect but it would hold up under a cursory examination. She only needed enough time to find Raven and escape, after that it wouldn't matter. With the body hidden, she went to the door and checked to see if she was correct and it was unlocked. It was.

Opening it, she stepped out into the hallway, unsure which way to go. Creeping slowly down the hallway, she looked at the multitude of doors, wondering which one Raven might be behind. The sounds of grunting and groaning came to her, the grunts and groans of people having sex. When she reached the end of the hallway, a guard rounded the corner and for a second both man and woman stared at each other. Then Cindy smiled and lowered her dress, exposing her firm breasts to the man. The guard gaped in awe at the two perfect globes of flesh exposed to him, his mouth falling open slightly. He had seen breasts before, but Cindy could have been a supermodel in another life, so to see such perfection was quite a distraction from the normal, sagging tits he was used to.

He was so distracted he didn't snap out of it until Cindy was a foot from him, her hand coming out and around to bring the glass shard across his throat, slicing his neck open and severing his jugular and voice box in one smooth motion. His hands went up to his neck as blood spurted out, replicating the death scene with Madam. Cindy didn't have time to wait for the man to die. She opened the closest door and shoved the man inside, his limp body doing what she wanted. The room had been silent, no sounds of grunting or other sounds of sex.

As the man tumbled into the room and Cindy kicked his legs inside to close the door, she looked up to see Raven sitting on the bed, wearing similar attire to Cindy's.

"Well, it's about time," Raven said haughtily. "I was about to set out on my own."

"No need," Cindy said and quickly explained to Raven the last few minutes.

When she finished, Raven nodded and grinned wryly. "If you hadn't killed that bitch I would have," she said as she got up to help Cindy remove the dead guard's clothes. He was armed with a handgun and a knife. Cindy took the gun and Raven the knife, then they split up his clothes. Cindy took his blood-saturated shirt to wear, not liking the sticky feeling, but not waiting to be running around in a skimpy dress. Raven took his pants which were too big but were better than just the dress she wore. She cinched the worn leather belt as tight as it would go around her waist.

"We need to hide the body," Cindy said.

"The bathroom, in the tub," Raven said and they picked up the body and carried it to the small bathroom, dumping it unceremoniously in the tub, then drawing the plastic curtain that had a mural of fish on it, different-sized bubbles filling in the picture between the assortment of marine life.

Raven grabbed a white towel and quickly wiped up what blood drops she could and Cindy did the rug trick again to hide the worst of the blood. What blood was in the hallway couldn't be helped, as it had splattered the walls and floor, which really made the whole thing of hiding the body irrelevant. But Cindy hadn't had time to think, only act, and now they had wasted precious seconds hiding the body for nothing. Once the body in the bedroom Cindy had vacated was found, then all bets were off and the hunt would be on for her, and no doubt Raven as well.

"Come on, Raven, we need to find the others and get the hell out of this place. I hear there's some kind of show going on tonight at what's called 'the arena' around here," Cindy said. "If the others are gonna be anywhere, it's a good bet they'll be there, too." Her face took on a look of disgust. "Frankly, spending even one night in this wacko camp is one too many if you ask me," she added, heading to the door. "This way."

"Right behind you," Raven said, flexing her fingers in preparation of doing more killing which would no doubt be necessary.

Chapter 18

Mary closed her eyes and braced herself as Murdock slid himself inside her, his right cheek pressed against her right cheek, the stubble on his face causing her skin to become irritated as his head moved up and done in rhythm to his body. He smelled like sweat and cigars and it made her want to vomit. Each time he slid into her, the top of her head would hit the headboard on the bed, but Murdock didn't care and Mary knew better than to complain.

This was the second time in fifteen minutes that he'd fucked her, and though it was distasteful, she had to admit it was better than the first time.

When he'd arrived in the room she'd been put in, he'd told her to undress and get on the bed. The pet zombie had been there, too, and was there even now, standing at the foot of the bed, as if it was watching them have intercourse. Mary half-expected the zombie to pull out its decayed, limp penis and begin masturbating. She knew if she tried anything, and even if she survived in killing Murdock, the zombie would be on her before she could escape. A year ago, she'd been captured by cannibals and taken to an abandoned hospital. There she had been tied to a bed to be raped. She had stopped that rape and had killed her attacker by ripping his throat out with her teeth. She still remembered how it felt to feel the hot blood cascade over her face and neck, covering her in its sticky heat, how it tasted on her tongue, salty and coppery.

"Do you like it, baby? Huh? Tell me how good I am," Murdock whispered into her ear.

"I'm not going to do that," she said, her voice tight.

Though Murdock was a large man and in other times she might have easily been aroused by the size of his member, this wasn't one of those times. Murdock may have been a brutal man on how he ran the camp, but at least he wasn't into pain—giving or receiving—with his sex. That was a saving grace for Mary. Murdock had made her lie down and then he had gone down on her, working feverously with his tongue in her thick mound of brown hair. Though she was being taken against her will, she had to admit in being slightly embarrassed at her grooming skills of late down there. Before the dead walked, there had been a time when she was always neatly trimmed, but lately there had been too many things to worry about—such as staying alive—to worry about grooming her pubic hair.

Not that Murdock had minded. The man had used his tongue like a pro and Mary had even found her breathing getting faster. It wasn't that she was turned on, it was simply her body reacting to stimulation. Of course, Murdock had taken it as a sign that she was enjoying herself.

Then he had climbed on top of her, and after putting on a condom, which she was incredibly thankful of, he'd begun fucking her. If she had to be raped, then this was the way she would have wanted it.

Murdock began to thrust faster, his breathing coming in heavy spurts. Then he thrust one final time and rolled off her, now breathing heavily.

"That was nice, baby. Don't worry, you'll come to love it soon, I promise," he huffed.

"Don't hold your breath," she replied.

He merely chuckled and padded off to the bathroom to shower. The water was stored in a small water tower on the roof. "Now don't go anywhere," he told her. "Jasper wouldn't like that."

"Jasper?" she said more to herself than anyone else.

The zombie stared at her, its eyes emotionless. If 'Jasper' had heard its name, the large zombie gave no sign.

A few minutes later, Murdock exited the bathroom and he gestured for her to go inside and wash up. "There's still warm water, but not much. Sorry, the tank on the roof isn't that big."

She blinked at him, amazed at his callousness. He'd just raped her after all, even if it hadn't been violent. But if she'd tried to refuse then, yes, it would have become violent. Only her instincts had told her to go with it, to suffer it out and hope for a chance to escape. Still, she needed a shower badly and did as he directed.

Ten minutes later, feeling a hundred percent better, despite having had forced sex, she exited the bathroom to find clothes waiting for her. Nothing special, jeans, a cotton shirt, a light jacket and a pair of sneakers.

"These should fit, I think," he said. "All your stuff was still wet so I'm having it laundered. Your boots will be dried-out near a fire, and when they're dry I'll get them back to you."

He was so polite, she wondered if this was the same man that had ordered a prisoner tossed into a pit and eaten by rats, or the same man that had taken her and the rest of her group captive.

"Thank you," she said flatly, feeling guilty for saying it. He was her captor after all. Just because he was polite didn't mean he wasn't a bastard, like so many others she'd come across. Mary remembered a time when she and Cindy had been captured by a crime boss in New London, Connecticut. He'd planned on having his way with them both but she and Cindy had escaped, then joined up with Henry and Jimmy, and together they had escaped the naval base the crime boss had called his own. She never knew what had happened to the man and didn't really care. She hoped he was dead.

There was a knock at the door.

"Yeah, what is it?" Murdock called.

A man in a worn business suit opened it. "Sir, the arena is filling up. It's almost time."

"Ah yeah, I was having so much fun here I almost forgot. Thanks, Willy." The door closed and Murdock turned to watch Mary, who was getting dressed. He smiled as he watched her shimmy into her jeans, admiring her shapely ass. He felt a stirring down below but ignored it. He could fuck her later, after the show. Now it was show time, time to give the people of his camp some entertainment. It was why they followed him. It reminded him of the ancient Romans—which was where he'd gotten the idea from— how if you gave the lower class Bread and Circuses, they would be content and wouldn't bother trying to usurp you.

"That was Willy, he's the man I have who keeps track of the numbers of running the camp. He figures out how many slaves and fighters I have at any given time. I tell you, running this place without him would be so much harder. He was an accountant in the old world, how about that?"

"Interesting," she said, acting disinterested. Still, any information was worth hearing—but she didn't want Murdock to know that

"Come on, Mary, I have a surprise for you tonight."

"Oh, and what's that?" she asked as she slid on her shirt. She felt so much better with clothes on. She sat on the bed and put on the sneakers.

"A little entertainment. Should get the blood boiling."

"Not interested." This time she really wasn't.

"Oh really? And what if I told you that your two male friends will be there?"

That got her attention. "Go on."

"Oh no, my dear, it will be a surprise. But I promise you that you'll enjoy it. If you're ready we can leave."

She stood up and walked over to him. He held out an arm for her to slide her hand through, and though it made her cringe to even touch him, she did it.

They went to the door and exited the bedroom, walking through the house. Before they were outside, Mary saw a room with a door open.

Inside the room was a table, and on it were the companions' weapons and backpacks. She spotted Cindy's M-16, Jimmy's shotgun and Henry's Glock. All looked shiny and oiled. On the wall were other firearms, an assortment of handguns and assault rifles. If she was correct, she'd just found Murdock's armory. It made sense that the man would keep it in his own home, that way he could keep an eye on the guns twenty-four hours a day.

A man stepped out from behind the armory door holding Sue's .22. He was cleaning the muzzle with a brush. Upon seeing her watching him, he closed the door with a loud slam.

She made a mental note where the room was, knowing it was valuable information. If she could get there unattended, maybe she could get hold of one or more of the guns, kill Murdock, and try to free her friends.

It was a slim chance but she knew she had to maintain hope. Henry would get them out of this mess; he had in the past and she had confidence he would this time. She just needed to survive that long and use the chance to escape if one came up.

Murdock escorted her to the main door of the house and out into the night, Jasper following right behind Murdock and Mary like a loyal hound dog.

"Trust me, Mary," Murdock said with a smile. "Once you see what I have in store for you and the people of this camp tonight, you'll never forget it."

She said nothing in reply, though the chill that ran down her back said it all.

Sue was put to work immediately upon being brought to the head matron of the kitchen and laundry departments. There had been no room for her in the kitchen so Sue had been put to work washing laundry in the pond. There were five other women with her, all well in their sixties and early seventies. Sue felt out of place with them, as she was only in her forties.

They were a gaggle of hens, talking about this person and that person, who was sleeping with who and who was hoarding food and what guard was unhappy with his shift and who wanted to leave, but knew if they tried and got caught it would be the end of them. They seemed to know everything about the camp. Not all of them talked however.

Mostly it was only a few who did the lion's share of gabbing, the others just nodding when it was appropriate. Sue had been introduced to them earlier and she had told them her name but she had already forgotten all of their names except one—an old woman called Rose.

"How come there are no guards watching us?" Sue asked.

"Oh, they don't bother with us. They think we're too old to do anything bad, I guess," Rose said. "We don't usually get help as young as you, Sue, but the boss must've decided you were a tad too old for the brothel."

"You know, Sue, you're lucky you ended up with us," another old crone said.

"Oh?" Sue replied.

"Hell yes. If you weren't here you'd be at the whore house getting screwed every night by the men that go there." She shook her head. "Some of them boys like it rough—a lot rough."

"Two of the people I came with were sent there," Sue explained. "Their names are Cindy and Raven."

All the crones shook their heads in sorrow.

"Poor girls are in for a hell of a time. Might have been better off they'd been killed before they got here, the camp I mean," Rose said.

"Oh, Rose, you're always making it seem like such a bad thing over there," one of the old women said. "It's only sex, and maybe a few slaps or a punch sometimes when one of the men gets too rough. It's better than being out there in the desert, dying of dehydration and running from those damn dead people."

"That's a matter of opinion," Rose said in a huff.

"I hear another one of the women she came in with was sent to the boss' house," one of the crones said, a bitter old thing with only one remaining tooth and hair so thin it was like wisps of a spider-web.

"Yes, her name is Mary," Sue said. "Do you know anything about what will happen to her?"

One-Tooth began to laugh, the sound reminding Sue of the wicked witch in The Wizard of Oz.

"That's easy," Rose said. "She's gonna be the boss' slut. He takes one from time to time when he wants to."

"It's good to be the king," One-Tooth laughed, the others join-ing in.

Sue sent out a prayer to Mary, Raven and Cindy, hoping they would be okay and wishing she was with them, despite knowing what their fate was.

"Where is everyone going?" Sue asked, changing the subject upon seeing people walking through the camp in pairs of twos and threes, and sometimes in larger groups. All were laughing and seemed excited about something. From where she was doing the laundry, she had a good vantage point of most of the camp.

"Oh, they're all goin' to the arena," One-tooth said.

"Aye," Rose agreed. "There's gonna be a good show there to-night. Once we finish up here we'll bring you there, Sue. You'll like it."

"Yeah, I hear some of the men you came in with are gonna be the stars of the show," One-Tooth cackled.

"Do you mean Henry and Jimmy?" Sue asked while ringing out someone's long johns. They were so stained in the crotch that in the old world it would have been easier to simply toss them out and buy a new pair. But no one was making long-johns anymore so no matter how dirty or stained, they would be washed and dried.

"Sure, if that's their names," Rose said, the one-tooth geriatric nodding in agreement beside her.

"Harry and Timmy, sure is. They's gonna be fightin' tonight," One-tooth said.

Sue was going to correct the old woman on the names and then decided why bother. It didn't matter anyway.

"Gonna be a hell of a show," One-tooth said with an all-gums grin. "Sure to be blood."

"Then we need to finish up this load or we'll never see the show!" Rose said, the rest of the gaggle of hens all nodding.

"That's right! Everyone shut the hell up and start workin' instead of talkin'," One-tooth said, despite the fact that *she* was the worst of the bunch.

Sue began to concentrate on working faster as well. If there was a chance to see Henry and Jimmy, and possibly Mary at the arena, then she wanted to be there.

Because she was concentrating on her work and not watching the camp around her, she didn't see the two shadows skulking past her, each with large hats on to hide their features and bulky clothes. It was impossible to tell if the shapes belonged to male or female forms and they were gone before anyone might have noticed them, just two more patrons going to the arena.

Sue did finally look up once to check her surroundings, but the two shadows were long gone, lost amongst other shadows. She focused on her work again, knowing soon she would be at the arena.

She wondered how Henry and Jimmy were doing and hoped that at least for now, they were safe.

Chapter 19

At the moment, Henry and Jimmy were most definitely *not* safe. As the two men stood with their backs against the locked door of the shack, the shuffling shapes moved ever forward.

"This doesn't look good for us, Henry," Jimmy said as he raised his fists, prepared to go down fighting. The stench in the shack was unbearable and it was all he could do to keep from gagging.

"I hear ya, buddy," Henry said, readying himself for the battle—if the battle meant being torn apart limb from limb—to come. But the figures suddenly stopped moving, and stayed a few feet away, their bodies still hidden in the darkness.

"What are they doing?" Jimmy asked.

"You're asking me?" Henry replied.

"Well, fuck this, I'm not waiting to be eaten, I'm taking the fight to them," Jimmy said softly, so only Henry could hear. Then he let out a scream and charged the first figure, drawing back his right arm and curling his hand into a fist. The blow struck the shadowy face right on the chin.

"Owww, hey, why'd you do that?" the shadowy face yelled, slinking away from Jimmy and into the further darkness. "Fucking asshole punched me," the figure muttered.

Jimmy stopped cold, amazed at what had just occurred. "What the fuck?" was all he could manage to say. "It talked."

"Of course he talked," another figure said. "What are you, some kind of retard?"

"Ah, Jimmy, wait a second." Henry walked up to his friend. "I think we made a big mistake here. These aren't deaders," he said, referring to the figures. Someone lit a match and the small circle of brilliance banished the shadows to the deepest corners of the shack. Jimmy and Henry got their first good look at the figures they had thought were the living dead. There were seven of them. Their clothes were covered in filth, some not much more than rags. Their arms and faces were filthy, too, their fingers dirt-encrusted. Eyes were sunken in from lack of food and water, and a few had wounds that had begun to fester, giving off a sickly odor that suffused the air, overriding the redolent body odor already there. They already looked like the living dead, only they were still alive.

"Jesus," Jimmy muttered. "Not by much though. What a sorry looking lot of bastards."

"Fuck you, too," the man Jimmy had hit said, annoyed. "You don't look so hot yourself there, ya know. We'll see how *you* look after a few days in the arena."

"The arena?" Henry asked.

"Yeah, the arena. What? You don't know about it?"

"We're new in town," Henry said sarcastically, only Jimmy getting the joke.

"Well, you'll be findin' out soon enough, laddy," an older man said, his voice thick with an Irish accent. "From what I heard the guards talkin' 'bout through the walls of this here buildin', you and your friend there are the star of the show tonight."

"What show? What the fuck are you taking about?" Jimmy demanded, losing patience with the entire group of men.

All the men began to laugh, an inside joke if there ever was one.

"Shit, you really don't know, do you, kid," one of the men said. He began coughing heavily, a mist of blood flowing from his mouth. He had pneumonia, and wouldn't last to see the end of the week. Not that he knew this. He thought he had a bad cold and would get over it. But with no medial care and barely enough food and water to survive, his body was fading fast.

"Know what?" Jimmy asked. "Shit, will you fuckers stop being so damn cryptic and just spell it out already."

"Oh, laddy, we could do that. But you see how we live here." His Irish brogue even was heavier than before. He was a big man and still looked powerful, unlike some of the others. "They barely give us enough food and water to live on, and when we're not in the arena, we're sitting in our own filth waiting for the next time they let us out of here. So we have to take our amusement where we can. And, pally, you two are it right now."

"Let it be, Jimmy," Henry said softly so Jimmy could barely hear him. "These guys have lost it, we're not gonna get anything more out of them."

"Yeah, I hate to say it, but I have to agree with you there, Henry," Jimmy said.

Henry pointed to a corner of the shack where the floor was relatively clean. They went there and sat down, backs pressed to the wall, legs pushed up before them, and arms resting on their knees, hands hanging limply before them. The match burned out and the shack was returned to relative darkness, the seven men moving back into the shadows to sit or lie down. A few could be heard talking but most went to sleep, too exhausted to do anything else.

"This sucks. What the fuck are we gonna do, old man?" Jimmy asked, squeezing his hands into fists. He hated not knowing what was coming next, and hated being kept as a prisoner even more.

"We wait," Henry said, then he leaned his head against the wall and closed his eyes, knowing anytime there was a chance to rest needed to be taken advantage of.

There was no way of comprehending exactly how long Henry and Jimmy waited, as in the dark there was no way to tell time, but if Henry had to guess, he would have picked two hours, give or take a few minutes.

The door to the shack was pulled open and moonlight streamed inside, causing Jimmy and Henry to close their eyes, the wan moonlight too bright for their eyes after so long in the darkness.

A shadow blocked the doorway for a second. "Come on, assholes, it's time," a guard said at the door, then he stepped back and out of the way.

Henry and Jimmy got to their feet, stretching cramped muscles, then exited the structure. Behind them, the filthy group of men followed, all shuffling their feet as if they were zombies.

"We going to the arena?" Henry asked one of the guards.

The man nodded, a smile on his face. "Shit yeah. Gonna see what you're made of, stranger." He gestured with his assault rifle. "Get moving, and if you try anything, my orders are to shoot you in the leg. You're going to the arena alive, one way or the other."

"No, I won't go," one of the filth-encrusted men said. "Just kill me now. For the love of God, show some goddamn mercy."

The man received a blow to the lower back and he collapsed on the ground.

"Get up, asshole, or so help me I'll break your legs and drag you to the arena," a guard warned.

"Come on, Petey my lad," the man with the Irish brogue said. "There's nothing to be done about it. Best we go and make our stand like men." He spit at the guard's feet. "Not like these cowards, doin' Murdock's biddin' like a pack of wet-nursed kiddies."

The guard snarled angrily and raised his rifle to crack the defiant slave on the forehead when another guard stopped him. "Don't do it, Lenny, let the arena deal with his wise mouth."

The guard lowered his weapon, nodding. "Yeah, you're right. Fucker's just tryin' ta get me ta kill him and end it quick like."

"All right, move out, all of you," the lead guard ordered, and with Henry and Jimmy in the lead, they began walking, flanked on all sides by men with guns.

Jimmy leaned in close to Henry so as not to be overheard. "We should jump a couple of these assholes, take their guns, and make a break for it before we get to this arena they keep talking about. Whatever it is, you know it can't be good for our health."

Henry scanned the men guarding them, watching how they moved. None of them were derelict in their duty, all keeping their eyes locked on the prisoners. Even if Henry and Jimmy managed to take down two guards, they would be gunned down long before they had a chance to use their captured weapons. He told Jimmy as much.

"But we gotta do something, Henry," Jimmy pleaded, his hands curling into fists. "This shit can't go down like this. We gotta find the girls; who knows what's happening to them right now."

"Don't you think I know that, Jimmy? Damn it, if there was a chance in hell of us escaping right now, don't you think I'd be the first one to try it? But there's not, we need to wait for a better chance."

"You two, shut the fuck up. No talking," a guard snapped, his eyes going from Henry to Jimmy.

Henry stopped talking and the two warriors walked for a minute in silence, then Henry leaned in close to Jimmy and said, "I'm worried about the girls, too, but for now, I think we need to concentrate on saving our own asses. Then, if we're still alive in the morning, we can help the women."

"Well, it still sucks," Jimmy spit angrily.

"Jimmy, I couldn't agree with you more."

Chapter 20

The prisoners were led through the camp until they were brought to a holding pen, the chain-link walls of a hurricane fence more than adequate to keep them inside. There was a ceiling as well, also made of chain-link wire so there was no chance of simply climbing the fence to escape if an opportunity arrived. The churned-up dirt on the ground, still moist from the rain the previous day, was darker in many places. Once inside the pen, Henry bent down and touched one of the spots, the tips of his index and middle fingers coming back tinged red. Sniffing them, he made a disgusted face as he wiped his fingers on his pants, knowing it was blood.

Henry and Jimmy went to the north side of the pen, where they could see a large, lighted circular area surrounded by stadium seating. Unknown to Henry or Jimmy, this was where the summer camp guests once held joyful events, such as the talent show or camp Olympics. Now the area was used for far more sinister reasons. Torches were spread out every ten feet to give light to the crowd. A few of the crowd had hand-held flashlights as well, a few more carrying glass camping lanterns.

The seats were filling up fast with the denizens of the camp. All walks of life had arrived, from the lowly kitchen workers, to some of the whores from the brothel—only the ones that were content with their new role in life and wouldn't try and run—to the elite of the camp, as well as any guards that were off duty.

The events held at the arena were looked forward to by the residents of the camp, something to enjoy, like seeing a play in the time of Shakespeare. Without television or the internet, entertainment had gone back to its roots.

"Jimmy, look, there's Mary with that guy Murdock," Henry said, pointing to a section in the middle of the stadium seating. Mary was sitting quietly beside Murdock in a special raised podium, her jaw taut, her brown hair pulled back away from her face. She didn't look pleased with her present situation, but she also didn't look as if she was hurt physically.

"Shit, that is her," Jimmy said. "Well, at last we know she's safe."

Henry didn't reply, not seeing a reason to.

Murdock was sitting in a large Victorian chair with purple upholstery in the center of the podium. There were smaller chairs on either side of him. Mary was on his right side and another woman was on his left—she was older than Murdock. Perhaps she was some kind of matriarch, a mother or an aunt.

Not that it mattered to Henry.

Murdock's pet zombie was standing directly behind him, its leash wrapped around the ornate carvings on the top of Murdock's chair. The podium was ten feet off the ground, too high to be reached without help of some kind.

The crowd was loud, talking and laughing amongst itself. The energy through the audience was powerful, as if there was an electric charge in the air. A battery-operated CD player was connected to a loudspeaker with cheerful band music playing, the latter running on car batteries that were charged by the use of solar power. Henry had seen the panels on roofs as he walked through the camp. Most of the cabins seemed to have them.

Henry watched Murdock while he chatted with others surrounding him, some standing behind him and others further back. It reminded Henry of a king at his court with his chosen few around him.

"Look at that asshole up there, sitting like he owns the fucking world," Jimmy said, as if he'd read Henry's thoughts.

"Yeah, he seems like he's really full of himself," Henry said, wrapping his fingers through the chain-links and gripping the fence.

"What's the big surprise in that? It seems like every time we meet someone like Murdock, they're always full of shit with grand designs. Just one more tin-pot dictator in a sea of them. No matter how many we've killed there's always one more around the corner to replace the dead ones."

"Then we'll just have to keep killing them until there's none left," Henry said, his knuckles turning white as he griped the fence. If only he could reach out and grab Murdock by the throat and squeeze the life out of him.

Murdock stood up, waving his hands in the air for the crowd to be silent. The CD player was turned off and slowly the crowd quieted down. They knew what the stoppage of the music meant and were looking forward to it, so they were happy to oblige and cease the chatter.

A man to Murdock's left handed him a bullhorn and he flicked it on, the expected static crackling as he exhaled through the mouthpiece. "Welcome, my friends, to the arena. And let me tell you, I have quite a show in store for you tonight." Murdock raised his voice at the end, wanting to get the crowd excited.

Vendors had begun walking through the crowd, hawking food and drinks. One man was calling out that he offered peanuts, another saying he was selling jerky.

It was like a circus and Murdock was the ringmaster.

The crowd began to clap, hoot and holler as Murdock finished his speech. Cheering came next, Murdock raising his hands over his head and basking in the accolades.

"But first..." he yelled out, trying to quiet the crowd. "But first before the main event, let's get the show going with a group battle. And to make things interesting, what say our gladiators fight barehanded!"

The crowd began to clap and cheer again.

By the pen, five guards went to the door and opened it, all aiming guns at the prisoners. "You, you, and you," a guard said, pointing out three of the filth-encrusted-men. "It's time to fight."

One of the men was the one Jimmy had first punched upon being tossed into the shack, another was the man with pneumonia, and the third was the man with the Irish accent.

"Come on, laddies, let's go show them what we can do," the Irish man said. "Let's kill those undead bastards."

The man with pneumonia coughed heavily but he joined the Irish man, as did the one Jimmy had punched.

Henry took a step forward to one of the guards, all guns swinging his way. "What about me and my friend, I thought we had to fight," Henry said.

"Don't worry, stranger, you will. But you and your buddy are the main event. Murdock likes to save the best for last. Till then, watch the show and see what's in store for you both. Now step back or I'll make you step back." The guard smirked and raised his gun higher so that the muzzle was only inches from Henry's face.

For a second Henry stood defiant, his hands closing into fists. He wanted to wipe that smirk off the guard's face by taking his head from his shoulders, but the deadland's warrior knew if he so much as tried, he would either get a bullet to the face or a rifle butt to the gut.

Henry stepped back. "This isn't over, you know."

The guard smirked even more. "Yeah, I think it is." He turned to the three filthy men. "Okay, you three, let's move. Get in the arena and fight."

The men did as they were told, the muzzles of assault rifles following them at every step. The man with pneumonia tried to slow down, as if his legs didn't want to carry him into the arena. A rifle butt to the back caused him to fall to his knees, where he then received help from the other two men and was carried away to the arena.

"What do you think's gonna happen next?" Jimmy asked when Henry joined him at the fence. The pen door was closed and locked and the guards had walked away, only one remaining to watch the prisoners and make sure they didn't try anything.

"Don't know, but I can tell you it's not going to be good," Henry said.

"And here they come, our warriors, ready to do battle with the evil walking dead!" Murdock called out, his voice distorted by the bullhorn.

The crowd cheered and a spotlight snapped on, illuminating the three men in the center of the arena.

"Don't they look brave? Give them a hand!" Murdock coaxed. "Okay, folks, let's not keep our warriors waiting any longer. I'm sure they're eager to do battle. If you'll all turn your attention to the far side of the arena, here come the walking dead!"

The spotlight shifted from the three men to the far side of the arena, where another pen made of wood was located, this one set back amongst wooden walls ten feet high. A door slid up, similar to what would be found at a rodeo when releasing a bull with its rider, and out stumbled a dozen zombies.

The arena was coated with six inches of sand, the softness of it making it hard for the zombies to walk. As they shuffled their feet across the giving sand, they left long trails behind them.

"Come on, you men, do ya want ta live forever?" the Irish bloke cried out, rallying his two friends. A half-hearted cheer followed, as the three men spread out to fight the zombies.

"Jesus H. Christ, Henry, three against twelve. It's gonna be a fucking massacre," Jimmy said.

Henry couldn't argue with his friend's assessment. The zombies didn't spread out, but came at the three men in one large group, only splitting up at the last second when the men moved apart.

The crowd in the stands roared with excitement, loving every second of it, knowing blood was coming, that it was inevitable. The man that Jimmy had punched was the first to go down. He tried to fight but was quickly surrounded, the sheer amount of bodies simply too much for any man to resist. He was swallowed completely by a mass of decayed flesh, the zombies hunched over the fallen man.

Then the screams began as the man was torn limb from limb, gutted as if he was a heifer at the slaughterhouse. Blood spilt onto the sand to be absorbed into the fine grains and the man's yells for help quickly diminished.

Next to go was the man with pneumonia, but he didn't go down before doing some damage to the zombies first. Though sick, he had some combat training, and he used it now, grabbing a zombie, spinning it around and wrapping his hands around its head, then jerking the head to the side. He snapped the neck, severing the spinal column from the brain and decommissioning the ghoul.

As the body dropped to the sand, he spun around, albeit slowly thanks to his health, and grabbed another ghoul, doing the same thing. He was on the third one and had just managed to crack the spine when he was taken down by four ghouls at once. He kicked and punched but was already far past his limit of strength and was soon being torn apart. In a macabre way it was a blessing that he died quickly, as now he wouldn't have to suffer till the end of the week before dying, due to his poor health and straining lungs.

The Irish rogue was last to go down, and he gave as much as he got before finally being dragged to the sand and eaten. Two more prone zombies were by his side, their skulls caved in thanks to the Irish man's meaty fists. But the man was weak from hunger and couldn't put up much of a fight when too many came at him at once.

The crowd cheered as he went down, the last of the three men, and Murdock sounded an air horn, announcing the end to the first match.

"Wasn't that exciting, people?" Murdock's voice boomed out over the arena thanks to the bullhorn.

The crowd cheered its reply, some stomping their feet on the wooden stands, shaking it and threatening to take the entire structure down in one massive swoop.

"But that was nothing compared to the fight to come. We have two strangers that have volunteered to fight those zombies, to see if they can overcome the living dead."

"Volunteers, what the fuck is he talking about?" Jimmy snarled. "I didn't volunteer for shit."

"You tell him that when we're out there, Jimmy," Henry said. "I'm sure Murdock'll apologize and tell you it was all a mistake, then he'll let us go," he said sarcastically while shaking his head. "It doesn't matter what he says. We're here and we're gonna have to fight. But we have an advantage over those poor bastards that went down and the ones behind us." He pointed to the remaining filth-encrusted men, who were watching the arena with dull eyes, sad to see the loss of their friends, and knowing they could be next.

"Yeah, what? I'm all ears," Jimmy said.

"Well for one thing, we're not half-starved. We're still strong 'cause we're new here. That's a big advantage in that arena over these poor slobs."

"True, but that won't get us free, even if we take down the deaders we face," Jimmy pointed out.

"Yes, I know, but I've been studying the arena itself while the fight was going on and I think I have a way out of here, but we'll need to act fast."

"Go on."

"First we need to fight whatever's thrown at us. Once we do that and win, that's when we can put my plan into effect, and only then."

"So you're saying we're gonna have to go out there and fight, no matter what?" Jimmy asked, already knowing the answer and none too happy about it.

"Yeah, buddy, I'm afraid so."

Jimmy set his jaw, his eyes creasing in anger. "If that's what it takes to get us out of here, to find the girls and split, then I'm with you. What's the plan?"

Henry began laying it out, and as he did, Jimmy slowly began to smile, liking every second of it.

Chapter 21

"It's time," a guard said by the open door of the pen. "Come on you two, let's go."

Henry patted Jimmy on the shoulder for encouragement and the two men exited the pen.

"Good luck," one of the filth-encrusted prisoners called after them.

"You'll need it," said another.

The two warriors were led to the edge of the arena, where they were shoved into it. Henry glanced over his shoulder to see that the guards were still there, their weapons aimed at him and Jimmy. Around the arena, at ten foot intervals, were more armed men, all there to make sure the fighters didn't try to escape.

The seven remaining zombies were still occupied, feeding on the bodies of the three slain prisoners.

"And here they are!" Murdock yelled through the bullhorn. "Two strong warriors, ready to battle with the living dead. Give them a hand, folks, tell them how brave they are!"

The crowd began to cheer, a few booing for the hell of it. Jimmy flipped them off, then leaned in close to Henry so he could be heard. "The deaders aren't paying any attention to us, now's a good time to take the fuckers out."

"I couldn't agree more. These people want to see a fight, to see blood. What say we take that away from them?"

Henry and Jimmy ran across the arena, straight at the seven feeding zombies. The crowd cheered, thinking the battle was about to begin. Henry was first to reach the seven ghouls. He picked the closest one and ran at it, kicking it in the head as it was leaning over to feed on a corpse's small intestine. The zombie was knocked to the sand where it flopped around. Henry raised his left boot high and brought it down hard on the still-chewing mouth, dislocating the jaw and sending bloody teeth spraying across the sand. He raised his foot a second time and brought it down on the nose of the ghoul, caving in the skull and sending brains squirting into the sand.

Jimmy took down the next zombie by picking up a severed arm and using it as a club, beating the ghoul down and finally caving in its skull. Meanwhile, Henry went to another feeding ghoul, grabbed it by the ears and started turning, spinning the head like it was the cap on a beer bottle. Cartilage and muscle began to snap and break until the head came off clean, the spinal cord dangling and twitching beneath the decapitated head. Henry threw it away from him. He was close to the stands, so the head went into the crowd, bouncing onto the lap of an unlikely patron. The bloody teeth of the still active head snapped at the patron, who screamed and stood up, the head sliding off his lap to fall between the stands. It lay under the seats in the dirt, the mouth still opening and closing, the eyes moving left to right as it tried to understand why it couldn't move, that it was now just a head.

Jimmy took out two more zombies by snapping their necks, and Henry grabbed a femur and stabbed another in the eye, jamming the wide bone into the ghoul's eye socket so hard that the socket cracked from the force of the object.

Jimmy found a bleached skull buried in the sand and he began using it as a bludgeon. He did this over and over, and only relinquished his weapon when the skull crumbled into shards from taking a beating.

In no time, all the zombies were down and Henry and Jimmy stood in the middle of the carnage, breathing a little heavy from their exertions but none the worse for wear. Henry glanced at Murdock to see that the boss of the summer camp wasn't pleased.

Murdock waved one of his lackeys to him and whispered in the man's ear, then the man ran off on some errand. Murdock finished giving his command and his eyes went right back to glare at Henry and Jimmy.

Henry had a feeling whatever Murdock had told the lackey, it had to do with himself and Jimmy. He doubted it was good news.

The crowd began to boo, not pleased with the results. They wanted to see blood, and not the blood from the living dead. They wanted to see *human* blood spilled across the sand.

"Now, now, my friends," Murdock said through the bullhorn. "The show hasn't even begun yet. This was only a warm-up, to let our two warriors flex their muscles. The true event is still coming."

138

The crowd quieted down some, hope that blood would still be spilled making them excited and optimistic.

"And now, back from the dead and ready to battle for your entertainment, I give you the greatest warrior this camp has ever seen. If you will all direct your attention to the right..."

The music started up and the spotlight shifted to the far side of the arena, where the door was sliding upwards. Using cattle prods, the guards were forcing a large figure of a man out into the arena.

"Oh shit, is that who I think it is?" Jimmy said, his eyes going wide at the large ghoul coming out of the zombie holding pen.

"Yeah, I think it is," Henry said. "It seems that even in death you still keep working for Murdock around here."

"Clap you hands for none other than Redbeard the Great!" Murdock yelled, the crowd going wild for their favorite.

Redbeard looked around, his dead eyes taking in the stands, the people that were out of reach of him. The head swiveled slowly on his shoulders, and when his eyes fell on Henry and Jimmy, they locked on to the two men, who were easily attainable. Redbeard's hands were gone, severed at the wrists, to be replaced by ten inch blades, the hilts embedded into his arms.

So though he had no hands, each time Redbeard tried to reach out and grab something, the knives would slice through the air, which sang from the razor-sharpness of the blades. He wore a leather tunic half-an-inch thick over his chest and stomach, the bottom hanging down over his genitals, making him look like some Spartan gladiator fresh to the arena. He roared a challenge at Henry and Jimmy and began shuffling forward, his arms swinging left and right, the blades moving in tandem, cleaving the air with each step.

"Shit, Henry, was this figured into your plan?" Jimmy asked, taking a step backwards.

"No, but we'll make do. It's not like we have a choice."

"Yeah, but this guy was a handful when he was alive, and now he's a fucking deader," Jimmy said, pointing out the obvious.

"Split up, and stay out of reach of those blades," Henry said, moving to the left while Jimmy slid to the right.

"Yeah, I kind of came up with that on my own, old man, but thanks for the tip."

The two warriors separated as far apart as they could. Each time Redbeard would head for one of them, the other would throw objects found in the sand at him, distracting him.

This went on for a full five minutes.

"How long are we gonna keep this up?" Jimmy called to Henry as he threw a severed hand at Redbeard's back, causing the large ghoul to spin around, roar with what sure seemed like anger, and then come for Jimmy.

"As long as we have to," Henry replied, tossing a severed foot at Redbeard. The foot hit the giant zombie in the back of the head and bounced off. Reheard spun around, waving his left arm at what he thought was an attack. The blade hissed through the air yet again, a sound Henry was growing to dislike.

"Come on, fight you two, or we'll shoot one of you and then the other till you do," one of the guards called out from close to the two warriors. The guard had just lowered a two-way radio from his ear, where he had received orders from Murdock directly, or one of the boss' lackeys. "You fight or you die, those are Murdock's orders."

"Screw you, asshole!" Jimmy yelled at the guard.

For a reply, the guard shot twice at Jimmy's feet, the two bullets kicking up a spray of sand, the threat all too real. "You have one minute to engage or I shoot you, asshole," the guard said.

Henry ran around the arena and joined Jimmy. "It looks like we don't have a choice here, we gotta fight him." They were backing away from the zombie as they talked, always moving to keep their distance.

"With what, our hands?" Jimmy asked, holding his hands out palms up. "Jesus, Henry, this guy is huge."

"I guess so. Our hands is all we have. But listen, I've been studying Redbeard as he moves around. He's still powerful but he's a lot slower now. We can use that to our advantage. When you were a kid in the schoolyard, did you ever get behind someone's legs on your hands and knees and have someone else push them over so that they trip over you and fall on their ass?"

"No, I wasn't a bully, but I get what you're sayin'. Why, you want to try it?"

140

"Sure, it's as good as anything else, isn't it?" Henry asked. "If we can get him on the ground, we can try and step on his arms, then kick him in the head till his skull gives out."

"Okay, I'm faster than you so I guess I'll get behind him."

"Good, when I tell you to, run around to his right, and when you're in place, I'll shove him back. But give me a chance, I need to avoid those damn blades of his."

The crowd was cheering and some were booing, wanting the show to get going. Henry glanced at the guard that had shot at Jimmy to see the man was growing impatient. Henry knew they needed to act now or risk being shot.

"Hey, Redbeard, over here, come and get me!" Henry called out, waving his hands in the air to get Redbeard to come for him. While Henry did this, Jimmy started shuffling to the side, trying to come around and flank the zombie.

Redbeard moaned and began moving towards Henry, who picked up a severed arm with most of the meat chewed off it to use as a weapon.

Jimmy got so that he was out of Redbeard's view, and he began moving closer, making sure to stay behind the zombie where he couldn't be seen. Redbeard walked closer to Henry, who bent over and grabbed a handful of sand, and when the zombie was only a few feet away, he threw the sand in the zombie's face. "Now, Jimmy, do it now!"

As Jimmy ran in and dropped down behind Redbeard, who was flailing his arms, upset that he couldn't see, Henry dove in, used the severed arm to block a down-swinging blade, to then use his shoulder to shove Redbeard backwards.

The crowd went silent, watching in awe. No one had ever fought like this before and it fascinated them.

It would have worked perfectly if not for a bad turn of events on Jimmy's part. As Redbeard went down, the zombie's arms were still flailing the entire time, and his right arm swung around and the flat of the blade struck Jimmy on the left temple. If it hadn't been the flat of the blade, Jimmy would have been dead, but as it was he was immediately knocked unconscious from the blow. He slumped to the sand like a slaughtered pig after getting shot in the head with a bolt gun.

Seeing the plan fall apart, Henry disregarded it and ignored Redbeard, instead running to Jimmy, dropping the severed arm, grabbing Jimmy's feet, then dragging the limp man out of Redbeard's way. Just as Jimmy was pulled way from Redbeard, the zombie's flailing arm came down, the blade biting into the sand, missing Jimmy's head by an inch.

Henry dragged Jimmy to the edge of the arena and left him there to recover. He stopped and turned to face the young guard, who was standing only a few feet from Jimmy's prone form. "You touch him and I'll make it my mission to kill you, you got me?" Henry snarled at the young man, who was barely out of his teens.

The guard only nodded, intimidated by the muscular warrior who fought like a Viking and wasn't afraid of dying.

The plan to escape was on hold until Jimmy was up and about again, so Henry had to stall, and keep fighting Redbeard. He could only hope Jimmy would wake up soon, before Murdock grew tired of watching Henry dance around Redbeard.

The large zombie was on his feet, stumbling around blindly, blinking to clear his eyes. Henry had to wonder how that worked. After all, Redbeard was dead, and he doubted the zombie's eyes watered when irritated. Whether the ghoul would remain blind was unknown at this time, but either way Henry had to make the show look good.

He ran at Redbeard, then shifted to his left and plowed into the zombie, making the giant ghoul stumble. Redbeard lashed out, his arms reaching out. Henry ducked low, the blades slicing over his head, so close he felt the air distort with their passing.

He punched the zombie in the stomach, the ghoul not so much as grunting from the blow. Redbeard swung his left arm around and Henry had to leap back and roll twice before coming up in a crouch. If he hadn't maneuvered himself as quick as he had, he would have been eviscerated right there and the battle would have been over.

Redbeard was gaining his sight and Henry saw the zombie turn to look right at him. Henry looked past the ghoul to see Jimmy slowly stirring at the edge of the arena. Just a little more time and Henry could finish this.

Picking up the severed arm, he threw it at Redbeard, the stump where it had connected to someone's shoulder hitting the zombie right in the face. Redbeard growled loudly and stomped towards Henry, who had to back away and figure out a plan of attack.

Like a wrestler sparring with a foe, Henry started jogging around Redbeard, the crowd in the stands yelling at him to get in there and fight. Henry ignored the taunts, focusing on Redbeard. When Henry reached Jimmy, he called out to him, "Jimmy, get up, man, I need you up and moving around. Come on, snap out of it!" Then he ran off, not wanting Redbeard to come to close to his fallen friend.

Henry picked up a handful of sand, thinking he would do the same trick again, but when he began moving closer to Redbeard, one of the guards shot at his feet. Henry spun around to face the guard who waggled a finger at him. "Nah-ah, Murdock says once is enough."

Henry looked up at Murdock sitting on his makeshift throne to see the man smiling and shaking his head. He drew a finger across his throat, then pointed at Redbeard. The warning was clear, Fight or be killed. Henry shifted his gaze to Mary, who locked eyes with him and nodded, her eyes screaming that she supported him and was wishing him the best.

"Henry, I'm okay," a voice said from behind him.

Henry looked over his shoulder to see Jimmy on his feet. He was a little wobbly but he took a few steps forward. "I just need a minute to get my bearings. Everything's kinda fuzzy."

Henry saw the dark bruise on Jimmy's forehead and winced, knowing it must be painful. "The sooner the better, pal, we're running out of time." He had to dance away from Redbeard who had gotten too close, thanks to Henry shifting his attention to Jimmy.

Henry studied Redbeard again, his mind racing with how to take the large zombie down. He had no weapons other than human remains and that wouldn't be enough to kill such a big ghoul. He needed something stronger, something that could cut flesh.

But the only thing in the arena that could do that were Redbeard's blades, the ones sticking out of the zombie's wrists.

Henry glanced over at Jimmy to see how his friend was doing. This time, Jimmy was standing tall and he gave Henry a thumbs up.

"Let's do this, I'm ready," Jimmy said and he slowly began to move towards the podium where Murdock and his entourage were located.

To anyone watching, it simply looked as if Jimmy was trying to flank Redbeard, but that wasn't what he was doing at all. It was time to set Henry's plan into motion and hopefully if it worked, they could escape from the arena and then the camp.

"Okay then, it's time to end this. Remember where I said to meet up if we get separated," Henry said and ran over to the pile of bodies still in the middle of the arena. He quickly tore off some useable pieces of cloth from the corpses of the three prisoners killed earlier, ignoring the blood soaking the material. When he had enough, he wrapped them around his hands, making sure his palms had a good half inch of material covering them.

With a nod to Jimmy, to make sure the younger man was getting into position, Henry ran at Redbeard, sprinting by the time he reached the zombie.

Redbeard moaned loudly and tried to grab Henry, the blades sweeping out in a criss-cross pattern. Henry dropped to the ground and slid under the blades as if he was sliding into home base, and when his boots hit Redbeard's feet, he pushed up on his arms off the ground and came up literally inches from the zombie. Henry spun around so that his back was to Redbeard and he reached out and grabbed the blade jutting out of Redbeard's right wrist. The material on his palms protected Henry from being cut, and with all his might, he grasped the blade and yanked it free, using his body weight to push off Redbeard's torso.

The blade came out with a sickening squelch, taking muscle and tendons with it. Henry tossed the blade in the air so that it flipped over once, and caught it by the thin metal hilt. Then he turned and moved to his left so that he was standing side by side with Redbeard. In one fluid motion, with the blade down by his knees, Henry brought the blade straight up so that it entered right under the zombie's chin about two inches in, then continued upwards, slicing off his lips and nose and then the eyes. The zom-

144

bie's face had been carved clean off, leaving behind a red welt of muscle and cartilage.

The carved-off face fell to the sand, landing face up, looking like a rubber mask.

The zombie went wild, now fully-blind without eyes, its mouth opening and closing as it roared with anger or fear or whatever the undead sensed before they were about to die for the final time.

Henry took a step backwards, and blocked the remaining blade Redbeard had as the zombie swung at him blindly, then Henry raised the blade he was holding high and jammed it into the center of Redbeard's missing face. The tip of the weapon slid in easily through the nasal cavity and then into the brain.

As the brain was penetrated and then the spinal cord, the large zombie dropped to the sand like a bag of potatoes, all function gone before the body was fully prone. Henry wasn't there to see it, however, as he was already in action.

The second he knew Redbeard was done for, he yanked the blade free of the brain and started running directly at Murdock, knowing he only had seconds before the shock of the kill had sunk into everyone watching, especially the guards.

The crowd was going wild as Redbeard went down, and many jumped to their feet, clapping and yelling. For just a few precious seconds, there was complete chaos in the arena, no one fully understanding what had happened. In the history of the arena, no gladiator had overcome the zombies, all had been taken down and fed on.

Murdock was sitting in utter shock at the sight of Redbeard being put down, his mind not believing that a mere man, and an unarmed one at that, could overcome his living dead monster that he had taken so much time and thought in creating.

Jimmy was waiting for Henry directly under where Murdock was sitting, and as the deadlands warrior ran at him, Jimmy clasped his hands together like a step and got ready.

Running at top speed, Henry leaped up and his right foot went into Jimmy's clasped hands. Jimmy then pushed up with all his strength, giving Henry the extra lift he needed to reach the lower lip of the podium.

His body slapped the wood and Henry's arms grabbed hold of the edge, which was more difficult due to the fact that he still held the blade taken from Redbeard's right arm.

But his desperation and the adrenalin flooding his system gave him strength and he used it now, pulling himself up and rolling his body over the edge and onto the podium, landing directly at Murdock's feet.

For a second no one moved in the podium, all eyes on Henry.

Then the moment was broken by Murdock. "Don't just stand there, you fools!" he yelled to the guards standing behind him. "Shoot the bastard!"

Assault rifles swiveled in Henry's direction as the men prepared to fire.

Chapter 22

Just before the guards could begin firing at Henry, Mary jumped from her chair and punched the guard standing beside her. As the man rocked back from the blow, she grabbed his assault rifle. Before anyone knew what was happening, she turned it on the other guards, shooting them in a strafing pattern. In the small confines of the podium, the bullets were deadly.

One guard wasn't so easily hit and he prepared to return fire at Mary, who from her position couldn't see him. Henry stood up and used the blade he carried as a dagger, throwing it underhanded at the man. He'd learned this more than a year ago, taught by a weapon's master in one of the town's he and the other companions were passing through. He'd then practiced countless time, one time in the basement of an abandoned house he and the others were staying in. That night had been trouble when a pack of wild dogs had attacked them.

He'd used the same knife trick once before to stop the leader of the shopping mall from killing a woman he'd fallen for. It was years ago, when he was trapped on the roof of the shopping mall. He hadn't stopped the man from killing her, but his knife trick had allowed him to have his revenge.

The heavy blade wasn't made for throwing, its weight more than off, but it still managed to stab the guard in the stomach. He let out a warbled cry as the blade impaled him and that was enough to cause him to hesitate before shooting Mary.

Henry was moving right behind the blade, and when it hit the guard, Henry was there, yanking the assault rifle from limp fingers and using the butt of the rifle to send the guard to the floor with a crushed nose, blood spewing from the man's face.

Then, leveling the assault rifle, Henry began shooting anyone still alive on the podium, including Murdock's pet zombie Jasper, who Murdock had just ordered to attack Henry.

Murdock ripped Jasper's mask off, letting the zombie breathe, so to speak, then Murdock jumped out of his seat and ran out of the podium, through the curtains at its rear and away from the scene of carnage.

Henry tried to shoot Murdock but the older woman who had been sitting by Murdock's side got in the way, absorbing every round while the boss escaped.

The bullets slammed into her body, making slapping sounds with each impact. Her body shuddered from the barrage before crumpling in a bloody heap on the floor of the podium.

Jasper began walking forward, his arms reaching out for Henry, who was already turning to face the massive zombie. Jasper made Redbeard look like a midget, and though undead, the muscular arms could still break Henry in two.

Henry swung the assault rifle around, stitching the zombie from crotch to neck with high-powered rounds. After reaching the neck, Henry then went back down to the midriff, where he continued to fire until the clip ran dry.

The bullets cut into the dead flesh like the proverbial hot knife through butter, taking out chunks of meat with each round.

Finally, there was nothing left to support the upper portion of the giant zombie and the top part collapsed, falling off the lower part, the body separating into two distinct pieces at the waist.

No sooner did the upper part hit the floor, then Henry was popping in a new clip taken from the dead guard. He aimed at the floor and Jasper's head and began firing again, the head exploding in a dark mist of blood and bone matter.

All around the podium it was chaos as the crowd tried to run, terrified from the gunfire and death erupting around them.

On the ground of the arena, Cindy, Jimmy, and Raven were holding off the guards, having killed more than half, thanks to being better shots. Cindy hit a guard in the eye, the man's head snapping back, the back of his skull blowing out before the dead man crumpled to the ground. Jimmy shot a man as he popped up from hiding, taking off his ear in a lucky shot. As the man cried out in pain, Cindy sent a bullet through his open mouth, killing him instantly.

Raven fired indiscriminately, keeping heads down and just being a nuisance to the camp's security force. Though Raven didn't like guns, she had learned to use them at an early age on the farm she'd lived on, and though she wasn't a perfect shot, she could handle herself if need be.

Up in the podium, Henry shot the last guard and went to Mary. "Are you all right? Are you hurt?"

"No, I'm fine," she said.

"That was amazing what you did to Redbeard down there. I've never seen you fight like that bef..."

"There's no time for that now, Mary," he said quickly. "Jimmy's down below, get to him and find the others. Jimmy knows where we to meet up." Henry didn't know that the others were already with Jimmy, all but Sue, but she'd seen Cindy and Raven join Jimmy in the arena and was looking for her chance to join them.

"Why, where are you going?" Mary demanded. "We're almost back together again. We can get out of here now."

"And we will, but not before I kill that son-of-a-bitch Murdock." Before she could stop him, he was dashing through the rear curtain of the podium, down a set of stairs, and onto the ground, racing through the camp on his hunt for Murdock.

Mary watched the curtain flutter briefly, then shook her head, knowing there was no talking him out of it, even if she'd had the chance. Men and their revenge, she thought. Sometimes it was so foolish.

Repositioning her rifle in her hands, she went to the edge of the podium, and looking down into the arena, admiring her vantage point, she began firing at the guards still shooting at the companions. From her position, the guards had little cover and it wasn't long before the holdouts were either killed or they retreated.

When the firing stopped, Mary dropped a rope made up of the curtain down to Jimmy and the others and they quickly climbed up into the podium to join her. Which was a good thing, too. In one of the guard's haste to run when the bullets began flying, the zombie pen had been left unlocked and even now the walking dead were shuffling into the arena to feed on the warm meat lying just about everywhere,

Sue, seeing the companions climbing into the podium, ran out of the stands and around the edge of the arena, finally joining them in the podium after climbing the stairs and entering through the curtain.

"Sue, oh my God, it's you!" Cindy cried out, hugging her briefly. "We were just saying we had to find you, too."

"Find me? You guys made it awfully easy to find you." She looked around, checking to see if Henry was there, but not seeing him. "Where did Henry go? I saw him up here before I ran around the back of the arena."

"He's gone after Murdock," Jimmy said, who'd found out from Mary only moments ago.

"Then we have to go after him, he might need our help," Sue said, concerned for her man.

"No, we're not doing that," Jimmy said. "He told me to find as many of you as I could. He gave me a place to rendezvous with him if we got separated."

"But..."

"No buts, Sue, those were his orders and I'm following them," Jimmy said, his voice brooking no rebuttal. Sue went quiet.

"Then we better get moving. There'll be reinforcements coming soon to see what's going on," Mary said. "These weren't Murdock's only men." She referred to the dead guards in the podium and arena. "Oh, and I have some more good news. I know where our own weapons are being kept. We need to stop by there first on the way to meet Henry."

"Then let's do it," Jimmy said, taking charge now that Henry wasn't around, the others deferring to him easily.

They looked at one another for a split-second, then with Jimmy in the lead, they filed out of the podium and into the camp, while behind them, the screams of the dead and dying filtered into the air as the escaped zombies began to feed.

Chapter 23

Henry chased after Murdock, the man always staying just out of target range. Rounding a cabin, Henry had to jump back when Murdock retuned fire. Chips of wood struck Henry in the face but he ducked back quick enough to avoid serious harm. Bending low, he swung the assault rifle he carried around the corner of the cabin and began firing. He didn't know if he was hitting anything, but for now he wanted to keep Murdock on the run. He fired two short bursts, then waited for a response.

Seconds ticked by and nothing happened, so he risked a peek around the corner. He half-expected to feel a bullet penetrate his skull. Sucking in a breath of air, he charged around the corner, zigging and zagging to create a more difficult target.

There was no retuning gunfire, Murdock had run away again.

Henry did the same, jogging warily, his eyes darting back and forth as he searched for Murdock. The man might have escaped then if not that he stopped again and tried to pick off Henry before Henry knew he was there.

Fifty yards ahead, pressed against the side of another cabin, Murdock was waiting for Henry. When Henry stepped out from around a building, keeping low, looking the wrong way, Murdock leveled his pistol and fired.

The bullet hit Henry in the side, but only scraped his flesh, tearing a long groove in his skin. The second he heard the shot, Henry was already dropping to the ground, which was what saved him form a fatal gunshot wound.

"Damn it, why won't you fucking die!" Murdock screamed, shooting three more times, the bullets zipping over Henry's head like angry hornets. One came so close to his head that he felt the wind from the bullet's passage.

"You first!" Henry yelled, returning fire as he rolled behind a pile of firewood.

Cursing loudly, Murdock turned and ran again, Henry following quicker this time.

The game of cat and mouse went on for another five minutes. The part of the camp they were in was empty, everyone having attended the fights at the arena, so there were no guards to assist Murdock.

Henry wasn't complaining, and he knew if he wanted to kill Murdock, this would be his only chance. If Murdock managed to get to the part of the camp where more of his men were, then Henry would soon find himself vastly outnumbered.

Rounding another building, Henry saw Murdock was much closer this time. Cutting across a small garden, he closed the distance even more. Murdock heard Henry's heavy footfalls, so he turned and shot over his shoulder. The bullets went wide, Henry not even ducking this time.

There was a set of outhouses at the far end of the path Murdock was on, and he dashed around the farthest one on the left, Henry right behind him.

Henry raced around the outhouse to then halt, Murdock standing only a few feet away, his pistol aimed right at Henry's chest. He had Henry cold, all he had to was shoot.

Cursing his carelessness, Henry gripped his assault rifle tighter, his knuckles turning white. He had made a foolish mistake and was about to pay for it with his life.

"You should have known better than to cross me," Murdock said, then pulled the trigger, only instead of a bullet leaving the muzzle, there was nothing but a dry click. Murdock's face said he already knew this. "It's empty, as you've just seen. I might have wanted to shoot you but I couldn't even if I wanted to. I guess I should have kept better count, huh?" He smiled slightly. He dropped the gun to the ground, shaking his head. "So, what now? Are you going to shoot me down like a dog or are you going to put down that rifle and fight me like a man." He spread his arms out invitingly, then reached around to his back and pulled out a seven inch knife he'd had there, dropping that to the ground, too. "As you can see I'm now unarmed. Come on, I saw you fight in the arena, surely you can take me. Don't you want to fight me to see who's the better man? Don't you want to teach me a lesson, beat some sense into me; make me pay for everything I've done to you and your friends?" He took a step forward in what looked like a genuine

152

show of comradeship. "You know, I fucked Mary good. She was so sweet, so warm and wet. I'm sure she'll tell you about it later." He flashed Henry a wide and knowing smile. "So, what's it going to be? Shoot me like a dog, or fight me like a man."

Henry glared at Murdock, his hands gripping the rifle so tightly that it was amazing the metal didn't begin to compress. It would be so easy to put down the rifle and fight this man hand-to-hand, to put his hands around Murdock's throat, to squeeze the life out of him.

So easy.

But magnificently foolish.

In the end, the answer was simple, after all, this wasn't some cheesy action novel where the characters had to fight because the book needed the hero and villain to battle, or some poorly-written movie that needed a large fight scene at the end.

This was real life. And in real life, things didn't always go the way you wanted, and sometimes even the good guys died if they pushed their luck.

"I pick dog," Henry said coldly and fired one round into Murdock's head, the bullet penetrating his face right between the eyes.

Murdock's head snapped from the force of the bullet, the rear of his skull blowing out blood and brain matter. He dropped to the ground. The look of astonishment on his face that Henry had shot him was there, plain as day.

Though it would have felt good to beat Murdock senseless before killing him, Henry knew that the risk was still there that Murdock could have won.

That risk wasn't worth Henry's life.

With Murdock's legs still twitching in death, Henry walked away, satisfied that yet another enemy was gone for good.

Chapter 24

With Mary in the lead the companions went to Murdock's house, the door unlocked as it usually was. There had never been a reason to lock it, as the camp was completely under Murdock's thumb and normally at least one guard would have been there. Once inside, they headed straight for the room where Mary had seen their guns.

The room wasn't empty, the door partially ajar. Jimmy was the first over the threshold.

"Hey, what are you people doing in here?" the man Mary had seen before demanded. He was sitting at a workbench, an assault rifle in pieces before him—he was fixing the firing mechanism. He began reaching to the top of the bench, where a loaded revolver was.

Jimmy didn't reply, instead picking up the butt of the assault rifle and striking the man in the forehead with it. He went down like a ton of bricks, unconscious before he landed on the floor.

"Okay, everyone take as much stuff as you can carry," Jimmy said.

"Wow, will you look at all of this stuff," Cindy said, her eyes going wide at the sight of so much firepower. She found her M-16, the notches she'd put on the stock easy to identify, then she began loading magazines into a rucksack she found under the workbench. Jimmy was elated to find his shotgun and .357 Colt Python, both clean and oiled, and his hunting knife, too.

Sue found her .22 and ammunition for it, and she began shoving bullets into her pockets from the cardboard boxes they were in. By the time she was finished, she had large bulges in all her pockets, front and back.

Raven grabbed a .45 and an assault rifle, knowing the others would want them later, and Mary found her .38 and plenty of ammunition for it. But the prize of the day was when she spotted Henry's Glock under an oil-soaked rag. The pistol had been cleaned and oiled and was ready to be fired. Five clips were next to it, all full, and she took these and tossed them into a backpack, then turned to the others, who were just finishing up, including Jimmy, who was stuffing as many grenades as he could into a backpack. Nothing worked better to destroy the living dead than hand grenades.

"Are we good?" Mary asked everyone, and was greeted by nods and smiles. It felt good to be armed and loaded for battle. Nothing was worse than feeling helpless.

"Let's get going, we still need to meet up with Henry," Jimmy added and exited the room first. As he stepped out of the room, he found three guards were standing there before him only a few feet away, but they seemed as surprised as he was upon seeing that there were strangers coming out of the armory.

"Hey, who the fuck are you peop…" one of the guards began, already swinging his assault rifle around from off his shoulder, when Cindy stepped past Jimmy and sprayed the three men in a figure eight pattern with her M-16. Their bodies twitched and danced a jig of death before they were blown back against the wall, then each man slid down to the floor, leaving a bloody streak on the wall.

"Come on," Cindy said with a sly grin. "Time's a wastin'."

"Man, I love you," Jimmy said to her.

"I know, babe, same goes for me. In fact, if we ever get two minutes to ourselves, I have something to tell you."

"Oh yeah?" Jimmy asked. "What is it?"

"Not now, babe," she said. "It's not the right time."

"Are we going to keep talking or are we leaving?" Mary asked.

"Yeah, you two can kiss later," Raven added, smiling slightly.

"Be nice, Raven, they're in love," Sue said, smiling. Her thoughts were on Henry and their own relationship.

"Yeah, yeah, I hear you, let's move out," Jimmy said, and with him leading the way, they exited the house and made their way through the summer camp.

"Damn it, Henry's not here yet," Jimmy said when they arrived at the rendezvous.

"What do we do?" Sue asked.

"Simple, we wait for him to show up," Jimmy replied.

Cindy took a good look at Jimmy and saw the bruise on his temple, finally taking it in. In all the chaos she'd seen it but hadn't given it any thought. "Oh, babe, that looks bad." She touched it, only putting light pressure on the bump but Jimmy winced just the same.

"Ouch, shit, Cindy, don't touch it," he yelped.

"My poor baby," she cooed. "Does it hurt?"

"Only when I laugh," he snapped, annoyed. Then he kissed her on the cheek and said, "Sorry, I didn't mean that. Yeah, it hurts, and I have a giant headache. Other than that I'm fine. It'll take a lot more than a giant zombie with swords for hands to take down Jimmy Cooper."

"You said it, lover," Cindy said and hugged him, which was followed by a wet kiss on the lips.

There were more screams coming from around the camp, much more than there should have been, and all the companions were on edge.

"I wish Henry would get here soon," Mary commented. "I really want to leave this place."

"Shit, heads up," Jimmy breathed. "We got deaders at six o'clock."

The entire group turned to look in the direction Jimmy said simultaneously, their guns coming up in unison.

"Where the hell did they come from?" Cindy asked, leveling her M-16 at the undead mob coming right at her.

"Who cares?" Mary yelled. "Just shoot them!"

Standing side by side, the five companions began firing, even Raven using her newly-acquired assault rifle, knowing her added firepower was needed. She made quite a sight, a thin sixteen-year-old girl holding a bullet-spitting rifle, her black hair flying out behind her as the weapon spit hot death.

In seconds, more than a dozen ghouls were shot down, each one with a headshot, but more were following right behind them, and more after that.

"Henry better hurry the fuck up or we're gonna have to leave his ass behind," Jimmy said, shooting three ghouls in the chest with his shotgun from no more than five feet away. The bodies were blown backwards, the middle zombie getting the worst of the blast and nearly becoming cut in half. "These deaders don't look like the ones from the holding pens, these looked wilder; just look at their clothes."

He was right. Some of the animated corpses looked brand new, but their clothes didn't match what the people in the camp wore, while some had clothes that were no more than rags hanging off their gaunt forms.

So that could mean only one thing, that these zombies were coming from somewhere else and there were a lot of them.

Suddenly, in the back of the undead mob, bodies began falling over, and a second later, a hole appeared in the crowd. Henry had arrived, and he was shooting his way through the zombies.

He never slowed when he reached the companions, only glancing at them briefly, relieved to see that everyone was accounted for. There was no time for a reunion, as more and more zombies were surrounding them as the horde flooded the camp, taking down anything living.

"Let's go, something's happening in the camp. There's deaders everywhere," Henry said.

"No shit, old man, tell me something I don't know," Jimmy spit.

The group turned as one and ran in the direction there were the least amount of ghouls.

"What happened to Murdock?" Jimmy asked Henry as they began running.

"He's dead," Henry said flatly, looking at Mary as he said it, the one glance speaking volumes. "He can't hurt anyone ever again."

She nodded, smiling a thank you. "Here," Mary said, handing Henry his Glock.

"My gun, where'd you find it?" Henry asked.

"All our weapons were being stored at Murdock's house. We got them back and our gear before coming to the meet-up point."

"We grabbed some other shit, too," Jimmy said. "We even have some grenades now."

"Good, we might need them before long," Henry said, and pointed to the mob of zombies ahead of them. "Use two of them now to clear us a hole, Jimmy."

Jimmy reached into his pack and pulled out two grenades, pulled the pins, and threw them at the crowd of zombies.

The small orbs flew through the air to land in the center of the ghouls. One ghoul looked down at the orb that had fallen before it, curious as to what it was. It bent over, studying the grenade as it wobbled back and forth before coming to a stop. Then the seconds ticked down and the grenade erupted an instant before the second one did, blowing the zombie and the others around it into bloody pieces, some gobbets of flesh no larger than a quarter. Bodies were blown to hell, pieces raining down to splatter on the ground with wet squelching noises. The companions raced through the hole in the undead line, heading straight for the Nevada desert.

But there were more bodies to fill the gap, and in no time the undead were giving chase, albeit moving much slowly than the companions' running gait. Thirty minutes later, the six friends had reached the top of a ridge and after charging down the opposite side, found that they were finally leaving the undead behind them. As long as they kept moving, the living dead would never catch up.

"Do you think anyone in the camp survived?" Sue asked.

Henry didn't care, and said as much. "They were all an evil bunch if you ask me."

"Not all of them were, Henry," Sue rebutted. "Some just went along with it, like the old women who did laundry with me. They had no choice but to do as they were told."

"Sue, have you heard the saying about how good men doing nothing is all it takes for evil to thrive or something like that?"

"That's easy for you to say," she said, clearly growing angry. "So, what? You expect old women to pick up guns and overthrow some dictator with a giant zombie as a pet? Not everyone is like you, you know. Some people are fine with keeping their heads down and simply trying to survive."

Henry didn't want to debate the issues of good and evil in his fellow humans, so instead he said, "You should save your breath for running, Sue. As long as we're being followed we need to keep moving."

"For what it's worth, guys..." Mary butted in. "I think you've both have good points."

"Thank you, Mary, that's good to know," Sue said, appreciating some solidarity from one of her friends, even if it was only in the spirit of keeping the peace.

Henry picked up his pace, catching up to Jimmy who was in the lead, running at a steady jog that the others mimicked. "I think we should keep moving for another fifteen minutes and then take a rest, you agree?"

Jimmy glanced over his shoulder to see nothing behind him but the ridge and desert on all sides. "Yeah, sounds like a plan. We must have lost them by now."

"Hey, guys, look over there. Is that a body?" Mary called out.

No more than twenty feet away, lying flat on the ground face down, was a small lump that stood out against the dark sky. Now that they were clear of the camp, the moonlight bathed the desert in an eerie yellow glow that made it seem almost like dusk.

"We don't have time to investigate, Mary. Whatever it is, leave it," Henry said. "If it's human, whoever it was is no doubt already dead. There's nothing around for miles."

"I don't care, I'm going to see," Mary said and veered off from the group.

"Here we go again," Henry said with a weary sigh. He waved the others to follow him, as he followed Mary. "I wonder what trouble she's gonna get us into this time," he said under his breath.

Lazarus stood in the middle of the summer camp, surveying the death and carnage around him.

He was shirtless. His torso still had the puckered wounds where he'd been shot, and he knew they would be there forever.

He didn't care.

After realizing that he didn't feel the weather, that terms such as *hot* and *cold* didn't matter to him, he had taken the shirt off and tossed it away. He didn't need clothes at all actually but despite being ruler of the dead, he still held onto a modicum of morality and had decided to keep his pants on, as well as his shoes, which protected his feet from harm. He might not feel pain but if he stepped on a jagged rock, it would still serrate his flesh, which wasn't a good thing when your body didn't heal.

All around him stood his army, as well as new recruits taken from the camp. Lazarus had let a few of the zombies feed on some of the kills, wanting to make sure they kept their energy up.

Though zombies didn't need to feed, fulfilling their craving for human flesh was never a bad thing in his eyes.

The only negative to this recent campaign was that Lazarus had seen through the eyes of his zombies that six humans had escaped his army and had run off into the desert. Some of his followers had pursued them but Lazarus had called them back when it was clear that the six humans had outdistanced his zombies and were long gone, lost in the desert.

But he wasn't pleased by this, not at all. He had seen the six humans shooting down his army like a scythe to wheat and then the two grenades arcing through the air. He'd seen through the one zombie's eyes as it had looked down at the grenade, and had experienced the white hot flash as the grenade exploded and vaporized the zombie and the ones around it.

He didn't know who these six humans were, but he knew they had killed far too many of his soldiers to simply be left to escape. They needed to pay for what they'd done...with their lives.

He knew which way they were going and no doubt, being on foot, they would have to stop at the next settlement they came across. He pulled out a folded map covered in dry blood splatter and searched for the next settlement. It was Indian Springs, and it was only twenty miles away. His army moved slow, barely a fast walk, but he would be there by tomorrow afternoon, evening at the latest. Then he would destroy the town and the six humans at the same time.

His plan was going perfectly so far and he didn't see any reason for that to change. The humans simply had no defense against a coordinated attack from the living dead.

And why would they? His intelligence was his secret weapon.

Nothing would stop him from achieving his goals. One day soon, he would be the ruler of the world, a dead world of his making. The entire planet united under one banner.

Nothing could stop him—nothing.

Chapter 25

With Mary still in the lead, the group reached the small form lying in the dirt before the others.

"Oh my God, it's a child," Mary said upon dropping down beside the child. "It's a small boy." She rolled him over. He looked exhausted, his eyes barely open. "Do we have any water?"

"Here," Sue said, handing her a water bottle. "Luckily it was still in one of the packs. No one had gone through them yet at the camp."

"Drink this, honey," Mary said, placing the lip of the plastic bottle to the boy's lips.

He drank greedily, his eyes fluttering as the water rejuvenated him. "Who...who are you people?" the boy asked, his voice hoarse.

"We should be asking you that first," Henry said, bending down close to the boy. "What are you doing out here alone in the desert? Where're you from?"

The boy coughed some and then sat up, his spirit strengthened as his body did the same from drinking the water. He took the bottle from Mary and finished it off, wiping his mouth with the back of his hand. "I'm Tommy. My town, it was attacked by walkers. The people tried to fight them off, to shoot them but there were too many to stop. They...they killed everyone, my sister, my mom and dad, too. My whole family's gone. I managed to get away. The walkers chased me but I was too fast for them." He began to cry, but he was so dehydrated that no tears fell.

"How many deaders were there?" Jimmy asked. Tommy looked at him, not understanding the term 'deader.'

"I mean walkers, kid, how many walkers were there?" Jimmy explained. "Shit, there had to be a lot of them to overrun your town and I know I haven't seen that many in one place in a long time."

"That's true," Sue said. "They're thinning out. Or at least it seems that way."

"Yeah," Cindy added. "Lately, the deaders are more spread out than ever. I can't remember the last time I saw a horde of them, especially a horde so large it could take down an armed town."

"Well, I saw what I saw and I was lucky to get away," Tommy said, angry that the adults didn't believe him, especially when he'd seen it for himself. "That wasn't all I saw, there was one walker that could talk."

"What? Okay, kid, now you're making shit up," Jimmy said.

"Am not," Tommy replied, indignant. "There was too a walker that could talk. He seemed to be controlling the other ones, makin' them do what he wanted. I swear it's true. He said he was going from town to town and taking them over and killing everyone." He began to cry hard now. "That zombie killed my mom and dad, my little sister, why would I lie about such a thing?" he wailed.

Henry left Mary with Tommy and he waved the others a few feet away so they could talk without the boy hearing.

"If what that kid says is true, we may have just found out about the biggest threat ever," Henry said. "If there's really a deader out there that can think and talk, and somehow control the rest, it could be unstoppable."

"Yeah, but what're the odds the kid's telling the truth?" Jimmy asked. "It could be all in his head."

"Maybe, but that seems pretty farfetched to me," Henry said. "That boy has lived with deaders for years as a threat, he knows what they are. I saw the look on his face while he told us his story. If he's making it up then that kid's one hell of an actor. He definitely *believes* what he told us. Besides, we've all seen some strange stuff since the dead began to walk, so to simply dismiss what the kid says as false would be a mistake, especially without investigating it first."

"Okay, then if we're gonna take what the kids says as true, then I have something to add," Jimmy said, his mind working overtime to explain what Henry was considering as truth. "Henry, remember all those zombies we saw back at the summer camp right before we got out of there? You know, the ones wearing really old clothes or brand new ones? Shit, some even looked like they'd just been turned," he said upon considering Henry's words.

"Yeah, what about them?" Henry asked.

"Well, if those were the advance deaders of this thinking zombie then that would explain why there were so many inside the camp all of a sudden. Hell, it was like they came out of nowhere.

They didn't just straggle into the camp, they came in all at once. I know it could have been a coincidence but..." He trailed off, leaving the rest of his idea for the others to consider on their own. "It does back up the kid's story of an attacking horde."

"But it could still all be a load of crap and the deaders in the camp were just a coincidence," Cindy said. "This kid might be delusional or something. I'm not saying deaders didn't kill his family, but maybe he's imagining the whole thing. I mean, what really happened to him before we found him? You know, like he's in shock or something."

"That's a good point, Cindy," Henry agreed. "I don't want to go running around the desert telling everyone we meet that there's a thinking deader controlling some kind of dead army. People would think we'd gone nuts."

"Then what do we do?" Sue asked, glancing over her shoulder to look at the boy. He and Mary were talking quietly.

Henry rubbed his chin, feeling the start of a beard growing. He'd been so busy running and fighting that there had been no time to shave, and at the moment he didn't know when there would be either. "There's really no choice in the matter. We need real intel on what the kid said, we need to know whether it's true or not."

"How do we do that?" Jimmy asked.

"That's simple, Jimmy. The others will stay here and rest up with the kid, while you and me go back to the camp to see if we can catch a look at this talking deader."

"Well, Henry," Sue said. "That's sounds fine but did you see your side? You're bleeding."

Henry glanced down at this side where he'd been shot, the wound only a flesh wound. The bleeding had stopped almost before it began but all the exertion since had opened it and there was a spot of blood about three inches wide on his shirt.

"I'm fine, Sue, really." Murdock shot me but it missed. "It's only a nick," he said.

"Maybe so but you're not going anywhere till I clean and bandage it. You of all people know how dangerous an open cut can be," Sue said.

With a weary sigh he nodded, seeing the look on her face and knowing it would be easier to submit rather than protest. She was in 'mother mode' and when she got like this there was no talking her out of it. "Fine, but make it quick. That horde isn't going to wait for us, you know."

An hour later, Henry and Jimmy lay perched on a ridge overlooking the summer camp. Henry was peering through a set of binoculars, the plastic housing cracked in half a dozen places. The binoculars had taken a beating since coming into the possession of the companions.

The stench of rotten flesh permeated the air, floating up from the camp thanks to the direction of the wind, which was blowing directly at the two warriors. The camp was aflame in many places, and with the moon shining bright overhead, it was more than adequate illumination to see within the camp.

"Well, old man, what do you see?" Jimmy asked impatiently by Henry's side.

"I see a lot of deaders, that's what I see," Henry said. "But I can't make out anyone specifically."

They'd been there for over an hour, searching the camp for signs of the so-called zombie king. From where they were perched on the ridge, they had an excellent view of almost the entire camp, other than a few places where cabins blocked their line of sight. Henry was about to pack it in when he said, "Wait a second, something's happening." He watched as a shirtless zombie strolled into the center of a gathering crowd of living dead. From a cursory glance there had to be over five hundred zombies in the crowd, but that wasn't all of them. Scattered throughout the camp were hundreds more. A guess on the number of undead had to be over a thousand, and that was Henry being reserved in his count. He had no doubt there were even more, maybe even up to two thousand, when all were accounted for.

"What's happening?" Jimmy asked. "Come on, tell me. Shit, I wish we had more than one pair of binocs."

"Well, we don't so deal with it." Henry passed on what he was seeing. "Damn it, there are survivors in the camp. They're not doing so good, though," he said as he watched the shirtless zombie

164

tear out each of the survivor's throats to let them bleed out, then let them rise from the dead to shuffle into the crowd. "Christ, there's a deader making more of them. Whoever or whatever he is, he has the virus inside him. When he bites and kills people, they come back as deaders."

"Let me see," Jimmy said and Henry relinquished the binoculars. Jimmy looked where Henry pointed and soon enough was taking in the grim scene. "Maybe we can take the fucker out. One bullet to the head would sure save us all a lot of trouble."

"I agree, Jimmy, but we'd need some kind of sniper rifle to hit him from here and that we don't have. The range is simply too damn great."

"So then let's get closer."

"No way. It's too risky, and we can't stay here and hope for a better opportunity. If that horde moves out, we'll have a hell of a time staying ahead of them. Christ, that many deaders will cover a mile wide when it marches. No, we're better off hightailing it out of here and get to the next town to warn them. Hopefully, if they believe us and don't either lock us up outright or kill us, and they have a good barrier to the outside world, and with some preparation, maybe we can hold off that army or even destroy it."

"That's a lot of if's Henry. You know that, right?"

"Yeah, but it's all I got at the moment. If you have any better ideas, I'm all ears."

Jimmy considered this but after only a few seconds he shook his head. "No, you're right; we're not left with a lot of choices here and trying something now with just the two of us and maybe dying for it if we fail isn't worth it. Hell, this isn't something I would have thought we ever would have to deal with. I mean, sometimes I thought it looked like the deaders were getting smarter but nothing like this."

There was the sound of someone moving through the scrub behind them. Both warriors jumped up and spun around, their weapons aimed at what they assumed would be advancing zombies, but both men held their fire by just a millisecond when they saw that it wasn't ghouls before them, but three survivors from the camp.

A man in his late fifties and two women in their forties moved out of the cover of the scrub, their hands held high. The women wore attire that made them look as if they had come from the brothel.

"Don't shoot us, we mean you no harm," the man said, the fear in his voice apparent.

"Who are you?" Henry demanded, his Glock never wavering. On the ground beside Henry was an assault rifle he'd taken with him but he ignored it upon getting up, knowing it was quicker to draw his Glock.

"We're...we're from the camp. We managed to get out alive," one of the women said.

"Barely," the other woman said.

"Then you're probably only a few that did," Jimmy said. "You armed?"

"Not really," the man said and slowly and cautiously pulled out an old 9mm pistol from behind his back and placed it gently on the ground. "It's not loaded. I found it next to a dead body as we were running from the camp. I assume it belonged to one of Murdock's men. There was no time to find any bullets for it. Hell, we barely had time to escape with the clothes on our backs as it is."

"Do you know what happened down there? Did the living dead break loose of their pens at the arena?" one of the women asked. "There were so many. I didn't think Murdock had that many of them."

"He doesn't, or didn't," Henry said. "Murdock's dead, if you didn't know it."

"No, we didn't," the man said. The women didn't seem to care one way or the other.

"We've been spying on the camp," Henry said. "Believe it or not, there's a deader that's leading that horde down there." He then quickly filled the three refugees in on what Tommy had said and that Henry and the others were going to try and reach the next town before the undead army reached it, then warn the populace and try to man a defense.

"You three can come with us if you like," Henry offered.

The man put up a hand for Henry to wait a moment, then he and the two women began to talk in hushed tones. For a full minute they went back and forth, and Henry was about to demand an answer when the man finally quieted the two women and turned to Henry and Jimmy with his hands spread before him in an apologetic gesture.

"No thank you," the man said. "Though we do appreciate the offer. But we've decided that if the town that you're going to is the next place those dead things are heading, then we'll go in the opposite direction."

"But there's only open desert in that direction," Jimmy said.

"Maybe so, son, but we've all seen enough dead people to last us a lifetime. We'll take our chances in the desert."

"Suit yourself, it's your choice," Henry said, not caring where they went. He only offered for them to join his group out of pity.

"Could I maybe make a request from you before we all part ways?" the man asked.

"Depends. What is it?" Henry asked.

The man gestured to the empty pistol on the ground and Henry nodded that it was okay for the man to pick it up. Henry's eyes locked on the man and the gun the entire time. The man retrieved the gun, then popped out the empty clip to show Henry he wasn't lying. "Like I said, it's empty. I was wondering if maybe you could spare me three bullets, you know, in case things get bad out there in the desert and we don't make it."

Henry looked at Jimmy who shrugged, the gesture telling Henry it was entirely up to him.

Henry looked at the man and his sad, weary eyes, then at the two women beside him. Under the dirt, grime and fear, they were still beautiful women. With a sigh, he reached into his pocket and pulled out three rounds, then placed them on the ground at his feet while gathering his assault rifle and other gear he'd taken with him on the recce.

"Don't go near these until me and my friend are out of sight," Henry said, his warning clear.

Before the man could begin saying his thanks, Henry and Jimmy were on the move, blending into the scrub to be lost in the shadows of the night.

Chapter 26

"Look, they're coming back," Mary said, seeing Henry and Jimmy running up the road, the night surrounding them like a living thing. It had been hours since the men had departed and she was getting to the point that she was going to take Raven with her and set off to search for the two men. She was relieved to see them now. When Henry and Jimmy had left, the others had set up a small camp off the path they'd been on in a circle of brush. From where they were they were hidden from the road, but not so far that they wouldn't see Henry and Jimmy return.

Everyone was standing by the time Henry and Jimmy reached the others and the two men were handed bottles of water to quench their thirst.

"So, what the story?" Cindy asked, going to Jimmy and kissing him, Sue doing the same to Henry. The couples hugged briefly before getting to the business at hand.

"It doesn't look good," Henry said. "The kid was telling the truth."

"Told ya I was," Tommy said. He wasn't crying anymore. Though still sad at the loss of his family, he was a tough kid and bounced back quickly. Now he wanted revenge for his family.

"So what do we do now?" Sue asked, worry clear on her face.

"What we said we'd do," Henry said. "Pack it up. I want us on the move in five minutes. The more of a head start we have the better. Jimmy checked the map he's carrying and Indian Springs is the next town. It's a good hike from here, so we'll need to move fast."

Everyone got to work packing up their supplies, and three and a half minutes later, they were on the move, jogging at a good pace.

Henry wiped the perspiration beading his forehead as he jogged in the middle of the companions. A few hours later and the group was still going strong, only stopping for five minute intervals to rest and take in water or pee.

He glanced to his left at Sue, who was holding up well. Her breasts bounced up and down in what to Henry was an arousing sight, as she placed one foot before the other in what seemed like infinite repetition, and he felt a surge of pride that this strong woman was his, and that she loved him and he her. Sue's body was almost solid muscle. When he'd first met her there had been a little fat here and there, such as what would be found on a middle-aged housewife that didn't exercise much, but now, after being on the road for over a year, running fighting and surviving, her body had grown lean and hard with muscle, her skin tanned like Henry's from the sun. She was truly beautiful, and Henry knew, even is she hadn't been such a beauty, he would love her anyway for who she was inside.

She noticed him looking at him. "What?" she asked.

"Nothing, just seeing how you're doing," he replied with a smile.

"I'm okay, but I can't say the same for Jimmy," she said. "I think that blow he took to his head is taking its toll on him."

Jimmy was in the lead, though his arms seemed like lead weights by his side, the pack on his back looking as if it had become heavier with each passing minute.

"He's fine," Cindy said, dropping back a little at hearing Sue talking. "I just checked on him. He's fatigued but he says he can still run."

The sun was up and had been for almost an hour. Henry missed the night. Though cold, it had made their travels easier, despite being dangerous. He shielded his eyes with his hand, gazing off at the horizon and a heat mirage that appeared to be nothing more than a shimmering pool of mercury.

The group was running on the highway, as it was the quickest and most direct road to the town. Normally, Henry would have chosen a more indirect route, to make sure raiders or slavers wouldn't come across them, but time was of the essence so he was risking a direct approach. Anyone who traversed the deadlands knew that traveling on an open road was asking for trouble, and doing so without a vehicle was even worse.

On the right side of the road, the land sloped downward, to a dry riverbed filled with rocks and scrub. To the left, the land inclined upward, until finally reaching a ridge covered in yellow grass; what was on the opposite side was unknown. For all Henry knew the ridge could be hiding a hundred slavers or five hundred zombies, or there could be nothing there at all but austere land that went on for miles. Or there was an oasis, with a clear pool of water and trees with branches ripe with fruit. Either way, the unknown tickled the hairs on the back of his neck and it made him super-alert.

He wasn't entirely concerned with the lack of defensive cover, for though they were vulnerable, if anyone tried to attack him and his friends, the enemy would be seen long before they arrived, which would give the companions time to prepare for the fight. Most travelers weren't as well armed as the six friends, and anyone who tried to take them down would be in for a surprise, not that it would stop them from trying.

But none of that mattered now, all that mattered was time, which there wasn't enough of. If this zombie king wasn't stopped, Henry knew that before long he would swarm over the entire state and beyond. Henry also knew if the monster wasn't stopped, before long there would be nowhere safe to go to escape his dead army.

The idea that a thinking zombie had somehow appeared and was leading an army was puzzling to Henry. It made no sense. From every ghoul he had ever seen, none had ever shown signs of truly being capable of speech, let alone rational thought.

And even if everything he'd seen was completely true—and he had no reason not to accept what he'd seen with his own eyes—how could the lead zombie control his army? Zombies didn't understand speech, they didn't take orders, and to control such a massive army of undead soldiers seemed impossible. In a human army, there would be generals, captains and lieutenants, men to relay orders from one squad to another, but here, it seemed that the entire army was being controlled by a single entity, or that was what Henry believed from witnessing the zombie king in action.

How it was happening was something Henry couldn't fathom, but maybe in time the explanation would show itself.

Tommy was gulping greedily from a water bottle a few feet before Henry, so he moved up behind the boy and tapped his shoulder. "Take it easy on the water, son, you don't want to drink too much too fast. We need to conserve it for now."

"Sorry, Henry, I'm just so thirsty."

"I know, son, and when you get to Indian Springs you can drink your fill, but for now we all need to conserve what we have."

The boy nodded and handed the bottle back to Cindy, who reached around to her pack and returned it there.

"How're you holding up?" Henry asked Tommy.

"I'm okay. I like to run. Me and my sister do it all the time. I mean we used to do it all the time."

"Hey, Henry, there's something up ahead on the road," Jimmy called out, slowing his pace a little, the others doing so as well. "It looks like a man." Henry jogged up to Jimmy and then the entire group slowed until they were just walking. Glad for the rest, they sucked in air and wiped sweaty brows. They shielded their eyes from the glaring sun, as if by their willpower alone they could make it go down and stop cooking them like turkeys in a convection oven.

Henry pulled out the binoculars and focused them on the lone man, who was sitting in the middle of the road in a plastic beach chair. There was an open, tattered beach umbrella connected to the chair to keep the sun off his head. On both sides of the man there was nothing but flat land and some sparse brush that couldn't hide a snake, let alone an ambush. The land slowly turned into high ridges so that the only practical way past the man was by using the highway; to try and go overland would add precious hours to their trip that they didn't have.

The man looked like he was sleeping, but then slowly, he raised his head, opened his eyes, and looked right at Henry, smiling widely. Or so it felt to Henry, who lowered the binoculars and filled in the others on what he'd seen.

"One man alone, it doesn't feel right," Henry said after explaining the sight of the man.

"But what else could it mean? What would be the point of being there?" Sue asked.

"That's a good question," Henry said. "One we don't have an answer to right now."

"We could go around him," Mary suggested.

"No, there's no time for that," Henry said. He glanced back at the small figure of the man, then at Tommy, who gazed up at Henry with large, trusting eyes. "We're just going to have to keep going and see what he wants."

"Maybe he doesn't want anything," Cindy said. "Maybe he just needs a lift."

"A guy in the road wants something, that's for sure," Raven added.

Henry nodding at her insight. "She's right," Henry said. "No one sits in the middle of the road leading to Indian Springs unless they're after something. The only question is: what could that be? Being alone, he can't strong arm anyone unless they're traveling in ones or twos and if they have a vehicle all bets are off." He rubbed his chin, scratching his light beard. "This makes no sense."

"Then we have two choices," Mary said. "We can try and go around and waste time or go right up to him and ask."

"Then we go ask," Henry said, not wanting to waste any more time. "But everyone stay sharp, weapons ready in case things go south. There's another piece to this puzzle, we just don't know it yet."

The decision made, the group began walking towards the man on the horizon.

Chapter 27

When Henry had seen the man through the binoculars, he hadn't been able to fully take in his size and appearance other than from a cursory standpoint. But now, as the deadland's warrior grew closer and the man stood up, Henry was able to study him better.

The man had a wrestler's build, with a shaggy beard and a bald head. He wore a pair of camouflaged pants and black boots, and a gray t-shirt that showed off his heavily-tattooed arms. Snakes and dragons writhed up and down his powerful biceps and danced on his neck where the shirt allowed the artwork to be seen. There was a hint that his entire torso was covered as well, by the way the tattoos peeked out from beneath the shirt. His muscles rippled beneath his skin as he flexed his arms and waited for the companions to reach him.

"That's far enough, strangers," the man said, holding up his left hand in a stop motion, his right holding a rugged-looking shotgun that had seen better days but still seemed serviceable.

Henry and the others stopped twenty feet from the man, their guns drawn but aimed at the ground. Henry held the assault rifle he'd taken from the camp in his hands, and though the barrel was pointed at the pavement, it was clear by his posture that it would come up if the burly man so much as looked as if he was going to try something.

Henry didn't like the situation, and by the way the man stood there so confident, Henry had a feeling that the man had an ace up his sleeve. Henry glanced from side to side at the barren land around him, but still saw no signs of an ambush. Not even a salamander could be seen moving under the harsh sun.

"Who are you?" Henry demanded.

"Well, now, the way I see it, that should be my question for you people," the man said. "I suppose you're on your way to Indian Springs, am I right?"

"Maybe we are and maybe we aren't," Henry replied.

The man chuckled. "Don't want to say, huh? That's okay. We both know that's where you're all headin' Nothing else around here for miles so there's nowhere else you could be goin'. Especially on foot."

"What if we are?" Mary inquired.

"Well there, sweetcheeks, if you are, then you gotta pay me a toll. See, this here's a toll road." The man grinned wickedly.

"A toll road, huh?" Henry asked. "I have to ask, as there's six of us and only one of you. What stops us from just shooting you down and moving on and to hell with your toll road?"

"Well, stranger, you could try, but I promise you it won't work out the way you think."

"Can I ask what the payment is for passage?" Sue asked, always the diplomat. She figured if the toll fare wasn't too steep, it might be better to simply pay it and move on as there was no time for idle banter or bargaining.

"Well now, seems as you got four women in your group, what say I take two as payment and then the rest of ya can move on."

"That's not gonna happen," Henry said, gripping the assault weapon tighter, his eyes creasing to slits.

"It's not huh?" the man said, stepping to the side of the road a little. He did it casually, looking down at his feet as he moved, as if he was just a person who didn't like to stand still for too long. He was doing his best to look relaxed, but Henry could see the steel coils of muscle beneath the man's skin flexing. "So tell me, stranger, what stops me from killing you all and then taking what I want anyway?"

"That's easy," Jimmy said. "You wouldn't be able to 'cause we'd gun your ass down; you'd be a very dead fucker."

"You think so, huh?" the man laughed.

"I don't like this, Henry," Mary said out of the corner of her mouth. "There's something fishy about all of this."

"Yeah, I know what you mean," Henry agreed. "But for the life of me I can't figure out what this guy has up his sleeve."

"Last warning, strangers," the man said. "Give me the women or you're all dead."

"Forget this guy, Henry," Jimmy said. "Let's shoot the fucker and move on, we don't have time for this shit. This guy must be crazy from heatstroke or something."

Henry stared at the tattooed man, seeing the way he was standing, his posture tall, cocksure of himself. He wasn't scared in the slightest that he was outgunned five to one. That overconfidence made Henry nervous.

"Sue, take Tommy and move to the rear of the line, and if anything happens, run for cover."

"Okay but I don't underst..." she began but was cut off.

"Don't talk about it, just do it, okay?"

"Sure, okay, I hear you," she said and took Tommy by the hand.

"Everyone, begin backing away, move up the road the way we came," Henry whispered.

Still twenty feet away, the tattooed man couldn't hear Henry. "Last warning before we take them from you," the man said.

That's when Henry knew the man was far from alone out the in the middle of nowhere. The man had said 'we', not 'I.' It had been a slip of the tongue, something anyone might do if they weren't alone but were pretending to be.

"Everyone, run, now! Back the way we came!" Henry yelled, but it was already too late.

As the companions turned to flee, on both sides of them, on the shoulders of the road, the ground burst upwards, spraying dirt in all directions.

A dozen men and women, all grizzled and filthy, exploded from the ground, jumping out of the holes they'd been hiding in, the tops covered with a thin piece of plywood, the soil then spread over them to camouflage the spots perfectly.

Half of the ambushers were armed with guns of assorted calibers, and the rest carried melee weapons, everything from a two-by-four with nails in the tip to a simple lead pipe. Many were dressed in old, faded leather, and Henry saw that a few wore necklaces of human body parts.

One even had a necklace made of human ears, each one shriveled and dried to the consistency of beef jerky. It was a testament to how many people the man had killed since the dead began to walk. Another of the attackers had a face that looked as if the man had been run through a meat grinder. Where the nose should have been there was nothing but an open, weeping wound, mucus dripping out of the hole to roll over his cracked lips to splatter onto the ground. One of the women attackers had a face covered in makeup, so much that she resembled a circus clown, with bright red lipstick smeared over her lips, overlapping onto her face and cheeks so that her lips looked three times larger than normal. Her face was covered in white pancake makeup too, her eyebrows looking like they had been painted on with black magic marker instead of eyeliner. Her leather vest was halfway open, her ponderous breasts literally overflowing out of the vest, as if they would not be contained by mere clothing and wanted to be free of their prison at all costs. Her long black hair was filled with snarls and pieces of debris, rounding out the picture of a madwoman.

Henry took all of this in with less time than it took for the dirt to fall back to the ground. "Take out the ones with guns first, the rest are secondary targets!" he yelled, swiveling the muzzle of the assault rifle at the first raider he saw carrying a firearm.

As Sue pulled Tommy to the side and dropped down in an impression in the earth—the ditch made from flash-floods—the rest of the group did as ordered, bringing their weapons around and firing in a deadly arc.

Jimmy killed the man they'd been talking to with his shotgun, the pellets blowing a large hole in his torso. The man went flying backwards to land on the pavement spread-eagled, knocking his lawn chair over when he fell. Spitting blood, he stared up at the hot sun and waited for death to take him. His umbrella fell over and rolled off into the barren desert, the wind carrying it further away with each second.

The companions split up to make harder targets, rolling to the ground and firing faster than the raiders could follow. Within the space of ten seconds, half of the raiders were down and bleeding, if not outright dead.

The only advantage the companions had was that they hadn't been taken by surprise as much as the raiders had hoped. Usually, when they popped up, the travelers standing in the road were flabbergasted and were either killed outright or taken prisoner to then be sold to slavers for a hefty fee.

But not the group before them now.

Instead of pouncing on simple civilians, men and women who barely could fight and only wanted to survive another day, they found themselves in a battle with a well-honed unit of mercenaries, men and women who had experience with firearms and knew how to use them.

The leader of the raiders saw this when half of his men went down in the span of seconds, so he did the only thing he could. He blitzed the companions, yelling, "Attack, kill them all!" as he and the others ran at the group at full speed, heedless of their lives.

Henry and the others tried to shoot them down but the raiders were too fast, and though a few of the attacking men and women received minor gunshots wounds, none were killed outright.

In less time than it took the wind to blow the beach umbrella into the desert, the gunfight had become a hand-to-hand battle.

Chapter 28

The raider with a meat grinder for a face came at Henry, yelling at the top of his lungs while waving a steel pipe over his head. Henry tried to shoot him, but the man jumped out of the way at the last second, all the bullets missing him but one, and that round only grazed his side.

Before Henry could swing his assault rifle around and try again, the man was on him, knocking the rifle to the ground to then lunge at Henry with murder in his eyes.

Henry grappled with the man then bent to the side, letting the raider trip over his lower leg to fall to the ground. As the man got up, screaming incoherently, Henry reached down and pulled his sixteen inch panga from its sheath. When the raider came at him again, Henry stepped in and sliced the razor-sharp edge of the panga across the man's throat. The skin parted easily, a warm cascade of gushing blood spilling forth. The man gagged and grabbed his throat with his free hand, dark crimson slipping between his fingers to splatter the ground in thick droplets. Henry kicked the man out of the way and searched for another enemy.

Meanwhile, Jimmy found himself dealing with the man with no nose, both of them falling to the ground in a heap of limbs as the man attempted to stab Jimmy with a small knife.

With both his hands locked in a grip with his attacker, Jimmy used the only weapon he had left—his teeth. He sank them into the man's wrist, tasting sweat and grime, but he held on, despite wanting to gag. The noseless raider screamed and his fingers released the knife, which Jimmy grabbed and slid into the raider's chest. The feeling of the blade going in was indescribable, the softness as the blade penetrated flesh and muscle, to then get hung up on the ribcage, before sliding between two ribs and into the man's heart. Jimmy watched the light go out of his enemy's eyes, then he shoved the corpse off him and got to his feet, ready to fight the next raider.

The rest of the raiders were surging forward, doing their best to kill the companions. Any plans for capturing the women were gone now, replaced by simple bloodlust and revenge for the death of their fellow cutthroats.

Mary, Cindy and Raven were holding their own, taking down any attacker that got to close, either by gun or blade. Off to the side, no one saw Sue and Tommy, the pair safe for the moment.

With a guttural yell, the woman with too much makeup charged at Henry, screaming at the top of her lungs. She was holding a machete, and she swiped it back and forth, attempting to eviscerate Henry, who blocked each blow with the panga. The woman was lost in bloodlust and barely tried to protect herself, her sole focus on gutting Henry.

After Henry blocked a swipe, she took a step backwards, raised the machete over her head in a chopping motion, then came at him again. Henry could see there was no way to stop her without killing her, and that he needed to take her down fast, before she got in a lucky blow.

Careless of her life, she dove in at Henry, who instead of backing away, moved forward into the charge, taking her by surprise. Before, whenever she had gone crazy in a berserker rage, her victims had stepped away, awed by her ferocity, but Henry had learned a long time ago that to charge in when the enemy expected you to run would take them off guard.

Henry was on her in a moment, face to face with her before she could bring the machete down. He used the panga like a spear, stabbing her right in her open mouth. Like a sword swallower that had messed up and the trick had gone horribly wrong, the panga slid into her throat, slicing her esophagus, larynx and voice box to bloody ribbons. She fell to the side, the panga then slicing sideways, through muscle and tendon and finally flesh, severing her head half off her shoulders. She slid to the ground, blood gushing from the mortal wound, but miraculously her head was still alive, the eyes moving back and forth, the nose twitching under the face paint, the eyebrows flaring in pain and the terror death.

Henry used his boot to push on her chest, then he pulled the panga free, blood drops flinging into the air to pepper the ground with red dots. In the Nevada heat, they would be dry in seconds. The woman was already dead, she just didn't know it yet.

Henry turned and began brawling with a gutshot man with a mohawk and a scar running down the side of his face that didn't realize he'd been shot, such was his rage. As they fought, changing blows, Henry got past the man's guard, slamming the panga into his stomach and then pulling up and to the side. The man's insides spilled out onto the hot ground, greasy entrails gently sliding across the pavement like live eels. The man stopped fighting and stared down in shock at the gaping wound. He dropped the knife he'd been holding and tried to scoop the intestines back into his body, heedless of the dirt he was forcing in there, too. His hands were cradled around his belly, but despite this, greasy ropes of intestine slid forth to squirt out and splash onto the ground. He slumped to his knees, looked up and locked gazes with Henry. "I can't die, I just can't," he blurted out in horror. "I've killed every-one I've ever fought, no one can beat me."

"There's always a first time," Henry said softly and slid the panga across the man's throat, making sure he died fast rather than the slow death of a gut wound. With blood shooting out of the wound five feet into the air, Henry stepped away and moved to see who else he needed to kill.

And just in time. A fat woman topping six feet in both height and girth, and wearing a leather jacket that was so big it could have been used as a blanket for a normal-sized person, had spotted Sue and Tommy and was making her way to them.

Sue looked up as the fat woman's large shadow fell over her and Tommy and Sue gritted her teeth in defiance.

"You're dead, bitch," the fat woman spit. "You first, then the runt." She raised a club made from a piece of scrap wood, the end covered in dried blood and dried gobbets of flesh and brain matter.

Using her .22, Sue shot the woman three times, the small caliber bullets hitting the woman in the stomach and lower chest. Though small spots of red appeared on her torso, the woman appeared to be fine.

"Huh, it tickles," she said with an evil grin, then knocked the gun from Sue's hand with the club. Stepping forward, the woman raised the club high to bring it down on Sue's head and crush her skull into a red paste.

Sue's eyes were gaping wide as she stared upward at her impending death. There was no escape. No way to stop the giant woman from killing her.

But before the club could come down and end her life, Sue stared in amazement as the fat woman began to flinch, her face taking on a look of curiosity, as her eyes rolled back into her head. Then she began to topple over, a felled tree taken down by a lumberjack. Sue rolled out of the way at the last second, pushing Tommy aside as well. The fat woman landed on the ground hard, a massive cloud of dust puffing up around her body. Sue went to her knees and gazed down on the back of the fat woman, seeing more than half a dozen spots of blood from bullet entrance wounds.

"You okay?" Cindy called from across the road, her M-16 still aimed in Sue's direction. Cindy had seen the fat woman going in for the attack and had shot her six times in the back. The woman's girth was too thick to allow the bullets to have exit wounds, but the rounds were more than enough to take the behemoth down once and for all.

Sue waved and smiled, signaling she was okay. Cindy nodded and moved off to deal with any stragglers, the raiders down to their last few men. They were brave but weren't as skilled as the companions, and their superior training had won the day.

Henry was dealing with the last two raiders even as Cindy searched for another target. The two men ran at Henry, each holding a knife. Henry had two blades as well. In his right hand he held his faithful panga, and in his left was a nine inch Bowie knife he'd taken from a previous vanquished enemy. Just before the men reached him, Henry dashed forward, ending up between the two men. He dropped to his knees, sliding across the ground as the raiders' blades slashed the air over his head. Henry used the two knives he held to hack at each of the men's knees just as his enemies' blades stabbed forward, missing him completely. Ripping the panga and Bowie knife upwards, he hacked at the men's groins, even as their legs were buckling from the wounds they'd received. As they went down, Henry's arms locked tight, the blades slicing upwards into their stomachs and then higher, only stopping due to the their ribcages.

On his knees, his arms spread wide, with a man hanging on each arm by a steel blade, and blood gushing out of them to splash onto Henry's bare arms, the deadland's warrior looked like something out of a history book, a berserker gone mad on the field of battle. Henry's face was set in a scowl of anger and hate, the desire to kill these men, men who only wanted to hurt his surrogate family, to destroy all that he had left, had overwhelmed him. With an angry roar, he thrust upwards, parting the ribcages of both men and opening their chests wide, their intestines and internal organs spilling out onto the hot ground. Simultaneously, he yanked his arms back, the blades coming free with a sucking motion. The Bowie knife had a small hook on the end of it, the upper half of the blade serrated, so it would cause even more damage when it was withdrawn. The two raiders tumbled to the ground, dead before their bodies had fully settled.

Spitting blood that had slid into his mouth from being splashed, Henry stood up, flexed his powerful muscles, and turned to see who his next foe was, what man or woman was ready to die by his hands.

It took a few seconds for him to come to the realization that there were no more enemies, that the battle was over and that he and his friends had won. He blinked a few times, and as he did, his face relaxed, the anger washing away. Reason filled him and he shifted his gaze from Jimmy, then to Cindy and Mary and so on.

"Is everyone all right? Anyone hurt?" Henry called out, sucking in air as he wiped his sweaty brow with the back of his hand, leaving a streak of bright red blood in its place. His shirt was soaked through with sweat and blood, as was the rest of the groups clothing. The temperature had to be in the high nineties or low hundreds, easy.

"I'm all right," Mary called from the side of the road.

"Me too," Cindy yelled, breathing heavily.

"I'm fine," Raven added.

"Good to go, old man," Jimmy said, walking over to Henry. "That was some kill you just did."

Henry nodded. "It had to be done; these bastards had to die, no way around it."

"Hey, you're not gonna get any argument from me," Jimmy said.

Sue and Tommy walked across the road and joined Henry and Jimmy, as did the others. They all looked around themselves at the blood and death, at the bodies.

"So no one's hurt?" Henry asked again, the reply from the group being that everyone was fine. A few cuts and scratches here and there but nothing serious.

"Okay, then fan out quickly and see if there's anything useful we can take from these guys," Henry directed, pointing at bodies as he talked. "Take any blades that are in decent shape and guns and ammo from any of the bodies that have one. We should be able to use them in trade when we get to Indian Springs." Everyone began to fan out to search the bodies. "And be careful. Someone might be playing possum and we don't need any accidents. Make sure they're dead before you start searching the corpses."

They got to work, ransacking the bodies for anything of use. Henry walked over to one of the holes in the ground and peered down into it. The hole was shallow, less than four feet. The raider that had occupied it must have been sitting down, and with the wood covering the hole, it must have been hot as hell in there. He had to wonder how long the raiders had sat in their holes, waiting for the signal to attack. Still, he had to admit, it was mighty clever. He wrinkled his nose when he saw the small bucket at the bottom of the hole filled with feces and urine. So as well as being hot as hell in there, it must have smelled terrible.

"Hey, I found something over here!" Cindy called from behind a large copse of scrub brush fifty feet off the road. "Come here, you guys gotta see this!" She was beaming happily and Henry realized that if there was danger present, Cindy wouldn't have looked so amused.

He and the others jogged over to her, and when they rounded the brush, they were all pleasantly surprised to find an old El Camino, the paint faded, the tires bald, but for all purposes it looked like a running piece of machinery. The ground had been excavated a few feet where the car was parked and with that added to the scrub brush, the car was virtually invisible from the road.

Jimmy went to the driver's window and reached inside, seeing the hotwired job someone had done. He twisted two wires together that were clearly there for that reason and the engine rolled over, coughed once and then surged to life, the patched muffler making it sound like a diesel truck rather than a car.

"It looks like we're in business," Jimmy said with a grin. "No more walking for us."

Henry patted Cindy's shoulder. "Well done, Cindy, you've saved us a lot of time. With a car, what time we've wasted here can be made up in no time. Okay, everyone get their gear and let's load up. Jimmy, drive this heap onto the road so we can pack up faster."

"Will do," Jimmy said and got behind the steering wheel, the driver's door creaking loudly due to ungreased hinges. Studying the dashboard and the knobs and switches, he moaned, "Ah, man, there's no A/C in this piece of shit."

Chapter 29

A short time later, the six companions plus Tommy were on the move again, driving away from the ambush site. No sooner did they leave then the scavengers of the desert began to appear to feast on the dead flesh of the fallen.

Though the muffler on the El Camino had been patched multiple times in the past, it was still rusted-out and filled with holes, the car sounding so loud everyone winced from the noise. Jimmy sat behind the wheel, and beside him was Cindy in the passenger seat. The others were in the rear bed. It was too hot to cramp three people inside the car, and Jimmy and Cindy enjoyed a few moments alone, or as alone as they could get given the constant danger they were always in.

"Jimmy, I have something to tell you," Cindy said hesitantly.

"What, babe?" Jimmy asked, fiddling with the tape deck, which didn't work no matter how much he fussed with it. He was aggravated by this. What sane person drove around without tunes to listen to?

"I don't really know how to tell you," she said, drawing out whatever she wanted to say.

"So then just say it. We don't have any secrets, right?" Jimmy had given up on the tape deck and was playing with the radio. He didn't expect to find an operational station, but it just felt right fiddling with the dial as he drove down the open road. Other than a few cars pushed to the side, the road was wide open, and he was going a steady thirty miles per hour. He wanted to go faster but the muffler became deafening if he sped up so he had subconsciously settled for thirty.

"Well, it's not that easy," she said, biting her lip. She sighed heavily, psyching herself up. "Okay, here goes. I'm..."

"Jimmy, slow down, we got vehicles up ahead heading right for us!" Henry yelled from the rear of the vehicle.

"Will do. They look hostile?" Jimmy yelled out the window.

Henry was standing up behind the rear window with his hands holding onto the roof of the car, and he could see farther than

Jimmy down the long highway. "Don't know yet. Pull over and we'll let them come to us. But keep the engine running in case we need to make a fast getaway."

Jimmy did as instructed, steering the car to the shoulder of the road and coming to a stop, the muffler thankfully dying down in pitch to only a low rumble.

"Did you want to tell me something, babe?" Jimmy asked as he peered through the front windshield, his attention barely focused on Cindy.

"No, Jimmy, it can wait, we've got more important things to deal with right now."

"Cool," Jimmy said and opened the car door to crouch behind it, the matter already forgotten. Henry, Mary, Raven, and Sue with Tommy, climbed out of the rear bed and onto the road, staying behind the rear bumper. Cindy sighed again and got out of the car, checking her M-16 while the others did the same with their weapons.

Up the road, the two vehicles Henry had spotted came over a rise and began to move closer.

"Have your weapons ready but keep them lowered till I say different," Henry said. "Maybe for once we'll meet people that don't want to kill us." They were all behind the El Camino, using the vehicle as cover in case the new arrivals were hostile.

"That would be a nice change of pace," Mary said grimly.

The cars slowed down when they were within fifty feet of the El Camino and by the time they were thirty feet away, they stopped in the middle of the road, front bumper to front bumper, thereby blocking the road. One was a Ford Mustang, the other an Oldsmobile Cutlass. Both cars needed paint jobs desperately and one had a quarter panel fender pushed in from an old accident, the paint flaking and rust peering out from under the chips.

Four men got out of each vehicle and lined up behind the cars, each of the eight men holding a battered but serviceable firearm. Henry spotted one man wielding a KG-99 assault pistol, two others carrying Remington hunting rifles, and another holding a Glock similar to the one Henry carried.

"Don't move and put your weapons down!" one of the new arrivals yelled. He was a short man with a handsome face and wavy blonde hair. He looked to be in his thirties.

"I could say the same thing to you," Henry replied, shifting his assault rifle slightly to the side. He thumbed the fire-sector switch to full auto, though he was still hoping this might end without a battle. Stranger things had happened.

"We've got you outnumbered," the man said.

"Only by two men. I'll take those odds in a firefight if I have to," Henry said.

The man paused for a second, then began talking to the man beside him. Finally, he looked back at Henry and the others and said, "How 'bout you tell us where you're going?"

Henry didn't see why it mattered if he shared his travel plans so he decided he had nothing to lose by answering the man. "We're on our way to Indian Springs."

"What's your business there?" the man asked.

Henry debated if he should tell him about the talking zombie and his undead army. Would the man believe him? Hell, even Henry didn't believe it and he'd seen it for himself. He figured a little white lie right now would be a good thing. "We have items to trade: guns and extra ammo for food and lodging. We've been on the road a long time and figured it would be nice to be with other people for a while."

"We don't need any of that, so if that's all you got, you should just keep on moving," the blonde man said.

"That's not all we have," Henry said. "We have important info for your mayor or whoever runs your town."

"Oh really. Then tell me and I'll pass it on," the man said.

Henry shook his head. "No way. Trust me, your boss is gonna want to hear what I have to tell him and if he finds out you didn't let us pass on our info, I highly doubt he'll be pleased. I'll tell you this. If you don't let us through, your entire town will be wiped out in a matter of days, maybe less."

"Bullshit," another man said. "These people are raiders, pure and simple. I'd bet a week's pay on it.

The leader of the eight men began talking with his partner again, then said, "We're from Indian Springs, actually. We came out here after getting reports of a firefight a little while ago. You know anything about that?"

"Maybe," Henry said carefully.

"We've had a problem with a band of raiders. They ambush people on their way to us, usually they kill them and take all they have. We've been trying to find and take them down, but they keep moving. So far we've had no luck."

"What do these raiders look like?"

"Most wear leather. Half have guns, the rest carry clubs and the like. One woman wears so much makeup she looks like a carny clown, and another fella has got no nose, just an open sore on his face."

"Don't forget the fattie. That woman is so fat I wonder how she wipes her ass," another man said.

"We were ambushed not long ago," Henry explained. "But we won. It sounds like the people you described. I remember the woman in makeup; I killed her myself."

"I saw the fat woman, Henry," Sue said. "Cindy killed her before she could get to me and Tommy."

"I killed that guy with no nose," Jimmy said.

Henry pointed behind him down the road. "There's your answer. The bodies are lying in the road a few miles back that way if you want to check."

"No shit?"

"No shit," Henry said.

All the men began to talk amongst themselves at the news that the raiders were dead. The man talked to his partner again, then said something low to the rest of the men. Then slowly, the other men lowered their guns.

"Well then, that changes everything, mister. You've done Indian Springs a big favor if you took down those damn raiders. Tell you what, relinquish your weapons and we'll escort you back to Indian Springs."

"Sorry, pal, that not gonna happen," Henry said. "Listen, I'll say it again. My friends and I have important business with your leader. Now let's cut this back and forth shit and get to the town. Every second wasted here is one less your town has remaining."

The blonde man began talking to his partner again, the rest of the men looking at them curiously. They wanted to know what was going on. Were Henry and his group of friends or enemies?

"I need to call and talk to the boss and fill him in on what you've told me," the man said. "You and your friends got names?"

Henry debated telling the man his name, as well as the other companions, but once more, in the end, he decided it didn't really matter. As far as he knew, all his enemies were dead. "The name's Henry Watson. That's Jimmy, Cindy, Sue, Mary, Raven and the boy is Tommy."

The blonde man began talking into a two-way radio, and everyone stood around, staring at each other. The standoff was becoming something else now, and though that could change at a moment's notice, no one seemed to mind. After more than two minutes of talking back and forth on the radio, the blonde man called out, "You people stay where you are, my boss is coming out to see you. He should be here in a few minutes."

"Fine, I guess we don't really have a choice in the matter," Henry said.

"No, you don't."

The sun glared down on the heads of the group of people in the middle of the road. Henry stayed on constant watch, letting the others rest in the shade of the El Camino. Finally, another vehicle arrived, a beat-up Ford pickup. It pulled up behind the first two cars and stopped. Three men were inside in the cab; two guards and the driver—the driver being the boss of the town. The driver climbed out slowly and squinted at the harsh sun, his already dark skin even darker thanks to the sun. He wore a Stetson hat low on his head, which concealed his face from Henry and the others.

He slowly walked up to the blonde man, said a few words to him, patted his shoulder, then strolled past the cars, out to the open road and over to the El Camino. Behind him, all the men put their weapons away, the blonde man telling them the standoff was over, that the companions were friends.

The driver of the Ford stopped a few feet from the front bumper of the El Camino and took the hat off his head so that the companions could see his face. He had a wide smile on his face as he nodded to Henry and the others. "Well, Henry, aren't you going to say hello?"

Henry's mouth fell open, as did Jimmy's, Mary's and Cindy's at the sight of the black man with a shaved head before them.

"No fucking way," Jimmy said.

"I don't believe it," Cindy added.

"It's impossible," Mary mumbled.

Henry stepped out from around the El Camino and walked over to the man before him, a wide smile on his face as well, one so large it looked as if Henry's face would remain frozen that way forever. "Well, I wouldn't have believed it if I hadn't seen you with my own two eyes," Henry said. "I'd have thought you'd be long dead by now."

"Not yet, Henry, I've got a few more years left before I'm going to meet my maker." He winked. "Or so I hope."

The two men shook hands.

Chapter 30

On the drive to Indian Springs, Henry and Mary sat in the cab of the Ford pickup with a man they hadn't seen in years, and never would have believed they would have seen again, let alone all the way from the east cost to Nevada. Jimmy and the others were in the El Camino, which had a quarter tank of gas in its tank and was useable for a good hundred miles, if not more.

"I still can't believe it's you, Sam," Henry said as he stared out the windshield at the road ahead.

Sam Foree nodded, agreeing with the assessment completely. "I know. In a million years I never thought I'd see you or Mary again." He was a tall black man a little over six feet, with a shaved head and a good physique, his broad shoulders the moist predominant feature. He'd been a roofer before the deadly rains came and had become the leader of the small town of Pittsfield, Virginia. "The last I saw you two, and Jimmy and Cindy, Pittsfield was in ruins and myself and the survivors of the town were driving away as it began to rain."

"So how did you end up in Nevada?" Mary asked. "It's a long way from Virginia."

Sam shrugged. "Once I left Pittsfield, myself and the other refugees began to roam around. Back then there were more walkers, and as you know it wasn't safe to stay anywhere in one place for too long."

Henry nodded, as did Mary. Back then, years ago, things had been very different. For one thing, the rain itself had been infected with the zombie virus. If it touched skin, the host would die immediately to then revive as one of the living dead. But then the rains became safe and only the threat of the zombies had to be dealt with. Back then, a bite from a ghoul wasn't contagious, other than the usual things to be concerned with, such as infection, and was no different from a dog bite. But then the virus mutated within the zombies until to be bitten by one would kill the host in days, to then have them revive as a zombie. It had been a long road to where Henry and the others were now, and though life was far from perfect, there had been hope that the zombies would eventually fade away. But now, with a zombie king leading a massive undead army, it looked like trouble was coming back even harder than before.

"We lost many of our group as time passed," Sam continued. "Months after leaving Pittsfield, there were only twenty of us left. We crossed paths with a local trader and he let us join his convoy. He traveled all across what was left of the United States, trading with towns. Eventually, he ended up in Utah, where the entire convoy was attacked by a large horde of walkers. Only myself and a few others managed to escape in one piece. We wandered then, much like you and your friends, Henry, and eventually we ended up here in Nevada. When I came to Indian Springs to stay for a while and rest, I decided it was a decent place to live and figured I'd stay. The group I was with moved on, leaving me behind. I got a job on the security force and eventually I worked my way up to town leader, much like I did in Pittsfield. And that's it, that's pretty much my story." He glanced at Henry and then Mary. "So how about you two? What brings you and your friends to my part of the country? I saw you have new people in your group, too."

"Yes, there names are Sue and Raven and the boy is Tommy. Sue is the blonde," Mary said "She's Henry's girlfriend, actually."

Sam's eyebrows went up. "Oh really? Good for you, Henry. I have to say I'm envious of you. I haven't met anyone like that, though I've had my share of flings." He glanced at Mary. "What about you, Mary? Are you and Jimmy an item yet?"

"What? Oh God no. Jimmy is with Cindy," she said. "Do you remember Cindy, Sam? She was from Pittsfield, too."

"Sure, I remember her and her uncle who owned a bar," Sam said.

"Listen, Sam, there's more important stuff to deal with right now than a walk down memory lane," Henry said, changing the subject. "Your town is in danger, grave danger, only I don't know if you're gonna believe me when I tell you from what exactly. I have to say, knowing you already may be the icing on the cake. If I had to explain it to someone I'd never met, well, hell, me and the others would probably be branded as nutjobs."

"Well, I know you, Henry," Sam said. "As well as your friends, so if you tell me something, I don't see any reason not to believe you. But you have to understand something. I haven't seen you in years. I have no way of knowing if you're on the level, that you're not working for someone else. Sorry, but it's a hard world and only fools trust another blindly—no offense."

"None taken. I hear you, but still…" Henry began but was cut off.

"So I hear you took out the raiders that have been plaguing my town. That goes a long way with me, by the way," Sam said.

Henry shrugged. "We didn't have a choice, Sam. It was either them or us."

"Sure, and you picked you. I would have done the same." Sam began to slow the pickup as they approached the barrier leading into town.

Unlike many other enclaves Henry had come across that had built tall walls out of either cement or debris, such as old cars and tires, Indian Springs had fifteen foot tall, twin hurricane fences with razor wire on top surrounding it, a six foot space between the fences. Inside the outer fence was wooden scaffolding that went along the fence in both directions. Here, men walked along the platform on guard duty. At the main entrance there were two wooden towers with M-60s, the black muzzles poking out of small windows. With one on each side of the entrance, it created a crossfire that no one could survive, a no man's land kill zone that would be death to any attacker. Any scrub or foliage of any kind had been cleared away from the fence up to twenty feet, so that no enemy could use it as cover or to sneak up on the fence.

Spotlights could be seen as well, but as it was daytime, they were pointed down and not in use. A large, chain-link gate was on wheels so it could be rolled to the side to let any traffic in or out of town, four men with rifles standing guard. It was all very efficient.

"We're here," Sam said. "So what say you save your news till we can all get washed up. That way I can gather my staff and security chief and you can tell everyone at the same time. That way if there are any questions, they can be answered right then and there."

"Well, I really think you should hear me out now," Henry said but Sam wasn't listening.

"Excellent. Once we're inside, I'll have you, Mary and your other friends brought to the main hotel. Wait till you see this place, Henry," Sam beamed proudly. "We have power from solar panels and have tapped underground water. We even have a good stock-pile of fuel, though we try not to use it other than for security patrols outside the perimeter." He talked as if the town was a child and he was its proud father. "You'll see. The people here have managed to make an oasis in the middle of the Nevada desert." He stopped at the gate, the other vehicles pulling up behind him, and began to talk with one of the guards as the gate was opened. While he did, Henry whispered to Mary so Sam couldn't hear: "God, Mary, why won't he listen to me? We don't have time for this shit. Get washed up? Dine with his staff? We need to tell them what's coming so they can prepare."

"I agree with you," she said. "But don't rush this. An hour wasted now so we can ease into it might make all the difference. If we just blurt it out, it's possible Sam might think we're lying or worse, crazy."

"Then he can send a patrol out to investigate."

"Sure, but he won't even bother if he doesn't believe us. I think you need to play diplomat here for the rest of us. All the lives in this town and ours too are depending on us making Sam believe what's coming."

Henry sighed. "Fine, but I don't like it."

She smiled and kissed his cheek, the bristles scratching her lips a little. It reminded her of her father. "I know, but this is one situation that you can't fight your way through. You need to be tactful."

The gate was opened and Sam finished talking to the guard. "You guys looking forward to a shower and a good meal?" he asked Henry and Mary.

"Sure, can't wait," Henry said, speaking for himself and Mary.

Chapter 31

The six companions and Tommy were dropped off at local hotel, getting three rooms total, where they were able to shower and rest until dinner. Sam had called ahead and had picked up the tab so no payment was necessary to the hotel owner.

The toilets worked as well through an elaborate system similar to the Romans, and Jimmy remarked how weird it felt sitting on an actual toilet instead of crouching down in a bush somewhere. Cindy tried to talk to him again, wanting to share something important, but no sooner did she exit the bathroom after showering, than Jimmy was fast asleep in the full-sized bed. She decided to let him sleep. Laying down beside him, she kissed him on his cheek and fell asleep in less than a minute.

Henry and Sue showered together, and after making slow love in the shower, they moved to the bed for round two, then had fallen asleep in each other's arms.

Mary and Raven shared a room with Tommy, and after both women had washed and used the facilities, followed by Tommy, they had all sat together talking, none of them wanting to sleep.

Three hours after being dropped off at the hotel, a man was sent to knock on each of their doors, to then wait and escort them to Sam's home, which sat in the middle of town over an old furniture store. It looked like a New York loft, a wide open space that had been split up into sections depending on what use it was for. In the center of the massive room was a large table where Sam ran town meetings from.

When Henry and the others arrived, and after a brief introduction to the staff of six men and women that Sam ran the town with, dinner was served—fresh roast pork and canned vegetables—and then coffee and dessert—which consisted of apple pie made from canned apples. No one complained and the six companions and Tommy ate heartily.

Each time Henry tried to broach the subject of the undead army, Sam would stop him, telling Henry that they would discuss business when the meal was over. This aggravated Henry to no end, and only Mary sitting on his right—and Sue on his left—stopped him from standing up and exploding, calling everyone at the table a goddamn moron and storming off to let the town fend for itself. But he knew the residents of the town would have no say in what went on at the dinner table, so he held his tongue, despite his right hand curling into a fist in frustration beneath the table. It appeared Sam had become a bureaucrat, as were the six men and women he associated with.

Finally, after the dessert dishes had been cleared away, Sam turned to Henry and said, "So, Henry, you've wanted to tell me something all day. It's time. Just what is this information you simply have to share with me?"

"It's about damn time, Sam," Henry muttered. "We've come to warn you. There's over a thousand deaders coming south to level this place. They've already destroyed that summer camp twenty miles or so from here. Do you know the place?"

"Of course I know of it. A man named Murdock is in charge there. I hear he likes to pretend he's back in the Roman Empire," Sam said with a chuckle, the others on his staff doing the same.

"Yeah, well, not anymore he doesn't," Henry said, keeping the true fate of Murdock a secret. There was no reason to share with Sam that Murdock had died by Henry's hand. The zombie army was more than enough of a reason. "He's dead, as well as everyone else that lived in that place."

There was a low murmur from the six men and women sitting at the table as they talked amongst themselves upon hearing this news, and Sam raised a hand to quiet them.

"That's quite a story, Henry," Sam said. "Like I told you before, only a fool blindly trusts another man without proof. Do you have any proof of this army of the dead? My scouts have seen or heard nothing and surely an army of that size would have been spotted by now."

"Not when it destroys everything in its way. There's no one to tell the tale," Mary said. "But we do have proof, Sam. Tommy here is a survivor from another town. He barely got away. We found him dying of thirst in the desert." She wrapped her arm around Tommy, who was seated beside her.

"Is this true, boy?" Sam asked Tommy.

"Y...yes sir," Timmy stammered, intimidated by the tall black man who was clearly the boss of the town. "The talking zombie killed my family. It's true. I heard him talk myself!"

"No kidding?" Sam said with a grin. "The zombie can talk?"

"It's true," Henry said. "Jimmy and I tried to get back to the camp and see this son-of-a-bitch for ourselves. We figured if we could kill the lead zombie that was somehow in charge then we could end it right there and then, but we couldn't get close enough for a kill shot. We saw him with our own eyes, though. He was shirtless, and I saw him waving his hands around as if he was talking to the deaders, but we were too far away to hear anything. The deaders looked like hell as if they were listening, too."

"He's not lying," Jimmy added. "I saw the fucker, too. He was controlling the deaders like some kind of Messiah."

"Look, Sam," Henry said. "You don't have to believe us but think about it. What would be the reason why I'd lie about something like this? By tonight or tomorrow at the latest, we'll know whether it's true or not. I'm not asking you to risk men or sound an alarm; all I'm saying is fortify your defenses and have all your men on high alert for the time being."

"That'll cost me a lot of money, Henry," Sam said. "Or what we use around here for currency. I'll have to pay a shitload of overtime to my men and spend a lot of the town's resources, plus it'll cause a panic as soon as I spread the word to fortify us, and all in the hopes that you're not making this up for some reason, that you're not from a rival town and trying to trick me somehow. Remember, I haven't seen you or your friends in a very long time. The past is the past. People change."

"You're right, Sam, and you don't have to believe what we're telling you, but think about the ramifications if what we're saying is the truth. Think about the people of this place when more than a thousand deaders show up at your gate? By then it'll be too late to even try to stop them."

Sam sat back and glanced at the other six men and women that made up his staff, searching their faces. "Well, people, do any of you have an opinion about any of this?"

"We'll go along with whatever you decide, Sam," a man with a thick beard and sad eyes said, the other five staff members nodding in agreement.

"You've done a good job of leading us so far," a black woman in her sixties said. "We'll back you whatever you want to do."

Sam stood up. "Thank you, all of you, for having so much faith in me as always. I'll try not to let you down." He looked at Henry, then Jimmy, Cindy and down the line, finally settling his gaze on Tommy. The two locked eyes for almost a full thirty seconds as Sam tried to see into the boy's mind, to decipher if what he said was true and not a story. Finally, Tommy shrank back and their eyes broke contact. "Okay, Henry, I'll do as you say and I'll begin getting our defenses up to snuff even more than they are now as soon as we're done here," Sam said. "But I warn you, if this is a hoax, if you and your friends are up to something that I can't discern right now, even our shared history will be irrelevant."

"I hear you, Sam," Henry said. "You won't regret this."

"Hmmph, I sure as hell hope not."

Chapter 32

It was a little after midnight on the same night Henry had told Sam about the coming undead horde. Surrounded by over two dozen zombies armed with an assortment of firearms, Lazarus climbed to the top of a tall ridge a mile from Indian Springs. The rest of the army was gathered at the bottom of the ridge and in other tactical places, the land behind the ridge covered for more than half a mile with bodies.

Many carried guns and others held melee weapons. If anyone with olfactory senses that still worked had been in the area, the stench of rotten flesh that filled the air from over a thousand zombies would have been overwhelming. Massive clouds of blow-flies filled the sky, resembling thunder clouds, the flies feeding on the undead flesh, laying eggs which in turn became maggots, which became flies, the entire cycle of life taking place over days as the dead army marched across the Nevada desert.

Across the distance, Lazarus admired the twinkling lights of Indian Springs, as the town fortified its defenses, the place was a hive of activity, despite it being well past midnight. Spotlights swept the perimeter in a cross pattern, while men walked along the platform within the hurricane fence. There was so much light it was as if night had never fallen, and inside the town it was still day. No one slept within the small town this night.

"The humans are expecting us," Lazarus said to a zombie by his side. The zombie was once John Cummings, formerly from the small town of Bishop, Nevada. Now John was a mindless creature that was driven by hunger.

"Someone warned the people of that town we were coming it seems," Lazarus said, tapping his chin with a pale finger. "There's no other explanation." Beside him, John drooled like an idiot. Lazarus sighed, "I simply must find some more intelligent friends. I mean, it's nice that you're a good listener, John, but it would be even better if you'd say something once in a while."

John moaned softly, his eyes reflecting the multiple twinkle of lights from the town.

"Yes, I know you want to go there," Lazarus said, telepathically sensing John's feelings, such as they were. All around Lazarus, the other zombies did the same thing, gazing off at the lighted town with hunger. "But we need to wait until tomorrow afternoon. Right now, every man and woman that can hold a gun is on the lookout for my army, but by tomorrow, with the sun at its peak, they'll be growing tired and complacent from their constant hyper-vigilance. Drained after a long night and day of inaction, they'll be even easier to defeat."

John made a soft moaning in reply, the ghoul's fingers flexing, as if John could just reach out and grasp the flickering lights.

Lazarus understood John's needs, the hunger that burned in the pit of his stomach, as it did in the entire party of undead that Lazarus had made come with him to the top of the ridge. It burned inside Lazarus, too, but he held it in check. Not all the zombies had made it to the top, and there were a few mangled bodies at the bottom of the ridge, after rolling down it ass-over-elbow.

Lazarus knew he was the only thing holding the zombies back, from simply moving down the ridge and directly at the town, where they would sub-sequentially be gunned down by the concentrated firepower of the town, even as the zombies attempted to satiate their hunger.

Lazarus spread out his mind and touched the thousand plus of dead soldiers he had at his disposal. He saw the groups of zombies that had been instructed to surround the town from all sides, but were held back, and for now were hidden from sight outside the main perimeter. He told his army that no matter what the humans did, there would be no escape, that no matter how many zombies were killed, Lazarus always would have control of the battlefield. Death was coming to the resident of Indian Springs, whether they liked it or not.

The entire town would sleep on edge this night, expecting an attack that would never come, and then, as the sun beat down on them tomorrow, Lazarus would spring his trap, closing it like a vise over the beleaguered town.

No doubt night patrols would be sent out to search for the coming army. These patrols would be dealt with quickly and quietly, a light snack for his zombies to feed on, and when the patrols didn't return it would only add to the fear suffusing the town.

Lazarus moved in close to John, so close that he could see the maggots squirming in John's nose, the zombie rotting quickly due to the heat.

"Don't worry, John, there'll be victims this night and their blood will be drunk by us all." He sent out a mental picture of the carnage to come and the zombies on the ground shuffled back and forth, as if they were anticipating the coming slaughter. Pale fingers gripped gun butts and gnarled digits flexed on triggers. Lazarus had instructed his army how to use guns and clubs, and though it was a strain to keep his soldiers in check, so far he was doing it. He'd found that the more he used his power, the stronger it became.

He gazed up at the sky and the twinkling stars, the image resembling the town's glinting lights, then back at the town. He laughed and raised his arms over his head. "It's all mine, all I have to do is reach out and take it. Tomorrow the humans will know pain and suffering like they could never imagine, and when we're through, our army will grow in numbers. We're unstoppable. I'm unstoppable." He lowered his arms so that they were level with the ground and opened his hands so that to him it looked like the town was resting in his palms. Then he snapped his hands closed into fists.

Soon, my friends. Soon we will feed, he thought to his army.

All around him and down on the ground stretching out beyond the ridge, every zombie took a step forward in unison, the earth trembling slightly with the impact of more than a thousand pairs of feet.

Lazarus began to laugh maniacally, reveling in his power. Though still a thinking entity, becoming one of the walking dead yet maintaining his thoughts from when he was human had made him completely insane, a psychopath that now controlled thousands of zombies.

Even if Lazarus had been able to realize this and consider his sanity, it was doubtful he would have cared.

Chapter 33

Sam lay awake, staring up at the white ceiling of his bedroom, counting the cracks for the thousandth time. He was alone this night. Most nights he had a woman with him, one of many that found him attractive, whether due to his powerful body or his position in the town. Either way was fine with him. When it came to sex, emotions weren't relevant.

Love was another story but so far he hadn't been able to find a woman that made him feel like a teenager, swooning at the sight of them.

Looking at the glow-in-the-dark hands of the ticking clock on the nightstand beside the bed, he sighed heavily and sat up. Padding to the bathroom, he urinated and washed his face from the pitcher sitting next to the sink, then went back to bed to try and rest.

He knew sleep wouldn't come, not when there was the possibly of an attack by a horde of living dead. He'd left orders with his second-hand man, a fellow by the name of Jake, who did everything for Sam from checking on his laundry to making sure he had enough toilet paper in the bathroom. Jake was in direct contact with the lead guard on the wall, that man in touch with the rest of the watch posts.

Sam had gotten a radio call an hour ago that two patrols were overdue from returning after scouting outside the town. When asked if Sam wanted to send out more patrols to search for the two lost ones, Sam had declined to do so, deciding that enough men had been lost already. Maybe in the day time he would change his mind. Had the patrols been attacked? he wondered. Possibly. Or it could be a simple breakdown of their vehicles, but the odds that both cars would go down and no radio contact from either, well, that was highly improbable.

He shook his head, trying to shake the memories of when he'd been in Pittsfield free, remembering when the entire town had been overrun by zombies. Was it possible it was going to happen again? Was Henry correct that a massive undead army was coming right for his town? Surely having a town that Sam was in charge of wiped out by the living dead was a once in a lifetime event.

Time passed fitfully and soon Sam was gazing out of the floor-to-ceiling window across the room at the newly-born sunrise just beginning to spill into the loft. Other than a few calls from outside as men communicated with one another on fortifying the towns defenses, there had been no gunshots, no screams of fear. There had been no attack this past night, no one had come to wake him and now it was dawn.

Had Henry been lying to him? Was it all a hoax of some kind? Sam couldn't fathom what would be Henry's end game but here it was morning and no attack.

Deciding there was no use staying in bed any longer, he got up and dressed, then headed out into the town to check on things. He made his way to the main gate, where his head security chief, Frank was overseeing the men. Frank looked exhausted, bags under his eyes, and Sam knew the man had been up all night.

"Sam, it's good to see you," Frank said when he spotted the boss of the town coming his way.

Sam was wearing his Colt Python on his right hip, his pockets full of extra rounds. "Morning, Frank, I take it you had a quiet night."

"Yes, sir," Frank said, the two men shaking hands. "Other than the two patrols not returning and a report of gunfire from the north quadrant, it's been quiet—too quiet."

Jake ran up holding a cup of coffee and handed it to Sam, who nodded thank you and took it. That was Jake; like a ghost the man would appear, giving Sam exactly what he wanted. Sam swore the man could read his mind sometimes.

"No one saw anything, no attack at all?" Sam asked.

"No, sir, and even the reported gunfire could have been thunderclaps from heat lightning," Frank said. "Some was spotted around the same time the gunfire was reported."

"What about the two patrols? Opinions?" Sam asked Frank, who shrugged his shoulders.

"Don't know, sir. You said the new arrivals took care of the raiders so it's probably not them that ambushed our men, but then if not the raiders, who?"

"That's what I was thinking. Okay, if they're not back by noon, send out a search party. Tell them not to engage anyone they find out there, but to report back as soon as they find the missing patrols."

"Yes, sir, I'll see to it."

"Where are Henry and his friends?" Sam asked.

Jake spoke up this time. "They're at the south wall, helping with the defenses."

"Good, then that's where I'll be. Henry and I have some things to discuss. Zombie army my black ass." He headed off, leaving Jake and Frank to watch him go before each man turned and went off in different directions.

Lazarus lay on his back on the ground near the town of Indian Springs, satisfied with the way his plan was taking form. He was covered in dried mud and nearly invisible to the naked eye. The morning sun beat down on him, cooking him, but he felt nothing, for only the living knew discomfort. In his hand was a .45 pistol, taken from some unknown killed victim.

Reaching out with his mind, he stared out of the eyes of thousands of zombies, his mind collating the images and processing them into one massive picture.

It had taken hours for his army to slowly creep up on the town, all of them crawling across the ground, their bodies camouflaged with mud and scrub brush. Some zombies were buried six inches deep in the dirt, covered up by others. It had been a wonderful idea when it came to him and he filled with pride even now to see it come to fruition.

Though very close to the perimeter fence, the bodies were hidden in plain sight, as they blended perfectly into the environment, and unless one of the guards walking the perimeter fence looked in exactly the right place and knew what to search for, his army was all but invisible. He had put them there the previous night, using the cover of darkness to move them closer to the town. Now they laid in wait, and only Lazarus' willpower prevented them from getting up and attacking the town. Seeing the humans on the fence, the zombies wanted to feed, only Lazarus mind holding them in check.

With the sun having risen a few hours ago, it was nearly time to drop the hammer on Indian Springs, and Lazarus savored the anticipation.

He knew the best way to overtake the town was to form a concentrated attack on one section of the fence near the main gate with most of his army, and at the same time have smaller groups of zombies attacking other sections of the perimeter fence to draw firepower away from his true target.

Once the fence was knocked down and the perimeter breached, his army could swarm inside and begin the slaughter; there would be nothing that could stop him. It would be an absolute victory for him, as it had been each time he'd taken an enclave.

A tremor ran through his hidden undead army as they fought to be free of Lazarus' will and attack the town of humans, wanting to feed so badly it was all they could think of in their befuddled brains.

He strained to hold them back, his mind pushed to the breaking point. This was the first time he had to control so many minds, and he found it hard to concentrate as he maintained control.

Lazarus sent out a thought, telling them to wait just a little longer. He did this for two reasons. The first was so that his soldiers could attack at the most optimum time, when the sun was at its peak and roasting the heads of the humans as they worked outside.

The second reason was all too personal. He held them back because he didn't want their lives wasted as cannon fodder; he did it because he loved them. They were his people and it was his job to protect them from themselves. If he made them wait for the appropriate time, then many more would be saved from being gunned down and the victory would be all but guaranteed.

It was almost time, and as the leader of his people, he would lead them into battle to destroy their enemies.

Chapter 34

Sam found Henry and the rest of the companions exactly where he'd been told they were: at the south wall. Tommy had been given to a husband and wife that had lost their son a few years ago from pneumonia. The couple were more than happy to take in Tommy. Sue had been sad to see the boy go, but she knew the life the companions led was not good for a young boy. With a hug and a kiss, she had bid the boy farewell.

Henry and Jimmy were directing men on how to set up a cross-fire when Henry spotted Sam. He told the men he'd be with them shortly and walked over to Sam, Jimmy right behind him. The rest of the companions were busy doing whatever they could to help fortify the town's defenses.

"Morning, Sam, sleep well?" Henry asked.

"Of course not," Sam replied. "I laid awake all night waiting for the alarm of this so-called impending attack. How about you?"

"Jimmy and I grabbed a few hours around two this morning, same with Mary and the others," Henry said. "We'd been going hard and fast for days, and it finally caught up with us. If we hadn't slept when we did, we would've probably fallen over from exhaustion."

Sam only nodded at this, his mouth set into a deep frown.

"They'll be here, Sam," Henry said. "They're coming; the only question is when."

"If you saw what we saw, Sam," Jimmy added. "You'd know it's true."

"Yes, but I didn't see what you saw, Jimmy, which is why I'm so skeptical," Sam said angrily. "The entire town is in chaos, women are holding their children closely, terrified of this coming attack. No work is being done other than fortifying our defenses. And it looks like it's all been for nothing. I knew I shouldn't have listened to you. A talking zombie," he scoffed. "It's ridiculous even to say it out loud."

The blonde-haired man the companions had first met on the road walked up and joined the discussion. "I recommend I take a patrol out to see what's going on out there, Sam. Surely if this massive army is coming, I should be able to see some sign of it."

"That's a good idea, Mike," Sam said. "Gather three men of your choosing and set off at once."

Mike nodded and ran off, calling out to men he trusted, that could handle themselves in a fight.

"You think that's wise?" Henry asked. "I heard two patrols didn't come back last night."

"Maybe they deserted," Jimmy suggested. "At the thought of a massive deader horde, they just took off and never looked back."

"My men wouldn't do that, Jimmy," Sam said, his eyes creasing in defiance of his men. "My men are loyal."

"Sure they are. All men are loyal till they're not anymore," Jimmy said sarcastically.

Sam glared at Jimmy but he didn't reply, then he looked at Henry and said, "Come with me to the main gate, Henry. We'll watch Mike and his boys head off. Who knows, maybe they'll report back with some news this time."

"Fine, just let me gather Mary and the others and we'll meet you there in a few minutes."

"Okay, Henry, but don't keep me waiting." Sam turned and strode off, not waiting for a reply.

Henry and Jimmy watched him go.

"Does Sam seem different from when we last saw him?" Jimmy asked.

"A little. He's a bit more intense now," Henry said. "This world will do that to a man. Hell, Jimmy, none of us are the same people we were back when the shit hit the fan and the world went into the crapper."

Jimmy smiled. "Hey, speak for yourself. I'm still the awesome Jimmy Cooper that everyone knows and loves. In fact, I'm like a fine wine; I've only gotten better with age."

Henry flashed Jimmy a sideways glance, seeing that Jimmy meant what he said, standing tall, his ego in full swing.

"That's your problem right there, buddy," Henry said. "You believe your own hype. Come on, let's get the girls and meet up with Sam." He turned and walked away, leaving Jimmy alone.

"My own hype?" Jimmy said to Henry's retreating back, though low enough so that Henry wouldn't hear. "Shit, I'm fucking awesome; you're just too damn old to appreciate just how much." Then he followed Henry, pouting slightly from his rebuke.

Fifteen minutes later, the patrol exited the main gate. Up on the platform, Henry, Jimmy and Cindy watched it depart. Down on the ground, Mary, Sue and Raven waited, talking while sitting in the shade of the platform.

The pickup truck didn't stick to the road, but veered off to go into the desert in the direction the summer camp was located. The plan was to drive there and see if there was any activity. But as soon as the pickup turned off the road and began bouncing over the rough terrain of dirt and rocks, it became stuck in the dirt, the rear tire spinning and spitting small rocks and soil.

"Shit, we're stuck," the driver said to Mike, who was sitting beside him. In the rear bed the other two men waited.

"What do you mean, we're stuck?" Mike asked. "Stuck in what?"

"How the hell do I know," the driver replied. "Must be a sink-hole or something."

"Just gun it and get us free."

The driver did as he was told, the rear tire spinning even faster.

Back at the main gate on the platform, Sam watched the pickup come to a halt. "What's Mike doing? They've stopped," Sam said

Henry was studying the vehicle through his own binoculars. "I think they're stuck in the dirt, maybe a sinkhole or something." He studied the surrounding terrain, frowning. "Is it me or does the ground look weird out there."

"It's you," Jimmy said, his eyes not seeing what Henry did as he had nothing to magnify the land with. "Looks fine to me."

The pickup truck spun its rear wheel faster, the engine redlining, but it wouldn't break free, the rear end sinking even more. Then red splatter began to shoot out of the sinkhole instead of dirt, painting the ground behind the vehicle dark red.

Sam blinked as he watched, not understanding what he was seeing. "What the hell is that?"

"I don't know but it isn't good," Henry said, starting to get a bad feeling, though he didn't know why. It had to do with the terrain. It did look different now that he studied it but he couldn't put his finger on the exact reason. Was the land more uneven than before? In the pickup, the rear tire ceased spinning and Mike hopped out of the cab to inspect the rear end. When he bent down to examine the hole the tire was trapped in, his eyes went wide when he saw the gaping cavity of a body, the tire having eaten through the rib cage and into the organs to then splatter the churned guts out behind it.

"What the hell?" Mike said, not comprehending what he was seeing. He slid to the side some and his eyes followed the body to where shoulders could be seen. It was as he stared at this spot that the dirt shifted slightly and a face appeared.

"So what's the verdict, Mike?" one of the men in the rear bed asked. "Are we going to have to push or what?"

Mike was about to reply when the face suddenly sprouted eyes that popped wide open to glare at Mike. The mouth opened next, yellow teeth gleaming in the sun, as an arm reached out and grabbed Mike's lower leg. Mike screamed in shock, surprised by a moving body with no insides reaching out and grabbing him. He jumped back and fell onto his butt, the arm ripping free of its socket from his weight.

"Mike, what going on?" the driver called. "Should I step on the gas again?"

Mike was about to reply, to tell the men to get out of the pickup, that there was something very wrong with this picture, when all around the vehicle, the ground began to shift and move on its own, bodies spewing forth as if the very land was birthing them.

Up on the platform, Sam, Henry, Jimmy and every guard stood in amazement, barely able to believe what they were witnessing.

"Oh my God," Sam gasped. "What's happening out there?"

Henry pieced it all together in seconds and he didn't like what the end result was. "What's happening is the reason we haven't seen an army of deaders coming for the town. It's because they're already here. They've been hiding in the ground. They must have crept up on us last night and dug in when it got dark."

"But that's impossible," Sam said. "That would mean they were thinking beings, and that they were able to stay that way until given a signal to move."

"That's what I told you, Sam," Henry said. "The deaders are being controlled by an intelligent leader. One that can think and reason." No one on the fence platform had fired a shot at the zombie army; they were too amazed at the sight before them. All around the town perimeter, bodies slowly rose from the ground, particles of dust cascading off their clothes. It was possible if the zombies had remained still, standing tall, but not moving, that the staring match would have continued indefinitely, but then one zombie near the front of the line raised an assault rifle and aimed it at the platform where a group of guards stood dumbfounded.

All was silent before the zombie squeezed the trigger, then all hell broke lose as the ghoul began spraying bullets back and forth, taking out half the guards before the rest ducked for cover. But then, like a signal had been given, as the first shots echoed off into the desert, every zombie holding a firearm began to shoot, and with a loud moan that resembled a war cry, they began to march at the town, firing as they walked.

Henry, Jimmy and Sam dropped to the wooden platform as bullets zipped by overhead.

"What the hell!" Sam yelled. "They can use guns!"

"It's news to me but not that surprising," Henry said.

Sam saw that some of his men weren't shooting back, but were hiding behind blast shields. "Fire at will, everyone, commence firing! Pass it down the line. Shoot those damn walkers!"

Frank could be heard bellowing at his men to begin firing, while other men used the few hand grenades saved for just such a dire need. Explosions ripped through the zombie force as the animated corpses stumbled forward, the undead enemy heedless of bullet or explosions. Mike and the men on his patrol had been taken down quickly, bodies swarming over them until the men were lost from sight. All four men were torn apart and fed on within seconds.

"Shit, Henry, what the fuck do we do?" Jimmy called out, holding his shotgun tightly in his hands.

"We kill the enemy, that's what," Henry said. He rose up and began firing with his assault rifle. When the magazine went dry, he let the rifle hang down by his side from its shoulder strap, pulled his Glock, and began firing again. "We have to hold them back or everyone in this town is dead—including us!"

Chapter 35

Lazarus hanged back and watched his army surge forward, shooting as they covered the distance to the main gate. He hadn't wanted to spring the trap so early in the day but there had been no choice. The patrol had ruined everything. When the zombie under the rear tire of the pickup had opened its eyes, Lazarus had seen through those eyes, too, and had watched the man shrink back in fear and amazement.

Then it was time to act, before more men came out of the town to investigate. But he wasn't worried, surprise was still on his side, and as he watched his army rise from the ground, and saw the men lined up on the platform staring in shock, he knew the battle would be his eventually.

Molotov cocktails made of gasoline and pork fat were thrown from the platform to douse the zombies in liquid fire. The zombies flailed and moaned as they burned, their dry clothes catching easily.

Lazarus could feel the imaginary flames on his body as he reached out and touched the minds of his burning followers, then he closed it off quickly. Though the fire didn't hurt him in a human sense, memories of his old life were still there and when he was human, being consumed by fire would have been excruciating.

Once the initial wave of zombies reached the main gate, it split up into three sections, while above the M-60s fired into the shifting bodies, blowing many to pieces and severing the arms and legs of others. Just as he planned, the guns swiveled to try and destroy the separate parties, and that was when he sent even more of his undead soldiers at the gate, swarming against and pushing on it. But the humans were smart and a transit bus was driven in front of the gate to reinforce it.

Though the fence buckled, it did not give and the zombies pressed up tight against the chain-links began to be crushed, the force of the pressure behind them actually making the brittle flesh on their bodies slide through the links to fall onto the ground inside the perimeter in bloody chunks.

Lazarus directed his zombies to shoot at the twin gun towers, the barrage of bullets making the men inside stop firing and duck for cover. He sent a mental command for his force to charge forward, and they did as they were told, heedless of bodily harm. More Molotovs and grenades were thrown from the platform behind the fence, blowing wide holes in the zombie horde, which caused the surge to weaken. Body parts and blood rained down on the undead army, coating them in gore.

Lazarus wasn't happy, and seeing that though he might win eventually, his losses would be so great that it would be a detriment to his plans of world domination.

He sent out a telepathic link to his army and rallied his troops, sending them surging forward one more time, only this time as well he was rebuked. This went on for more than an hour of continual fighting but he couldn't break into the town. He knew that if his army stayed out in the open for much longer, it would be annihilated by the humans' superior firepower, either by fire or explosions.

Frustrated at the loss of so many of his followers, he sent a mental order for a retreat. He needed to reformulate his plans. This town had been ready for his dead army and in so doing, had been able to thwart his advances. He needed to think. To come up with another plan, for brute force wasn't enough to destroy the town.

His army fell back but only so far, and Lazarus instructed them to make a ring around the entire town, thereby blockading it. No help would be coming thanks to a messenger trying to sneak out of the town under cover of night.

On the platform along the fence near the main gate, a few shots rang out. Lazarus made his zombies hold their fire. They weren't good shots at the best of times, and they were too far away to do any damage even if they could.

Making sure to stay out of sight himself, Lazarus began moving through the rear force of his army as he stared at the town with hatred in his eyes, trying to come up with a better idea on how to take it.

One advantage he had that the humans didn't was that he had all the time in the world, and if he had to, he could wait months if not years and starve the town out.

Sooner or later the town would be his; it was just a matter of time.

"They've retreated," Sam said, watching the zombies moving away from the fence.

"Yes, but they're not leaving completely, it looks like they're only pulling back to regroup," Henry said.

"Come on, let's go to the gate and see how it looks," Sam said and turned and climbed down off the platform, the companions following right behind him.

Mary, Sue and Raven joined Henry, Jimmy, Cindy and Sam by the main gate. All around the gate, the odor of burning bodies was strong, mixed with the offal of blown-apart bodies. Everywhere they looked, there was nothing but blood and body parts, corpses piled ten high.

Sam was talking into a two-way radio as he received reports from other posts across the town. When he had heard the last one, he lowered the radio and looked at Henry and the others. "My God, they have us surrounded. I have reports of bodies thirty deep on all sides."

"At least they couldn't get inside with us," Jimmy said hopefully. "We can be thankful for that."

"That's true," Sam said. "But we lost a lot of men. Those walkers may not be the best shots in the world but by luck alone they managed to shoot too many people for my liking." He shook his head. "I still don't believe that walkers are using guns. It's incredible." He saw that Henry was looking out at the undead army with binoculars. He seemed focused on something. "What's up, Henry?"

"I don't think they're doing it on their own. Normally they could never use guns," Henry said. "I've been watching one of the deaders, the same one I saw back at the summer camp, the one I think is their leader. He's definitely somehow able to control the rest of 'em, though for the life of me I have no idea how he's doing it."

"Then let's take the fucker out," Jimmy said. "Maybe this time we can hit him."

Henry shook his head, but never stopped looking through the binoculars. "No, Jimmy, he's too far out of range and he's always hiding behind other deaders. I think he knows we might try to pick him off. The bastard's smart all right. Too smart. Still, we could try." He lowered the binoculars and looked at Sam. "Do you have any sniper rifles in town? Something with range and accuracy to take the bastard out?"

"No, I wish we did," Sam replied. "We had some in the armory of the town's police force long ago but they're long gone now. Probably taken with the cops who bugged out and decided not to stay and try and help get things under control."

"Damn it, that would have solved all our problems right then and there," Henry said. "Well, it looks like some of the deaders are still in range of us though. Tell any of your sharpshooters to start picking them off. Any we take down now will be ones we won't have to deal with later."

"Sounds like a good idea," Sam said and got on the two-way radio to give the instructions. A few seconds later, sporadic gunshots rang out as guards took potshots at the closest zombies.

"How long can they keep this up, the siege I mean?" Sue asked.

"Well, they're dead, so like...forever," Jimmy said.

"Maybe they can but we can't," Sam said. "We only have so much food to go around. The town was never set up to handle a siege of this magnitude. We don't have that much food stockpiled as we trade with other towns for our supplies, though we do have all the water we need thanks to the underground wells."

"How much food do you have exactly?" Mary asked.

Sam thought for a moment, tallying figures in his head. "A week or so. Longer if we begin rationing."

"That's probably not a bad idea," Cindy said.

Sam got on the two-way radio and called Frank, then gave the man instructions to begin the rationing of food until further notice.

"What about sending someone to one of the closer towns for help?" Mary suggested to Sam, who shook his head sadly.

"I'd like to," Sam said, "but we're totally surrounded. A messenger wouldn't make it a hundred feet out there before being surrounded. We're totally cut off from help."

Henry had been silent while looking through the binoculars again, letting the others talk around him, but his face had taken on a certain look that Mary knew well.

Mary saw this and tapped his shoulder. "I know that look, Henry. You're coming up with a plan."

"What is it?" Cindy asked.

"Yeah, spill it, old man," Jimmy added.

Henry peered through the binoculars for ten more seconds while everyone watched him, then he lowered his arms and looked at Sam, then Jimmy, Mary and the others one at a time. His gaze fell on Mary again and he said, "Yeah, Mary, you're right, I do have an idea on how we might be able to end this siege, but it's more of something to do as a last resort, not now when things have just begun."

"So, spill it anyway," Jimmy prodded.

Henry shook his head. "No, not yet. My idea would be suicide for the man who did it. I'll keep this to myself for now."

"You know, Henry, I could make you tell me your idea," Sam said.

Henry smiled. "Well, Sam, you could try."

Chapter 36

Three days later and there was no end in sight to the siege.

The zombie army had attacked Indian Springs three more times, one time each day, but they were forced back each time. The problem was more zombies were arriving each day, attracted to the noise of the battle.

To prevent the bodies from being used as steps to gain access to the top of the fence, Molotovs had been thrown at the corpses, and in so doing, funeral pyres were burning twenty-four hours a day. The smell of burning flesh suffused the air, and no matter where someone was in the town, the stench was always there.

Sam held a war meeting on the status of the town on the end of the third day. The news wasn't good. Food stores were down by half, which wasn't bad, but the worst part was how low on ammunition the town was. After three days of battle, bullets were already at a premium and only a few grenades were left, and those used only in the direst of circumstances.

More men had been killed in defense of the town and now mothers and young sons manned the perimeter fence. In a few more days, anyone who could hold a gun would be conscripted. Morale was low, and most people in the town had come to accept that soon they would die and that the siege was only prolonging the inevitable.

Sam tried to muster morale but there was really nothing he could do. Even if he wanted to lie about the town's predicament, all anyone had to do was look out past the fence and see the undead army to know the situation.

On the morning of the fourth day, the companions were having a sparse breakfast when a runner came to them. He was a young boy of no more than thirteen with wavy brown hair and freckles. "Sam wants you people at the main gate right now," the boy said.

"Why, is there another attack?" Mary asked, dropping a biscuit covered in a teaspoon of honey. The jar was empty, the teaspoon being the last of it. With so many mouths to feed, items were running out by the hour.

"He didn't say, he just told me to get you there on the double," the boy said, then ran off to tell others the same thing.

Gathering their gear, the companions went to Sam. As they walked, they took in their surroundings.

"People look scared," Cindy said as they walked.

"Can you blame them?" Mary asked.

"If we can't end this siege soon we're all in big trouble," Henry said. "Not only is starvation an issue, but there's the concern of people freaking out and trying to run for it. All it takes is for one fool to try and slip out of the town to let in the deaders by the hundreds."

When they arrived at the main gate, the group climbed the ladder to the platform to join Sam and Frank. There, the companions were greeted by another sight they thought they'd never see.

Fifty feet from the gate stood ten zombies, each one holding a small white flag mounted to a stick—the material made from an old shirt. All were shirtless, their pale skin soaking up the sun's rays like a sponge. All around the ghouls, bodies were still strewn about. The fires had gone out and now only smoked fitfully. Buzzards were everywhere, hopping from corpse to corpse, feeding on the decayed meat. Ants swarmed over bloody bodies, feeding on the putrefied flesh, then taking small chunks back to their ant holes. The circle of life was continuing even here on a battlefield of death.

One of the zombies from the group took ten steps forward while waving its white flag, and when no shots rang out, it moved another five feet.

"Humans," the zombie said in a gravelly voice, barely more than a whisper. "I am Lazarus. I control the army of the dead and I'm feeling merciful this day. Throw down your weapons and open the gate, let us in. I promise you a swift death. But be warned, continue to defy me and you will all suffer more pain than any of you could ever imagine."

Sam looked at Frank and then Henry. "I don't believe it," he said. "That zombie is talking. It's actually talking." His mouth hung open slightly as he stared at the ghoul holding the white flag.

"Watson, is that the lead walker you told us about?" Frank asked.

Henry shook his head as he gazed down at the lone zombie. "I can't tell. It could be. The one I saw was shirtless, but so are all of them."

"The fucker's holding a white flag, are we really gonna honor that?" Jimmy asked. "I mean, it's a goddamn deader."

Sam stared at the zombie as it waited patiently for his answer. He scratched his chin and made a decision. "No, we're not, to hell with that. Frank, tell one of your best shots to take that bastard out. A head shot if possible."

"Will do, Boss," Frank said and began talking into a two-way radio.

Seconds passed, only the sounds of a town in peril carrying into the air behind the companions, then one shot rang out from the second tower.

The zombie's head snapped back and it dropped to the ground, brain matter glistening in the sun as it spread out on the dry dirt.

No one moved, everyone waiting with held breath to see what would happen next.

After a full three minutes passed uneventfully, another zombie from the pack of ten stepped out and walked forward, waving the white flag before it. When it reached the prone, head shot zombie, it stopped and looked up at the platform of men.

"Humans," the zombie said in an equally gravely voice. "I am Lazarus..." The zombie repeated the same speech verbatim and then stood there silently, waiting for a response.

"What the hell do you make of that?" Sam said to Henry and Frank.

"Ventriloquism?" Frank wondered.

"No, it's not that," Henry said.

"Then what is it?" Jimmy asked.

"That's the million dollar question, isn't it," Henry said.

"What do you want me to do, Boss?" Frank asked Sam.

"Take that one out, too," Sam said.

Frank spoke into the radio and a second later another shot rang out, the zombie slumping to the ground with a hole in its head.

"But the white flag," Sue said, believing they were breaking protocol. "Maybe we should honor it."

"To hell with the white flag. The flag is for humans, not zombies. I'll be damned if I'll negotiate with a dead thing," Sam said angrily and Sue took a step back, feeling she'd overstepped her bounds.

Henry reached out and touched Sue's arm, nodding to her that it was okay. She smiled wanly and crossed her arms over her chest protectively.

Everyone waited nervously to see what would happen next, and a few seconds later, another shirtless zombie broke from the group and walked up to its fallen brethren, another white flag held in its hand, the material fluttering in the wind. On closer inspection, there was dark spots of dried blood on the flag.

"Humans, I am Lazarus. I control..." the zombie began but was abruptly cut off by Sam, who signaled Frank to have the ghoul killed.

"That's it," Sam said from the platform. "Frank, have tower one take out the rest of them."

Frank spoke in the two-way radio and a second later the M-60 in tower one began to chatter, the heavy rounds digging up the ground before striking the zombies.

The bodies were blown apart by the barrage, limbs flying off, torsos exploding outward from each bullet, the white flags they held going off in all directions. The M-60 fired for a full five seconds and when it ceased, all the zombies were down and in bloody pieces, barely recognizable as once being human.

No one said a word, everyone waiting to see what would happen next.

Finally, from the crowd of zombies standing out of range of the gunfire, one more zombie appeared. This one was a child of no more than five, with long brown hair and a cherub's face, even though the boy had been dead for weeks and rot had set in. Slowly, its small legs carried it across the uneven terrain until it reached the seven dead zombies with flags, then it walked around the bodies and only stopped when it was standing in the center of the first three fallen emissaries.

"You've made your choice, humans, and it's the wrong one. Now prepare to die," the small voice said, sounding sweet and innocent despite coming from a dead thing.

Henry stepped up to the edge of the platform and leveled his assault rifle at the small ghoul, then fired on full auto. The small body danced as slugs struck it in the groin and worked their way up the tiny chest, finally hitting the neck and head. The body was blown backwards, where it landed in a heap of gore and cracked bones.

"That's our answer!" Henry yelled. "Keep on sending them and we'll keep on putting them down!"

Another zombie stepped forward from the crowd, and when it reached the lump of meat that was the child, it said, "Look around you, humans. My army is growing every minute as more undead followers come to me from miles around. You can't last forever, sooner or later you'll die from hunger, but before that you'll be too weak to fight. Then I'll simply come in and take the town and the humans within it. But I won't be so forgiving then. If you want mercy, give up now and let me in, embrace death, it's not the end, it's only the beginning."

"Kill that bastard," Sam hissed and Frank relayed the order, the zombie being taken down with a head shot a moment later. "Tell them to shoot at will from now on, too. I'm done talking with dead things." Sam turned and left the platform, climbing down to the ground, where he took a meeting with some people of the town.

A minute after the zombie was killed, another came out of the crowd and began walking towards the main gate. This one barely made it halfway before it was killed.

Another appeared and that one was shot the instant it was within range of the marksman's bullets. The answer was clear, the town was done talking.

After five more zombies made an attempt to reach the gate and were sub-sequentially destroyed, the ritual finally stopped.

From his place in the back of the battlefield, hidden behind a crowd of his brethren, Lazarus frowned deeply as the last of his envoys were killed.

He'd just learned the trick of using his ghouls as a mouthpiece and had wanted to try it out. He'd never really believed the humans would have agreed to his terms but it didn't hurt to try anyway. Each time he experimented with his powers he found out even more about them.

Which only went to show how truly great he was. He knew it was true that he was destined to rule the world. Only before he continued his dominion, he had to deal with the annoying town of Indian Springs.

Once more he sent his army at the town, an ocean of undead flesh swarming at the gate and surrounding the hurricane fence topped with razor wire. The battle was brief, lasting only a half hour, before Lazarus once more pulled back his army.

As his followers retreated, hundreds more of his army that had been destroyed were left to rot on the ground, feeding the buzzards with new kills.

Flames burned anew as corpses smoldered and cracked in the heat of the fires, and there were new holes blasted in the ground where grenades had gone off. Bodies looked as if they had been tossed into meat grinders, the M-60s having done their job well. As the zombies pulled back, the smoke was lifted by the wind and blown high into the sky.

Though he had lost many of his soldiers he also knew he was slowly whittling away at the town's resources. Their ammunition wasn't infinite and sooner or later they would run out. When that happened, Lazarus would send his army forth again and this time there would be no stopping it.

When that time came, he would be victorious, and the humans would die painfully before joining his undead army as new recruits.

But he knew he would be here for a while so he decided it was time he had a proper throne. Sending out a telepathic signal to some of his soldiers, he instructed them on where to find the parts to make the throne, then he sat down on a boulder and contemplated his next move.

Chapter 37

As the undead horde fell back yet again to lick its wounds, the town took stock of its supplies. In a meeting at Sam's home, Henry, Jimmy, Frank and a few others of Sam's trusted staff sat at his dinner table. Because there were only so many seats at the table, Mary, Cindy, Sue and Raven sat off to the side, watching the meeting and talking amongst themselves. If some of Sam's staff hadn't been women, she would have protested that they had been made to sit off to the side because they were female. She was almost disappointed that she wasn't able to voice her opinion.

"We're dangerously low on ammo," Frank said. "If they attack again, it's highly likely that we'll run out of ammo and grenades in the middle of the fight."

"Damn it," Sam growled, slamming his right hand palm down on the table, causing everything on it to jump half an inch. "This can't be happening."

"I'm afraid I have more bad news for you, Sam," one of his staff said, a man with dark hair and a thick mustache. He looked Palestinian or perhaps Serbian with his dark skin and thin lips. "Our food stores are even lower than we first thought. Weevils have gotten into the wheat and flour reserves. It's all inedible."

"Christ, what else can go wrong?" Sam yelled before calming down, knowing he needed to keep a level head to deal with the present crisis. "How much food do we have left then?"

The man shrugged. "If we cut rations by a third we'll have enough for four more days."

"And by that time we'll all be too weak from hunger to be able to fight the deaders off," Henry said, frowning. "We're all expending a maximum amount of energy in each battle, most of us going without sleep, and we're taking in a fraction of the calories we need to survive. We can't keep waiting for someone to come and save us; it's pretty obvious that's not going to happen. We're on our own here."

"Tell me something I don't know, Henry," Sam said. "What I need is a solution to this problem. We have thousands of walkers out there and no way to destroy them all."

"Maybe we don't have to kill them all," Henry said.

"What does that mean?" Sam asked.

"It means that I came up with an idea a few days ago on how to end this siege, but I wasn't about to try it then. See, it's probably a suicide mission," Henry said tentatively.

"Well, let's hear it first and then I'll make my decision," Sam said. "At the moment we're out of options."

Henry quickly laid out his plan, and when Sue heard it, she jumped up and ran to him. "You're not really thinking of doing that, are you? You can't, it's insane," she cried out, the concern on her face apparent to everyone who looked upon her.

"It's my idea, Sue," Henry said. "I can't make anyone else go but me."

"That's a hell of a plan, Henry," Sam said, shaking his head. "It's damn ballsy of you. But do you really think it'll work?"

"Well, shit, Sam, there's no guarantees, but I can't think of any other way to end this. Hell, I'll take any other ideas if someone has them. I'm not looking to be a martyr here."

"If you do this, you're not going it alone, old man," Jimmy said. "You'll need help; eyes to watch your back."

Henry turned in his chair and looked Jimmy in the eyes. "Thanks, pal. I'd be lying if I said I didn't want you there with me guarding my back, but you need to stay here and keep the girls safe."

Mary stood up and joined Sue, as did Cindy.

"We don't need Jimmy to take care of us, Henry, but that's beside the point," Mary said. "You're not really considering doing this? Why, the chances of you making it in and out of there alive is incredible."

"Well, we are near Las Vegas, what better place to beat the odds than here?" Henry said with a slight grin. "How is Vegas, Sam, what's it look like?"

"It's covered in sand and filled with nothing but walkers, a ghost town. It fell quickly when the rains came," Sam explained.

"Don't you try and change the subject, Henry, and don't you smile and pretend this isn't serious," Sue said. "This is life and death here and I don't want to lose you."

"Perhaps, Sue, but if we don't try Henry's idea, sooner or later we're all going to starve," Sam said. "Or worse, the perimeter will be breached, and as you know, there's no way in hell we can stop that tide of dead flesh once we run out of ammunition." He locked gazes with Henry. "Your idea is crazy, I'll give you that, Henry, but if there's a snowball's chance in hell that it might work, I say go for it."

"But he can't, it's..." Sue began but Henry cut her off.

"No, Sue, I've given this a lot of thought, trust me when I tell you this," Henry said, his voice low. "If there was no chance in hell of this working then I wouldn't even consider it, but I've been watching the deaders out there. I think it'll work."

"But we've never tried something like this before," Mary said. "How do we know the deaders won't recognize you as food?"

He sighed. "That's the chance I'll have to take."

"When do you want to do this?" Sam asked.

"As soon as possible," Henry replied. "Delaying will only add to the pressure of waiting. Besides, if I fail, then it gives you more time to try and come up with another plan of action."

"Well, you're not going in there alone, Henry," Sam said. "I'll send two of my men with you. You'll need them. I'll tell Frank to ask for two volunteers."

"One volunteer," Frank said. "I'm going, too."

"So am I," Raven said, finally speaking up.

"What?" Sue said. "Raven, no, you can't."

"Yes I can, Sue," she said. "I'm fast, Henry will need that." She crossed her arms over her chest and set her jaw. "I'm going and that's final."

"No, Raven, you can't go," Sue protested feebly, but Henry put a hand on her arm.

"Sue, she's right," he said softly. "If someone has to accompany me, Raven is the best one for the job. She's small and fast and if I fail, she's the next best chance to complete the mission."

Sue was crying now. "But what if neither of you comes back? Henry, I can't lose you, not after finding you."

Sam cleared his throat. "Henry, why don't we give you, Sue and your other friends the room so you can talk about this some more, it seems there's some disagreement within your ranks. I have to make my rounds on the perimeter fence, see how the men are doing, and my staff has other chores that need attending."

"Thank you, Sam, that would be much appreciated," Henry said.

Sam stood up, as did his staff, and they began shuffling out of the room. When Sam was at the doorway with Frank by his side, he paused and glanced back at Henry. "Oh, one thing before Frank and I go."

"Yeah?"

"When did you want to do this thing?" Sam asked.

"Tonight, right after it gets dark. No reason to hold off any longer than needed," Henry said. His attention focused on Frank and he said, "Frank, can you get us all the equipment we'll need to make this happen?"

Frank chuckled. "That's not the problem, hell, there's more than we need lying all over the place; the problem is putting it on us."

"One thing at a time," Henry said. "They say you can get used to any smell after a while, I guess we'll put that to the test."

"Yeah, I guess we will. See you in a few hours," Frank said and left. Sam hung back for a fraction of a second as he watched Henry and Sue talking to Jimmy, Cindy, Mary and Raven, then he stepped through the doorway and closed the door behind him.

Sue protested some more, as did Jimmy, Cindy and Mary, but Henry stuck to his guns and didn't give in, nor did Raven. The two stood side by side while the others tried to talk them out of Henry's idea, but finally they all gave up, realizing there would be no changing the two warriors' minds.

"So, you're really going to try this?" Jimmy asked when it had been established that there was no way to change either Henry or Raven's minds.

"Sure am, pal. I know it's risky but when has anything we've done not been?"

"This is a real Hail Mary, you're doing, you know, Henry," Cindy said. Then she looked at Mary and added with a grin, "No offense to you, Mary," referring to the saying *Hail Mary*."

"I didn't take it that way," Mary said. "But I have to agree with Cindy, this is a really wild chance you're taking. If one thing goes wrong, if your assumption is false, if you manage to do what you say and then become trapped; there are so many variables here. What happens if you're wrong?"

Henry's face grew serious, his eyes creasing into slits as he spoke in a calm yet authoritive tone. It brooked no argument, but relayed that his mind was made up, that he knew the risks and was going to try for it all. "Then I die, Mary, simple as that. We all die sooner or later; the trick is to make it later and not sooner."

"Amen, brother," Jimmy added and held out his hand for Henry to shake, the two men clasping hands and shaking briskly. "I'm done arguing about it. Just tell me what I can do to help you and Raven make this shit happen."

"There's not much you can do other than wish us well. Oh, and feel free to say a few prayers for us," Henry joked.

"Why, you getting all religious on us now?" Cindy asked, attempting to lighten the mood.

"No, not really," Henry said. "But right now I figure Raven and I can use all the help we can get."

Chapter 38

Night had fallen an hour ago and the residents of the town had never been busier shoring up their defenses. The companions were also busy as Henry got ready to head out on his mission, but first he needed to be *prepared*.

"Put some more on him, there's an empty space over here," Jimmy said to the worker, pointing to Henry. The worker did as instructed, grabbing a heaping pile of rotting intestines and draping it over Henry's left shoulder. The greasy, bloody ropes slid around his body like electric eels in a kitchen sink that were waiting to be prepared for food. Henry gagged, his eyes closed as the gore slid under his shirt collar and touched his bare skin. After sitting in the bucket for hours, the intestines were cold and they chilled him to the bone. It reminded him of rancid pudding, well, pudding he'd decided to rub all over his body after it went bad, that is. He decided he needed to think of something else, anything to take his mind off what was happening to him.

He thought back to two hours ago when he'd spent some private time with Sue in a room at the hotel, talking, trying to make her see sense to why he had to do the mission. She still protested but eventually she grew tired and had fallen into his arms, crying. He'd hugged her close, feeling her gentle sobs on his chest, and he had to admit that he was also pretty choked up with emotions. But he stayed strong, keeping his feelings under control and deep inside him, bottled up, where they had to stay until the mission was over.

"I love you, you know that, right?" he'd whispered into her hair as they'd sat on the edge of the full-sized bed, hugging.

She'd pulled away a little and had gazed up at him, her eyes filled with tears. "Of course I know that. I love you, too, that's why this is so difficult. It's so damn hard to let you go."

"Hey, I'll be back. Don't I always come back?"

She nodded slowly.

"And with Raven by my side I can't lose, right?"

She nodded again.

"Then be strong, and have faith that like the other times, I'll get through this in one piece and win."

She wiped her nose on her sleeve, then sat up and scooted away from him. She used the tail of her shirt to wipe her eyes of tears. "God, I must look atrocious," she sniffled.

"Not to me. To me you look like the most beautiful woman in the world."

She laughed. "You're just saying that, you old charmer."

"Come here, I'll prove it to you." He held out his hand and she took it and he pulled her close. He moved his face down to hers, parting his lips just a little.

"Oh, Henry," she whispered, feeling his muscular arms wrap around her, as well as something growing within his pants. They kissed, gently at first, but soon tongues were entwining and clothes were being ripped off.

It was a quick lovemaking, for there was no time for anything else, and in less time than either of them would have preferred, they were breathing heavily while getting dressed again, but both looking happier than they had in quite a while. Sue had a glow to her face.

As she was looking down and fumbling with the buttons on her shirt, he pulled her close and again and kissed her hard, one more touch of passion before it faded into obscurity.

"You better come back to me, Henry Watson," she said, breathing deeply.

"Of course I'm coming back, Sue. I have to. Maybe before, when things were different, before I met you that might not have been the case, but now...with you...I have something to live for. Hope for the future."

They embraced one last time and he said, "Come on, it's time to go meet the others."

"Wow, what a smell," Cindy said from nearby, breaking Henry's reverie of his time with Sue and snapping him back to reality. Cindy had a hand over her nose to try and staunch the aroma of dead flesh. Mary and Sue were also holding their breath, and though they wanted to leave to take in fresh air, they stayed, wanting to support Raven and Henry before they left on their dangerous mission.

Henry, Raven, Frank and another man named Wayne all stood side by side just behind the main gate. Three workers from the town butcher had volunteered to do the 'dressing' of the three men and one teenage girl. Up to their elbows in blood each day, to them the gore in the five buckets was nothing new, even if it was human, but to the people watching, it was utterly disgusting.

The five buckets were filled with dismembered zombies, organs the specialty as they made great parts to use to hang on Henry and the others. Jimmy was the only one who wasn't entirely affected by the disgusting situation. Wearing a pair of latex gloves like the other three workers, he dug his hands into a bucket of offal and then pulled out wet, glistening organs. His hands overflowed too much and the organs began sliding from his fingers to splatter back into the bucket with loud, wet plops. Jimmy dug into the bucket again and this time grabbed a little less so he had hold of them.

"Here, ya go, Henry, you need some more on your head," Jimmy smirked and placed a kidney on his friend's head. The kidney balanced there for a few seconds and then slid off to splatter onto the ground. "Hmm, it doesn't seem to like it there, but no worries, I have an idea." He went to a small table where there was an assortment of gear and other supplies. Choosing a hook and some twine, he returned to Henry and picked up the kidney. He acted as if he was trying to get it clean of dirt by blowing on it, as if that mattered, then he used the hook and twine to weave it through the organ, before attaching it to Henry's chest. "There—pretty as a picture." Jimmy smiled and took a step back to admire his handiwork.

The three workers finally finished with Frank, Raven and Wayne, and everyone stepped back a few feet to see how the three men and Raven looked.

"How's it feel?" Mary asked, doing her best to hide her look of disgust.

"Like a giant baby puked all over me, that's how," Henry said flatly. He went to the table and picked up his Glock and panga, then placed them on his person. He hated having the gore touch his beloved weapons but there was nothing he could do. It had to be done. He wasn't carrying any other weapons, figuring there was no need. He knew he needed to get close to this zombie king to take him out and if the Glock couldn't do the job then it wouldn't matter anyway.

Raven joined him, frowning deeply. "It's squishy," she said of the organs covering her and picked up a .45 pistol and a seven inch hunting knife. Henry had made her carry these weapons, otherwise she wouldn't have been allowed to go. There was only one chance at taking out the zombie king and if Henry failed, hopefully, Raven, Frank or Wayne could get the job done. Hundreds of people's lives were hanging in the balance if the group of four failed in their mission.

Frank and Wayne were armed as well and the four, gore-covered warriors joined together near the main gate.

"I'd shake you hand, Henry, but you know..." Sam said, wiping his palm on his hip out of instinct. The four warriors smelled terrible, and blowflies had already begun to buzz around their heads.

"No need, Sam," Henry said. "You can thank me when I return and have washed this stink off me." He glanced at Frank and Wayne, both men nodding in agreement, then Henry smiled at Raven who nodded curtly. "Is the distraction ready?" Henry asked Sam.

Sam nodded. "All I have to do is give the order and we'll start shooting and throwing Molotovs. In the chaos you four should be able to slip out of the town unnoticed and blend into the mob."

"Good," Henry said. "Just make sure we don't get shot by friendly fire."

"I've told all the men to keep an eye out for us," Frank said. "They have strict instructions that unless they can make out the face of the zombie they're going to shoot, they need to hold their fire until confirmation is made that it isn't one of us. That's about all I can do if we want to blend in."

"It'll have to be enough," Henry grunted. "Okay, let's get into position." He held out his hand for Frank to shake. "Good luck, for all of us."

Frank shook the proffered hand, so covered in gore himself that taking Henry's hand and shaking it wasn't an issue. Then he frowned. "We don't need luck, we have these," he said, holding up his assault rifle.

"I'm itchy, let's get this show on the road," Raven said.

"I'm with her," Wayne added, speaking up for the first time. "Wet stuff is sliding down the crack of my ass and I can tell you in all honesty that it isn't a nice feeling."

The four warriors waved goodbye one last time to the people watching and Henry blew Sue a kiss, then they moved across the lot until they were at the main gate, where a small hole had been cut into it so that the four warriors could slip through.

"Frank, give Sam the signal to start the distraction," Henry said and Frank nodded, stepping back a few feet and waving to get Sam's attention, the boss of the town holding a two-way radio to give the orders.

"I was wondering something, Henry," Wayne said, wanting to pass the time talking to cover his nervousness.

"Yeah? What?" Henry asked.

"Well, this whole thing about getting covered in blood and guts. Where did you come with the idea? Does it really hide us from the walkers?"

Henry shrugged. "Beats me if it works. I read it in a horror book once, long before the rains came, or maybe I saw it in a movie. I don't really remember. But looking back, I think it worked out pretty well for the people covered in the mess."

Wayne swallowed the lump in his throat, his eyes opening wide. "You mean you have no idea if this is even gonna work? That we don't take three steps outside the gate and that the entire army doesn't see us and attack us?"

"Yeah, pretty much," Henry replied. By his side, Raven was snickering. She was used to Henry's seat-of your-pants plans, and so far they'd always worked out in the end, even if they did detour slightly before coming to that conclusion. She liked watching Wayne squirm.

"Uh, I think I changed my mind about this," Wayne said, panicking. "I think I want to stay here." As he finished his sentence, weapon's fire began to go off and explosions filled the night as the guards on the platform began to attack the zombies, though the horde was doing nothing but standing immobile, and would stay that way unless Lazarus told his army to attack.

"That's our cue, let's move out," Henry said, grabbing Wayne by the scruff of his shirt and dragging the man behind him.

Frank followed next, then Raven. Wayne only had time for a quick bleat of fear, then they were all running through the hole in the fence and into the night, while around them, the world shook with fire and bullets.

Chapter 39

With the world exploding around them in a blazing inferno of chaos and smoke, Henry led Raven, Frank and Wayne across the no-man's land between the perimeter fence and the first line of walking dead.

"No talking once we're amongst them," Henry whispered to the others. "One word from any of us could be enough to blow our cover—and slow movements only. Deaders are slow, so we have to be, too. Stay in character or you're dead. Use hand signals to communicate."

The others nodded, understanding completely. There would be no hope of rescue if they were discovered. One false move and they would be torn apart in seconds, dying very painfully. Henry had already decided the second he felt he was discovered and there was no hope of escape, that he would put the muzzle of the Glock in his mouth and eat a 9mm bullet.

The zombies barely moved, mostly shifting from side to side. Henry assumed they were immobile because all the explosions weren't even close to any of the horde. Henry hoped the leader of the ghouls would think the town was going mad, attacking thin air in the hopes of scaring away the zombies.

It was a terrifying moment when Henry slid between the first row of zombies, their dead flesh brushing up against him. He took slow, plodding steps and kept a wary eye on Raven, who was right behind him. But he wasn't worried about her. If any one out of the four of them could move like a cat, it was her.

Henry had no idea how deep the horde was, so he paced himself, slowly taking step after step. He did his best to move around the bodies before him, but every once in a while a ghoul would stumble into him. He would stop moving, close his eyes, and wait for the ghoul to turn and wander away. One time, a zombie walked into him so that they were face to face. Henry's nose was no more than an inch from the zombie's, and he held his breath for fear of being discovered. They locked eyes, Henry's dark blue ones and the ghouls bone whites, and it seemed an eternity before the ghoul finally turned away and stumbled back into the shifting throng of dead flesh.

Letting out a silent sigh of relief, Henry glanced at Raven and she nodded she was okay, then they began walking again. Frank and Wayne followed close behind them. Wayne wasn't doing so well, and being last in line, no one could see he was falling apart. The constant press of dead flesh on his body was making him lose it. He was doing his best to stay calm, but with each passing second he was getting closer to cracking.

The four, gore-covered humans had to go in a circuitous route, due to large clumps of zombies that were so thick it was impossible to traverse them. Only by using the perimeter fence as a reference could Henry make sure he was heading away from the town. He didn't know where he was going exactly, but he figured Lazarus had to be somewhere in the back of the army, where he would be safe from attack.

More than an hour had passed before the first problem showed itself.

It was Wayne, who had finally lost control of himself. The first Henry knew there was a situation was when he heard yelling over the moans and shuffling feet of the dead. He stopped walking, Raven coming up against him. She almost opened her mouth to ask what was wrong, but Henry placed a hand close to his lips to silence her. Frank saw what was happening then, and with Henry by his side, the two men tried to calm Wayne with hand signals, but Wayne wouldn't listen. Before anyone could stop him, he began yelling at the zombies. "Get back, get away from me, damn you!" Wayne cried out. "No, I can't do this. I thought I could, I really did, but I want out! I want out of here right now! I want to go back to town!"

Frank was gritting his teeth in frustration, waning to speak desperately, to help Wayne, who was having none of it. Frank tried to grab Wayne, to control him; he even tried putting his hand over Wayne's mouth to silence him, but all he got for his trouble was Wayne sinking his teeth into his palm.

"Ah, Jesus, Wayne, that fucking hurt!" Frank screamed, ripping his hand back from Wayne's mouth, the man's teeth now coated in blood—Frank's blood. Wayne had taken a good chunk of meat in his bite and Frank's hand splattered blood on nearby zombies when he yanked it back. Immediately, every zombie around the two men turned to face them, smelling the fresh blood and attracted to their yelling.

Henry knew before the first zombie laid a hand on the two men that the men were already dead; they just hadn't gone through the suffering part yet.

Wayne was the first to let out a scream of pain when a zombie sank its teeth into his left arm. He roared in agony and surprise and shoved the ghoul away from him. Drawing his firearm, he began to shoot at anything that got in front of him. Only the dead were behind him too, and before he could take down more than three ghouls, he was overwhelmed and brought to the ground. His screams began in full force then as he was torn apart, gutted and fed on.

Frank tried to push his way through the throng of dead flesh, but he tripped over a zombie's foot and fell onto the ground face first. Pushing himself to his knees, he tried to crawl under the legs before him, but after making it less than six feet, he came face to face with a half-zombie with no legs. The ghoul was propped up, its arms holding it upright. Frank stared at the decayed face, the missing lips, the extra large teeth, and he tried to back away. Only he couldn't move; bodies were crammed behind him. He never got a shot off with his gun before the half-zombie was on him, then other ghouls figured out there was food right below them and they bent over while others went to their knees to begin feeding on the dying man. Bright arterial blood spurted out in all directions as Frank began to die horribly.

Henry and Raven stood stock still, not wanting to attract attention to themselves. Zombies moved past them to reach the two screaming men, their arms brushing Raven and Henry and threatening to knock them over.

The screams stopped eventually and only the sound of mastication filled the air.

Henry saw a zombie with Wayne's head moving away, its hand scooping out glistening pink brains to shove them into its mouth greedily.

With a bitter taste in his mouth, Henry waved Raven onward. They still had a mission to complete.

It took another three hours to finally reach the destination Henry was searching for. Both Raven and he were exhausted, the sheer stress of being in the middle of an army of undead too much for even their iron wills.

Before the two warriors, about a quarter mile from the town, was a high ridge, and cut into the ridge from centuries of exposure to harsh weather was a large crevasse a hundred feet wide and eighty feet deep.

Henry and Raven pushed through the undead crowd until they were in the second row inside the fissure. Here, they had the perfect vantage point to see the spectacle before them. After taking in the sight, they looked at one another, their eyes saying the same thing: Could this really be true?

In the center of the fissure, tucked in the back, was a throne of human body parts, which in turn was resting on a giant pile of corpses, all of the cadavers gutted. Made from arms, legs and torsos, the throne was held together with anything from twine to tendons to intestines, the makeshift bonds taken from the dead bodies. The pile of corpses was four feet high, made so that bodies lined the front like steps. Gore and pus seeped out from under the pile to spread out across the dirt. Most of the slime had soaked into the ground, but there was simply so much that even the earth began to refuse to accept it.

But if that wasn't enough to make Henry's mouth drop open in amazement, there was still the fact that there was a zombie sitting on the throne. Finger bones had been tied together to fashion a crude crown on its head and a wreathe of ears and noses adorned its naked chest. On either side of the throne stood a perfectly-still zombie, each one looking like a statue.

So here was the fabled Lazarus, Henry decided as he took in the zombie on the throne of body parts. Though the face was pale and decayed, the visage of the man the ghoul had been in life could still be made out. The eyes were closed, and the face looked as if the zombie was concentrating or contemplating on something only he could know.

236

Henry reached down to draw his Glock, then began to push forward through the first row of ghouls. Raven was right beside him, her .45 gripped tightly in her hand. It had been agreed on beforehand that Henry would take the shot and only if something happened to him would she attempt to shoot the zombie.

Henry was sweating like a pig under his gore costume and he could feel every blowfly crawling across his skin, feeding on the caked-on blood coating him.

He was bringing his Glock up when suddenly every single zombie in the crevasse went to one knee, as if they were bending low for their king, their heads bowed down so that they were looking at the ground.

Raven and Henry found themselves standing there, the only two *zombies* still upright. They stood out like the proverbial sore thumb.

Acting fast, Henry went to one knee, Raven following suit, both their heads facing down. But it was too late, the damage had been done. A full ten seconds passed without a sound and Henry snuck a peek, raising his head slightly to see what Lazarus was doing.

The zombie's eyes were open and looking right at Henry and Raven. The gaze wasn't one of hunger or of blankness either. The gaze was filled with intelligence.

Knowing it was now or never, Henry jumped up and raised the Glock, firing three times before he was fully standing. He knew his aim was true, that in less than a second, Lazarus would have half a head and the controlled siege on Indian Springs would be over. Sure the town would still have to contend with the zombies, but without an intelligence controlling them, even their vast number could be dealt with in time.

But things didn't go as Henry had hoped. Before the first bullet could reach Lazarus, the zombie standing on his right side lunged in front of him, taking the three bullets in the chest and head, as if he was a government agent assigned to protect the President of the United States. The suicidal zombie shook with each bullet before collapsing onto the pile of corpses, rolling down the steps made from cadavers until finally coming to rest at the bottom.

Amazed at what he'd just witnessed, Henry froze for a split second, but his reflexes snapped him out of it and he adjusted his aim and fired three times again. Only this time the other zombie on Lazarus' left side jumped before its king, absorbing each round before crumbling onto the stairs.

Cursing his luck, Henry tried to shoot again, and now Raven had raised her gun, knowing it was time to add her firepower to his, but neither had the chance to squeeze the trigger. Before either could get off a shot, the zombies surrounding them jumped up and grabbed the two humans, holding their arms tightly. Henry squeezed the trigger on the Glock once while being restrained, shooting the closest zombie in the foot and blowing all five toes clean off its foot. The ghoul didn't so much as flinch at the lost digits. Raven managed to fire her .45 twice, but only managed to shoot a zombie standing in front of her, its body blocking Lazarus from her sight. Henry and Raven's weapons were then ripped from their hands and body to be tossed aside, including his panga and her hunting knife.

Trapped in the clutches of the dead, they tried to break free, but there were too many hands on them. Henry kept waiting for the zombies to attack, to begin tearing him and Raven apart like they had done to Frank and Wayne, but it didn't happen, they were only restrained.

Then, Lazarus stood up slowly and began to clap, the dull sound echoing in the hollow fissure. Calmly, he began to climb down the stairs of corpses, stepping over the zombie that had absorbed bullets meant for him. When he reached the bottom body-step, he walked on the back of the other zombie shot dead to then cross the short distance until he was standing before Henry and Raven.

A malevolent smile creased the zombie's cracked lips and a shiver went down Henry's spine. He wasn't facing a typical mindless enemy; this time he was facing an enemy that was intelligent...and already dead.

"Did you really think it would be that easy?" Lazarus said to Henry, the smile never leaving the pale face.

"Well, yeah, I kind of hoped it would," Henry said, his voice flat. Many times since the dead began to walk Henry had been terrified. Sometimes he had been so scared he could barely move. But each time, he did move. He overcame his fear and did what had to be done. He never gave it much thought, only that he had no choice, for not to act would have meant death. Henry had never considered that a real hero, a man brave beyond means, was the man who though frightened, still did what had to be done, regardless of the consequences or fear of bodily harm.

"You make jokes at a time like this," Lazarus said. "When you're so close to death, a painful one I might add, and all you can do is make wiseass remarks."

Henry forced a grin. "Call it a coping mechanism."

"You never had a chance, you know. From the second you and your three companions entered my little hideout, I knew you were here."

Henry's eyebrows went up in curiosity despite himself.

"Yes, that's right. I didn't know who you were or anything so detailed but I could sense two minds that weren't like my undead soldiers. They felt different somehow. But that difference was enough to allow me to separate you from my followers."

"You sensed us?" Henry repeated, his mind working overtime. Then it all came together: the zombies with the white flags speaking like each one was Lazarus himself, the way the undead army seemed controlled by an outside force, as if there was someone instructing them on what to do, telling them how to use firearms.

"You can read the deaders' thoughts, can't you? Somehow you can tell them what to do."

"The fucker's telepathic, Henry," Raven spit, her jaw taut, her eyes alight with anger and hatred.

Lazarus shifted his gaze to Raven, nodding at her words. "The girl is correct. That's exactly what I am, and each passing hour I become more powerful."

From behind Henry and Raven came the sound of explosions and the staccato of gunfire. Henry tried to turn his head out of instinct but he was held too tight to move more than an inch. Lazarus noticed Henry trying to turn around and the smile on his face increased tenfold.

"Ah, you hear the sounds of battle. Yes, I've sent my dead army to attack the town once more. This time I won't stop until the town is mine."

Henry's thoughts went to Jimmy, Cindy, Mary and Sue, his concern for them so strong that Lazarus was able to pick up on it. The images of the four friends appeared in Lazarus' mind and he nodded, "You have more friends in the town, I see. They're like you, not from the town but part of it nonetheless. Hmmm, I'll tell you what. I like you, I like your style. As a favor to you I think I'll have my soldiers bring your friends here. Then you can all die together."

"Fucking deader," Raven hissed and then suddenly broke free of her captors, slipping free of their hands as if she was coated in grease. She lunged forward, her right hand slashing at Lazarus' face. Her razor-sharp fingernails cut deep into his cheek, leaving a long gash from his left eye to his lower jaw.

"Get her, you idiots!" Lazarus screamed at his zombies, falling back and cupping his hand to his face out of instinct, as if he was human and felt pain. But it was fleeting and a moment later he'd regained his composure and was standing tall once more. He gingerly touched the gaping wound on his face, his lips curled into an aggravated frown. Congealed blood seeped from the wound to drip off his chin.

Raven tried to get away but was quickly surrounded on all sides; there was no where to go. She sliced decayed flesh off of zombies with her fingernails and punched and kicked anything within her reach, but in a matter of seconds she was caught and held fast. Her eyes glistened like a wild animal's, and her neck bulged with veins as she fought to free herself again.

Henry tried to break free too while Lazarus was distracted, but the zombies holding him hadn't lessened their hold on him in the slightest. His muscles tensed beneath his gore-covered clothes; all he could do was watch Raven fight for her life as tears welled up in his eyes, knowing it was hopeless.

Lazarus stepped up to Raven so that he was mere inches from her. "I was going to make you suffer for a long time, both of you, but it appears I underestimated you." He touched the seeping wound on his face. "I'm dead, you know, this won't heal. From now on I'm going to have to live with this mark you gave me, girl."

She smiled, baring her teeth. "Good, you can always think of me when you see yourself in a mirror, you ugly fuck." She began to laugh.

Henry didn't know what was coming next, nor could he have imagined it, and even as Lazarus lunged forward, his teeth sinking deep into Raven's neck and tearing out her carotid artery, Henry's mind tried to tell him that what he saw wasn't possible. Raven, so strong and powerful, quick as a cat and always the victor of any fight, was now being slaughtered like a lamb.

"No, you bastard, no, Raven!" Henry screamed, trying to fight free of his captors once more, only to be held even tighter.

Lazarus took a step back as blood shot out of the two inch wound in Raven's neck. She couldn't say anything. Bright red bubbles seeped from her mouth. She was drowning in her own blood. Coughing and spitting, all she could do was wait till the end. Her eyes began to glaze over and her gaze shifted to Henry.

He tried to read something in her eyes, hoping she was attempting to send him a message, but there was nothing there but pain and loss as she felt herself falling into the black void of death.

"Raven, no, damn it! Lazarus, I'll fucking kill you! You're dead, you hear me, dead!"

Lazarus chuckled at Henry's threats. "Ah, but you're too late. I'm already dead. Or did you forget?"

Raven had gone limp, her head hanging low. Blood still spurted fitfully from her neck wound, and then it stopped altogether, her heart finally running out of plasma to keep her body alive. She let out one last gasp filled with red froth, then she was gone.

"Raven, Jesus, Raven, no, you can't be dead!" Henry yelled, his voice on the verge of cracking.

Lazarus swiveled his head to face Henry, his eyes locking onto his prisoner. The zombie's lips and chin were coated in Raven's blood. "You're next."

Chapter 40

"But before I change you, too, I think I'll keep you around for a bit," Lazarus said to Henry. "After all, it's not like I have people to talk to anymore." He saw that Henry wasn't listening to him, the man's attention focused on Raven. "Wait for it, Henry, this is the part I love the most," Lazarus said, gesturing to Raven. He'd learned Henry's name when Raven had informed Henry that the zombie was telepathic. Lazarus preferred using Henry's name; it made it seem so much more personal.

Still locked in the standing embrace of the zombies, Raven's body began to shiver, to twitch as undead life flooded through it. Slowly, as if it was painful, she raised her head up so that she was looking at Henry.

Her face was a blank slate, her eyes now glazed over, and Henry saw nothing of the vivacious warrior she once was.

Raven was gone, her body now nothing but a lifeless shell.

Over the years, and many times the companions had sat around a campfire, discussing life and death. Each of them had made a pact to the others, that no matter what, none of them would ever be allowed to become a zombie, that if it ever came down to it, each of them would put a bullet in one another's heads so that they could rest in peace. But here Henry was now, looking at Raven as she became a zombie, and there was nothing he could do to stop it.

"I can hear her thoughts, Henry," Lazarus said. "She doesn't know you anymore. She's mine now, body and soul, if there really is such a thing as a soul."

"You bastard!" Henry snarled. "Kill me now, because if I get the chance I swear to God I'll kill you!"

"Ah, but you won't get that chance. My zombies are many, and even if you were to somehow break free of the ones holding you, there are many more that would stop you." He went over and picked up Henry's Glock. "I'll keep this as a souvenir," he said and slid the pistol into his waistband.

Raven's .45 was given to one of the zombies. The panga and knife were left on the ground where they'd been tossed. Lazarus walked over to the dead zombie that had sacrificed itself by being hit by Henry's bullets that had been meant for Lazarus. He gestured to the still corpse. "This was John. I liked him. I turned him myself." He spun to face Henry. "And you killed him, you naughty boy."

"Screw you, you bastard!" Henry spit. Veins bulged on his forehead and neck from his hate and anger, his arms flexing as he tried to break free of the zombies holding him. If only he could get free, for even a second, he would snap Lazarus' neck and die a happy man as the zombies tore him apart.

The explosions and gunfire coming from the town had died down and Lazarus smiled contently. His eyes rolled into his head and he seemed to go into a trance. Henry stared at Lazarus, the deadlands warrior's mind creating violent ways of killing him.

Lazarus stayed that way for more than twenty minutes, immobile, not so much as moving an eyebrow or a finger. The zombies around him stayed still as well.

Only the ones holding Henry reacted each time he tried to break free. Henry had over half a dozen ghouls holding him, some on their knees wrapping their arms around his legs while others did the same to his arms and torso. He was truly trapped. He could get no leverage in order to break free. Even his head was immobile, a zombie taller than him holding his head close to its chest, as if the head was locked in a vice. The smell of decayed meat was terrible but Henry barely noticed. Once in a while he would glance at Raven by shifting his head to the side an inch, but then would have to look away. The guilt he felt for her fate was too much to bear right now. He felt responsible for her death and revival. He vowed to put a bullet in her head if he had the chance, to honor the promise he'd made to her over the campfire.

At the end of the twenty minutes, Lazarus snapped out of his trance. He blinked and looked around, as if waking from a nightmare. "Good news, Henry, my army has taken the town. Most of it is in flames and my soldiers are even now killing the townspeople. I let them eat a little of each one, you know, that way the victims revive to join my army. It's a great way to recoup my losses, which I hate to say was great this time around. This town was very resistant to me I have to admit but in the end I won." He walked over to

Henry so they were a mere foot from one another. "I always win." He tapped Henry's cheek with his palm, a playful slap.

"That's supposed to be good news?" Henry asked. "You just killed hundreds of people. You're a monster." His thoughts went to Sue, Jimmy, Cindy and Mary. Were they dead or alive? Had they managed to escape the town? Or were they even now nothing but body parts, or worse, were they the walking dead like Raven? The thought of not knowing their fates added to the guilt he felt for Raven's death, a massive well of emotions that threatened to overwhelm him. He bit his lip, letting the pain fill him, giving him something to focus on other than the loss of his friends.

"I'm a monster?" Lazarus said, touching his chest as if in indignation. The necklaces of ears and noses shifted when he did this. "What about you? How many of my kind have you killed, hmmm? Do you even know?"

"That's different," Henry said.

"Not to me. To me you're nothing but a murderer, who kills my kind as if we were nothing but ants."

"How can I kill what's already dead?" Henry snarled. "You and your kind are an abomination. The world is shit because of you damn deaders, and now you want me to act as if you're somehow equal to human beings? Well, forget it, that's never gonna happen."

"That's where you're wrong, Henry, we're not your equals, we're better." He sent a mental order to one of the zombies holding Henry and it placed its hand over Henry's mouth, silencing the man.

Satisfied that he'd gotten the last word, Lazarus strolled off, leaving Henry alone with an undead Raven and a mob of the living dead. After a few minutes, Henry's mouth was released but there was no one for him to yell at. Frustration built within him and he screamed as loud as he could, his voice filled with sorrow and hate. Ever since he'd been thrown into a world of walking dead, he'd managed to come out ahead each time he'd found himself in a bad situation. But this time was different. This time he couldn't see any way out of it. As he stared at Raven, he began to believe that this time would be different, that this time he was going to die, or worse, join Raven as a zombie. When his voice finally grew hoarse and he was spent, he stopped yelling and settled down. He couldn't sit due to the zombies holding him, but he let his body go slack to rest. With nothing else to do, he stared at the zombies securing him and waited for what would come next.

Despite his horrifying situation, Henry managed to drift off into a restless sleep, due to the exhaustion of the past few days. Even a man with an iron will needs to rest once in a while. Nothing stopped him from drifting off, not the smell of rotting human flesh in the hot sun, nor the moans of the zombies surrounding him. He floated in and out of consciousness, images of Mary, Sue and the others flashing across his mind's eye.

Raven was there, asking why he'd let her die, and what he was going to do to avenge her. Visions of Jimmy and the others filled his head, ones where they were either torn apart by ghouls or were walking corpses themselves, stumbling around aimlessly in the burning town of Indian Springs until Lazarus called them to him. From there they would follow the zombie leader across the country, killing and turning all who crossed their path.

Henry was pulled from his nightmares by the sound of human voices, ones he recognized. At first the voices meshed with his dreams, his friends calling out to him, but then he opened his eyes to see that his nightmares had become reality. Before him, to the left side of the throne of body parts, were Jimmy, Cindy, Sue and Mary. Each was tied to a wooden post that had been driven into the ground, the dirt around it churned up but more than solid enough to hold the posts in place. Nearby, zombies with no flesh on their hands stood by dumbly. Their skeletal hands were caked with dirt and Henry figured it out immediately that these ghouls had dug the holes for the posts, which had been taken from the town, and had once been used for a fence. Two more zombies stood nearby, holding the companions' weapons and gear. Torches had been lit around the throne to push the darkness away. Henry gazed up at the sky between the walls of the fissure to see that it was now night.

"Look, he's awake," Jimmy said when he saw Henry stirring.

"Oh Henry, thank God you're alive," Sue cried out, from beside Jimmy.

"We thought you were dead," Mary piped in from beside Sue.

"Henry, no one has seen Raven," Cindy called from beside Mary. "Where is she?"

It broke his heart to tell them but he gestured with his chin to their far left. "She's there, in that group of deaders."

Four sets of eyes followed Henry's gesture and gasps and shocks of horror came from them when they spotted Raven amongst the zombies.

"Oh, God, no," Sue cried, the tears flowing harder than they already had been. "Oh Raven, I'm so sorry."

"How did it happen?" Mary asked.

"That bastard Lazarus did it right before my eyes," Henry said. "That son-of-a-bitch is mean, I'll tell you that much. But it's good to see you all. I thought you were dead or worse, walking around as deaders."

Jimmy was furious to be captured and he strained to free himself of his bonds with no result. "Shit, Henry, your plan didn't work out as you hoped, huh? Wish it had though, maybe then we wouldn't be in this mess. A few hours after you and Raven left, the deaders came at us hard. Just like Sam said, the townsfolk ran out of ammo and it wasn't long before they were fighting hand-to-hand. Then the fence collapsed south of the gate and that was all she wrote. They swarmed in and overran the entire town. Shit, I doubt if anyone but us made it out alive and even that's a mystery."

"I agree about that last part. Not that I'm complaining to see all of you, of course," Henry said. "In fact, I can't tell you how relieved I am to know you're alive, but how did you guys wind up here with me?"

"That's the weird part," Mary chimed in. "We were surrounded on all sides and were about to be taken down when we ran out of ammo, but before they attacked, they suddenly stopped and one of them spoke to us. It told us if we came along quietly we wouldn't be killed."

"And you listened?" Henry asked.

"Well, shit, old man, what were we supposed to do? We were outnumbered a hundred to one and we were out of bullets. I didn't think we had many options left, do you?"

"No, I guess not, but still..."

"What? You wanted us to go down fighting, am I right?" Jimmy asked. "Well, we decided every breath we took was worth it. At the time it seemed the right call to make. Now? Maybe not so much as I doubt we're here for a birthday party."

"Okay, fine, forget that part. What about Sam?" Henry asked. "Is he..."

"Dead," Cindy said. "I saw him go down under a dozen deaders. He put up a hell of a fight, too, before they got him."

Henry shook his head. Another friend lost to the walking dead. "He was a good man."

"Yeah, well, he's dead and we're alive," Jimmy said. "So if you don't mind I think I'll worry about my own ass right now. The rest of you should, too."

"We have to get out of here," Mary said. "We need to find a way to escape, Henry."

"But there is no escape, people," Lazarus said, walking into the open from between a group of zombies. In his waistband was Henry's Glock; his face was covered with fresh blood from recent kills, the few victims taken from the town. "I heard everything you said, you know. Every one of my soldiers is a conduit to my mind. What they see I see, and I hate to break it to you, but I only halted your deaths inside the town so you could have a much grander one here. You see, I like to play with my food, and when my soldiers kill all the townspeople, there's nothing left for me to enjoy."

"Fuck you, you goddamn deader," Jimmy spat. "Already dead or not, let me get my hands on you and I'll make sure you're dead for good."

"Ah, such bravado, even in the face of complete hopelessness. Now, I suggest you shut up or it won't go well for you."

"Screw you, you piece of shit. Why, I bet when you were human you were nothing. Let me guess...an insurance salesman? An accountant, maybe? Hmmm, wait, I bet it was some job like a janitor or a garbage man."

That hit a nerve and Lazarus sent an order to a nearby zombie. The ghoul stepped out of the crowd of hundreds and walked over to Jimmy, then it tore off its shirtsleeve, balled it up, and shoved it into Jimmy's mouth to silence him.

"There, I think that's enough from the peanut gallery." Lazarus looked at Sue, Mary and Cindy. "If any of you utter so much as a single word I'll do the same to you, too." He smiled, which caused the weeping wound on his face to open slightly, looking like a vertical mouth. "Or perhaps I'll just tear out your tongues to make sure there's no further chance of hearing from any of you."

Henry was furious but he remained silent. Asking questions such as *What do you want from us?* or *Why are you doing this?* seemed redundant. The truth was that Lazarus was doing these things to Henry and his friends because he could, because he had no conscience. Torture gave him pleasure and that was it.

When no one spoke Lazarus nodded slowly. "Good, that's very good. Now, on with the show. Before my undead army and I move on to my next conquest, we're going to play a little game." He looked at Henry and the smile on the zombie's face was enough to make any man, no matter how strong of character, shiver with fear. "Do you want to play my game, Henry?"

"Do I have a choice?" Henry hissed.

"Why no, you don't actually. You see, I'll play it with or without you, but your friends might last longer if you agree to play."

"Then I guess I'm in," Henry growled, his hands clenched into fists.

"Good." Lazarus walked over to the tied companions. His right hand caressed Cindy's left cheek first. She cringed but said nothing, knowing what would happen if she did. Lazarus glanced at Henry and the zombie creased his eyes, then he did the same for Mary and Sue, each time studying Henry's reaction as he touched their faces. "I see it's these two you cherish the most, Henry. I can feel the emotions within you. It's so strange, actually, I'm so used to dealing with the dull minds of my followers, to now feel a human's thoughts is rather revitalizing." He thought for a moment. "I wonder if in time my powers might become so strong that I can control even the minds of humans. Now that would be interesting. I could make them come to me before I slaughtered them and turned them into soldiers for my dead army."

Jimmy was going crazy, struggling to break free of his bonds and spit out the filthy shirt in his mouth. He wasn't going to give in for anything. Lazarus could kill him but he wouldn't stop fighting until he was dead.

Lazarus ignored the struggling Jimmy and walked around the four, trust-up prisoners to stand between Sue and Mary. He raised his arms and placed a hand on each of their shoulders, the gesture almost friendly. "If you pick one to die, I promise to set the other one free. I'll release her unharmed far away from here, but if you don't choose then they both die, to then become part of my army. So, Henry, what's it going to be? Life for one or death for both." His smile disappeared and his face became serious. "You have one minute to decide."

Chapter 41

Henry blinked in shock at what Lazarus had just said. There it was, right there for him to decide. After Lazarus had killed Raven with no hesitation, there was no doubt in his mind that the zombie would do as he said. But still, how could he ever make that kind of decision? How could he save one and sentence the other to a fate worse than death? How could he ever choose between Mary and Sue?

Mary was the daughter he'd never had. They had been through so much over the past few years. They had a bond that was so strong that even spoken words couldn't be used to truly explain it. But then there was Sue. He loved her deeply, had made love to her more times than he could count, their bodies becoming one as they forgot the horrors of the world and simply reveled in each other's company. So many nights, after the others had gone to sleep, they had sat by the campfire talking, or when he had been on guard duty while the others slept, she had kept him company long into the night. She knew things about him no one else in the world knew, the last person to know his so intimately being his late wife Emily. If a person could have two soul mates in this life, then Sue was his second after his late wife.

And now he was being forced to choose between Sue and Mary.

All this rushed through his mind in the space of seconds, but still he couldn't decide what to do. It was the hardest decision of his life. Who should he save? And even if he chose one to die, would Lazarus really do as he said and set the other one free? For all he knew, this was all an elaborate joke, the zombie already saying how he enjoyed playing games. And what would happen to Jimmy and Cindy? Surely Lazarus wouldn't free them. The zombie was evil incarnate, his promises were less than worthless.

But then, if there was even a chance, a slim one at that, shouldn't he take it and save one of them? His indecision only grew worse as he considered his choices.

"Tick-tock, tick-tock, Henry," Lazarus said, growing impatient. "Your minute's almost up."

"I…" Henry began but then stopped, not able to do it. "Damn it, you bastard. How can you make me do this?"

"It's easy, Henry. One lives and one dies. Eeny-meany-miny-moe; pick one that way if you must. I really don't care, but I'm hungry so if you don't choose in the next few seconds, I'm going to have them both for dinner."

"It's okay, Henry, you can pick Mary. I understand," Sue said, risking speaking despite the warning not to.

"No, Henry, you love Sue. You lost Emily, you can't lose her, too," Mary rebutted.

Lazarus smiled, enjoying the angst on Henry's face.

"Ah, such selfless women, it's such a shame one of them will be dead in the next minute."

"Stop this," Cindy demanded. "Kill me instead and leave them alone!"

Lazarus chuckled at this. "Don't you worry, my dear, your turn is coming, as is your big-mouth friend." He pointed to Jimmy, whose eyes were so wide they were about to burst from his head, he was so filled with anger. He screamed something but it was intelligible with the rag in his mouth. "Remember, there are four of you. This game can be played twice," Lazarus teased.

And there it was. Once Mary and Sue were dealt with, the game would be played again with Jimmy and Cindy.

"That's it, Henry, time's up. Choose one now or I slaughter them both." Lazarus went to Sue and yanked her head to the side, exposing her neck. "Does this one live or die?"

"I choose…" Henry stuttered, not able to say it. He'd made a decision, and though it broke his heart to do so, he had no choice. "I choose…"

Everything had gone quiet, as if even the zombies watching silently wanted to know the answer to this daunting question. Cindy and Jimmy leaned forward slightly, amazed that Henry was going to actually pick one. Mary's eyes were wide, a lump in her throat as she waited to hear if she was going to live or die. Sue had tears in her eyes, sobbing silently as she waited to know if her death was imminent.

Lazarus was smiling, loving every second of it, his power sensing Henry's suffering as the warrior made a decision that would haunt him for as long as he lived, the guilt of sacrificing one person he loved to save another something that might very well break him as a man.

"I choose..." Henry said again, drawing it out, as if some miracle might suddenly happen to save him from this terrible decision.

A bright light suddenly lit up the night sky, as if a light as big as the sun had been turned on and then off. It was so quick that if someone had blinked they would have missed it.

And then, as if some deity had flicked a magical switch, every single zombie—with the exception of Lazarus—simply dropped dead, slumping to the ground to lay still.

There was the sound of thousands of bodies hitting the ground, the rustling sound almost hypnotic, and then there was nothing but silence for miles.

Lazarus let go of Sue's head, his face taking on a look of worry, his eyes darting back and forth. "My undead army, I can't feel them anymore. I can't feel any on them anywhere. All across the world, it's as if they've all disappeared in the blink of an eye. But how? It's impossible." He took a step away from Sue and Mary and raised his hands to his head, as if he could force things to go back the way they were only seconds ago. "They're all gone, every single one of them, all dead, gone."

When every single zombie dropped dead, Henry suddenly found himself free of his captors. Though he'd wanted this for hours, he was as amazed as Lazarus when it happened. There had been no sound, no explosions, nothing to explain this event; just one second every zombie was active and then they weren't. He looked down at his feet to see some of the pale faces of the dead. There was nothing in those open eyes but death, true death. They were now only corpses. Whatever had animated them with life was gone, sucked out in the blink of an eye.

But the amazement was short-lived and Henry's warrior's instinct kicked in almost immediately. He looked up, over at Jimmy and the others, and a still very active Lazarus, who was mumbling to himself.

Like a bull charging the hated matador, Henry took off running directly at Lazarus, who snapped out of his stupor at the sound of Henry's footsteps. Acting far faster than something undead should have been able to, Lazarus reached down to his waist and pulled Henry's Glock from his waistband, then leveled the gun directly at the charging man.

The deadlands warrior didn't so much as slow or weave, his mind only set on one thing: kill Lazarus.

The zombie fired at Henry, but his aim was off and the bullet missed Henry's head by inches. Henry never slowed, but powered on even faster, crossing the distance between them in less than three seconds. His right fist was already coming around as Lazarus tried to shoot Henry again.

Henry managed to reach Lazarus first, his right fist connecting with Lazarus' chin. The zombie went flying backwards, the Glock tumbling from his hand to land in the dry dirt ten feet away. But he didn't fall down, and regained his balance and charged Henry a second later, the two meeting like gladiators in the Roman arena, something Henry was all too familiar with as of late.

They grappled, Lazarus grabbing Henry's right arm and trying to throw him over his back, while Henry kicked out with his right foot, cracking Lazarus' knee and sending the zombie to the ground. Lazarus didn't cry out, as he felt no pain, but he still couldn't stop his body from failing him with a shattered kneecap.

Henry pushed the advantage, sending a roundhouse blow into Lazarus' face, the impact of fist on skin almost enough to snap the zombie's neck. Lazarus rode with the impact and fell to the side, his arms holding him up. When he turned to face Henry, he saw a haymaker coming right at him. The fist connected with the zombie's nose and the cartilage lost out. Though his nose was pulverized, it shattered in a way so that the shrapnel didn't go into his brain.

Swinging out with his free arm, Lazarus wrapped his hand around Henry's ankle and yanked as hard as he could. Henry went horizontal and hit the ground on his back, hard, the force of the landing knocking the air from his lungs. Lazarus jumped on top of him, but Henry bucked his hips, tossing the lighter zombie off him. Lazarus fell back and Henry jumped to his feet, kicking out with his right foot and connecting with Lazarus' jaw. The blow dislocated the zombie's jaw and sent teeth flying off in all directions.

Henry used his foot and pushed Lazarus onto his back, then he dropped down on the zombie's chest. He wanted to begin punching him, to pulverize that face, but even in his haze of anger he knew that could be deadly for him. The infection of a zombie was in its bite, and even one of Henry's knuckles being cut by the remaining teeth in Lazarus' mouth could do Henry in. So he leaned over Lazarus' head and picked up a fist-size rock, then raised it high in the air.

"You can't kill me," Lazarus spit, the words slurred due to his broken jaw. "I'm a god, I'm immortal. I can't die."

"Let's test that theory, shall we?" Henry hissed and brought the rock down as hard as he could, the blow so powerful that it caved in Lazarus' face. But Henry wasn't done yet. Raising the gore-caked rock, he brought it down again, and did this four more times, until Lazarus' face was nonexistent and there was nothing left but a wet pile of pulped brains and skull fragments.

Seeing his enemy was vanquished, Henry dropped the rock and leaned back, his breathing coming in gasps. When he began to hear voices, at first he didn't understand where they were coming from. Then he turned his head to see Mary, Sue and Cindy, as well as a still-muffled Jimmy, calling out to him to be freed.

Standing up on shaky legs, he stumbled over to them. He went to one of the fallen zombies that had their weapons and gear, took Jimmy's Bowie knife, and used it to free the others. As soon as Sue's bonds were severed, she jumped at him, hugging and kissing him, ignoring the disguise of dried blood and gore still covering his body and clothes.

"Oh my God, Henry, thank heavens you're all right. I was so scared." She kissed him some more until he pulled her off.

"I know Sue, but I think the others would like to be untied, too, don't you think?"

"Huh, what?" she said and then turned to see Mary, Cindy and Jimmy glaring at her. "Oh, of course, what was I thinking?"

"Here, you do it. I have something else to do." He handed her the knife and she took it, quickly going to work on Mary's bonds. Jimmy was telling her to take the damn rag out of his mouth but no one could understand him because, well, he had the rag in his mouth.

Henry moved away from Sue and the others, heading straight for the last place he'd seen Raven. He found her quick enough, half-buried under another zombie. He dragged the unknown ghoul off her and scooped her up into his arms. Tears had already begun to fall from his eyes now that he was holding her still form. He walked back to the others, surprised by how light she was. He'd always known she was petite but holding her like this, it felt as if a strong breeze would rip her from his arms.

When he reached the others, he gently set her down in a clear area. Mary and Sue joined him, while a free Cindy had taken the knife from Sue and was cutting Jimmy loose. As Henry, Mary and Sue knelt down by Raven, Jimmy's annoyed complaints could be heard behind them.

Mary brushed Raven's dark hair off her pale face. "Oh, Henry, I'm so sorry she didn't make it. She was a great girl." Mary was crying, the tears flowing freely.

Sue was sobbing openly, too. Having known Raven the longest, seeing the girl like this was like seeing her own child dead before her. "Poor, Raven, I can't believe she's gone."

"She put up a hell of a fight before she did, I can tell you that," Henry said. He looked up to see Jimmy and Cindy joining them. Jimmy was shaking his head at the sight of Raven, and he wiped an errant tear away.

Cindy was sniffling. She wiped her nose on her sleeve, then touched Raven's face. "We'll miss you, Raven, I hope wherever you are, that it's better than here."

"Amen," Sue said.

"Henry, are you sure all these deaders are well, you know, dead?"

Henry looked around at the corpses. "They're dead enough for my taste. Why, you complaining?"

"No, of course not, it's just...well, I don't know. They just dropped dead, like that; one second they were alive—well not alive but active anyway—and the next..." He snapped his finger. "Dead."

"Jimmy, I have no idea what just happened here and to tell you the truth, I really don't care. All I know is that except for Raven, we're all alive, and considering what we just went through, that's still pretty damn good." He sighed heavily. "Though I wish Raven had made it, too." He glanced at Lazarus' body, wishing he could kill the bastard again for what he'd done to Raven.

"We need to bury her, give her a proper funeral," Sue said, her tears falling onto Raven's chest.

"I couldn't agree more," Henry said. "When Raven and I left the town to go on the mission, I spotted this nice place with trees and a view of the desert close by. What say we clear out any bodies we find there and bury her in that spot?"

Sue nodded. "That's sounds wonderful. I think she would have liked that."

Henry scooped her up again, holding her gently, like a baby. "You guys get our gear from those bodies over there. Sue, will you make sure my Glock and panga are there too, please."

"Sure, Henry, of course."

It didn't take long for them to gather their meager supplies, and once they were ready, they headed out of the crevasse and onto the desert plain. Walking was hard, as there were bodies everywhere, covering the desert like a meat carpet. The buzzards were many, feeding on the decaying meat, the zombies having putrefied to perfection for the buzzard's distinguishing palates.

Eventually the group made it to the clearing. There were a dozen bodies spread around the area and Henry set Raven down and the five of them began to clear the area, dragging the zombies well out of range of the burial site. Once finished, they had to take on the arduous task of digging a grave. Henry got to work immediately, working like a man possessed. His side hurt from where the bullet Murdock had shot at him had grazed him, but he relished the pain, letting it fill him with hate for what the zombie had done to his friend. Jimmy helped, too, and half an hour later they had dug a decent-sized grave while the women prepared Raven by combing her hair and fixing her clothes as much as possible.

Henry climbed out and gently carried Raven to the open grave. Then he climbed down into it and laid her flat. With a helping hand from Jimmy he climbed out of the hole. The others joined him and they all gazed down at their lost friend.

"Okay, guys," Cindy said. "I need to say something. No matter how bad it seemed to get sometimes, no matter how dire the situation, we always got out alive. I never really thought one of us would die."

"I know what you mean," Mary said. "Ever since I joined up with Jimmy and Henry, it seemed like we were always one step away from death, and each time we escaped to fight another day."

"A lot of that is because of Henry, isn't it?" Sue asked, hugging Henry's arm and putting her head on his shoulder.

"Thank you, Sue, but I can't take all the credit," Henry said. "Whatever we did, we did it as a team."

"Who's gonna say something before we cover her up?" Jimmy asked.

"I will," Henry said, the others nodding that it was fine. "Okay, this will be short and sweet. We all knew Raven and that she didn't talk much. She never said five words when three would suffice so I'm gonna wrap this up the same way she would have. She was tough, beautiful and a hell of a fighter. She was fearless and could fight like a she-demon. She'll be missed more than she could ever know. I think I speak for all of us when I say there will always be a small hole in our heart knowing she's not with us anymore." He picked up a clump of dirt and dropped it into the grave. It landed on Raven's chest and broke apart. "Ashes to ashes, dust to dust. Farwell, Raven, we love you; you'll be missed."

"Amen," Mary said.

"Amen," Cindy muttered.

Sue was crying and she couldn't speak, she only shook her head and turned away.

Jimmy began using his feet to push the dirt back into the hole, Henry joining him. After a minute they got down on their knees and used their hands. It took fifteen minutes of hard work to get all the soil back into the grave. When they were done, they stood up and wiped their hands on their clothes. Mary and Cindy had made a cross out of found wood and Mary stuck it at the top of the grave. Cindy had carved Raven's name in it. It was crude but most people in the deadlands never even got a grave, let alone a marker, so by the companions' standards, Raven was doing all right.

"Where to now?" Jimmy asked, breathing a little heavily from the exertion. The moon was full and it lit the world in a pallid glow.

"Back to Indian Springs," Henry said. "I want to see how bad it is there. Besides, we need transportation. That's our best chance of finding some. Agreed?"

Everyone nodded. Henry could see in their faces that none of them really cared where they went at the moment. They were all emotionally and physically drained and filled with grief for their lost friend. Henry could lead them off a cliff and no doubt they would follow without question. Henry knew how they felt, but he was doing his best to stay strong. The others looked up to him and he wanted them to see the strength in him that they all needed to keep going. Sure they'd lost one of their own, but they were still alive and they needed to keep moving, to keep living.

But Henry knew later, when he was alone with Sue, he would finally be able to let his guard down and let the night overwhelm him. But it would be many miles down the road before that would happen.

He thought about the zombies and how they had simply collapsed like that. It made no sense, but he pushed the thoughts on the subject from his mind as soon as they arrived. He wasn't a medical doctor or a professor and even if he was, it was possible he still wouldn't be able to figure out what had killed them. But the zombies were dead for good and that was what mattered. He tried not to think about how fortunate he and his friends were for the timing of the zombies' dying. Even another minute could have cost Sue or Mary her life. But worrying about things you had no control over was a waste of energy, so he turned his mind to more important things, such as getting to the town and finding what they needed to survive. Besides, sometime you made your own luck and sometimes luck was simply there.

The town was in ruins, corpses everywhere. Many and been burned, the sweet smell of charred human flesh cloying the back of the companions' throats. This wasn't the first time they'd have to suffer through that odor, nor would it be the last.

They began scavenging what they could find, and though there wasn't much left, there was more than enough for five humans. Henry even found a working shower in a home that hadn't been burned near the center of town. Though the smoke was thick in the air, he still managed to bathe quickly and change into new clothes

Sue had found in a closet, relieved to be able to wash the gore from his skin. When he emerged from the home in new attire with Sue by his side and no longer covered in gore, he felt like a new man.

The others were waiting for Sue and Henry after scavenging what they could find. With Jimmy in the driver's seat of a bright red Chevy pickup with flames on the sides, oversized wheels, a double-wide rear bed and a cab with two rows that sat the five of them comfortably, they were all more than ready to put the town of Indian Springs behind them. The air conditioning even worked, which was a gift from God Himself as far as Jimmy was concerned.

Henry and Sue climbed into the back seat. Jimmy put the transmission into drive and drove out of the burning town, the bright halogen headlights cutting through the smoke and darkness. The ride was bumpy for the first half mile, as there were corpses everywhere, remnants of the zombie army. The sound of the tires squishing and pulverizing the bodies was something the companions looked forward to putting behind them, and eventually the road opened up and was clear.

For a while no one spoke, each of them lost in their private thoughts. It felt weird leaving a place without Raven, the taciturn girl who'd only spoken when it mattered.

Henry looked out the window at the austere desert, the far off ridges that blocked the dark horizon, and he thought of those he'd lost since his adventure had begun years ago. There had been many friends who hadn't made it, and no doubt as life continued, there would be many more, but what mattered was that though a part of the body might have been missing, the body as a whole would continue ever onward.

Henry took Sue's hand in his and kissed it; she leaned close to him, resting her head on his shoulder. Cindy was doing the same with Jimmy, and Mary was pressed against the passenger door, gazing wistfully out the window.

Every now and then the pickup would drive past a corpse laying in the road, the zombie having dropped dead where it had been standing. It was an odd sight seeing the prone body, the headlights of the pickup illuminating it before passing it by. The bodies weren't the oddest thing though, which were a common occurrence in the deadlands, but to see no zombies active anymore was almost eerie.

"Hey, Henry, I've got a question for you," Jimmy said, finally breaking the silence. The road ahead was wide open and he was going a good thirty-five mph.

"Oh yeah? What about?" Henry inquired and hugged Sue closer. He didn't want to think about how close he'd come to losing her this time. Losing all of his friends...his family.

"Back there when we were tied up, Lazarus gave you a choice. Sue or Mary. You never told him your choice. I was wondering who it was? Who'd you pick to live and was gonna die?"

"Jimmy, how could you even ask him that?" Mary said, the shock in her voice apparent.

"What? It's a valid question. He had to make a decision and he was about to when the deaders suddenly dropped dead. I want to know." He glanced in the rearview mirror to see Henry's piercing eyes looking back. "So, old man, what's it gonna be? Who'd you pick to live and whom was gonna die?"

Henry managed a sly grin. "I'll never tell."

"What? Oh, come on, help me out here. Mary and Sue, one or the other. So who was gonna live and who was gonna be worm food?" Jimmy prodded.

"Jimmy, you can ask me a thousand times and a thousand times I'll tell you the same thing. I'm not talking, now why don't you concentrate on the road before you get us into an accident."

"That would be just like Jimmy," Cindy joked. "Getting us into an accident when we're the only vehicle on the road for a hundred miles."

"Hey, I'll have you know I'm a damn good driver," Jimmy snapped, offended now that everyone was teasing him. "I aced my driver's test when I took it."

"You probably just got lucky," Mary laughed, glad that the subject had been changed. She hadn't wanted to know the answer, having a feeling knowing it might be detrimental to the group.

Henry sat back and let the others argue playfully. It was true though, he had made that fateful decision and would have given it to Lazarus if things hadn't happened the way they had. So though he knew the answer to Jimmy's question, he would never tell anyone. That would be a secret he took to his grave.

"Okay, enough about me and my driving skills," Jimmy said, "I want to talk about the deaders dropping dead again. I want to know how it happened. Something like that, well, it seems kind of crazy. Don't you guys think? And how do we know it's happened everywhere and not just out here in the desert?"

"It's possible this was an isolated incident but I highly doubt it, Jimmy," Henry said. "That light in the sky we saw before they collapsed was from space or the upper atmosphere. Whatever did this turned them all off at the exact same moment. We won't know for sure if they are all dead till we get out there and explore the country more, but I bet they are dead."

"Maybe it was just their time," Sue said, offering a suggestion. "Maybe someone up in the heavens finally threw us and the world a bone and killed them, giving the world back to mankind."

"Do you think we'll ever know what happened?" Mary asked.

"No, Mary, I doubt it," Henry said. "I mean, think back to when it all began. We still don't know how it started. All we knew was that it had and we had to deal with it or die. This is probably no different. And you know what I say?"

"What?" Cindy asked.

"I say who the hell cares. They're gone and the world is ours again, that's all that matters."

"Huh, some world," Jimmy said. "There's still cannies, slavers and raiders to name a few; the world is far from a paradise."

"One thing at a time, Jimmy. Take it one day a time," Henry said.

"Okay, uh, guys, I have something to share with all of you but most importantly with Jimmy," Cindy said loudly so that everyone shut up.

Jimmy glanced at her. "Oh yeah, babe, about what?"

She sucked in a deep breath, as if she was psyching her self up to say something important. Jimmy, concentrating on driving, was oblivious to her discomfort.

"Jimmy, I've wanted to tell you this for a while now but I've been waiting for the right time. But hell, lately there's never the right time. So I feel right now, with all of us alive and for the moment safe, is as good a time as any."

Jimmy began to look concerned, as did some of the others.

"You're starting to worry me, babe," Jimmy said. "What is it? Are you okay, is something wrong with you? Are you sick? Is it..."

She cut him off as he wasn't going to stop talking and quickly blurted out, "I'm pregnant."

For a few seconds the words hung in the air, no one saying a word. Then Jimmy's face went stone blank and he slammed on the brakes, the Chevy sliding across the road before coming to a stop. In the distance, there was the hint of light of the coming dawn.

"Did I hear what I think I heard?" Jimmy asked. His face had lost all color and he was as pale as a zombie.

Cindy nodded. "Uh-huh. If I had to guess, I'd say I'm at least two months along. I don't know for sure, of course, it's just a guess." She began to look worried and tears sprouted in her eyes. "Are you...are you happy about it?"

Henry and the others remained silent, seeing that this was a moment between Cindy and Jimmy, though they all stared at Jimmy, waiting for his reply. Without saying a word he put the transmission into 'park' and stared out the front windshield

"Happy?" Jimmy asked. "Happy?" His face slowly took on color. Then a wide smile creased his lips and his eyes went wide with happiness. "Of course I'm happy. I'm gonna be a father?" He pulled Cindy close and kissed her and then everyone inside the cab was talking, clapping Jimmy on the back and hugging Cindy.

After five minutes of joviality, Jimmy calmed down enough to put the Chevy into drive and continue down the road. The mood was light inside the cab of the pickup, everyone basking in the good news.

"So, Jimmy, you're gonna be a father, how 'bout that. I tell you, Cindy, I hope that baby has your looks or that kid is going to be one ugly baby," Henry joked.

Everyone laughed except Jimmy, who was frowning at the jibe. But he was never one to take one lying down when it came to Henry.

Jimmy had spent years honing his craft on teasing and aggravating Henry. "Oh yeah, old man? Well, if I'm gonna be a father, then that makes you the grandfather, how 'bout that?"

"Ha, he's got you there, Henry," Mary laughed.

"I'm gonna have to start calling you Grandpa from now on instead of 'old man,' " Jimmy said with a grin. He watched Henry frown in the rearview mirror and knew he'd gotten him good.

"You do and I swear you won't live long enough to see that kid grow up," Henry said. He tried to sound angry but he faltered halfway through and began to chuckle.

"So Cindy," Sue said. "Do you have any names picked out yet?"

"No, not yet, but since everything's that's happened, I now know the name if it's a girl."

"Oh yeah, what's that?" Jimmy asked.

"If it's a girl we should call her Raven."

Everyone went silent and Sue muffled a sob of sadness and joy simultaneously. "I think Raven would have liked that," Sue said and reached over the seat to touch Cindy's shoulder. Cindy raised her hand and squeezed Sue's hand in response, the two sharing an unspoken moment.

Jimmy pulled Cindy close and hugged her with his right arm, his left hand on the steering wheel. "That sounds fine with me, babe," Jimmy said. "Kind of perfect actually. Raven Cooper. It has a ring to it, doesn't it? Like it could be the name of a movie star."

"Agreed," Henry said. "It's a beautiful name."

Everyone relaxed, and silence filled the cab once more, but this time it was layered with hope.

The road cut through the desert, the lone Chevy its only occupant as it drove headlong into the coming dawn.

The night had been banished and a new day was dawning, the horizon tinged with red and orange.

It was the first sunrise on a world free of the living dead.

Epilogue

"Report. Did it work?" a deep male voice asked in Russian over a loudspeaker mounted to the wall of the underground bunker buried deep in the heart of the Soviet Union.

"According to my reports, General Ivanov," the woman scientist replied in Russian, "all the missiles exploded perfectly and in perfect synchronization."

"That's not what I asked you, Professor Romanoff," the voice said, now sounding more than a little aggravated. "I asked you if it worked. Is the reanimated dead plague finally over?"

"I...I won't know for sure until I can bring up satellite coverage," Romanoff said. I'm getting information now; just give me a few minutes."

"Fine, but if you know what's good for you, no longer than that." The transmission was cut off.

Professor Susana Romanoff began crunching numbers, and when a soft beeping began on her console, she punched in a code and a large screen before her lit up, showing the eastern seaboard of the United States. Other screens began to light up as well, each one covering different parts of the world. One was showing her Mother Russia, another Japan, while another showed Australia. She began her work, analyzing the data and images.

She was the last in the line of scientists and professors that had been working on a way to stop the walking dead for years. Ever since the first data had come in from an American scientist, a Professor Keagan, from the Midwest in the United States, that man sending her information from a secret project codenamed Deadwater, surviving men and women of science had struggled to find a cure for the undead plague.

Nothing had worked on a global scale until Romanoff had figured out that an EMP pulse set at the right frequency would shut down the electrical impulses in a zombie's brain but yet not hurt electrical devices such as computers and cars like a standard pulse would do.

She had been the one person to figure out that the brain of the living dead was affected mostly in the hypothalamus, which was the old brain, where mankind's deepest most primitive instincts lay.

It had taken more than a year to set everything up, to have the missiles programmed to the exact specifications, but now, as the data came in and she crunched the numbers, she began to smile.

When she was assured of her information, she pressed a button on her console and the man's voice came on immediately.

"Yes, report," General Ivanov demanded.

Prof. Romanoff smiled widely, a smile of pride and congratulations. "I have confirmation, sir. The plague is over. The reanimated dead have been destroyed for good."

"Excellent," General Ivanov said. His voice was filled with power, of a man who was in control of others, and wielded his authority like a living thing. "Now that we don't have to fight the dead, we can concentrate on more important things, such as invading the United States and adding it the glorious Soviet Republic. And let me say, Prof. Romanoff, it's long overdue. Since the cold war, I've been waiting for this moment, for Russia to finally become the superpower it was always destined to be, to crush the Americans under the might of the Soviet Union."

"Yes sir," Prof. Romanoff said.

"Soon..." General Ivanov said, though the man seemed to be talking more to himself than to Prof. Romanoff. "Soon, the Americans will feel the wrath of the USSR and they will long for the days when the dead walked the earth."

Where the Dead
Never Sleep

UNDEADPRESS.COM

CLAN OF THE BIGFOOT

ANTHONY GIANGREGORIO

Lightning Source UK Ltd.
Milton Keynes UK
UKOW032306220313